PRAISE FOR AV

"...this book's appeal comes down to its intriguing world-building...and its varied cast of characters."

— JAINE FENN, AWARDING-WINNING SFF
AUTHOR

"Sabina...is very sharp and funny. She really leaps off the page."

— LIZ WILLIAMS, BEST-SELLING SFF AUTHOR

AWAKENING MAGES

AGE OF ACADEMICIANS II

MARIA HERRING

For Bilbo
(my cat, not the hobbit)

Book 0 in the *Age of Academicians* series

Discover the first orc
Discover the first Mage
Discover the truth about
the academy

ORIGINS reveals the secrets
that were kept hidden
from the humans of Tauré
throughout the Ages.

Get Your Free Gift Now!

Claim your FREE BOOK here: https://www.mariaherring.com/free-book/

MAGELANDS

DRAYKE

*S*till not home yet.

Rain cannoned into the stagnant, weed-choked waters of the old moat, throwing up wafts of stink that stayed with Drayke even after he crossed it. Banker's Drive stretched on and on, no matter how many steps he took. Peering through the downpour, Banker's Gate in the near distance seemed remote, unreachable. The longest part of the journey yet, despite having trekked all the way from the Blasted Glade in the Fallen Forest.

How long had he been away? Almost two months. An eternity. He just wanted to get back to the Barracks and forget everything that had happened. Barracks that would be emptier and quieter thanks to this false quest. He scowled. Too many good Rebels had died needlessly. More at the final battle against the orcs in the Glade, until Audra…did what she did. He risked a sideways glance at her.

She looked different. Not because her expensive travelling clothes were torn and dirty. Not because her long auburn hair and small stature had changed. It was something within. Something inexplicable. And Drayke preferred to keep it that way. He couldn't unsee all he'd seen her do, but he didn't have to explain it. Better that way.

He set his eyes forward again. Banker's Gate was no nearer and he stifled a sigh. This was definitely the longest part of the journey yet.

OUT'KEEP HADN'T CHANGED. Still the same old shit in the streets. Same old beggars. Same old hovels. Same old market stalls clambering up the side of In'Keep's walls. Touters shouting, buyers haggling. Dogs and children chasing each other, doubling the noise, despite the heavy tithe the plague had claimed. Noise and smell, that's what Out'Keep was. And had anyone even noticed that the plague had ended? How could everything stay the same when so much change had happened?

The guard at Banker's Gate stifled a yawn as Drayke passed him, even though it was only a couple of notches past noon. No doubt still suffering the effects of over-indulgence at his local inn last night. If the useless sack even noticed how many Rebels were missing, he certainly didn't care enough to mention it. Drayke would inform the Prime Minister when he reached the palace that the quality of guardsmen employed by the city was lacking. But he had to get there first.

At least they were finally in In'Keep. The quiet wealth of the financial quarter enveloped him but did nothing to calm him. It only meant his thoughts weren't drowned out. Movement registered in the corner of his eye and he saw the lordling elf peel away from the group. He headed towards the mansions that housed the elvish families who controlled the city's economy. Of course, Drayke couldn't see them from here. They lay beyond the labyrinth of banks and other financial institutions that the clans had created from white stone and immortal arrogance. But where else would he be going? He had to tell his family that his sister had perished. When the few remaining Rebels had been brought back, she was the only one who'd stayed dead.

Faër of the Worthy Clan. He hadn't really liked her. All right, she'd been beautiful and she'd used it to great effect. He'd lost count of the times he wanted to wallop his men for lusting after her like dogs sniffing out a bitch in heat. But she'd possessed great quantities of that elvish conceit that grated on him. He hadn't wished her dead though. And certainly not by orcs, who had no business existing in the real world. No. For all his wealth and power, Drayke wouldn't wish to swap places with the lordling elf and break that news to the mighty Worthy Clan of Kingston City.

His gaze swept over Audra once more. Her step faltered a little when she noticed her friend depart, but she didn't call out to him. He didn't look back at her either, let alone offer a farewell. So not only elves died on the false mission then.

Soon enough the trees surrounding the palace, barracks and library came into view and all of a sudden the journey ended too quickly. Now he had to face the Prime Minister and explain what happened. Use words. The group had barely spoken to each other on the long journey back and that was as it should've been. Now, though, the Prime Minister would be full of the same questions that the Rebels had kept to themselves over the weeks and Drayke would be forced to answer them. He didn't know the answers. Didn't think anyone did. But he'd known from the very first day that he'd become a Rebel that his duty wouldn't be easy and he wasn't going to shy away now.

The trees thinned, the wooden enclosure appeared, and even before they reached the gate it was yanked inwards.

"Drayke Rebel Leader!" He winced at the sound. Not

because it was too loud, because it was too joyful. "We thought you'd deserted!"

He mustered a smile from somewhere. "Death before desertion, Claytun. Isn't that what I always taught you?"

The lad smiled. He was a good fighter, Claytun. Had a tactical mind. But he was young. He'd never have survived the mission. Pit fighting was a picnic by comparison.

"Where are the rest of the Rebels?" he said, swinging his eyes over the remains of the group. "Don't tell me you let them get their fill of whores before being welcomed back by their brothers!"

Drayke couldn't answer that. Claytun's face fell and he took a step back.

"I have to see the Prime Minister," he said. "Take these Rebels back to the barracks and see they're fed. They need rest."

Claytun nodded, all happy words departed. He watched his men leave. They'd find no comfort in the barracks. They'd be too empty and too quiet.

And now it was just him and Audra. She regarded him with eyes deep and blue. They'd always shown her intelligence. Now they showed something else.

"Let's go," he said. She walked on without a word.

THE PALACE LOOKED SHABBIER since he last saw it. The white stone was discoloured from the elements. Grey streaks ran down the facade from beneath the hewn window sills like dirty tears, an image only accentuated by the rain falling on them now. Perhaps it had always been this shabby. Perhaps it took time away to truly notice it.

Inside, however, was as decadent as he remembered. Thick-pile rugs in deep shades of red and purple carpeted the marble floor, crystal chandeliers draped the candles in the ceilings, and gold-framed paintings adorned every spare wall space. And then, of course, were the random chairs upholstered in silk that no one sat on, the objects of art carefully placed upon wooden tables made purposely for that single article, and golden platters people were supposed to look at, not eat from. He knew such items were made by a particular branch of the Academicians, artists of some kind, but he'd never been interested in such frippery.

Shortly after stepping into the atrium, a short and bustling man zipped over to them, a look of recognition on his face. Drayke had no idea who he was. Civil servant. Faceless to Drayke. Nameless.

"Rebel Leader," he exclaimed, clasping his hands before him, swaying back and forth on squeaking, highly-polished shoes. "We didn't know when to expect you back but it's an honour to be the first to greet you. The Prime Minister is in his chamber and will be delighted to see you. I'll bring you to him this instant."

Drayke nodded his acceptance and followed, despite knowing his way around the palace as well as any servant here. Better than. These shuffling, bustling people knew nothing. There was so much more to the palace than this staircase and this corridor leading to the Prime Minister's chambers. He'd wager a season's salary that this squeaking fool was completely oblivious to that.

He opened the chamber door for them, nodded his head as Drayke and Audra marched past him, then the Rebel Leader forgot he ever existed.

"Drayke Rebel Leader," said the Prime Minister, pushing himself out of his chair. "Welcome back. Do you have the artefact?"

"The mission was a success in that the plague has ended," he said, "but regretfully, I inform you that it was at the cost of many good Rebels."

"You can provide me with the details later. I asked for the artefact."

Drayke regarded the Prime Minister. Here was the man who embodied the beliefs of the entire city. That the few shouldn't benefit from the suffering of the many. It was why the original Rebels rose up against the royalty and ousted them from power. It was why they swore loyalty to their leader, who then became the first Prime Minister, and promised to protect the ideas of the new government. And in the Ages that had passed since that upheaval, the Rebels had kept that promise and remained loyal. Not once had Drayke questioned the orders of his Prime Minister, not once had he doubted his duty to the city. But here he was, this Prime Minister, after being told of the deaths of his most loyal subjects, asking for the artefact that had killed them instead of commenting on their loss. When had an object become more important than good men?

"Well?"

"There is no artefact," said Audra. The Prime Minister raised an eyebrow and looked at her as though she were a forward child, but he said nothing. "Neither you nor the Academicians will get your scheming hands on it because it never existed."

"I beg your pardon? There was no scheming!"

"Well done, you've missed the point entirely," said Audra, glaring at him. "Good men, friends, died for an artefact that didn't exist. The Healing Glass was a fabrication of the Mages."

A smattering of laughter rattled around the chamber from the ministers and Drayke looked from Audra to them and back again. She was unperturbed.

"Scoff all you like, but your own Rebel Leader will confirm it, as will Lord Worthy, who is even now recounting our journey to his clan. There are a few Rebels left who can also corroborate what you hear now. Unfortunately, the majority of the Rebels died during the mission, as did Lady Worthy. They died to save the city. They're dead."

The assembled ministers shifted uncomfortably in their seats and Drayke was glad.

"I'll send my condolences to their families," mumbled the Prime Minister.

"You've missed the point again!" said Audra, striding forward and slamming her hand down on the desk as she spoke. Even Drayke was surprised. "Mages are still among us. The plague was never real—it was merely a catalyst to throw us into this death quest of theirs! We're nothing but pieces in a game to them and they'll keep playing it if we don't stop them. Too many people have died already and it must stop *now*!"

There was silence. Then the Prime Minister cleared his throat. "Mages are relics of Ages past, Audra Academician, along with orcs. Now, I understand that this journey must have taken its toll—"

"You understand nothing, you bloated fool," said Audra, pushing herself away from his desk. "Revel in your ignorance for as long as you can, because I shall revel in demonstrating the depth of it. When you know how right I am, you'll regret it deeply."

She turned and marched out of the chamber, slamming the door with impressive power behind her. Drayke turned his regard back to the astonished ministers.

No. Audra wasn't the same woman at all.

SABINA

*U*sually, falling asleep is one of those experiences that's never really experienced. One moment you're lying in bed, thinking about falling asleep. The next, you're waking up wondering how come the night whizzed by so quickly. You don't feel anything.

Except if you get one of those almost-dreams where you trip over, or fall off a stool and your whole body jolts like it's just been struck by lightning. Sab hated those almost-dreams. She got them often enough to know she hated them.

So it took her a couple of moments to realise that what was happening to her right now wasn't even a little bit like an almost-dream.

Jolted awake, yes; but she hadn't been dreaming. And this jolt was lasting way too long. It was still going on. And it was…coming from *outside* her body…

She hadn't been dreaming before, but now images were coming thick and fast into her mind. Not dream images. Real images.

A battle between humans and orcs.

An angry human carrying a heavy sword.

8

Messina's head, chopped right off. The surge of power from that was incredible!

Nathaniel's head, also chopped off.

And lots of that delicious, pulsating power going… straight into the human.

Wait—what?

The Game was definitely over, Sab knew that much. Her body tingled with the fresh new inundation of power it always brought. But she was also pissed off, because it meant it was going to take her Ages to get back to sleep, and she had a really busy day tomorrow. Or later on today, more accurately.

Back up a moment—Messina and Nathaniel were *killed*. By that human, that, that Audra. What was that? Was that a name? And then she'd taken their power. How was that even possible?

"What the fuck's going on?" she grumbled to the dark room. Because that was what an exhausted body and mind wanted after the adrenaline-pumping, heart-racing influx of power; a confusing puzzle to mull over.

She whipped her blanket aside, disgusted at the world in general. She was going to have to get drunk now if she ever wanted to get to sleep tonight.

"Lights," she snapped. A sickly yellow glow suffused her cell and she immediately tripped over a shoe. She bellowed a wordless roar of exasperation and kicked away the offending item and its pair. She hated living in this mess. But not conforming to her family's notions of perfection really irritated them, and she hated them more, so…

As if on cue, the Patriarch's face appeared just in front of her. Ten times bigger than it was in real life and only a foot away from the tip of her nose, he was obviously going to explain that weird ending to the latest Game. She rolled her eyes, but his projection moved with them. Couldn't he just wait until morning, like normal people?

"All members of House Lix-Tetrax to Cirrus Level," his projection boomed. "Now."

"What, no please or thank you?" said Sab.

But only because she knew the projection couldn't hear her. He used magic to project an image of himself through his relatives' eyes, but it was a one-way system. Once his proclamation was over, his image dispersed in a flash of photons. Showy.

She got the message because, technically, she did have Lix-Tetrax blood in her, but that didn't mean she had to go, did it? She was way down in Stratus; none of the rellies up in Cirrus actually wanted her to turn up, did they?

But if she didn't go, she could guarantee that the Patriarch would find some way of punishing her for disobeying an order.

Well, hoo-fucking-ray. A chance to go to the upper level without getting kicked back down again for getting above her station. Although it did mean she'd have to find those shoes she'd just launched into the general mess.

Today couldn't get any worse.

THE ATMOSPHERE RAN ON MAGIC. Because it was the most powerful city state, it had a lot of magic. All this was thanks to the number of Mages who lived here. Mages contained magic—no, that wasn't right. Mages contained something that allowed them to use magic. Sab was perfectly capable of finding out exactly how it worked if she had any inclination, but she didn't. Accident of birth dumped her in the most powerful of city states. Accident of birth meant she was a Mage. Didn't mean she had to take an interest.

She lived on the lowest level of the 'Sphere, Stratus level, where the human slaves lived, because she was one of the Stratians in charge of them. She was in charge of making sure their numbers didn't drop below a certain amount, because an all-powerful city state like this one needed a lot of slaves to keep it functioning in the manner to which all the upper-level Mages were accustomed. She, and a few others like her, were the only Mages in the city to have a job, and that was purely because of their accidental births as well. But Sab wasn't about to complain. She much preferred the company of her Stratus companions compared to their upper-level counterparts.

But every now and then, those counterparts reached down and scooped them up for something or other, and Stratus denizens weren't really allowed to say no.

She couldn't find her other shoe. Bare feet it was then. Someone like the Patriarch wouldn't be kept waiting, and it was either turn up on time, or turn up appropriately dressed. He couldn't have both.

She stumbled out of her tiny cell, kicking at the clothes and detritus that wanted to follow her, or keep her from leaving. There was no door. None of the Mages down here had a door to call their own. Privacy was a privilege for the elite. The Stratians had to count themselves lucky that they had individual cells. At least they weren't all shoved together in one wailing, filthy mass like the humans were at the very bottom of the 'Sphere.

"Where are you going?"

Sab squinted up the corridor at the voice. It was Prisca. Official mother hen of Stratus level.

"Patriarch called," Sab replied.

"It's about the Game?"

"Obviously. Look," she raised her voice a little so the rest of the faces poking out into the corridor could hear her. "I'll let you lot know what's going on when I come back down. Right now, fuck all is all I know."

"Be careful, Sabina," said Prisca.

Sab snorted a sardonic laugh through her nose. That was Prisca's way of telling her to behave. Like it had ever worked before.

Her naked soles slapped against the tiled floor, always meticulously cleaned by the slaves, but probably dirtied far more by her feet than her shoes. Most people would likely be horrified to feel their skin stick to the surface, but Sab found the tickling sensation rather pleasant.

Ten yards or so later she was at the core. This was a shaft that ran through the very centre of the 'Sphere, depositing people at whichever level they requested. As she approached it, the magical barrier, a lilac fog that fried any non-Mage trying to pass through it, recognised her as a legitimate person and cleared. She stepped through into the cylindrical chamber.

"Cirrus level," she said with a sigh, leaning heavily against the glass at the back.

"State your reason," came the androgynous voice of the core.

"Patriarch's orders."

You couldn't lie to the core. Sab had tried to before, obviously. It just resulted in her being spat back out into the corridor. Somehow the core was able to check minds to see if passengers' words matched their memories, or orders, or whatever. Some Mages, in Sab's entirely non-humble opinion, were far too imaginative when it came to inventing magical devices.

"Confirmed," said the core.

And then movement. Not from outside the body, but right in the pit of the stomach. The core pushed and pulled its passengers up and down the levels at an astonishing rate.

Pole to pole, the AtmoSphere was five hundred kilometres long, the same at the equator. A monstrous city state that hovered above the ocean, defying gravity with magic alone. That was how come the other city states knew that the 'Sphere was the most powerful of all of them. It had extraordinary amounts of magic to waste on this ridiculously unlikely city structure. Sab couldn't wait for the day when the Patriarch's time at the top of the food chain was broken and the whole city splashed back down into the ocean. Such destruction! Let that be a lesson to him for being such a dick.

The levels between Stratus and Cirrus strobed past in a migraine of colours, but she was travelling too fast to see any details, despite the core's glass exterior. Twenty seconds later, the lilac fog cleared again and she stomped out onto the gleaming marble floor of the Patriarch's level. Cirrus. Exactly the same volume of living space as all their tens of thousands of slaves had at the very bottom of the AtmoSphere, but it was all just for him.

And this was the very first time in all her life that she'd ever been up here. She was probably supposed to feel honoured, or something. But honour could piss right off.

Look at this place! While the squirming, stinking slaves were hemmed in by steel, no light coming in at all except for whatever lamps the slavers brought in with them, this place was all glass and light. The sky beyond was still night black, but a sliver of moon smirked down at Sab from its lofty position in the heavens. She couldn't see any stars though, because floating orbs shone golden light everywhere. No shadows up here.

And just as the 'Sphere itself used up magic to defy gravity, so did the Patriarch's seat of power. He'd decided that regular floors that used stairs to connect them weren't inspiring enough. Instead, his floors floated free from any tethers, gently drifting across the open space like flat clouds caught in the fairest zephyr. The one closest to her displayed a fat leather armchair, several rows of bookshelves, and a little bonfire in the middle. No wood for it to burn, because obviously it was magic, but the flames danced merrily and sang in that popping, cracking way that normal fires preferred. Honestly. No one was on that level, and it clearly wasn't needed for heating, so what was the point in keeping that little illusion going? For the spectacle. The spectacle being the pointless use of continuous magic just in case someone spotted it. Sab rolled her eyes. She was the only one here, so—

Wait. She was the only one here. Either she'd got here before the rest of the family, despite having the furthest to come. Or…

"If you would deign to grace us with your presence, Sabina," said the Patriarch, "we can start our discussion."

Sab sucked at her teeth. She'd heard his voice all right, as though he was standing right in front of her. But she couldn't see him. And she certainly couldn't see anyone else, all waiting patiently for her, as they obviously were. So which of these floating dick measurers were they all on then?

She looked up. Of course. There was one bobbing away right at the top, right in the curve of the 'Sphere, rotating ever so slowly, so that those perched up there could get a perfect three-sixty of the world outside without ever having to leave their seats.

Well. She'd worked out where her extended family was. All she had to do was figure out how to get up there.

She stepped forward, keeping her eyes on the marble underside of the uppermost floor. She'd have to use magic to get up there. How like the Patriarch to force people to demonstrate their skill to all their peers. Fine. She was bursting at the seams with power anyway, what with that very special ending to the Game they'd all benefitted from.

She balled her fist, then visualised herself as bubbles. She flung her fingers apart and scattered her component atoms across the room, then coalesced right at the edge of the topmost floor. Safest place to do it; it was the only space up there that for sure was empty. The instant her shape reformed she took a step forward. Woozy was normal after a dispersion and she certainly didn't want the humiliation of toppling off once she'd finally made it to the top.

"Thank you for rushing to get here," said the Patriarch. "We've only been waiting a mere fifteen minutes for your attendance."

A mixed assortment of sneers and scowls from her kith and kin at that blatant sarcasm. All right, she'd see his sarcasm and raise him a dose of taking-shit-literally.

"You're very welcome, Patriarch," she said, then proffered a huge smile. "So kind of you to invite me. Have to say, *love* what you've done with the place."

"Sit down, Sabina," he said.

There was only one seat left. A little wooden stool, where the rest of them lounged across obese armchairs. Except for the Patriarch, of course. He sat straight-backed in a glimmering throne of gold and gems. Floating, obviously. He'd found his theme and he was going to smash it into everyone's faces just as hard as he could.

She looked at her stool, kept her face pleasantly blank and sat on it. A good couple of metres on either side separated her from her nearest and dearest, just to make sure that she knew that *they* knew she didn't belong up here.

There was a tut to her left. "You could've dressed for the occasion," said the obese armchair.

"It's the middle of the fucking night," she said agreeably, pulling out her tobacco and papers from thin air. "I was sleeping."

A furious face appeared from behind the wing of the armchair. "You're in your underwear."

"Which is perfect attire for sleeping," she squinted at the angry face while rolling a cigarette. "Emil, is it? I can never remember which one of you is which."

"You disgust me," he said, his handsome face ugly with fury.

"Aww, thank you."

"Enough," bellowed the Patriarch. "Sabina, we all know you are Stratian, but you can at least pretend to be civilised. You are of House Lix-Tetrax, after all. Put some clothes on."

She looked down at her grubby knickers and even grubbier vest. More holes than vest, really. Did nothing to cover up the scar tissue, caked-in grime and blood, or flayed skin at the top of her thighs and across her abdomen. She shrugged. Somewhere in her cell she had a pair of black trousers that weren't falling apart, and a black vest with fewer holes.

She imagined them as bubbles too, beckoned them to her with her fingers. A second later she was wearing them. Still couldn't be bothered to find her shoes. She looked over at Emil, flicked her thumb up, and lit her cigarette from the flame flickering there.

"Better?" she said.

He glanced at her forearms. "No."

She grinned at him through a plume of smoke. Over the years, she'd gradually stripped the skin off her forearms, from wrist to elbow, so that muscle, sinew and bone was constantly on show. Her hands, with their raggedy, filthy nails, looked like weird gloves. She'd started because she liked feeling pain. One Mage can't kill another, neither can they kill themselves. But it was astonishing how much pain a body could endure while that body was trying to heal itself.

Now, she liked the effect her skinless arms had on other people. She waggled her fingers, making the muscle fibres in

16

her arms ripple and twitch, then winked at Emil. He tutted and sank back into the flabby folds of his chair.

"The Game is over," boomed the Patriarch, obviously as tired of Emil's bitching as Sab was. "But Nathaniel and Messina are dead."

"I saw the images of their death throes," said some random family member. Everybody here was so perfect and beautiful that Sab couldn't distinguish one from the other. "But I don't understand how it could have happened."

"One of the pawns," said the Patriarch, "is a New Born."

A susurration of surprise rippled around the circle. Sab raised an eyebrow. Obviously the Patriarch's statement meant something to them.

"The fuck's a New Born?" she said, which earned her a few scornful chuckles.

"Oh, don't laugh at her," said Emil with insincere concern. "It's not like her mother had time to teach her much."

Genuine laughter flittered around the circle. She'd never give these thundercunts the satisfaction so she laughed right along with them.

"A New Born," the Patriarch interrupted, "is an aberrant human. One able to control magic."

Sab whistled long and low. "Shit on a stick. How'd that happen?"

After a slight pause the Patriarch said, "We are still uncertain of their origin."

"That's why they're called New Borns, genius," Emil said to her. "They're a new kind of human."

"Huh. Well, sucks for us, I suppose," said Sab, "having humans out there that can actually kill us off. Didn't know that." She turned to Emil. "So, what? They're like reverse mutants?"

His perfect face flushed. "Mutants are repugnant, but

they're still from the lines of Mages. New Borns are worse than repugnant. They're human."

"Yeah," said Sab. "That sounds fucking gross."

"What our family must decide now," said the Patriarch, doing a wonderful job of pretending that his important meeting wasn't being disrupted by two annoying idiots, "is what to do with her."

"Audra!" Sab shouted out. "That's her name, right? I kind of, felt it? Maybe. When the Game ended."

"We *all* did," said the Patriarch. "That's why we are here."

"What *can* we do with her?" said another nameless family member. "The human, I mean. Not that…embarrassment," he clarified, gesturing at Sab.

She rolled her eyes. "Well, it's not like we don't know where she is, is it? She's stuck on Taurë. Just go there and get her."

"She's a New Born, genius," said Emil, in what he probably thought were withering tones. "She can kill us."

"It seems to me," said the Patriarch, "that Sabina has offered herself up to aid House Lix-Tetrax in its greatest need by volunteering to hunt down our New Born enemy."

"What? Wait, I never—"

"And we thank you," the Patriarch continued over her protestations, "for undertaking such a dangerous mission for us. We will honour your name once you are dead."

Well, shit on a fucking stick. The day just got worse.

SQUIRREL

I felt her.

At the time, obviously, I didn't know who she was or why I was able to, but I know now it was Audra.

A month or so before, just as the warm season was packing for the off and the rains were coming in to take its place, I was walloped by power. I didn't know what it was at the time, but it was the opposite of what I'd felt when I took out the Chief's men. The opposite, but the same. The Chief's men were the victims of the storm that thundered inside me and ached for release—which it did with bloody consequences.

This time, the storm wanted to come *in*. And there was nothing I could do to stop it. I remember screaming. Mouse, my beloved cat, ran away from me and didn't come back for two days. Took a week for the poor mite not to flinch every time I spoke to him.

I didn't scream because it hurt. I screamed because I knew that at some point it would want to go back out again, and I didn't want to think of what might happen then. And I screamed because it felt good. I didn't want it to stop. No way that was a good thing.

As it turned out, that was when Audra killed off them two Mages who'd plagued Kingston and starved the Villagers. I still can't call them orcs. Orcs are from stories. And orcs were evil. From what Audra told me, the orcs she'd met were quite nice. Once the Rage had passed.

But that wasn't when I felt her. I felt her when she got back to Kingston. I'd been minding my own business, willing Mouse to catch a bloody bird so we'd have something to eat later, when I suddenly realised there was someone like me, near me. I spun around thinking they were just behind me, but alls I saw was the parched copse, barely clinging on to leaves that'd be ripped from their branches when the rains finally came. Of course, there was no one there. Which made no sense, because my eyes could feel them. I scrambled up the nearest tree, frightening away the bird that had been pecking at the rotting berries on the ground and earning a look of disgust from Mouse, so that I could look above the treetops and back towards the smudge on the horizon that was Kingston City.

Well, if someone had've walloped me with a coin-stuffed sock I wouldn't've known the difference. I couldn't *see* her, not like now, but I could still see her. She was walking along Banker's Drive. And she was a blob of red. I was seeing her aura.

At that point I had precisely two thoughts: *can she see* me? And: *I'm not alone!* I jumped out of the tree and pulled Mouse in close for a hug. I hadn't been happy for a long time.

"Fancy a trip to the big city, Mouse?"

He blinked his big yellow eyes at me.

"Let's go then!"

. . .

Now, it took all the way until the looming hill of Kingston City filled my vision and the stink of Out'Keep filled my nose until I finally came to my senses. The Chief was in there somewhere, no doubt still smarting after I'd done in Razor-Hand and some of his finest thugs a few months back. And the Chief was like a big fat jewel-bedecked spider sitting in the middle of his web of silk and money—he had cronies everywhere. And if they weren't paid cronies, there were certainly plenty of regular people who'd happily accept a handout in exchange for information. Within a notch of my arrival, the Chief'd know it and I'd be back in his lair and *I'd* be done in.

Orcs bollocks though, but I could feel her! Feel her with my eyes, see her with my stomach, hear her with my nerves. I had to meet her, speak to her, find out who—what—she was, and that need was greater by far than my fear of the Chief. All right, he'd kill me stone dead as soon as his eyes fell on me, but *she'd* be able to answer my questions. She'd be able to tell me what happened in my old house, how those men died, how my mum could walk again.

She could tell me what I was. And that was something that'd been torturing me every day since I left the city and called the trees my home.

"It's a big dirty place in there, Mouse," I said to my cat, busy washing his paws until I decided to start moving again. "Ready to go in?"

He swatted at a butterfly that dared to cross his path. He missed it. He wasn't nearly as good a hunter as he thought he was. But he'd kept me company ever since Mum'd gone and I loved him for it.

"Well, then. No point standing about out here looking in."

Could've used the gates, would've been easier, and it's not like they had guards on them these days—such expensive uniforms and weapons were saved for the inner gates. No one cared who got into Out'Keep, but Ancient Realm forbid any poor bastard got roughed up in the nice clean streets of In'Keep. So the gates were an option, but not a realistic one for me and Mouse. Barrow boys and fly-pitchers always crawled around the gates to catch the unsuspecting visitor unawares with their wares, and if they didn't buy anything, they'd always find their purse had mysteriously vanished the first time they tried to later on in their day. And it was them types of people as'd go straight to the Chief if they saw my face. Because I didn't doubt that there was a price on the head that it was attached to.

So once we crossed the sludge that made up the old moat, that meant we had to climb the walls. Luckily, we'd both got pretty good at climbing since living in the trees. A dreadful hunter Mouse may've been, but he was a bloody good climber. Especially when he climbed up my legs and on to my back, dug his claws nice and deep into my tunic so's he wouldn't fall, and let me do all the hard work. There were a couple of slips and missed grips here and there and Mouse voiced his disapproval with a soft mew in my ear each time, but we got to the top eventually with all our bones intact. And this was the easier of the walls. Once we'd passed through Out'Keep, scaling In'Keeps's walls would be much more interesting.

But first things always first. Away to the right I saw the straight line of Intellect's Path leading up to Intellect's Gate right into the Academician's Quarter. Away to my left was King's Route leading to King's Gate and right into the Royal Quarter. The nearer I got to that part of the city the more people there'd be asking what business I had there. But if I strayed too close to Intellect's Path I'd be dangerously close to Keep'Out Quarter, and that was the Chief's domain. Best I stuck to the middle then, working my way through the hovels and lean-tos that made up this quarter of Out'Keep and wound around and up and through each other with no sense of direction or privacy.

Mouse wasn't very happy about the excursion. He'd never seen so many people before, never heard the screams and shouts that made up their daily lives, the bangs and crashes that warned of imminent violence. Never witnessed the number of communal cook-fires, smelt the stink of unwashed bodies walking through shit-stained streets. I can imagine it was a bit of an eye-opener for him. He spent the whole time perched on my shoulder, hissing. The fact it was raining didn't help his mood much neither. But at least he wasn't walking along badly cobbled streets made treacherous with mud and water in his bare feet like me. Maybe I should've been hissing too. But I noticed the difference immediately: the plague had been a vicious cull. I'd never seen so much of the street before.

And then we reached the market stalls. Right behind those was Academician's Quarter, and in another life I'd worked nights in there, lifting things that were mere trinkets for the Academicians, but meant me and Mum could eat the next day. So I knew that behind one of the market stalls was a little crawly hole that a small thief could squeeze through instead of scaling the smooth white stone of In'Keep's walls. I knew it because I'd made it. It'd taken an Age, but it'd proved its worth. I could even remember where it was. Alls I had to do was get to it. The only thing was, every time I'd used it was during the dark of midnight when all the market-stalls were empty of seeing eyes that would wonder what a little boy was doing creeping around the back of them.

Now, though, it was day time. Even in the rain most Out'-Keepers would rather be outdoors than in, it seemed. I needed a plan to get behind the crowding market stalls. Thing was, I'd been out of the business for a bunch of months and I didn't know if my mind could come up with one any more.

Luckily, I didn't have to. Mouse, intrepid hunter that he was, caught sight of a market stall full of caged chickens and launched himself from my shoulder towards the biggest wire coop stuffed full of squawking feathers and caused a right racket. I remembered enough from the old days not to let a golden opportunity pass, so I made myself small and crawled beneath stalls and around feet until I reached the foot of In'Keep's wall, then scrabbled around a bit until I found the loose stone that hid my little tunnel. The warm season had kept it fairly dry in there, but I did disturb a nest of creepers that scuttled out of my way on their many legs. I paid them no mind though, because I was hoping that Mouse would realise I was no longer beside him and that he'd have to sniff me out. We'd become quite used to each other's smell since the day Mum left. I didn't want to leave the stone out of place for too long, so I was also hoping he'd get a move on.

He sauntered over a few moments later, mouth devoid of any catch and bearing a look that said he'd never intended to catch a chicken anyway. I drew him in by the scruff of his neck and put the stone back in place. Pitch dark it was, but we were both accustomed to such after moonless nights in the wild and it did nothing to hinder our short journey. On the other side lay the Academician's Quarter, and there'd be far fewer prying eyes and many more questions answered when I got there. I smiled in the darkness and shuffled forward as quick as I could.

I REMEMBERED THE LIBRARY WELL. Course I did. Last time I'd looked at it from these trees it'd been dry and dark, so the pillars had been less noticeable, as were the graven patterns along the window sills, but there's no mistaking a huge building like that. I also remembered it was shit-brickingly close to the Rebel Barracks, although even at this relatively early notch of the afternoon it was empty around there. Jumping out of the tree, I was ready to scarper across the grass towards the library, when I saw her.

She must've been in the palace because she came marching from that direction with a face more thundery than the weather, stomped her way to the giant wooden door, threw herself against it and disappeared from my sight again. Except for her redness. That I could still see faintly, even through the stone of the building.

I looked across at Mouse, shrugged, then ran after her, my shoeless feet making no noise whatsoever under the sound of the rain. I slipped in before the heavy door finally closed—with a very soft click considering its size—and Mouse rubbed up against my calf, letting me know he'd made it in too.

Didn't really have enough time to look around me before I heard voices, and they came from the library proper. I'd come out this way last time and I knew that the place was filled with standing shelves of books, plenty of places for a sneaking thief to hide. I dithered a little, uncertainty creeping up on me now I was so close to her. But finally the thought of someone coming in the front door to find a book and finding me instead got my feet moving again.

The inner door was silent when I pushed it, thankfully. I'd only taken a couple of steps before nerves failed me. I slunk into the nearest book alley to catch my breath, slow my heart and plan my next move. A thief's no good if he's panicking, and I was about as useful as a fingerless hand right now. Fortunately for me, Mouse understood the seriousness of the situation. Instead of going off to investigate the new surroundings, he sat himself down next to me, his tail winding around and over his front paws and looked entirely disinterested.

"Thank you, Jenna, it looks just as I left it." That was Audra. And her grateful tone sounded forced.

"It was a pleasure. It felt a little like a holiday actually, all nice and quiet with no Academicians running around the place. No wonder you like it here so much."

"Yes."

There was silence for a moment and I could feel the awkward tension from where I hid.

"So, did you find it? Is Kingston free of the plague?"

"It's free of the plague but at too great a cost."

Another awkward pause. Evidently this Jenna was aching with curiosity but Audra was reluctant to satisfy it.

"What happened out there, Audra?"

She sighed. "I'll be writing a very full paper on all that happened, which you'll be welcome to read. I can't bring myself to recount it now."

"No, of course, you must be exhausted after your travels. Go and take some rest. I can stay here a little longer while you—"

"Thank you, that won't be necessary. You must have other duties to attend to. Thank you again for all you've done in my absence."

"You're welcome."

We both heard the footsteps. Mouse stood and twitched his ears back and forth. But the girl called Jenna passed by our alley without even a glance. Me and mouse looked at each other, but our relief was short-lived.

"You'd better come out from there," Audra said. "I'm not fond of boys skulking in my library with their cats."

SABINA

"*I*f I might interrupt, Patriarch," said Emil, shuffling his perfect arse to the edge of his fat armchair. "Why should a Stratian get all the honour? And a *girl*! I mean…" He blustered like an idiot for several seconds while he tried to find the right words to convey his meaning. Any words probably. "Surely someone from a higher level should represent House Lix-Tetrax on such an important mission as this?"

Silence descended on the assembly like soap bubbles.

"I honestly do not believe," said the Patriarch underneath a perfectly sculpted, raised eyebrow, "that anyone else here would care to volunteer."

Various family members chuckled their agreement. Or probably relief. Venturing beyond the 'Sphere where their magic wouldn't be topped up whenever they wanted no doubt had their tiny minds aghast.

Oh, and the certain death thing. Sab was under no illusions as to why the Patriarch was happy to send her out after this New Born thing. This…Audra human.

"Well, I mean to say," Emil continued, "Cirrocumulus

level is renowned for their fearlessness. We invented the Dive. No one's as brave as we are, Patriarch. Except for you."

"Are you saying," said Sab, "that you want to come with me?" She finished her cigarette with a double toke and crushed the butt under the heel of her bare foot. The brief spark of pain made her smile.

"Urgh, skies above, no," said Emil. "Not *with* you. Against you." His face brightened and he looked up the Patriarch again. "Let's make it a race. Cirrocumulans versus Stratians. The winner, me, will be the one who saves Magekind."

So many questions. Like: did he think just getting to Audra first would somehow make him invulnerable to her? Didn't he understand that he'd have no access to human slaves to top up his powers the second they were beyond the Magelands? And how was it possible that she was related to such a fucking idiot, however distantly?

Obviously, she wasn't going to ask these questions out loud; she did hope that she could convey some of it by open-mouthed astonishment. By the looks of it, other family members were trying to do the same. Even the Patriarch had to blink a few times before speaking again.

"You are certain, Emil, that you want to undertake this…race?"

"Fuck yeah!" said Emil, boxing the air. Then he remembered himself. "I mean, yes please, Patriarch."

"But," said anonymous family member number 6 maybe. "You're an important member of House Lix-Tetrax. *She* isn't. *She's* disposable, isn't that right, Patriarch?"

The Patriarch inclined his head slightly in the affirmative. The bastard.

"You know, guys, I'm sitting right here. I can see *and* hear you." No one paid her any attention.

"You're a Cirrocumulan, Emil," said anonymous. "We can't risk losing *you*."

"Sabina's mission will give us time to devise a long-term strategy that will be certain to work," said the Patriarch.

Wow. Sab decided right there and then that she'd do everything possible, and impossible if it came to it, to succeed. Not because she particularly wanted to help her House, or her family, or any of the idiots living on the 'Sphere. But because she wanted to force-feed everyone sitting here their words. Until they puked on them. And then she'd make them eat their puke.

"Won't you all feel silly if I come back with Audra's dead body in tow," she said pleasantly.

"Not if I bring it back first!" Emil wailed. He drew a finger along his palm, then blood swelled. He threw a glistening ruby orb of it up into the air in front of her face. "Blood pact," he growled. "Seal it right now."

She copied his gesture and sealed the pact with her own blood before any of the rellies sitting in the circle could stop it. There was uproar, obviously, but no one could blame Sab for it. She was simply following a command from her higher and better. And they all knew it. The blood bubble burst, the droplets flying back into their hands and sealing up the cuts in their palms.

The Patriarch pinched the bridge of his nose. Even he couldn't undo a blood pact. It was how the Games were started every fifth Age, and it bound the competitors together until the Games were over. Only a surge of power, like what happened at the end of a Game, was enough to break a blood pact.

"What is done," said the Patriarch, "is done. And now that it has become a race rather than a simple mission, there must be rules."

"I have a rule," said anonymous, grinning smugly at Sabina. "Competitors have to pass through all three city states before reaching the border. They can't leave a city state until they have at least one new member on their team."

"Interesting," said the Patriarch.

"She's Stratian," anonymous said to Emil. "No one's going to risk their lives for her. But you're Cirrocumulan. They'll be queuing up to curry favour with you."

Emil turned to Sab and smirked.

"I literally couldn't give a shit," she said.

"And the first team to reach this New Born human wins," Emil declared.

"Or is the first team to die horribly at her hands," said Sab. "She chopped off Nathaniel's *and* Messina's heads. Didn't you see it? It was brutal. I'll gladly let you get to her first if it means—"

"The winning team," said the Patriarch, patience strained to breaking point, "is the one who brings her corpse back here."

"Can't we just kill her and leave her in Taurë?" said Emil.

Sab held up her grimy hands. "Knowing me, I'll probably cheat if we don't have to bring back proof. I'm insanely dishonest, you know."

"You Stratians make me sick," said Emil. "You bring nothing but shame to the AtmoSphere."

"Shame, yes," said Sab. "But also slaves. It's us lot down there that makes sure there are enough humans to power this great city. Without us, you'd literally be nothing."

Emil stood, hands clenched tight by his side. He loomed above her, so she smiled sweetly up at him. "I'm going to watch Audra kill you before I kill her and win the race."

"Good for you," said Sab. "I'll be rooting for you."

He spat at her, but she dispersed it before it reached her. Pain she liked. Other people's bodily fluids, not so much. Humiliation she stored up deep within her soul. It matured into rage, and that could be harnessed to do some wonderfully destructive things. She knew that, because she'd seen it happen.

"The blood pact is made," said the Patriarch. "The rules are set. You leave the AtmoSphere for Oceanwall as soon as you have found at least one new member for your team." He smiled at Sab. Well, he displayed his teeth at her, more accurately. "The Game is over. Now the Race is begun."

"WHAT A TWAT," said Claws. "He actually said that?"

"Those very words," said Sab. "Like it was some kind of Age-defining proclamation, or something." She giggled, grabbed her tobacco and papers out of thin air. "They have all this power, but none of them realise just how pathetic they all are."

"So when do we leave?" said Claws.

Sab paused, her freshly rolled cigarette halfway to her mouth. "You what?"

"Well obviously I'm coming with you."

"Uh-uh," said Sab, lighting her cigarette with her thumb. "I'm not getting you killed out there."

"Oh, fuck you." Claws swiped the tobacco and started rolling her own cigarette. "First, I'm a mutant, not a Mage, so Audra ain't gonna kill *me*. Second, you can't leave until you get someone else on your team. I want to be your someone else. Light it up."

Sab flicked her thumb. Claws drew on her cigarette. Smoke curled out of her cheek.

"Huh. Two good points. First, hadn't thought about that, but it's not just Audra we've got to worry about. Second, like I was going to follow their stupid fucking rules anyway."

Claws grinned, but it faded quickly. "Just let me come with you. Please. I hate it here. I hate it even with you in it.

Can't imagine how unbearable it'll be with you gone. Just let me escape. Please help me escape."

The pleading in her eyes was desperate. Tangible, even. Like Sab could've scooped up the air in front of her friend's face and tasted the bitterness that permeated it.

Claws was the most beautiful woman Sab had ever seen. Far more beautiful than those flawless upper-levellers because Claws's beauty was natural. She couldn't use magic to perfect herself like they all did up there, but she didn't need to. Six foot tall if she was an inch, with a lean, muscular body thanks to all the farming she did down here. Her black hair was as wavy as the ocean beneath the 'Sphere, except for the straight white streaks. There was a story behind each one of them, but poor Claws still hadn't got up the courage to tell Sab about them.

For a mutant though, being this beautiful was a curse. Claws had done everything she could to ensure eyes that looked at her turned away in disgust. She kept the left side of her head perfectly shaved, displaying the criss-cross scars she'd carved there over the years. And in her right cheek she'd cut a hole, big enough to see her teeth and tongue move when she spoke, which always freaked people out. Grossed them out too, when she was purposely not being careful when she ate anything in front of them. But in Sab's eyes, these mutilations just made Claws even more beautiful. They were the story of her survival. No matter how bad it got, she lived through it. Not like some people she could mention, but refused to talk about.

And now there was a chance to take her away from all of this. Get her out of the city that had turned this mutant into a ragged cut-out of a person. How could Sab refuse her?

"Of course you're coming with me," she said, leaning over and hugging her. "Don't know what I was thinking."

"Neither of you is thinking."

Sab looked up. There was Prisca, lurking in the doorway of Claws's cell, holding two steaming bowls.

Sab sighed in that melodramatic way that informs all listeners that the world is nothing but a huge vat of shit that doesn't understand anything. Then she said, "Is that porridge?"

"Course it's porridge," said Prisca, stepping primly over the mess carpeting the tiled floor. Claws had approved of Sab's rule of filthy thumb that kept other people away and had decided to implement it herself. She'd done so with impressive skill. The only other place in the whole 'Sphere that gave the gag reflex more of a workout was the slave pits.

"Eat up," said Prisca when she'd finally navigated the chaos and handed them a bowl each. "I've had mine. Ready to go when you are."

Two heads shot up and looked at the older woman.

"What are you looking at me like that for? You two will've cut yourselves to pieces before you even get out of the core if I'm not there to keep an eye on you. You'll never win the race if you're nothing but meat ribbons."

Claws laughed with a mouth full of porridge.

Sab chuckled, then said, "It's a death quest and you know it. The Patriarch's sending me out there to get rid of me. None of us'll get back here."

Prisca looked around the grotty cell. "I will miss this lap of luxury I've sat in all my life."

Sab snorted a laugh through her nose.

"But I promised your mum."

Now Sab looked Prisca in the eye. She had remarkable eyes. Pearl white irises ringed with black. She never blinked when she was being dead serious.

"Your mum knew she couldn't keep you safe down here. She couldn't even keep *herself* safe down here." Prisca looked across at Claws, smiled sadly, then faced Sab again. "I

33

promised her the day you were born I'd do everything in my power to watch over you. I never knew what she was going to do to herself," her unblinking eyes filled with tears, "but I'm buggered if I'm going to break my promise to her now. You're my girls, both of you, and I'm not letting you go on your own."

Sab nodded, finished her bowl of porridge in silence. Prisca always cooked for her two girls. The slave way, with fire and pots and stuff. Not with magic. Magic was finite, and the poorer you were, the more finite it was. She'd known Prisca forever. They didn't always see eye to remarkable eye on everything, but that was normal, right? No matter what though, she never stopped cooking for them. How could she've thought about leaving the 'Sphere without Prisca?

"Well, fuck me," Sab said. "Looks like I've got *two* members on team death quest."

"Watch your language, my girl."

"I suppose we'd better sort out the farms before we—"

"Fuck that," said Prisca. "We've got permission to leave the 'Sphere. I'm not staying a second longer than we have to."

ADÀM

*A*part from the palace, no residence in Kingston City was bigger than the Worthy Clan mansion. One look was enough to see that it had been commissioned a couple of Ages ago, just as Lord Worthy had made his clan the wealthiest and most powerful. He knew that nothing was better at demonstrating to commoners how wealthy and powerful a person was than the place in which they lived.

Sitting in the middle of the Financial Quarter, its immensity dwarfed all the other mansions. Indeed, the entire district grew up and was built around the Worthy mansion, like a king from the old Ages surrounded by his adoring peasants. Adàm stared up at it, feeling no gladness at having returned, at seeing his parents—in fact, he felt nothing at all. But he remembered. He remembered how Faër had claimed to hate the marble monstrosity in which they were born, what it symbolised, and how far it separated them from their mythical ancestors of the Ancient Realm.

Not so mythical any more though.

And he'd tutted and rolled his eyes at his stupid twin

sister before bounding off to the vaults to count the vast stores of family wealth. He'd loved money. He'd loved his sister. Now he felt nothing.

In the atrium was the fountain that Faër loved to sit by, trailing her fingers in the crystal waters, singing songs, pretending she wasn't the wealthiest person in the land. Their parents, when not obsessing over accounts, had often despaired of her Age-long fad, and every decade or so Adàm would tell them that it would pass soon enough. Now he could tell them that he'd been right all along. Her fad *had* passed. They would no longer need to worry that their only daughter wouldn't be continuing the family name due to her snubbing the modern elvish ways in favour of those from legends.

He plodded towards the staircase, as wide and winding as the streets in Out'Keep, trying to find a way of delivering the news to his parents, but failing entirely. People came up to him, spoke to him, but he understood nothing they said, so eventually they went away again. An Age passed while he climbed the stairs and trudged along the upper arcades, but all too soon he stood before the great portal that led into the beating heart of the Worthy clan's fortune. He had a key, but he wasn't sure he could remember how to use it. Wasn't even sure if he had it with him. He sighed, lifted a fist and beat it against the aged oak. The electric shocks of pain that forked out from his fingers along his forearm felt good. The booming thumps sounded good to his jaded ears. It was probably the first time ever that someone mistreated such a respected and important piece of furniture. He didn't stop pounding until the door slowly opened.

"Lord Worthy," said a servant. Not an elf. Servants were never elves. This was a human. "We weren't expecting you back today. But we're very glad you are."

He walked passed him. Gold and jewels, that's all this room consisted of. And ledgers. Lots and lots of ledgers. Many of them gilded and encrusted with jewels. There was also a mahogany desk the size and pomp of a banquet table with two matching throne-like chairs. That was where his mother and father sat. Each had a ledger before them, an opal ink pen in one slender hand and a golden goblet of expensive cordial resting at the other. They also wore twin expressions of surprise—a slight rise of an arched eyebrow.

"Adàm, my boy," said his father. "You caught us closing the last of the books. Why don't you come and join us? You've missed all the best ones, I'm afraid, but there are still some good ones left to get your teeth into."

"No, thanks."

"You see?" said his mother. "I told you allowing him to go off on an adventure would change him."

"Yes, my dear. Adàm, you haven't gone the way of your wayward sister, have you, old boy?"

"No."

Clearly they were waiting for more from him, but he still couldn't find his words.

"Out with it then, my boy, ink's drying up on my pen and it isn't cheap stuff, you know."

"Is everything well, Adàm?" said his mother, finally standing and moving away from the desk.

"No," said Adàm, then his voice cracked and the dam burst.

"Orc's balls, my boy, whatever's the matter?" said his father, joining his wife on the other side of the desk.

"Where's Faër?" she said.

"Still out dancing around trees, I shouldn't wonder. Isn't that right, old boy?"

Adàm shook his head. He wouldn't be able to keep it in

for much longer. Apart from the fact that he was pretty sure it'd rip him apart, he could also hear the twinge of panic in his mother's voice and the brittle jollity in his father's. Adàm had never cried before. No one from his clan had. Why would they? They were practically immortal and definitely wealthy. What could possibly make them cry?

"Faër's dead," he said.

"No, she isn't," said his father. "That's absurd. She's barely two hundred years old."

His mother, on the other hand, raised both of hers to her mouth.

"She was killed," said Adàm, forcing the words out between sobs. "By a Mage. Two of them. Two Mages."

And then he spent a desperate half-notch explaining to them what he meant. How the Healing Glass in the Blasted Glade had been nothing but a trap to lure them and the orcs into battle. How nearly everyone had been killed. How Audra had somehow defeated Nathaniel ScourgeMaster and Messina LandSlayer. And then how she'd been able to save everyone, including the orcs, but not Faër. Faër had died in his arms.

From their faces he knew they didn't understand half of what he said but he didn't much care. It was a relief just to tell them. No one had spoken on the way home. No one. Nothing had been explained or questioned. No one had apologised. Nor offered sympathy. It was the hardest part of a very strange journey.

"But she can't be dead," said his father again. "She's barely two hundred years old. She's supposed to continue the family name. She has duties as a Worthy elf that must be carried out. I absolutely forbid her to be dead!"

"How could young Audra save all the humans and...orcs?" said his mother. Her mahogany skin was drained of colour.

"If they were already killed in battle, how could she save them? Academicians aren't healers."

"No," said Adàm. "I'm not sure she's an Academician any more. She's a Mage."

HE LEFT them during the reeling silence of his pronouncement—the smell of wealth in that chamber nauseated him. The idea to visit Audra in her library popped into his mind but he dismissed it as quickly as it arrived. He had no wish to see her. Not that he blamed her for Faër's death—how could he? All of them had been fooled by that disguised old scholar Than and that cursed journal. All of them except Faër. Why didn't she say something sooner? Why keep all that knowledge to herself if she knew they were in danger? Why didn't she explain her distrust of Than?

He voiced a wordless cry of frustration and flung himself over the balustrade, landing softly on the marble floor of the atrium. There were far too many questions that he simply didn't have the answers to, and he was fairly sure that finding out wouldn't help him. All he knew for now was that he had to get out of this mansion. Once his parents came to terms with their daughter's death they would need to speak to him about succession. It wasn't a conversation he wanted. He left the mansion and wandered out into the pristine streets of the Financial Quarter, where wealthy elves moved with grace and speed to their next important meeting, dressed in clothes so luxurious, the cost of them would feed several Out'Keep families for many seasons. Some of them knew his family well and gave him a glance of recognition, probably assuming that his sister was up a tree somewhere. He knew precisely how they'd react to news of her death. They'd be annoyed that they now had to groom their sons for an entirely different elf and her family if they wanted to marry into a good one, while secretly hoping their daughters would be chosen for Adàm.

Walking back towards Banker's Gate, he didn't really know where his feet were taking him so he didn't try to stop them. And he didn't once look back.

"*W*hat's in the bag, Prisca?" said Sab, nudging Claws and smirking.

"Just some bits and pieces that might come in useful on the journey," replied their old friend. "Not least food."

"Aww, that's really sweet," said Sab. "It's like you don't even know we're leaving the 'Sphere to go to our certain deaths."

"Not going to mine on an empty stomach."

"So you're just leaving all the work to us then?"

A figure was in the middle of the corridor, a person-shaped blockage between them and the core. Woman, fairly young. Tried to look less disgusting than Sab looked, for all the good it did her. She obviously had a name, but Sab had never bothered to learn it. There was no point down here. What Sab definitely knew was that she looked well pissed off.

"Weren't you in the corridor when I came back from Cirrus?" said Sab. "Didn't you hear what I said? About the Patriarch sending me out to kill me off?"

Pissed-off puffed through her lips in disbelief. "Right.

41

And he just so happened to let you bring all your little friends with you."

"Don't know if you've met Claws before, but she's not that little."

"Yeah, and she's the best rape-racker I've got. You can't take her with you."

Ah. So Pissed-off was one of the slavers in charge. Prisca was too, but unlike this one here, she never let that minuscule bit of power over the lowest of the low go to her head.

"I'm not *taking* her," said Sab. "She's coming with me. Of her own free will. Well, except that it's been ordered by the Patriarch. You know what free will's like round here."

"Yeah, I do actually," said Pissed-off, taking a step forward and placing her fists on her hips. Her elbows scraped along the wall of the corridor. She was a big girl. "And that mutant belongs to me."

"Huh. Well it seems like we're at a bit of an impasse."

"Yeah, it—"

Bubbles. Sab flicked her fingers towards Pissed-off and dispersed her component atoms.

Claws gasped.

Prisca said, "What did you do?"

"Oh, she'll be all right in a few minutes," said Sab, walking briskly to the core, waving at a few heads poking out of their cells. She was delighted to see some of them flinch. "Come on."

"But I thought," whispered Claws. "I thought…"

"Look, she's not dead, all right? She'll be back in a few minutes. Hours? I don't know really. Ever since the Game ended I've been a bit unsure of my own strength."

The lilac fog at the core parted and allowed them access. Sab ushered her two friends through, then stepped in herself. There was just about enough room for the three of them in the cylindrical tube. Luckily, they were close friends.

As the fog coalesced once more, she took one last look at the corridor, with all those cells along it. It wasn't filthy or cold down here, and there was always food in the common room at the end, which Sab had avoided as much as possible. Everyone kept it so neat and tidy it made her sick. But compared to the slaves, the Stratians lived lives, long, long lives, in relative comfort.

And that was precisely why she hated it. The upper-level Mages gave them just enough to make do. Just enough so that they wouldn't think about turning around and saying, "Hey, you fuckers. How come we've only got this when you've all got fat leather armchairs and free-form fires on your floating terraces? Why's our magic limited when yours isn't?"

Because that's what they'd done, those upper-level bastards. Here was a race of people that was right at the top of the food chain. Humans were feisty, and fought like motherfuckery when they were scared or angry, but really they didn't stand a chance against a Mage. Mages were the strongest race on the planet. And you'd think, you'd *think*, that because they could all use magic, they'd live in an egalitarian society and lord it as one over the humans.

But no. Some bastard of a Mage had found a way to limit others' use of magic, so that even amongst the only magic-wielding race in the world, there was a fucking hierarchy. And she had no idea how it worked. As if anyone would ever tell her. They'd be way too scared to tell the Stratians how their magic was limited, just in case some clever little bitch like Sab herself reverse-engineered it.

But it meant the Stratians hoarded what little magic that was eked out to them once a year. Some of it going to healing themselves—slaves got vicious every now and then, so injuries were common. A lot of it went towards attempts at perfecting themselves as the upper-levellers did. You know, just in case some Mage came all the way down here to say to one of them, "Oooh, you're so beautiful, I must take you away from this squalor so you can live with me in wonder and luxury for the rest of your immortality."

Stratians. They were all fucking idiots. Wasting all their magic on hope.

"Sabina." An impatient elbow nudged her in the ribs.

"What?" She looked around into Prisca's lightly wrinkled face.

"You have to tell the core where to take us."

"Oh yeah." The fog was thick and purple in front of her and the corridor was gone. "Mind wandered, sorry," she said to her friends. Then, louder, "Terminal."

"State your reason," said the androgynous voice of the core.

"Because this is team death quest and we're doing this ridiculous race the Patriarch signed off on."

The briefest of pauses, then, "Confirmed."

Sab's stomach lurched.

"I'm sorry," said Claws.

"What for?"

"For making you stick up for me. Back there."

"You didn't make me do anything," said Sab, smiling. "Besides, it's not like you were going to say anything, right?"

Claws chuckled. Shook her head sadly.

"Anyway, that bitch was annoying."

"Maybe once I'm out of the 'Sphere I'll be a bit braver."

"That's the spirit," said Prisca. "A fresh start for all of us."

"Wow, you girls," said Sab. "You're astonishing…"

"Thank you," said Prisca with a smile.

"…ly stupid," Sab finished, and ducked out of the way of Prisca's backhand. "You know this race isn't going to end well for us, right?"

"Terminal," monotoned the core.

"See? Even the core agrees with me."

The lilac fog dispersed. The rising sun streaming in through the 'Sphere was blinding. Sab stepped out onto the platform.

Behind her, Claws said, "I can't."

She turned around. Through the hole in her cheek, Sab saw her friend's teeth were clenched tight. She also saw a lump of porridge lodged in there. But now wasn't the time for laughing.

"Look, I get it," said Sab. "It's big out there, and full of people."

"Not our people," Claws mumbled.

"You're not wrong," Sab agreed. "And there's no way we're going to cross the terminal without at least one of the bastards saying something about us that they think's funny or clever."

Claws tensed. Sab took her hands.

"But it's like, what? Ten minutes of our lives? And then we're off the 'Sphere forever. The Patriarch and his dick holders think they're getting rid of us, but they're not. They've handed us a free ticket off this ball of shit. That doesn't happen very often to our people, does it?"

Claws shook her head.

"Do you want to live an exciting new life with me and Prisca in the outside world away from all these wankers?"

Claws nodded her head.

"Good." Sab squeezed Claws's hand. "Me too. And do you think you can be brave enough to walk across the terminal with me so we can get to that new life?"

The briefest pause, then Claws nodded her head again.

"That's our girl," said Sab. "But we should probably do it pretty sharpish, because when the core spits you out we'll end up stumbling around up here like dicks."

This time Claws laughed. That was good. Laughter was

always strong enough to kick fear's arse. She flicked her eyes briefly to Prisca, who winked at her for a job well done. Then the three of them stepped out of the core and onto the platform.

The platform was just that. A narrow strip of thick glass tiles supported by a steel skeleton. No magic holding up this structure; the original architects of this ridiculous city obviously wanted something a bit more durably certain to hold up the innards of the 'Sphere. The steel scaffolding was everywhere in this enormous space, because the terminal was right at the equator of the city, and this platform ran along the central line of the equator. Meaning it was really fucking high up in the air. Scaffolding just to be sure, the architects had obviously said, but also it should be pants-shittingly impressive when people step out from the core and have their first look around.

Sure, some of the scaffolding had been decorated with winding, dangling vines or flowering shrubs, and the space was indeed criss-crossed with other platforms from different terminal quays—and even some boutiques and eateries, by the looks of it—but none of it detracted from the sheer immensity of the space. Sab's stomach jumped around uncomfortably every time she remembered she was on a narrow platform a hundred metres up from the next surface. Which was every other second. And it was narrow up here—Claws hadn't released her grasp of Sab's entire arm from the moment she stepped out of the core, and their feet literally had no margin of error. Luckily there was a flight of steps coming up, same steel and glass construct, so she wouldn't have to pretend to be fearless for that much longer.

"Skies above," said Prisca from behind them. "All that time cramped down on Stratus. Who'd've thought there'd be so much wasted space, eh? Where do we go now? Looks like there's loads of places to catch capsules from down there."

"Don't know," Sab said, concentrating furiously on the steps that were so close right now. "We'll have a look when we get down there, shall we?"

"Funny that they'd put so many stairs and walkways about the place, isn't it?" the old woman gabbled on. "All these Mages having to use their actual legs to move around. You'd think with all their vast wealth they'd just magic themselves about the place."

Huh. She hadn't thought of that. All this interminable eternity walking across this ridiculous platform with Claws doing her best to claw the flesh off her upper arm too, and she could've just…

Well. That was weird. She looked inside herself again. There was never that much magic in her stores anyway, except right now after the special explosive ending of the last Game. It was like a supernova right now. Usually it was like a cooling ember. Ha. Bet the Patriarch hated that. Couldn't take it back once it was put in. Anyway, the point was, she could see it, but she couldn't access it. If she tried to reach out to it, it repelled her away, like matching ends of magnets.

"It'a a magic dead zone," said Sab. "No one can use their magic here."

A couple of moments of silence from Prisca, then, "So it is. Well, now. Mind you, I suppose it makes sense. All these capsules, probably running off the stuff. Wouldn't want anyone tampering with them, would they? Especially not if one of our lot managed to get up here through the core." She cackled a little bit, then went back to oohing and ahhing at all the new sights.

"How can they make a place this big a dead zone?" Claws whispered.

"Dunno," said Sab with a shrug. Which made Claws grip even harder. "But if they can make sure that us Stratians only get the minimum amount of power needed to not keel over and die of exhaustion on the job, then I'm sure they can come up with a way of dampening an area in the 'Sphere."

Claws nodded. Then, "There's screens down there."

Now that they stood at the top of the flight of steps, Sab saw them clearly herself without any prompting, but Claws found talking a useful way of taking her mind off her all-consuming terror of, well, of everything that wasn't Stratus. And even then it was touch and go.

So she said, "Let's see if any of them tell us where we need to go."

"Where *do* we need to go?"

"Whichever city is closest to this one. How's your geography?"

Claws shrugged.

"Honestly," said Prisca. "I expected more from my girls than this. Oceanwall is the city nearest to us. Then it's Hinterland Deeps. After that, well," she shrugged with her face. "Fans and flying shit are in abundance."

"Oceanwall it is, then," said Sab. "So." She looked around the vast space, people bustling from quay to quay, stepping on and off the stationary capsules. They all knew exactly where they were going. "How do we get there, then?"

As well constructed as the terminal was, to Sab it looked chaotic. The quays above and below the equatorial line of the 'Sphere were crowded with capsules, the only transports that could take a Mage off the 'Sphere and to, well, wherever the Mages wanted to go. How was Sab supposed to know? She'd never been in one. From here, she saw that the quays below the equatorial platform ran east to west, stacked on top of one another, totalling five. Or maybe it was ten, because it looked like the capsules came in from the west on one side, and went out east on the other side. The capsules themselves were little bubble-like constructs linked together. Probably made out of some kind of light plastic so that less magic was needed to move it around. She looked up towards the platform she'd so recently tightroped across and saw that as below, so above. The quays up there seemed to mirror the quays down here. Looked like the Mages with plenty of power liked themselves some travelling. Lucky them.

"Well," said Prisca, sucking her teeth while looking at the screen. "I can't work out how that screen works, so…"

Sab drew her gaze down from the upper quays and joined Prisca's regard. Words and numbers flashed up and changed. The numbers were possibly times. But none of the words spelled out Oceanwall.

"Do you think," she said to Prisca, "that they're names of regions inside the cities, or something?"

"Could be, could be."

"Don't you know?" Claws whispered. She flinched just a little when they both looked at her. "Well, don't you?"

"How would we?" said Sab. "We've never been up here."

"Before today the terminal was just a word to me," said Prisca. "A mythical place that only happened to other people."

"So what are we supposed to do?"

Sab shrugged. "I reckon we just go down there, get on a capsule, see what happens."

Prisca nodded. "Solid plan."

Claws said, "But what if it's the wrong one?"

"We'll get on another one and try again. What's the worst that can happen?"

Not the right question to ask a mutant who'd lived her entire life in the 'Sphere, where only the slaves she farmed were below her on the social ladder. Sab linked her arm through Claws's and tugged gently at her.

"We'll be fine," she said. "We're here at the behest of our great and beloved Patriarch. We've got as much right to be here as any of these other fuckers."

"Besides," said Prisca, taking Claws's other arm, "maybe those capsules work like the core. Maybe they'll ask us where we want to go and they'll just take us."

Down on the main concourse a genteel hubbub settled on the trio, of wealthy Mages being polite to those from the same echelon they hailed from, resolutely ignoring those beneath them. Sab grinned hugely at all those who looked at her with disgust, knowing that her grotty teeth and receding gums would cause even more offence.

She hadn't changed out of the torn, black trousers and t-shirt she'd covered herself in during the family meeting, obviously. And there was Claws in filthy, baggy trousers that possibly used to be white or yellow, but were now mostly brown, and a shapeless black jumper with sleeves that went way past her hands but had holes for her thumbs to poke through. And Prisca. Fuck knew what Prisca was wearing. Random layers of grey material that were trying to be a dress? A bring-along blanket? Anyone's guess. Point was, all three of them couldn't have looked more out of place among these perfectly tailored, perfectly coiffed, perfectly made-up Mages, men and women, if they'd tried. Sab couldn't have been more proud.

"Oh look," said a voice from behind them, full of oil and smug. "Three slaves have escaped. Oh no, it's just a bunch of Stratians."

Emil. And judging by the toffy guffaws, he'd found his team too.

Sab turned. Yep. Emil, and five dicks. "Wow," she said. "You uppers have a distressingly low comedy threshold."

"What?" said Emil, scowling with incomprehension.

"I said, you're a dick."

All six of them looked scandalised. It was hilarious.

"You can't speak to us like that," said Dick #1, checking

with Emil to make sure this statement was correct. "You're just a Stratian. We're Cirrocumulans."

Sab blinked. "Oh—was that my cue to be, like, impressed or apologetic, or something?"

"Yes, actually."

"Well then," said Sab. "I'm a scion of House Lix-Tetrax, and we're all massively arrogant thundercunts so I don't have to say shit to you."

Dick #1 looked as though he would choke on his own tongue. Emil yanked him aside and Sab heard him hissper, "Skies above, Drusus, I told you about Sabina after the meeting—"

"*That's* Sabina? You said we were racing against Stratians!"

"She *is* a Stratian."

"But she said—"

"Just shut up, all right? And don't talk to her. I'll do the talking."

During the exchange, Sab grinned at Dicks #2-#5, flexed her skinless forearms at them, chuckled at their quadruplet expressions of horror.

Emil, chastising complete, spun back around to face her. He looked so clean and neat in his pristine trousers and pressed shirt. His ears and fingers glittered with jewellery. His blond hair was teased into wavy patterns that he probably thought were becoming. He put his hands in his pockets and adopted a pose that he likely intended to look casual with a little dash of intimidation.

"This is your team?" he said. "An old lady and some mutant?"

Claws's grip tightened on Sab's arm.

Dick #3 chuckled and said, "Emil, man, that's your sister Claudia."

Emil snarled. "She's not my fucking sister."

Claws whimpered.

"All right," said Sab. "So let's just pretend we've had our pissing contest, yes? We'll even say you won it. But now is probably a good time to find our capsule and get this race started for real."

"Everything's a joke to you, isn't it?" said Emil. "I get it—you're a joke, so you have to make everything else a joke, just to feel normal." He took a step forward, tried to cow Sab by towering over her. "But this race isn't a joke. This race is going to save Magekind. In the name, and for the honour, of House Lix-Tetrax, I'm going to win it."

Sab opened her mouth to speak. She was going to say that they were all going to die at the hands of this New Born Audra the moment she saw them coming, regardless of what House they came from, because Houses and names and honour didn't mean shit to this New Born human. She was going to say that just by getting off this fucked up 'Sphere, Sab and her friends had already won, because they'd finally have their freedom.

But Prisca got there first. "Well, what are we all standing around here for? Let's get on with it."

Emil and his dicks did some glowering and posturing, before finally swaggering off towards a capsule.

"We better follow them," said Prisca. Sab opened her mouth, but the old woman cut her off again. "I knew exactly what you would've said to those boys, and I'm telling you, if they, or anyone, knew—" she lowered her voice to a whisper "—that we just wanted to get out of the city they'd never let us leave. So keep your mouth shut. For us. Because the second they know we're not doing this against our will, we're right back down in Stratus. All right?"

Sab blinked at her. It wasn't often that Prisca gave someone a bollocking, so when she did, they knew they deserved it. And Prisca was right. This new race was only fun for the Mages if they thought the Stratians were doing it against their will.

Sab nodded. "All right," she said.

"Right," said Prisca, fixing her gaze on the strutting forms of their competition. "Let's get this over with."

SQUIRREL

"**W**ell, come along," said Audra. "There's no point pretending you're not there. I can see you, you know."

I looked down at Mouse, but he was staring at the opposite shelf of books as though he was actually trying to work out which one he wanted to borrow. I bent down and picked him up, was rewarded with a miaow of annoyance for my efforts, then shuffled out of the book alley and into the library proper.

It was then that I knew I'd seen her before—alls I could remember really was that mass of curly auburn hair, but even though it looked as though it hadn't been washed for a while there was no mistaking it. I hadn't really seen her face that last time I was in here, but the one looking at me now seemed pleasant enough in a grubby sort of way, although her eyes were a bit too penetrating. It was like they were telling me they'd seen more and knew more than I ever could in several lifetimes, so probably best not to mess with her. She was older than me by a good few seasons, but I was taller. That didn't really put me in any kind of advantage over her. Something was telling me she was stronger, and I believed it. I think it was probably her red aura. It was pretty potent this close up.

"That's better," she said, looking all around me briefly before settling her gaze on my face. "From the looks of you, I don't think you're here to borrow a book, are you?"

I shook my head.

"So let's start with names. I'm Audra."

"Squirrel."

She raised her eyebrows a little but didn't comment. "And your friend?"

"Mouse."

She smiled. It was supposed to be happy but she'd seen too much sad. "A cat called Mouse. Why not? He's very handsome."

"He knows it."

"So now we know who we are, why don't you tell me why you're here."

I nodded, but I had to think before I said my next words. *Because I saw you before you even reached the city this morning* just sounded ridiculous and I was afraid she'd kick me out before I got any answers. So I played for a bit of time by saying, "Umm…"

"Let me have a guess," she said, stepping closer. "It's because of this." She waved an arm in a wide arc around me.

"So I *have* got one then?"

The sad smile reappeared. "How did you think I knew you were here?"

I shrugged, and Mouse used the movement as an excuse to jump out of my grip. I called after him, but it'd never worked before so I don't know why I expected it to work then.

"He'll be safe enough," said Audra. "There's nothing in here but books. Yours is violet. What colour's mine?"

"You can't see it?"

"Can you see yours?"

I held up my arms and had a good look at them. They didn't look even a little bit violet. "Nope," I said. Then, "Yours is red. What are they?"

"Our auras, I believe." It was the first time I'd heard the word. I liked it. "Could you see any one else's on your way here?"

I shook my head.

"Nor could I. I think that makes us alike, Squirrel."

A thrill of relief tickled my chest—I wasn't alone any more! Although, there was still one obvious question. "What are we?" I asked.

Her face fell and her piercing eyes gazed far, far away. "We're Mages."

"Mages don't exist any more."

She looked at me like I was a stupid child then she looked away again.

"All right," I said. "We are, then. But that's a good thing, right? Mages had power and were heroes in all the old stories before they disappeared. Maybe we'll be heroes now."

"Have you used your power at all? What happened to make you realise you weren't the same as everyone else?"

The image of RazorHand and his two thugs smashing out through the wall of my old house came back to me. As did the memory of me squeezing the throats of two others until they died. I'd been fearful angry.

"I healed my mum's legs," I said.

"And was she grateful?"

She'd cut her own throat to get away from me. I shook my head.

"Come and sit down," she said, holding her hand out to me. "You look famished. I'll get some food and tea, then I'm afraid I'm going to have to tell you a little story."

I took up the offer even though I didn't feel particularly famished however much I looked it. And even though I used to love it when Mum told me stories, something told me Audra's wasn't going to be one where the hero came out on top.

So IT TURNED out that Mages were still alive and had been playing games with us humans for Ages and Ages. Deadly games that resulted in a battle with lots of death, and as the humans died the Mages' power was restored. Audra had killed two of them, Nathaniel ScourgeMaster and Messina LandSlayer, she called them, and that was what I'd felt: the mass expulsion of power from the dying Mages.

But it wasn't just humans in the game, according to Audra, oh no. Orcs, too. Orcs were still alive and well outside of stories in all. They'd been created by Messina for the express purpose of being used in the Game, and it was the consuming of blood that turned them wild. Raged, Audra called it. Like it was an illness. These days the orcs are harmless farmers and live far away from anyone, which is why we've never seen them. But Messina had tricked them into battle just like Nathaniel had tricked the Rebels into battle, and she got the orcs Raged up before she turned them loose on the humans. And they'd pretty much all killed each other by the time Audra'd found the two Mages. Normally, Mages couldn't kill each other, but Nathaniel had called her a New Born and was scared because he'd just seen her chop off Messina's head. Fear was the last thing he felt before Audra chopped his head off too.

Then she managed to save everyone who'd been killed by giving them back the life force that the two Mages had stolen, and she'd even been able to unRage the Raged orcs. The only person she couldn't save was her best friend, an elf called Faër. Audra looked so sad when she told that part of the story, and that was when I knew all of it was true.

But even though she'd told me her whole story, I still didn't understand anything.

"So if the Mages are bad," I said, "and we're a kind of Mage, does that make us bad? Because it seems that we've both tried to help people we love, and that makes us good, doesn't it?"

"There are so many questions, Squirrel, and I'm afraid I haven't yet got all the answers. But don't worry, I'll find them. I'd like to think that I'll use my new power to make things better, but how do I know if they won't just get worse? Are the Mages naturally bad people with power, or is it the power that turned them bad? There's much studying to be done."

I looked down at the remnants of our meal—only bread, cheese and some kind of fruit, but it was the most delicious I'd tasted for Ages—and was glad I'd eaten before she'd started talking. I don't think my body would've been able to digest the food as well as all the information she'd given me. I wished there was more tea though. I hadn't drunk any since leaving Kingston with my mum and I'd forgotten what an elixir it was. And it was one of the rare luxuries we allowed ourselves if I'd had a particularly gainful night and all our taxes had been paid to the Chief and Bear hadn't gambled or drunk too much of it away. Tea, a luxury. There were folk in In'Keep who drank several cups of it a day in porcelain mugs worth more than my life. Even Audra, in this library, had brought out an entire tin of it when she'd brought out the food, and poured a generous amount of the expensive leaves into the pot of hot water without even measuring it! Tea was nothing to these people.

But in Keep'Out Quarter, I knew one man who'd beaten his son to death because he'd knocked his mug of tea from his hands and wasted it all over the floor. And then he'd dragged his body out to the city limits and chucked it on the never-ending pyre with all the rest of the plague-ridden corpses like it was nothing. I know this because I'd just been about to pass over his roof on my way home one early morning. I heard the racket. Heard the blows and screams. And then I saw him leave his hovel, a fistful of the boy's shirt in one hand, mug handle minus the mug and its precious contents in the other. The boy's face was completely mashed to a pulp, but from the size of him and the ease with which his father pulled him, he couldn't have been more than about seven or eight.

And I didn't say anything. None of us ever did. Shit like that happened all the time and no one said anything, no one told the guards up at the Gates, no one got punished for it. I suppose the In'Keepers were happy for us to control our own population levels in our own way, because life was cheap in Out'Keep. Tea wasn't.

"From what you've told me," I said, an idea forming in my mind, "the Mages only play their Game because they've been immortal forever and they've got nothing else to do. There's no illness for them, no poverty, no deaths to mourn. For them, us and the...orcs were entertainment. But we can make a difference, Audra. Have you ever been to Keep'Out Quarter?"

She flushed red for a moment then shook her head, like she was embarrassed by that.

"It's a mess. There are more bad people than good, but even the bad'uns are only like that because they think it's the only way they can survive. We could change all that. You and me. Just by going down there and, and...wishing it! We could give kids food. We could heal people that have been beaten up, or got some disease from living in their own shit. Orc's balls, Audra, we could even just magic them up some money so they're not poor any more! These Mages, all of them have power, every single one of them, and so the power is no more special to them and theirs than…than tea is to you and yours. But here, there's only two of us what have power. It's special here. We can make a difference with it. A good difference."

While I'd been speaking her face had changed from one of uncertainty to a little smile of possibility.

"We don't just magic them up money," she said. "That'll reduce its value and make it worthless. Adàm taught me that the only reason why money is so valuable is because a few people have it and control it, while everyone else wants it but doesn't get it."

"Who's Adàm?"

"He was a friend of mine."

"Sounds clever."

"He's one of the richest elves in all of Kingston."

I raised my eyebrows. This woman knew some people, all right.

"Anyway," she continued, "magicking up more money won't help the poor in Out'Keep. We've got to give them the money that's already here."

"And we do that with magic?"

"We do that by telling the people in control that they aren't in control any more. They think they've got power because they have money and titles. But we have *actual* power. If we tell them that we're changing the way things are done here in Kingston, how can they possibly refuse?"

I grinned back at her. "You're not the kind of person who thinks small. I like that."

"We'll go right away." She took a step forward then stopped, looked at me then looked at herself. "But let's wash and change first. Even with all our power, you'll be astonished how little regard people up at the palace will give you if you turn up looking scruffy."

"We're going to the palace?" My heart fairly leapt up out of my mouth. They were big people up there. Couldn't even look at the Chief without wanting to piss myself, didn't know if I'd manage even opening my eyes in front of the Prime Minister. "I don't have any other clothes than these," was all I could squeak out.

"Don't worry about that," she said with a kind smile. "We'll run a few errands before we change the world. Shall we go?"

I shrugged and grinned. What else could I do?

SABINA

*C*laws bent down. "I don't want to get in the same capsule as those boys," she whispered into Sab's ear. Her breath was warm and smelled of rot.

Sab didn't know any Stratian who was bigger or stronger than Claws. Or one who was so afraid. Her heart broke a little for her friend.

"Urgh, nor do I," said Sab. "Did you smell them? Disgusting."

"Very expensive perfume," said Prisca.

"Chemical scents to hide their rotten nature," said Sab.

Claws giggled.

"Besides," said Prisca. "I doubt very much that they'd want to ride with us either. Gems as precious as them wouldn't be seen dead with the likes of us."

Claws nodded, mollified for now.

The boys strode up to a capsule, confident because they knew what they were doing. Made sense. They'd've been given all sorts of advice and instructions on how best to win the race that Emil had come up with in the first place. But it looked like the capsule they'd chosen was linked to a twin.

Couldn't possibly allow the Stratians to go off in one on their own, could they? Bollocks. No chance of fucking off on their own then. But if she'd thought of doing that, then so had the Patriarch, no doubt. He'd probably put all sorts of measures in place to make sure the Stratians stayed in the race. What fun Sab and her friends would have finding out what was in store for them.

Then Claws gasped. "But what if the capsule doesn't let me in? I'm a mutant. What if I don't have the right to travel?"

Huh. That had never crossed Sab's mind.

"Just because you can't do magic," said Prisca, font of all knowledge, "doesn't mean you don't have Mage blood in you. You're also a descendant of House Lix-Tetrax, remember. You've got as much right to be here as anyone else."

"But what if—"

"Trust me," said Prisca. "You're not the first mutant to be born here, you won't be the last. It's only humans that can't pass through magical barriers."

"What happens if a human tries?"

"A very wet explosion."

"Oh."

"But you're not a human, so it doesn't apply."

"I hope you're right."

"When am I ever not?"

It was a valid point, but it didn't stop Claws from hesitating at the threshold of the capsule behind the boys'. Sab had to give her soft tug to get her to step up onto it. No wet explosions ensued, and even Sab was relieved at that. She couldn't remember a time when Prisca was wrong about anything. But here the three of them were, legitimately leaving the 'Sphere, so there obviously was a first time for everything.

Prisca stepped on last of all, and Sab heaved a silent sigh of relief that her team was all together. They wouldn't win this race, they might not even get as far as Taurë, but she wanted to at least experience the joy of leaving the 'Sphere with her only friends.

"Welcome, contestants," said the voice of the capsule, as androgynous as the core's, but not quite the same. "Please take your seats and enjoy the trip to Oceanwall."

Sab cocked an eyebrow at her friends and they all took their seats on the plush bench that ran around the interior of the capsule. There was a little table in the centre with a mini forest of potted plants, and underfoot was a ridiculously thick-piled carpet. Favoured colour themes were cream and pale blue, and when the door slid shut, the plastic dome of the capsule deepened in colour, suggesting to Sab that, while they could still see out, people walking along the quays could no longer see in. The fact that she couldn't see inside the boys' capsule also gave her a clue. A somnolent hum filled the capsule and the quay started sliding away from them.

"Ooh, we're moving!" Claws squealed, clapping her hands together.

Sab and Prisca looked at each other and laughed. Neither one of them had ever seen Claws excited before. It was a sight to behold.

"We're leaving the 'Sphere, girls," said Claws, bounding across the capsule so she could see out of the back and watch the concourse slip away. "Shit on a fucking stick, we're actually leaving the 'Sphere!"

Sab watched with her for a couple of seconds, but what she really wanted to see was the world opening up before her as they pulled out of the terminal. Obviously, the view was somewhat obscured by the other capsule, but the opening was big enough to see. A wide circle cut into the structure of the 'Sphere, flashing red lights all around it just in case some Mage decided to take a walk on the rails and didn't realise they were about to walk off their city. Or something. Sab had no idea really.

Beyond the circle was white. Plain white. She saw little wisps of it floating into the circle, but that could've been the flashing lights making her eyes play tricks on her. But as the boys' capsule went through, there was a definite movement amongst that whiteness, like the world's softest implosion.

And then Sab's capsule was going through it. Into the white. There was nothing to see for several seconds, and then all three of them squealed as the sun appeared, full and high in a flawless blue sky, and scared the shit out of them.

"It's magnificent," Prisca whispered. Always the first of the three to settle down.

"It's so bright," said Claws, tears in her eyes. "No wonder they never let us out. Who'd want to go back after seeing something like that?"

Sab nodded. Then something made her look back. She caught her breath, then tapped Claws's knee and pointed out the back of the capsule.

"That was our home," Sab said.

Hanging in the air, suspended by the magic harvested from the slaves they farmed, was a gigantic cloud in the shape of a perfect sphere.

"Fuck me," said Claws.

"Language," whispered Prisca.

"It's kind of beautiful," said Sab.

There were a few seconds of silence, their unblinking eyes taking in the city that had been their home for all of their lives, but had never seen from this perspective.

Claws said, "It would be beautiful, if we didn't know what happened in there."

And then the capsule dropped.

After a few seconds of screaming, laughter erupted when

Sab realised they weren't about to plummet to their deaths. Then she saw what was beneath them.

"Look!" she cried.

The ocean stretched out before them, as wide as the sky above them, but a much deeper blue, decorated with little white triangles of waves, and fireworks of reflected sunshine.

A shoal of sea creatures breached the surface, pink iridescent skin flashing in the sun. Then they extended purple wings and skimmed across the ocean for several seconds before plunging back into the waves.

"What were they?" cried Claws.

Sab shook her head. "Never seen anything like it. Prisca?"

"First time off the 'Sphere for me too, you know. But they're called fish."

"Fish," said Sab. "Fish." It was a fun word to say. "How come you know so much, Prisca?"

"There they are again!" said Claws, her pointing finger jabbing at the capsule's widow. "I think they're following us!"

Sab laughed. "I think you're right."

"I never thought it would be so wonderful beyond the 'Sphere."

Sab's throat grew hot. She had to swallow several times to keep her eyes from leaking, and she pressed her forehead against the glass so her friends didn't see her discomfort. The sea creatures' extraordinary show was the perfect disguise. Claws was right—it was wonderful. All this time, a world of wonders had existed mere metres from where they'd lived. But it wasn't just that realisation that made her eyes prickle. It was knowing that the Mages had taken this world of wonders and turned it into something dreadful. As long as Sab and her two friends were part of this race, they'd never be a part of this world.

"What if we just ran away?" Sab said into the glass, her rotten breath bouncing back to her nose.

There was no response from her friends, so she looked around at them. Both were staring at her. But where Prisca looked aghast at the idea of going against the Patriarch, Claws looked at her as though she was stupid.

"We can't do that," said Claws. "We're on a capsule. We'd only be able to run around in circles."

"Not—" Sab began. "I mean, when it's landed, what if we just don't do the race? Who'd know? Those fuckers wouldn't care," she threw a thumb towards the capsule in front of theirs, "because they'd win the race. And everyone else on the 'Sphere would just think we've been killed out here. So let's just run away."

"Where to?"

"I don't know! I've seen as much of the world as you have! But it looks pretty big. Bound to be loads of places we could run away to without being found."

Prisca shifted in her seat. "I wouldn't underestimate the Mages, if I were you. Especially one as powerful as the Patriarch."

"Yeah, but," said Sab, "we're Mages too. We might not be able to keep a whole city up in the air, but we can find a place to escape to. Besides, the Patriarch wanted to get me out of the city. You didn't see his smug face—he thought he was punishing me by expelling me."

"He expelled you," Prisca said calmly, "because he's sending you to the New Born human. And what happened to Nathaniel's and Messina's power when the New Born killed them?"

"It came to us," said Sab. "And it must fuck him right off that scum like us have got so much magic now."

"Of course it does. And what do you think will happen to that magic if Audra kills you?"

Sab sighed. "It'll go back to them."

"That's why the Patriarch freed you for this race. He can't

control the surge after a Game, but he can control *you*. If you die, he gets your power. If you run away, he won't. Same goes for me. He knows that as well as I do."

"So does that mean," said Claws, "he'll know when we die?"

Prisca nodded. "Magic links us all together, to a greater or lesser extent. That's why we all felt it when Nathaniel and Messina died. But you," she pointed at Sab with her eyes, "are of House Lix-Tetrax. So is the Patriarch. Magic through bloodlines has a much stronger link."

"So what you're saying is that I can never get away from him?"

Prisca shrugged a shoulder. "He's in your blood and you're in his. He'll always be able to find you."

"Cities with fewer Mages are less powerful," said Claws.

"That's right," said Prisca.

"Which is why everyone hates mutants."

"Not everyone," said Sab.

Claws offered her a sad smile. "They hate us because we're powerless. How come magic doesn't work for people like me?"

Prisca's ice-white eyes considered the ceiling of the capsule for a couple of moments. "Don't know," she said. "We know magic works, we know it can do all sorts of things. And we each have our own ways of making it do what we want it to."

"I see bubbles and tendrils," said Sab. When Claws had fully opened her mouth to ask the obvious question, she added, "It's what my mum told me to do. See everything as bubbles and magic as tendrils."

"Interesting," said Prisca, eyebrow cocked. "She always was a clever one, your mum. Anyway, knowing it works is one thing. But as to the how and why of it... That's been lost to the Ages, I'm afraid." And just as Claws opened her mouth for a second time, Prisca said, "Don't pay any attention to the propaganda the upper-levellers spout. It's got nothing to do with being a special species, I'm sure of it." She sighed. "If I had the right tools and enough time, I could come up with some experiments…"

"Enough time?" said Claws, finally getting her words out. "You lot are immortal. You literally have all the time in the world!"

Prisca's eyebrow twitched. "How many slavers do you know that have time to themselves? Anyway, can't see many Mages that'd want to know how and why it really works anyway."

"Why not?" said Claws, frowning.

"Because real truth often has a way of gainsaying the preferred truths of the rich and powerful. It's what keeps them high and mighty. They're certainly not going to let a little thing like actual fact topple them. Ignorance and power make a Patriarch extremely watchful."

Sab huffed a frustrated sigh. "So we really are going to have to do this stupid race then?"

Prisca nodded.

"Fine. But can we at least keep our eyes open for possible escape routes?"

"I can't stop you doing anything with your eyes," said Prisca. "Now. Who would like an apple?"

DRAYKE

"*I*ndeed. A most interesting tale, Drayke Rebel Leader."

"Not a tale, Prime Minister," Drayke said. "It's a full account of the events which took place on the mission."

The Prime Minister nodded slowly, head twitching to the side now and then at a comment whispered by his ministers. It was clear from his expression that he hadn't believed a word Drayke had said.

"Orcs and Mages, Drayke? I expect elf-tale nonsense like this from that silly little girl , but you are my Rebel Leader. Now, loss of life was incurred and I understand that such can be distressing for one's mind. That, coupled with the fact that you failed in your mission—"

"Failed, Prime Minister?"

"Yes. Failed. Do I now have the Healing Glass in my hand? No. That was your mission."

"Prime Minister, I recall explaining that the artefact never existed. It was—"

"Precisely, Drayke—it never existed. Yet, I was made to believe it did by the Academicians and the elvish clans and that silly little girl. It cost a considerable amount of public money to provision that mission, and what return have we got from it? Nothing. Though I am now down a number of trained Rebels and it will cost more money in order to replace them. I am less than happy about that, I'm sure you'll appreciate. All because of an artefact that didn't exist. So do not expect me to believe that Mages and orcs have jumped out of history and back into the present day."

Drayke was often speechless, because he preferred silence to conversation. Speaking was a tool used for communicating orders or finding necessary information. Anything else was superfluous. Now, however, he was speechless because he couldn't think of anything to say. The Prime Minister was choosing to ignore him despite the evidence he'd presented. He was calling Drayke a liar. Or worse, accusing him of succumbing to fancy. Audra. This must be how she'd felt every day since she released her theory on the evolution of humans in Taurë. It wasn't a nice feeling.

"Stand there and glare at me all you want, Rebel Leader, but I shan't be swayed and made a fool of this time. Now you're back you have duties to fulfil."

"Yes, Prime Minister," he said. "And paramount of those duties is protecting the government from any threat. I tell you that these Mages are the biggest threat that we face. We cannot ignore them."

"Confound it, Rebel, there's no such thing! And even if there were, you said yourself that the two you *claim* to have encountered were thwarted."

"Yes, by Audra," said Drayke. "And she managed that because she displayed abilities—"

"Rebel Leader!" The Prime Minister slammed his fist onto his desk and launched himself up from his chair. "That is enough! You are dismissed!"

"Prime Minister, ministers," he said, mustering all the

respect he could, then turned and marched towards the door. What he would do when he walked through it, he had no idea. He was saved the decision, however, because once he'd pulled the door open he found himself face to face with the very Academician he'd just been talking about. And standing next to her was a very small, very nervous young lad.

"Hello, Drayke," she said. "Do you mind if we come in?"

SHE'D WASHED AND CHANGED, but that didn't make the Prime Minister regard her any more favourably. Drayke also noticed that he looked at the lad with unconcealed contempt.

"Who do you think you are, Academician, to come barging in here without leave or appointment?"

"Prime Minister," she said. "I come barging in here as a mark of respect only, though only tradition dictates you should be shown such. I, for one, think you deserve none."

The Prime Minister paled and his jowls wobbled as his anger mounted at her opening statement. Drayke tensed. This confrontation was not going to end well.

"How dare you!" the Prime Minister bellowed. "I am the most powerful man in this city, and as such—"

"I dare," said Audra, her eyes never leaving his, "because you have no power over me. You have no power over my new friend Squirrel here, either. It was a recent conversation with him that made me realise it."

"He looks plenty angry as it is, Audra," whispered the lad. "Don't make it worse."

She smiled at him and draped a hand on his shoulder. "Don't worry. They can't hurt us."

"Rebel Leader," said the Prime Minister. "Remove these two from my chamber."

Drayke stepped forward, but he wasn't going to touch

her. Not after what he'd seen her do. And the look in her eyes told him she knew it very well.

"My argument isn't with you," she said to him. "You're not a nice person, but you saved my life once and I haven't forgotten it. Besides, you only act on orders." She turned back to the assembled ministers. "My argument is with those giving them."

The Prime Minister laughed. "And I take umbrage at silly little girls who—"

"Be quiet," said Audra. And to Drayke's surprise, he was. "I'm here to inform you that you're no longer in charge. Your ability to rule is abysmal and an affront to the original Rebels who sought to change the unjust order of society. You're no better than the kings of old, who rewarded the rich with more wealth and allowed the poor to suffer. There's enough wealth in this city that no one should be living in poverty, enough food that no one should starve. My friend and I will see to it that the imbalance you've perpetuated is rectified and reversed."

For a long moment there was silence as the ministers shared looks of stupefaction, then the chamber erupted with their cackling. Yet Audra didn't look annoyed. She looked amused.

"Do you think we should demonstrate what we can do?" she whispered to the lad.

"Do *we* even know what we can do?" he whispered back.

Drayke frowned. We?

"Well, let's find out."

She closed her eyes, took a deep breath and released it very slowly. Then she flung her arms out towards the assembled ministers.

Whatever happened, happened far too quickly for Drayke to process. There was a flash of light, then the chamber was silent again, the laughter of the ministers cut off as completely as a severed limb. He looked, but didn't understand.

"What have you done?" he said to Audra.

"I don't know," she said, her tone curious. She walked over to them. He walked with her.

They were all still there, the ministers, but they were completely motionless. Their postures varied, for when they were rendered immobile they'd been in the throes of laughter. One clutched his belly, his eyes tightly shut. Another rocked back in his chair, mouth wide open revealing the rotten teeth at the back of his jaw. The Prime Minister was in the process of slapping one palm down on his desk and pointing to where Audra had stood with his other, while his face was fixed in an expression of laughing scorn.

"Are they dead?" said Drayke.

"I don't know," she said, reaching a hand out to the Prime Minister's face. "Oh no, they're not—did you see? His eyes just flickered. Can you hear me?" She bent closer to him. "Flicker your eyes again if you can. Good! Oh well, this is even better! You're conscious, you're aware, but you can't move. You thought yourself powerful, but you have no notion of what true power is. Power is a river that carries you away, but I am the river. It is a tiger that destroys, but I am the tiger. It is a fire that consumes you, but I am the fire. Now let me still your mind as I've stilled your body—I will make this city just again. And once I've done that, I may well free you to live among your equals. Won't that be nice?" She turned back to the lad. "I think that made our point fairly well, don't you?"

The lad said nothing. He was too busy gaping at the frozen tableau before him. Drayke couldn't blame him. The ministers may well have been laughing before Audra did... whatever she did, but now their expressions looked horrific.

"You can't leave them like that, Academician," said Drayke.

"And you can't tell me what to do, Rebel."

"Then I'll have to arrest you."

She looked at her hands. "You could try."

He looked down at her. There was a time when he'd only been intimidated by her intellect. He missed that time. "So you plan to take this city by force and punish any who oppose you with…that?"

Her face softened. "I don't want to take this city. I want to give it back to the people. It doesn't belong to only the rich and the titled, it belongs to all of us. We left Kingston to find a cure for the plague, and instead we've come back with a power that can change everything for the better! Why wouldn't you want to live in a city where everyone is fed and happy and equal?"

Because she was the only person who could wield that power. How would that ever be equal?

"Our next meeting is with the elves," she continued, looking and smiling at the lad but still addressing Drayke. "Now that there are no ministers who need protecting from riotous hordes, I think your position here is nullified."

He raised an eyebrow.

"You'll still be employed by the city though, don't worry. I want you to divide your men and send a group into each quarter of Out'Keep. Crimes have been committed there that need justice and I'd have you tell me of them. You no longer serve the Prime Minister, you serve the people."

"Is that an order?"

"Would it make you feel better if it were?"

"No."

"Then get along with you. We've got a lot of work to do. Cheer up, Drayke! This is a new era for our great city!"

He held the door open for her, followed her out and

closed it behind him. He paused for a moment, then locked it with a copy of the key only he and the Prime Minister had. No one must be allowed to see what took place in there today.

She and the young lad were almost at the end of the corridor by the time he started down it. A new era for the city, indeed. An era where everyone was happy, fed and equal. He might even have believed it if he hadn't seen her expression during her magic trick. He'd seen similar ones on the faces of whores every time he pulled out his money bag— lustful pleasure. Greedy joy. And he knew it meant that they would do just about anything to get their hands on the object of such desire.

It was an expression he'd learned never to trust.

SABINA

*T*urned out, even though the ocean was vast, it wasn't all that existed out beyond the 'Sphere. After a couple of hours in the capsule, it changed colour from a deep grey-blue, to a bright green-turquoise and the waves got bigger until they finally crashed against the beginning of dry land. It started off white as powdered bones, and then got greener the further inland they flew.

Just when Sab was starting to get a little bit bored of green, the capsule began slowing down.

"Arriving at Oceanwall in five minutes," said the capsule.

But Sab could already see it. "Shit on a fucking stick," she said.

"Language," said Prisca, but her heart wasn't in it. She was as glued to the window as Sab was.

"But how can anybody live in there?" said Claws.

"You'll find out in a couple of minutes," said Prisca.

Oceanwall. It looked exactly as it sounded. Rising up from the carpet of green was an enormous wall of water. Craning up as far as she could, Sab saw that the walls of the city tapered as they rose, hundreds of metres above the green carpet, until they met in the centre in one furious, splashing column of water. From there, water fountained back out, falling like rain back down to the walls, where it began its upward journey again. Because those walls that gave the city its name weren't still. They were as active as a waterfall, except that it ran upwards.

"Mages," said Sab, "really seem to have thing for defying gravity, don't they?"

It was possible that one of her friends was about to answer, but at that very moment their capsule plunged into Oceanwall and the whole universe turned blue.

"There's even creatures in here," whispered Claws.

She wasn't wrong. The wall teemed with variations on the theme of the pink and purple fish they saw flying out of the ocean, but their wings were much smaller and their colours more diverse. Many swam up to the capsule, gazed inside with huge black eyes and gaped with mouths that opened and closed with astonishment.

"Mental," said Claws. "They're like birds, but they live in water."

"They're not like birds at all," Sab scoffed. "They haven't got beaks or feathers. Or legs. And they're bodies are totally diff—"

"I meant," said Claws, giving Sab what she obviously thought was an evil eye, "that they *fly*. They fly in water with those tiny wing things, the way birds fly in the air."

"So, what? You're saying fish are just water birds?"

"Could be."

"That's ridiculous," said Sab. "They have a completely different name. Fish. And they're not flying in the water, they're swimming. That's what things do in water, isn't it, Prisca?"

Before Prisca could answer, the capsule cleared the wall

of water that gave this place its name. Sab got her first look at a completely new town.

The most astonishing thing she noticed was that it was all on one level. She took consignments of slaves up to different households in the 'Sphere all the time, and was so used to using the core that having an entire city made up of levels seemed the most natural way to organise one. How would the citizens know which social class they belonged to otherwise? Here, though. Here it was just flat. One flat mass of city cut into squares by lanes of water.

So, what? Did the slave farmers live in the middle? That would be the smallest part of the city probably, with the wealthiest households taking up all the space around the outside. But that didn't make any sense, because looking down, the buildings they were passing over now looked quite squat to her, and in the distance she saw that the buildings got taller and grander. In fact, from this height, it looked like there was one gigantic building right in the centre of the city that almost scraped the underside of the tapered roof of water. It would probably line up quite nicely with that fountain they had on the outside.

Ah, okay. That made sense. In Oceanwall, it wasn't which level you lived on that gave you your status. It was the size of your building. So that central monolith obviously belonged to the patriarch of the dominant House of this city, and all those other buildings around it, still huge but not as big, were the Emils of these parts. The further away you got, the less important you were. The Sabinas, Claudias and Priscas of Oceanwall. It looked so different to the 'Sphere, but it was actually exactly the same.

"Who's the dominant House in this dump then?" said Sab.

The two younger women looked at the older one expectantly.

"How is it that you two know so little about the main Houses?" said Prisca.

"I'm a mutant," said Claws. "No one tells me anything."

"And I'm lazy," said Sab. "And really don't give a fuck."

Prisca tutted.

"The question you really need to be asking," Sab continued, "is why *you* do."

Prisca rolled her eyes, although it was difficult to spot with those white irises of hers. "Oceanwall is controlled by House Forneus. Quite a recent ascendancy, as these things go. They're the ones that raised the wall and made House Lix-Tetrax sit up and take notice of them."

"Why would anyone want to do that?" said Claws.

Prisca shrugged a shoulder. "Houses rise and fall. Mages want more and more power. Everyone thinks the Game we play in Taurë is a new invention, but really Mages have been playing games for millennia. Sometimes they dress it up as politics, other times it's Games. But really it all just comes down to the same thing: who's got the most power."

Claws sighed. "Wouldn't things be nicer if magic didn't exist? Then there'd be no power to fight over in the first place."

Mutants and the human slaves'd certainly be happier if magic didn't exist.

"Well, you never know," said Sab. "Perhaps this Audra human will rid the world of it once and for all after she's annihilated us racers."

Claws and Prisca turned to look at her, various levels of disbelief on their faces, but she just shrugged at them. No point being coy about matters of life and death. Well, just death really. Besides which, the capsules were descending and slowing. Time to put on Game faces and put up with the upper echelons of this city.

The 'Sphere didn't really have a central meeting point for

— Actually, it may well have done, but Sab didn't know anything about it. She was Stratian. They weren't involved in general AtmoSphere events. The only thing she'd ever been invited to was that one and only family meeting that landed her in the race, and that wasn't really an invitation. It was a summons. Perhaps the Patriarch's uppermost level was the meeting place for everything that went on in the 'Sphere.

Anyway, it was irrelevant now. Her mind was only rambling because, where the capsules were coming to a stop right now, seemed to be a central meeting place for the citizens of Oceanwall.

It was a tiered square. The backdrop for it was the gigantic residence of House Forneus, a giant dick if ever Sab saw one. Around the square were variations on the theme of canals and streams, with mini-waterfalls sectioning off each tier. Every now and then, some brightly-coloured swimming creature would leap out of the water and plop back in. The hundreds of people gathered on the tiers paid them no mind whatsoever. This Sab found astonishing for two reasons: one; that everyone was so accustomed to these fascinating creatures that they could just ignore them. Two; there were *hundreds* of people gathered all over the tiers of the main square.

"What's all these people doing here?" Claws whispered. Sab heard the edge in her voice. The edge which meant that at any moment she would flip into full freak-out mode and Sab and Prisca would have their work cut out for them trying to get her back down to normality. Well, what passed for normality for Claws.

"Looks like the 'Sphere went to the trouble of letting Oceanwall know all about our little race," said Prisca, keeping her tone light. "That was nice of them."

"Are we going to have to talk to all those people?" said Claws.

"Nah," said Sab. "They probably just want to have a look at us. You know what it's like at the start of a Game, right? Remember when Nathaniel and Messina even came down to Stratus level before they went off to Taurë? I reckon it's just like that. They're not going to expect us to say anything."

"You sure?"

"Totally. No one really gives a shit. Listen, Claws. Mages don't need much of an excuse to throw a party. It's not like they've got anything else to do. I mean, yeah, you can bet your sweet little arse that Emil and his handful of dicks are going to give a bunch of speeches about how fucking awesome they are, but no one really cares. All this is just a minor distraction from the infinite boredom of immortality that is a Mage's life."

Claws nodded, but then she always did after Sab gave her a little pep talk. Didn't mean she'd taken any of it to heart and wouldn't lose her shit at any given moment. But at least Sab also had Prisca here to help keep an eye on her.

The capsules glided to a stop on the largest tier, which also happened to be right in the middle. Sab watched Emil and his dicks disembark, relishing the fact that they were surrounded by onlookers, giving the crowd what they wanted by waving and blowing kisses to all the women. The applause and cheering whoops were ridiculous. Sab rolled her eyes. She was fucked if she was going to do that.

"Out we get then," she said. "Claws, stay in the middle of us, if you like. To be honest though, I don't think anyone's gonna be paying us all that much attention with that lot out there."

Prisca snorted a derisive laugh through her nose. "Cirrocumulans and their constant need for attention."

Sab stepped out of the capsule. Underfoot, the terrace was a honey-coloured stone, and even though the tiers were pretty much swamped with cheering onlookers, she guessed that all of the terraces in this central square were made of the same stuff.

She took a deep breath. It was kind of a luxury to be in a place that didn't reek of unwashed bodies and human filth. The whole place smelled of water, and had a fresh dampness about it that was far pleasanter than the stifling air of Stratus. Mingling in with that were the layers of perfume that Mages so loved to douse themselves in. She gave a wry grin. She'd love to see some of their faces if they ever got close enough for a whiff of Sab and her two teammates.

Claws's hands snaked around her forearms, her fingers digging into the exposed muscles. It didn't hurt, not really. But when Claws's pointy nails scraped against the exposed ulna it sent little electrical pulses up her arm, which promised to have Sab grinding her teeth if it went on for too long.

"I bet all this a bit overwhelming for your slave, sorry, Stratian senses, isn't it?" said Emil, a smug grin smeared across his face.

Ah. This must be his attempt at some kind of trash talk.

"Are you kidding?" said Sab. "We literally wade knee-deep in actual shit down at the slave farms. This is nothing."

"It's actually quite pleasant," said Prisca, looking around and nodding slightly.

"And it's certainly a lot less crowded," said Sab.

"Although these buggers make a lot more noise," said Prisca.

"That's true," said Sab. "Slaves are far more well behaved when we rock into their place."

Emil huffed and puffed, then eventually turned away from them and carried on with his waving and kiss-blowing. He obviously needed people to give a shit about the things he said and did. Sab chuckled.

The air changed slightly behind her. She turned. The

capsules were taking off. Well, that was it then. No turning back, even if she'd wanted to go back to the 'Sphere. The only route out of Oceanwall now was whichever way the race took them.

"They're coming closer, Sab," hisspered Claws, squeezing Sab's forearm as she did so. "They're surrounding us."

"It's all right, Claws, you're all right. They're probably just going to spout a bunch of bollocks about how brave we are, or about how lucky we are to be doing this wonderful race for Magekind. You know what these lot are like for speeches and shit. It makes them feel important."

"Yeah, but why do they have to come so close to do it?"

"Well, you know," said Sab, raking through her brain to find any plausible reason that her friend might buy. "It's not like any of them are brave enough to take part in this thing. They probably just want to have a good look at those of us who are. You're braver than every single person here, remember that."

Claws smiled, but Sab could see through the hole in her cheek that her teeth were clamped together. A sure sign that she was doing everything in her power not to scream the city apart.

In the meantime, Emil and his right-hand man, Drusus, had marched forward to meet the oncoming crowd, both of them wallowing in the women that fawned over their perfectly constructed handsomeness. Sab took a couple of seconds to look over dicks #2 - #5. It was interesting that they'd hung back. She doubted it was because of the kind of anxiety that crippled Claws, which in turn was kind of crippling Sab's arm. Probably more out of deference. Cirrocumulans were fucking obsessed with hierarchy, so Emil and Drusus were no doubt a rung up the social ladder. Not that you could tell just by looking at them—they all had those perfectly gorgeous, even features that rendered all the uppers identical. For men, it seemed the popular look this Age was sun-bronzed skin, dark hair with a little wave running through it, and slightly beardy jaws. Just enough facial hair to give the impression that these were rugged men who preferred an outdoorsy life of adventure rather than submitting to vanity.

Sab chuckled. Wankers.

Still, despite their overall similarity, now that she looked closely, she could see they'd gone to pains to differentiate themselves a little bit. One of them was head and shoulders taller than the rest of them. One had gone to the effort of fashioning and tinting his hair so that it looked a little bit like a crown. One had…shit on a stick, one had actual wings folded against his back. She'd thought it was just some kind of pompous overcoat at first glance. Honestly, these people. And the last one smelled *incredible*. Sab inhaled deeply, then blinked a couple of times. That was certainly one way to make yourself stand out in a crowd of people that all looked the same.

And while she'd never stop thinking of them as dangling male appendages, she didn't like the thought that they all knew her name but she didn't know theirs. It was easily rectified. A little tendril of power would do the trick. She looked inward, sussing out how much magic she had to spare and was shocked again by the amount the Game had given her. She'd never had so much in her life! And the Patriarch would get it all once she died. Bastard. She released a little and let it snake out towards the four men. Prisca glanced at her, sensing the minute thread, but probably guessing what she was doing. Claws was entirely unaware, her focus still on the crowd around them.

All right then, who's who? As soon as Sab's magic neared them she saw their names glimmering around them like faint dust motes caught in a sunbeam. Well, she didn't exactly *see* in the conventional sense, with eyeballs and everything. It was more of a sensation. The tall one was Celsus—from Cirrostratus level. Huh. Obviously hoped that getting in the race would help him move up a level. The rest were Cirrocumulans, like Emil. She could taste their arrogance. The one with wings was called Detius, the one who smelled amazing was called Laelius, and the one with crown hair was Regulus.

"So?" said Prisca once Sab had recalled her tendril of magic.

She divulged the pompous names of their opponents. Prisca did nothing more than purse her lips while nodding once. A gesture which could've meant anything from *Thought as much* to *At least we'll all know who we are before we die horribly at the hands of a New Born.*

But there was no time for guessing because the crowd decided now was a good time to cheer. Sab looked up and around, expecting to see Emil performing some pointless display of magic to show off how much power he had, but actually seeing nothing more impressive than the assembled throng moving aside to let someone through.

"Buggeration," said Prisca. Sab glanced at her. The old woman looked decidedly uncomfortable.

"Who's that?" she said.

Prisca sighed. "It's the patriarch of House Forneus, obviously. And his bloody wife."

"No need to get snippy."

"Then don't ask stupid questions! Who else would cause the citizens to move aside in order for them to make a grand entrance?"

Sab opened her mouth to ask a bunch more questions that had exploded into her head after Prisca's peculiar reaction, but a honey voice filled the air around her.

"Oceanwall welcomes you, brave volunteers of the race!"

It was the patriarch of House Forneus. He looked…weird.

He had the normal one head, usual facial features, two arms sticking out of a regular torso. But that was where normality ended. His hair was shockingly white, long, and floated around his head as though he were actually floating in water. Despite the whiteness of his hair, his face looked young, but his skin was aquamarine, and where most men would have a suggestion of a beard, he'd opted for suggestions of scales. And while the glittering, expensive and immaculately tailored suit he wore fitted his arms and torso perfectly, it was his legs that made Sab blink rapidly. Because he didn't have any. He had waving, shimmying tentacles. Eight of them. The same aquamarine as his skin, but as glitzy as his suit. And they even had suckers. He glided towards them with a beatific smile splashed across his face.

"Shit on a stick," Sab hisspered out the corner of her mouth. "He's really taken the ocean theme to heart."

And his bloody wife was no better. She'd come dressed as a mermaid. Lots of pink and sparkles made up her tail, which propelled her through the air without touching the floor. A tiny waist and enormous bosom topped the tail, but a ridiculous explosion of blond hair erupted from her head and floated around her, somehow always managing to keep her boobs covered. Her face was beautiful, obviously, and she'd opted for a delicate coral blush to her skin. Both of them waved at and revelled in the adoration of the crowd.

Then, with no warning whatsoever, silence descended so abruptly that even Sab started.

"So," said the House Forneus patriarch, his mellifluous voice carrying well. "You have come back to us, Rusalka."

A susurration bubbled up from the watching crowd. Sab frowned. Who the fuck was Rusalka?

"Not through any choice of my own," said Prisca.

Sab spun to face her. Even Claws was pulled from her panic to stare at her.

"You know these people?" said Sab.

"Yes," said Prisca.

"Why'd they call you Rusalka?"

"Because," said the mermaid in a singsong voice, reaching out coral hands, "she is our only daughter."

JENNA

*N*o matter how many times she walked to the Academy, and even though she'd been an Academician for a good few years now, it always surprised Jenna that she was allowed to be a part of this elite group. Her parents were merchants, after all—from a long line of them. The mild surprise stayed with her constantly, but it never lessened her enjoyment of Library Walk, the meandering pathway that roamed from the main entrance of the Academy in Academician's Quarter all the way up to the library in the palace enclosure. Even when it was raining, like it was today, the willow-lined walkway was always a pleasure. The only thing that marred her mood a little was Audra's return.

Well, not her return—Jenna was delighted to see her again after two months. But Audra seemed…distant. She was the only Academician who'd ever left the Academy in the name of research, and she'd saved the city from a dreadful plague, yet she'd seemed so despondent. Yes, despondent was exactly the right word.

No, wait. Jenna wasn't considering everything properly.

While Audra was passionate about researching her theories, her father had just died before she went on the mission. In fact, Jenna's mother suggested that the only reason she went was because of that sad event. She'd been so dedicated to him. Nothing would've taken her away from his side, even something so urgent as finding a cure for the plague. And then, of course, she'd said that the cost of finding that cure had been too great. So yes, it was understandable that the poor woman wouldn't be skipping around in happiness on her return.

But world be buggered, Jenna had so many questions! While Audra was away, the whole Academy had been abuzz with her departure—not least because the Academy had granted it in the first place. Obviously, the gossip and rumours remained whispers, for no one wanted the Sages to hear of them, and nobody was brave enough to ask them directly even if they could get an audience with them.

She stopped and smiled as a soggy and bedraggled red squirrel ran across the path in front of her and leapt into the nearest willow, nestling deep inside a hole in the trunk to escape the rain. She knew how it felt, poor thing. She'd have to get a wriggle on if she didn't want to get washed away herself.

Turning the last little corner, the Academy finally came into view and it always made her smile. Made of the same golden stone as the residences in this quarter, it was probably her most favourite building in all of In'Keep. While the palace was magnificent, the architecture was complicated and ostentatious. And the elvish residences were impressive, yes, but they were built to demonstrate wealth and power. The Academy, though, was simple, built by simply laying stone upon stone and left unadorned by carvings or pillars or decoration, roofed with dark slate that glistened in the falling rain. Though Jenna doubted that it had been easy to construct, for it was colossal, and perfectly circular, representing the eternal nature of knowledge. The only ostentation was the great glass dome that soared from the very centre, where the Sages sat and thought their lofty thoughts.

Library Walk ended at the entrance to the Academy, a huge but plain oak door with no grand staircase leading up to it, just the end of the path. Above, etched into the lintel, was the Academy's motto: Truth, Unity and Harmony. This always made her smile too, not just because it was a lovely sentiment, but because all her years as an Academician had taught her unity and harmony were far from the Academician's main priorities. She would go so far as to say that the competition between the disciplines was fiercer than that of the market sellers outside In'Keep's walls.

The entrance lay on the meridian of the circle, and just as she was about to enter, a colleague exited and held the door open for her.

"You look a bit damp, Academician," he said with a smile, which she returned.

"I can certainly confirm that the rainy season's upon us," said Jenna. "I hope you won't be spending too long out in it. Thank you," she added, once she was in the warm and dry.

"Pass the day well!" he called as he pulled up his hood and trotted out into the rain. She was a little ashamed at not knowing his name, but the brooch at his throat had marked him out as belonging to Arts and Music, so it was no surprise really.

There was no atrium as such when one arrived at the Academy, it was simply the start of the continuous corridor that encircled the entire building, with the lecture halls and study rooms to the left so that they overlooked the central courtyard. She turned to her right and started her long walk to the History department, which was her discipline, but first she would stop off at the Philosophy department on her way round.

Inside was much brighter than out, because the corridor was lined with pinewood and varnished a lovely golden to match the stones outside. And even though there was a generous window every few strides, it was the lit oil-lamps placed between them that gave the place its glow, not to mention its quite specific smell. Sort of greasy, but not unpleasantly so, because it brought to mind cosy evenings tucked up at home during the cold season. Which in itself was odd, because she didn't have any oil-lamps at home— they were far too expensive to have with a toddler running around. Not to mention dangerous. A knocked oil-lamp would spill its contents and spread its flame. A candle usually snuffed itself out. Because no matter how high things were placed out of little arms' reach, those little arms always seemed to find a way to reach them. She smiled fondly. Thinking of her precious Calla never failed to make her do so, and she couldn't wait until her workday was finished so she could collect her from her mother and father's boutique.

"Oops, walked straight past it," she said to herself with a little grin.

She retraced her steps, then knocked on one of the identical pine doors that lined the corridor, each only differentiated by the little brass name plaque nailed into it. This one said *The Very Academic Konrad Sarkar*. He was her husband.

"Enter," he called. Then, "You should be in History, not Philosophy," when he saw it was her.

"I know, but I just wanted to say hello."

"I'm too busy, Jenna."

"I can see," she said, looking around at all the glass and metal experimentation equipment crammed into his space. He was a Natural Philosopher and she was very proud of him for that, even if she didn't really understand what he did. "What are you working on?"

He started to explain his experiment and she smiled. He was always happiest when he was talking about his work.

"Go away now," he said once he'd finished. "I'm expected to give a lecture on my results in a few days."

She nodded. "Sorry for the interruption." She walked slowly towards the door. She knew he was busy, but she just *had* to tell someone. "Oh! By the way, Audra's back."

"What's that?" He was starting to sound irritated.

"Audra. You know her. She left two months ago to find that Healing Glass everyone was talking about."

He stopped what he was doing and raised an eyebrow at her. "And she's back?"

Jenna nodded. "This morning."

"Are you sure?"

She smiled. "Of course I am! We were talking just now in the library. Although, it wasn't quite the conversation I'd expected, after all the time she's been away. And she looks so sad now, poor thing. She'll be writing a report of course, which I suppose everyone will scoff at as usual, but she couldn't bring herself to tell me anything about it, which worried me. You remember how passionate she was about her researches? And the two of us used to natter for notches about her theories before she left. She seems…different now."

"You saw her yourself? You actually spoke to her?"

Jenna frowned. "I just told you I did."

"Where is she now?"

"Still in the library, I imagine. She was exhausted, she needed to rest."

Konrad carefully put down the flask he held, quickly turned off all the burners and removed his gloves. "You must get her and bring her back here."

"Why?"

"Just do as your husband tells you," he snapped.

She watched him march across his research room, fling open the door and throw himself out of it. He never left her alone in this room—he was too afraid she'd break his expensive equipment. She frowned deeper at the closing door. That hadn't been the reaction she'd expected at all.

SABINA

"Our beloved daughter has come back to us!" cried the coral mermaid. She and her husband then turned to the gasping crowd, who promptly cheered on cue.

It was confusing as all fuck, but Sab was pleased to notice Emil's rapid blinking as he took in the scene. He obviously thought he'd be the one getting all the attention during this part of the race.

Another good thing about the revelation was that it even had Claws dumbfounded, which meant she'd released the death-grip on Sab's arm. She'd left behind deep dents in Sab's muscle fibres where her sharpened nails had dug in, but even as Sab looked at them, they healed right up. She could definitely get used to having all this spare magic in her. But now wasn't the time to get side-tracked.

"Um, Prisca," she started.

"Oh, by the way, my girls," said the older woman, turning to them with a brittle smile on her face. "There was something I've been meaning to tell you for a good long while now."

"Wait, let me guess," said Sab in a flat tone.

"You're not really from the 'Sphere, are you?" Claws said quietly.

Prisca shook her head.

"Then how come you're there?"

"And is that how come you know so much about literally everything?" added Sab. "It is, isn't it?"

Prisca's explanation was going to have to wait though, because now the cheering had stopped and the air behind Sab shifted. When she pivoted to look, the patriarch and the mermaid were right behind her.

"Shit on a stick," she hisspered.

Their attention was focussed solely on their daughter however. The crowd around them were silent in their rapture, just waiting for the next big surprise. What a great day this was for the citizens of Oceanwall. Oceanwallians? Oceanites? Considering the state of the two weirdos in front of her, they probably called themselves Fish.

"So," said Sab, taking a pointed step backwards. "The patriarch of Oceanwall and his wife, is it? I'm Sab, this is Claws," she chucked a thumb in her friend's direction, "and Prisca you know already. So what shall we call you?"

The patriarch swivelled his eyes down to Sab. He didn't move his head or any other part of his body. He just swivelled his eyes down until he was glaring at her. It was probably the single-most creepy thing Sab had ever seen.

"For one thing," said the patriarch, "you won't refer to me as the patriarch."

Huh. Unexpected.

"We're equal rulers, my husband and I," the mermaid chimed in. "Our devoted subjects call us the Lord and Lady."

"That's nice. Were they given a choice?"

"But," said the *Lord*. "As you are our celebrated guests, you can of course refer to us as Alpaloovik and Scylla."

"Why?" said Sab.

Prisca bent close to her ear. "Those are their names, Sabina."

Sab blinked. "I could probably manage Al and Silly." She looked up at Prisca. "Which one's which?"

"Now, everyone just wait a minute." Emil. Oh, yes. Sab had temporarily forgotten about him. "Why are you wasting your time on Stratians when you could be currying favour with Cirrocumulans? I am *the* Emil Lix-Tetrax—"

"Not all Cirrocumulans, though, are you?" said Sab. She pointed at Celsus, the tall one. "He's from Cirrostratus." The giant idiot blushed a violent red and tried to hide behind his betters. "Tut, tut, lying to a lord and lady."

"Shut your face, *Stratian*," said Emil. He was furious. His beautiful face twisted into an ugly scowl.

"Now, now, children," said the Silly mermaid. Sab raised an eyebrow. She didn't look any older than Sab did. Obviously, what a Mage looked like was no way to gauge their age —Sab was two Ages old herself. Prisca *looked* older than her, but that didn't necessarily mean she was. It just meant she wasn't using as much magic to iron out the creases. And no one ever asked each other how old they were. That kind of information was irrelevant to people who lived forever.

Unless a New Born human killed them.

Anyway, the point was, even though Silly was Prisca's mother, and even though Prisca looked older than anyone here, it was well rude of the mermaid to refer to Sab and Emil as children. For all she knew, they could be Ages and Ages older than her. No other Mage would dream of using such a term in public, but then, Silly was a lady of the dominant House. She probably felt like she could say anything because normal rules didn't apply to her.

Emil obviously didn't like being called a child because he was blustering so much he couldn't even get any proper words out. Sab chuckled.

"We've prepared a wonderful festival in your honour," continued Silly, utterly oblivious to her faux pas. "Now let us repair to our humble home and celebrate!"

"This might be a festival for you," said Emil, "but *we're* on a mission to save all of Magekind from a New Born." He pointedly only gestured to his lackeys. "We don't have time for any festivities."

"You're in our town now," said Silly, looking a little less merry. "You'll do as we say. Besides, you can't go on until you've got another team member, isn't that so? You'll get them at the festival. Now, do as you're told and come to our humble abode."

Sab saw the confusion in Emil's face. He wasn't used to being ordered around. And he certainly wasn't used to ridiculous-looking women having a scary edge to them. As pert and pretty as she was, there was something in her eyes... They were too wide, too unblinking. So were her husband's.

They were utterly insane. Mind you, you couldn't fuck about with your body as much as these two clearly had without it having some impact on your mental faculties. And who knew how many Ages they'd been using magic to deform themselves? Prisca probably did. Sab would have to remember to ask her about that when they had a private moment.

"But you," said Silly, fixing her too-wide eyes on Claws. "You're not one of us. You're not welcome into our home."

Al fixed his gaze on her too. "No, you're not. Rusalka," he swivelled his eyes to his daughter without moving his head. "You shame your House by aligning yourself with a monster."

Sab looked across at Claws. The poor girl was shivering with fright and Sab saw her teeth grind together through the hole in her cheek.

"She's a friend," said Prisca.

"How are you *still* a disgrace?" said Silly. "The monster says here. The rest of you come to the feast."

"Don't leave me!" Claws whispered, grabbing Sab's arm again.

"You'll be safer out here than in there with them," Prisca whispered back to her. "Trust me."

"Well that's comforting," Sab said to her. Then she turned back to Claws. "Look. We'll have a bit of food, then come right back. Promise. We just have to play along for a little bit longer. Until then, probably best just to do as we're told."

Sab had barely finished speaking when a section of the crowd broke off and separated the two friends. They formed a circle around Claws, then just stood there, silently watching her. Poor Claws was too terrified to move, and for that Sab was glad. At least she wouldn't have to worry about Claws running away. Sab had no idea what these people were capable of, but she had absolutely no desire whatsoever to find out.

And then Emil was behind her, pushing her towards the tower and away from her friend.

TRUE, Silly and Al were creepy as all fuck. But what creeped Sab out even more was the utter silence that descended on Oceanwall when the procession of racers, led by the lord and lady, moved through them towards the gargantuan tower in the middle of the city. They just... watched. No other movement except their heads as they followed the new arrivals and their leaders.

Sab looked behind her. It was a shame she was so uneasy, because she really would've enjoyed relishing the discomfort etched all over Emil's perfect face. He was clearly trying to maintain his swagger, despite the pegs that Silly and Al had busted out from underneath him, but it was difficult with his lackeys huddled so closely around him. And swaggering needed a roaming gaze of contempt across those the swagger was for, but Emil kept his gaze locked on the ground in front of him. Instead, Sab seared the image deep into her memory so she could take the piss out of him later.

For a reason she was uninterested in exploring, it made her feel better that the high and mighty Cirrocumulans were scared. Must've been difficult for them to process, a feeling like that. Not something they ever would've felt before. Unlike Stratians. Fear came with the territory.

But, you know. There was being scared, and then there was being creeped out. Sab had spent pretty much all her life being scared, because the slaves in the farms weren't a happy bunch. But being creeped out was new for her.

They finally reached the lord and lady's residence. It struck Sab how well suited to Silly and Al it was. From far away, and despite its overwhelming size, it looked attractive, all sparkling glass and gleaming metal. Get a little closer though, and you started to see things which made your skin crawl.

The plaza around it, for one thing, was frozen water. Not ice, because Sab could feel through her ragged boots that it wasn't cold. It was just still. Frozen in time. Not that creepy, until she looked down. There were faces down there. She'd thought it was just a trick of the light at first, but no. They were definitely faces. Hair floated around some of them, also frozen in time. And a couple of times she walked over hands pressed flat against the underside as though trying to push their way back out.

So that was the plaza.

The doorway leading into the building was no better. It was just a black hole. Sab couldn't see anything beyond it, which really didn't give her any incentive to pass through it. She knew Prisca and the others were just as reluctant as her, because no one had said anything since the procession began.

"So this was the family home then?" she whispered to Prisca out of the corner of her mouth.

Prisca said nothing, just gave her a quick glance then focussed again on the looming doorway in front of them.

"No wonder you never talk about it," said Sab.

"Stop talking," whispered Prisca.

"Why?"

"Because no one else is. Please just shush."

Sab shrugged and did as she was asked. And passed through the portal.

Blackness enveloped her so completely she felt like she'd been plunged into a viscous liquid. It coated her eyes and plugged up her ears. She kept her mouth shut because she just knew that if she opened it to speak or even breathe, the blackness would coat her throat and drown her lungs. It was bad enough having to breathe through her nose. Any minute now she was going to suffocate if she didn't get out of here. Except she didn't know how she was supposed to get out of here. She'd followed a couple of insane leaders and she was completely at their mercy. Because in here, it felt like the dead zone at the terminal in the 'Sphere. Even if she wanted to use her magic to escape, she couldn't.

She looked inside herself just in case... But no. She saw it inside her, but she couldn't reach in to get any out.

"Banquet hall."

Silly's voice was so unexpected and so out of place in the suffocating blackness that Sab opened her mouth and gasped. She instantly regretted it because she'd suffocate for sure.

Then her intestines were sucked out through her feet.

And then she was surrounded by decadence.

"Shit on a motherfucking stick," she said, then sucked down the fresh air.

Emil and his lackeys were clearly fighting to hold on to their pride as well. The only newcomer who wasn't affected by the last few seconds was Prisca.

"Not a fan of your family home," Sab said to her.

"You get used to it."

"Really? Don't think I want to."

"Welcome to our humble abode!" cried Silly, swirling around on her tail to face them.

"As you can see," said Al, no less proud than his wife, "the feast is ready for you."

He flourished with arms and tentacles towards a table that wouldn't have fitted inside Sab's cell back on the 'Sphere. It was laden with food, and considering all she'd seen so far, Sab wasn't sure she wanted to look too closely at it. But it seemed that wasn't going to be something she could choose. Not because it would be rude to decline... Something was definitely compelling her. She reached inside herself and noted that she was still unable to use her own magic, but this place wasn't a dead zone like the portal was, because there was definitely magic being used here. The finest tendrils wrapping around her in order to compel her to do...what? As she was told? Was this how the lord and lady controlled their city and had such an obedient population who cheered on cue and didn't speak out of turn?

But, no. Sab hadn't sensed this gentle compulsion outside. Just another thing she'd have to bring up with Prisca when they got out of this place.

"While House Lix-Tetrax appreciates all the effort you've obviously gone to on our behalf," said Emil. His voice was thin. "I think it would be better if we just continued on with the race."

His lackeys nodded, brave enough to demonstrate that

tiny bit of solidarity, but not brave enough to add their voices to his. Sab decided to add hers just because she knew it'd really piss him off.

"I agree," she said. "It's a bit of trek to Taurë. We'd better get a move on."

She looked over to Emil and smiled. He scowled back at her.

Not that it made the blindest bit of difference though — despite their brave words, the whole company were already at the table and, scraping back the high-backed chairs in order to sit down at places that had been pre-decided for them.

"Nonsense," said Al. "You're here now. You might as well eat." His words were pleasant but his face wasn't. "Sit."

They all obeyed. They had no choice. And it suddenly occurred to Sab why Claws wasn't welcome inside this giant symbol of the lord and lady's power. She was a mutant, or monster, as they'd so politely referred to her, and whatever compulsion was working on them would never have worked on her. It didn't give her any sense of relief knowing that she had no choice in what she did while she was here.

Worse was knowing that the lord and lady probably had a very specific reason for doing it. Admittedly they probably did it to everyone who came into their house, but that didn't ease Sab's mind even the tiniest bit.

She sat in the chair her body had scraped aside against her will, then shuffled herself forward so she could sit comfortably. Well, comfort was a strong word. Something was up with the chair—it shifted under her like it was trying to squirm away. A quick glance at Emil and his toadies showed her their discomfort too. Prisca's face showed nothing. But then, she was probably used to her parents' weird ways.

And that left only the food. The moment Sab and the

others entered the room, servants entered to load the table with an array of colourful cuisine. Sab didn't recognise a single solitary morsel of it. But just like the chair beneath her, she realised now she was actually face to face with the food, it squirmed.

She glanced up at a servant. His face was carefully blank, but no amount of training could erase the fear that stretched his eyes wide, or stop the tendons from straining in his neck. So, a slave then. Maybe he was just scared of his owners, and frankly, who wouldn't be? But something in Sab told her that he was also horrified at the food he'd just served up to the guests.

A translucent yellow blob on a gold plate right in front of Sab wobbled, shifted, and then a bulbous black eye stared up at her.

"Urgh!" she said, never one to worry about minding her manners. "What the *fuck* is *that?*"

Al chuckled a little. "A delicacy in Oceanwall. "Something we only serve up to our most honoured guests."

"Why? Don't you like having honoured guests?"

"Sabina!" hisspered Prisca.

"You're friend is very rude," said Silly, an almost believable expression of hurt across her coral face.

"I am sorry, Mother."

"That's a rare flab-fish in front of you, dear," said Silly. "The most expensive food you could hope to find here in Oceanwall."

"But it's alive," said Sab.

"Best way to eat them," said Silly, then stabbed her fork down onto her own plate with a squelchy clang. A thin squirt of yellowy blood covered her hand, then she picked the struggling, squealing flab-fish up to her mouth. It opened far wider than was pleasant to watch, and she stuffed the writhing creature into it. Bliss closed her eyes.

"Mmmm, tastes just like warm butter," she said, dribbling yellow juice over her chin.

"Then just eat warm butter," Sab said under her breath.

"All of you," said Al, "eat."

Sab had no choice. Her hand grabbed the nearest fork on the table, and plunged it into the black quivering eye that gazed up at her. It popped quietly. She'd never forget that sound for the rest of her immortality.

Well, it seemed that her body was functioning of its own accord so she didn't have to look at what she was doing. She squeezed her eyes shut, tried to do the same with her mouth, but all too soon she was chewing through rubbery blubber that really did taste like warm butter. It didn't help thinking of it like that.

"That's an interesting effect on your arms, Sabina," said Silly. "Open your eyes and tell me how you did it."

Sab did as she was coerced. "Just peeled my skin off over the long years of my life down in Stratus."

"Why?"

"Because I like feeling pain." She tried to stop her mouth from talking. "My mum killed herself so I've been punishing myself ever since."

Silly and Al burst out laughing, spraying masticated flab-fish over the table. "Mages can't kill each other, nor can they kill themselves," said Al.

"She didn't kill herself with herself," said Sab, trying to bite down on the words. "She got the slaves to do it for her."

This tickled Silly and Al even more. "How she must have hated you!" said Silly, then leaned across to her husband and licked a chunk of flab-fish off his cheek. "I was never overly fond of Rusalka, but I couldn't have a slave even *touch* me let alone kill me!"

"How did she manage it?" said Al, his eyes gleaming with avarice.

"She started a riot amongst them," said Sab, hating herself for being made to talk. "They ripped her apart."

"It must have taken so long to die!" said Silly, her voice breathless with laughter.

"It did."

"Why did she do it?"

"I don't know." For the only time in her life, she was glad she didn't.

"Oh." Silly's laughter stopped instantly, so did Al's. "Well, that's a poor ending to a hilarious story. You should fix that."

"I have a question," said Emil, "for the lord and lady of this magnificent House." He fidgeted under their twin glares, and Sab wanted to smirk at that but she was too relieved to be free of them.

"Ask then, boy," said Silly, still paying no attention whatsoever to linguistic etiquette.

After Emil had done bridling at being called a boy, he said, "We're to find another Mage to join us on our race. Will we have time to do that once we've finished this…delicious meal?"

"No," said Silly.

"We've already assigned people to you," said Al.

And that was it. Apparently, their good humour had passed. Sab was all right with that. Although listening to the squishy sounds of everyone chewing through live flab-fish was really gross.

Eventually, the meal ended, and Sab promised that she'd make herself throw up the second they were outside Ocean-wall. It wouldn't do the flab-fish any good, but it would make her feel a little bit better. But it already helped looking at the green-tinged faces of Emil and his stooges, knowing that their lives of privilege were no match for shit that was so utterly disgusting.

"Ceremony Room!" Silly screeched.

If not for the compulsion magic that was working on her, Sab knew that the yanking blackness would have been multi-coloured with her vomit. Anonymous groans told her that she wasn't the only one feeling that way.

A second later, the Ceremony Room smacked her in the face.

This place was making as much use as possible of the water-frozen-in-time theme that the plaza displayed, but here it was taken to extreme levels. The floor beneath Sab's feet plunged to black and midnight depths, but fortunately was broken up by the immobile forms of what used to be citizens in varying paroxysms of aguish.

She turned her head minutely to the side. "Were they punished for something?" she whispered to Prisca.

But Prisca didn't answer. The woman who'd been a mother to Sab ever since her own had left her, was too afraid to talk about her parents in front of them.

The walls of the Ceremony Room were just as disturbing, and spaced along them were giant, breaking waves, fixed in time. Flowing down from the middle of the ceiling was a vast, inverted fountain, that flickered its way through the spectrum of colours from palest blue to ocean black. The resulting light it threw across the cavernous space was probably meant to mimic sunlight on water, but it just made Sab feel like she was seeing a headache.

Citizens were clustered at the foot of the waves, shuffling closer together at the abrupt entrance of the lord and lady, while simultaneously erupting into wild cheering and applause. The husband and wife were directly under the inverted fountain, basking in the adulation. Sab, Prisca, Emil and his lackeys stood in a semi-circle before them. How did they know their masters were going to arrive at this particular moment? Unless they just waited here all the time, ready to praise the lord and lady when they made an appearance.

This place was even more fucked up than the 'Sphere.

"Silence!" Silly screamed, and instantly there was. "Now is the time for us to award these brave participants with another team member worthy of them."

"Rusalka," said Al. "Step forward."

Prisca stepped towards her parents, a perfectly tailored mask of politeness covering her face. "Mother, Father," she said in a voice Sab didn't recognise as hers. "Any honour you bestow on me is gratefully received."

"Of course it is, dear daughter," said Al, reaching out with one of his tentacles to stroke her cheek. She didn't even flinch, which was an extraordinary demonstration of will-power.

"To you, we present one of our best Mages," said Silly. "He's very powerful and is committed to helping you win this race."

"You're too kind, Mother."

"Kindness has nothing to do with it," said Al. And then the tentacle that had been caressing her cheek was suddenly squeezing itself around her throat. "You *will* win this race. It's high time AtmoSphere recognised House Forneus as the great power we are. Win this race, and bring that New Born human to us. Do you understand?"

"Yes, Father," said Prisca, though her voice was little more than a croak.

"How wonderful!" said Silly, and the Ceremony Room filled with clapping and cheering once more. "Stop!" she shrieked three seconds later, and they did.

Al slithered his tentacle off Prisca's neck and pushed her back towards Sab.

"Volos!" he boomed.

In the space between the competitors and the insane leaders, a form materialised. A huge form. Sab didn't know why, but something told her that their new team member was going to be a giant wanker.

It seemed to take an Age for the form to coalesce, but it was also instantaneous. It occurred to Sab that she was perhaps witnessing the end result of that yanking blackness she'd so recently experienced and despised. She blinked once, and was suddenly looking at a hulking beast of a man.

"I am Volos," said the beast, his voice deep and commanding. His eyes were fixed on Prisca. "And you *are* fortunate, for I am incredible."

Yep. Giant wanker it was then.

SQUIRREL

"Stop staring at me, Squirrel," said Audra.

We were in a carriage, a novel and somewhat uncomfy experience for me, on our way to the Financial Quarter. While she gazed out of the window, I couldn't take my eyes off her.

"What did you do to them?"

She sighed and looked at me. "I don't know. But they're not hurt, so don't worry about them. Not one of them ever worried about you, or anyone living in Out'Keep. They don't deserve your concern."

"I'm not concerned about them. I just want to know what you did."

"Me too. Somehow I doubt there'll be any books in the library about it though. I'll have to keep a journal. You should too."

I blinked. I had no intention of using whatever this was, let alone writing about it. Wasn't ready to tell Audra that yet.

"It's fascinating," she continued, looking back out of the carriage window. "Two months ago everyone thought that magic, Mages, Ancient Realms elves and orcs had died out, but it turns out they're all still very much alive. I wonder what else we've been wrong about?"

I shrugged, but I didn't think she actually expected an answer from me. I kind of expected an answer from myself—what was I doing here? Now, I'd used this magic exactly twice. The first time was to protect myself and my mum from RazorHand and his crew. The second was to heal Mum's legs. Both times ended with death. And both times... Well, they left me with a gnawing hunger inside that I decided not to think about. So far, it wasn't a great gift. Plus, I'd just seen Audra use it to imprison a bunch of rich old men inside themselves. So what, exactly, was I doing here with her? I could feel my face twitching as I tried to come up with any kind of explanation, but I couldn't. There was just a tiny little part of my mind that was screaming at me to get away. Go back to my little copse with Mouse and forget all about her. Forget all about magic. But I think...I think there was an even smaller part of me that was too afraid to do even that.

"When we get to these elves, are you going to stop them like you did them ministers?" I asked.

She laughed softly through her nose. "Don't be silly," she said. "I quite like some of them. Besides, we'll need them to move all the money around."

"Do what with our money, old girl?"

It was the one called Lord Worthy who spoke. I'd never seen elves up close—don't think anyone in Keep'Out Quarter had. Probably not even the Chief. Even though we all knew they were the richest folk in the city, the Financial Quarter was unofficially out of bounds to people of a thieving persuasion like me. No one ever really said why, it's just that they were elves, which meant they weren't human. And we just didn't know what they'd do if they caught us pinching stuff from their houses. If we even could've got in them in the first place. They were right beautiful, mind. Tall and thin—rich folk thin, not starving poor-people thin—with dark skin the colour of expensive wood and pale hair the colour of moonlight. Perfect bone structure. The kind of beauty that terrifies and keeps you away, rather than invites you in for a friendly chat.

Don't mind saying though, standing in that room with all them jewels and coins twinkling about the place, I fair thought my hands would explode if I didn't nick something quick. Obviously, I didn't. I was an opportunist, yes, but I wasn't stupid.

"Share it," said Audra. "My friend Squirrel here could tell you some shocking stories about the state of Out'Keep, but with all the money this city has, it needn't be like that."

"We thought perhaps you'd come to offer your condolences," said Lady Worthy, only a little bit more beautiful than her husband. "I offer you mine. I know you and Faër adored each other, Audra dear."

Audra closed her eyes for a moment, and I remembered that Faër was the friend she couldn't save at the battle of Blasted Glade. I looked back at the two elves—these were her parents. I suddenly felt really bad.

"I don't know why I couldn't save her," Audra whispered. "I'm sorry. But I can save this city. And I will. With your help."

"Adàm tells us you're a Mage," said the lady.

"So is Squirrel."

The lord and lady gave me a raised eyebrow each. Don't know if that signified interest, or worry, or what. Not very easy to read, them elves.

"So is it really help," continued the lady, "if we have no choice in the matter?"

"Why wouldn't you want to make things better for everybody?" said Audra.

"Economies don't work if you just give all the money away, old girl," said the lord. "They need competition, ambition, and lots of people working. If everybody has money, why would they work? Our economy would come crashing to a halt and then we'd all be poor."

"You invented the economy, Lord Worthy," said Audra. "You can make it do whatever you want. But *I* want you to make it get rid of poverty."

"I'm sure we could organise trusts to solve the problem, Audra dear."

"What's that now?" said the lord turning to his wife, frowning slightly. I guessed that meant he was furious. "We'll do no such thing! We've been running this city for four Ages, and I'll not have some ephemeral human tell me what to do with it, no matter how friendly she is with my family!" He turned back to Audra. "Out of the question, old girl."

"Well, if you can't learn to share," she said, raising her hands and wiggling her fingers, "then no one will have it."

I blinked, and when my eyes opened again all of the gold and jewels and money was gone. All that lovely, lovely money. Just gone.

"How did you do that?" I asked. "I didn't even hear anything let alone see it."

"I know!" Audra said with a delighted giggle. "I just thought it and it happened!"

"What have you done?" whispered the lord. His face was all slack. "Audra, what have you done?"

"I've taken away your money."

"Where is it?"

She shrugged and grinned. "I don't know how the magic works yet, but it's quite good fun finding out."

"We're ruined!" he wailed.

"You probably should've thought of that before, instead of just being greedy. Now, when you're explaining your sudden downfall to all the other elves in this quarter, you should probably mention I'll do the same to their money if it doesn't start pouring down into Out'Keep. Do you both understand?"

The lord looked aghast, but the lady merely smiled sadly. "I'd counsel caution in using something you don't understand, but I fear you won't listen."

"No need to worry about me, Lady Worthy," she said with a bright smile. "Now, we've all got many things to do today, so we'll take our leave. Pass the day well!"

I couldn't formulate any sentences until we'd left their mansion and were back in the carriage.

"You got rid of all that money!" I said.

"And they'll learn how difficult it is when you don't have any. This was the best thing for them. It'll motivate them into helping others as needy as they are."

"But they were your friends."

Audra laughed. It was a pretty sound even if it was unexpected. "A good friend of mine once said to me, 'Who needs friends when you've got power?'" she said. "And do you know what? I rather think he was right."

SABINA

"*W*e are honoured," said Prisca, lowering her eyes. "With you on our team, Volos, we can only win."

Sab scowled. "What the fuck, Prisca? We can't have this monster on our team! Think of Claws!"

"Not now, Sabina."

"Yes, now! We don't—"

She was rudely interrupted by a sudden flare of power. Volos was glowering at her, a crackling, seething ball of magic cradled in his hand.

"Give me the word, my lady," he said, his voice deep enough to rumble Sab's bones. "I will dismiss this one for you."

"Dismiss me?" said Sab. "What, like, get rid of? As in kill? Mages can't kill Mages."

"That's why he said *dismiss*," said Silly. "No, Volos, she's on Rusalka's team. Leave her be."

Volos growled, looked at the pulsating ball of magic held in his hand. Then he flung it up in the air. Sab waited for it to smash the upside down fountain to smithereens, but it stopped. She blinked. It bobbed there for a second or two, turning this way and that as though it were looking for something. Then it sped down into the watching crowd beneath the frozen waves. It engulfed someone fully before Sab could even discern whether the unfortunate bystander was a man or woman, adult or child—the wretched howling that emanated from it could've been any of them.

The other spectators had already scattered, and now the floor around the heaving, person-shaped blob of magic rippled.

Then it started swirling.

Then it funnelled up and engulfed the person.

Then everything was sucked back down into the floor, its surface as shiny and undisturbed as it had been a few mere moments ago. And as if that weren't sickening enough, the audience exploded with applause.

Sab had no intention of going over there to look, but she knew if she did, she'd see a newly-frozen person with terror etched all over their face looking back up at her. She shivered, suddenly guilty about leaving Claws on her own outside.

"Are they all mutants?" she whispered over to Prisca, just as the cheering stopped.

"No, silly girl," said Silly. "Our dear Volos just dismissed one of our courtiers. He so hates wasting his magic when it's ready to be cast."

"But if that person wasn't a mutant—"

"Dismissing isn't killing," said Volos. "That Mage is still alive. He's just suspended. And in a lot of pain." He grinned.

Silly giggled. Al chuckled.

"There's a lot of things I can do to a Mage that doesn't result in death," said Volos in a deep voice, bending down to look right into her eyes.

It had been a long time since Sab was scared of anything.

In fact, the last time she'd been scared was when her mum died and left her all alone in Stratus. This close to Volos's face, seeing the network of veins mapped out beneath his translucent skin, horribly contrasting with the sprouting tufts of dark, curly hair that covered his head, neck, jaw, and out of his nose, plus the oversized features on an oversized head, she wasn't scared now. Not exactly *scared*. Really fucking uncomfortable, would've been a much more accurate way to describe it. However long took to get to Taurë, it'd be a billion times longer with this monster as part of their team.

And poor Claws was going to spend every single second of it shitting herself.

Volos straightened up again, but didn't let his gaze wander from Sab. Nor did he let his grin slide. What was it with these people and their too-big mouths? She kind of missed the days when all she knew about privileged Mages was that they used their power to stoke the fire of their vanities. Here in Oceanwall it was clearly all about making yourself look as terrifyingly ridiculous as possible.

No fucking way she'd say that out loud to Volos's revolting face though.

She wasn't looking at him, but Sab felt Volos's eyes on her even as he lurched over to Prisca, taking up the stance next to his team mates.

"We will bring honour to House Forneus," he said, "and the lord and lady who preside over it. Audra the New Born will be yours."

Rapturous applause shattered the air for a few seconds then ceased.

Sab risked a glance at Emil. He was clearly disgusted by this turn of events—not even in his most perverted dreams would he have expected Sab's team to get landed with such a powerful ally. That look almost made having Volos on her team worth it.

Silly yawned, the back of her head almost touching the nape of her neck. "That patriarch in AtmoSphere said both teams had to get a new team member," she said, "so here is yours."

She clicked her fingers, the blackness yanked at Sab all over, and then she was back out on the plaza. It only took a few moments for the gathered citizens to realise their masters were back, and they broke out into a frenzy of cheering.

Sab tried to surreptitiously seek out Claws, but a servant shuffled across Sab's peripheral view, holding the hand of a... wait—was that a kid? One of the Mages in this mental city actually agreed to give up their *child* for this ridiculous race?

For a split second, a smug smirk pushed its way across her face—this was really going to piss Emil off! The Stratians got the enormous burly Mage man, and he got the little kid!

But then she made the mistake of reaching out a tendril to find out who the kid was. There was nothing. She should've been able to see his name, his age, what House he belonged to. Even slaves and servants had that information magically imprinted into them by their owners. But this kid had nothing. And that meant only one thing.

He was a mutant.

Shit on a stick. The poor bastard was never going to survive this race with the likes of Emil and his goons. On the 'Sphere, their ilk had turned torturing mutants into a fun spectator sport. There were stories that Claws still hadn't told her and Prisca because she simply couldn't bring herself to relive them.

"What is this?" roared Emil, stepping towards the lord and lady. Although the sudden hush of the crowd and the way they all stepped forwards as one made him stop. He glanced around nervously, then privileged indignation won out once more. "You're giving us a mutant? That's not fair!"

Al rose up on his tentacles, and it turned out he was horribly tall. "That patriarch of yours said the rules were to give each team a new member before they could move on. He didn't specify that it had to be a Mage."

"Lian is the shame of a very well-respected family here in Oceanwall," Silly continued, floating next to her husband. "They don't want him, so we're giving him to you."

"Be grateful," said Al. "My initial plan was to have you dismissed, but soft-hearted Scylla here," he caressed his wife's cheek with his hand, "couldn't bear the thought of hurting children. If you refuse the mutant, I'll have Volos dismiss you right here in the plaza."

Volos raised his hand, a vicious grin slicked across his face.

"No, no, that won't be necessary," said Emil, stepping backwards. "We're very grateful. Thank you lord and lady. I'm sure this...this Lian will be very...um, adequate."

"Well!" said Silly. "We've done more than we needed to, so get out of my city. Rusalka," she said, swivelling to Prisca. "Bring me back that New Born."

She clapped her hands once.

Sab felt as though she were simultaneously being flung across a great distance and bounced against a wall. When the sensation passed, she was standing on patchy grass, the walls of Oceanwall roaring upwards beside her.

"Wow," she said. "They really didn't want us to outstay our welcome, did they?"

"We should hurry," said Prisca. "Emil's team must be somewhere nearby and we can't have them getting to Hinterland Deeps before us."

Sab caught her arm. "You better get back to your old self soon. This new you, this Rusalka? Not a fan."

"We have to get a move on." She yanked her arm back and trotted away from the roaring walls.

Before Sab had a chance to speak to Claws and get her settled, Volos swung his giant, hairy arm around and grabbed a fistful of Claws's shirt, pulling her off her feet and towards his face.

"Mutant," he growled at her. She whimpered. "I *hate* mutants."

Sab picked up a rock and threw it at the back of his head. Brute like that would've had all sorts of spells in place to protect his hide against magic. But not against rocks. He bellowed incoherently, dropped Claws, and spun around to face Sab.

"Before you start issuing threats," she said, "let me just say that I don't scare all that easily." She pointed to herself with both thumbs. "Bottom of the heap, been shat on all my life. And pain doesn't frighten me either, you see?" she showed him her arms. "The more you hurt me, the more I like it.

She took a step forward and scowled up at him. "What I don't like, is giant dicks picking on my friends. Claws is essential to our mission—"

"She's a mutant," said Volos, then turned and spat on the sparse grass.

"That's right, genius, and guess what that means when we get to Taurë and come face to face with a New Born human with a taste for killing Mages?"

Volos frowned.

"Shit on a stick," said Sab, pinching the bridge of her nose. "It means the New Born won't kill *her*. Claws here will look just like any other human to the New Born, so she's our secret weapon." She reached up, grabbed a handful of Volos's shirt, and strengthening herself with magic from her reserves, pulled him down to her face level. "So if you touch her, or even look at her with a hint of malice, I'm coming right back here to tell your lord and lady that *you* single-handedly ruined their chances of beating House Lix-Tetrax in this race." She pushed him away.

"As soon as this is over," he rumbled, "I'll have my revenge on you."

Sab grabbed her arse with both hands, then regarded them with mock pity. "Well, now, would you look at that. Fresh out shits to give."

She linked her arm into Claws's. "I got you. Let's catch up with Prisca."

She hadn't got very far, Prisca. Probably caught up by the minor confrontation, because she was gaping at Sab with worry, with just a few hints of annoyance trying to creep in at the edges.

"Don't antagonise him," she whispered when Sab and Claws reached her.

"Know him well, do you?" said Sab.

"Everyone in Oceanwall does. That's why we don't antagonise him."

Before Sab could fire out a scathing retort, the whole world vanished.

JAYMES

*I*t wasn't a tavern, even though he'd had to pay for whatever slop the toothless wench had spilt into his tankard. A shit-hole, was what it was. Piss on the floor. Puke up the walls. Stubs of smokes everywhere. The place reeked of all that, plus the unwashed bodies crammed in here, bad breath, foetid liquor. And someone somewhere was smoking poison weed. Fucking foul.

And just the kind of place he'd been looking for.

Jaymes squeezed his tankard until the pewter groaned. Not only had he lost some of his closest friends on that forsaken mission, but now the Rebels had been disbanded. All thanks to Audra. That bitch and her Healing Glass. Healing Glass? Fucking thing didn't even exist!

When Drayke had said their new orders were to come into Out'Keep and find criminals, Jaymes had immediately come down to Keep'Out Quarter. Not because he intended on doing what that bitch told him to, but because he wanted to get drunk in the filthiest, roughest dive he could find. Get drunk, then start a fight.

Because he should be dead, for fuck's sake! He'd died! He

knew he did, because he'd felt it. That orc's rusty, twisted blade had pierced his stomach with excruciating pain, pain which worsened when it was pulled back out, spilling his guts over the barren ground of the Blasted Glade. Guts which were then trodden on by his comrades and squashed into a bloody, shitty jelly. Then he'd fallen to his knees in the shit and blood, which was just the right height for another one of those orcs to start eating the flesh right off his face. Then blackness, blissfully, had taken him.

Only to be woken up with that bitch's face staring down at him. What had she done? All the pain was gone. There were scars on his body, but definitely no gaping holes where his guts had slipped out. And his face was whole. Almost whole.

When he'd looked around he saw his friends scrabbling up from their hands and knees looking just as confused as he felt, friends he'd seen fall before him with their throats slit, or pulled down by the weight of orcs eating them alive. How could they possibly be getting up after that? How could he?

Because that bitch had done something to them! And did she explain it to them on their way home? No. She'd been wrapped up in her own selfish grief at the death of that elf woman. Too selfish to realise that there were men who needed to understand why their rotting corpses weren't now nourishing the sterile earth of the Blasted Glade.

So fuck it, if he wanted to fight, he'd damn well fight!

He downed his drink, ignoring the foul taste and burning sensation down his throat, and launched himself off his broken stool. Holding court in the centre of the room was the ugliest man Jaymes had ever seen. Uglier than himself even. And covered in almost as many scars. Here was a cunt who liked fighting. Jaymes walked right up to him, swung his arm back as far as it would go, then punched the ugly fucker right in the face.

He fell backwards off his stool onto his arse, his cronies staring down at him and then back up at Jaymes as though they couldn't quite work out how the two events were connected. All of them looked so comical with their expressions of surprise plastered on their plastered faces. In another lifetime Jaymes would've roared with laughter.

Today though he just sneered. And for a heartbeat or two there was utter silence before the cronies jumped into action and onto him, fists pumping and punching his head, chest, belly. With each blow that landed, there was pain, but it didn't bother him. He could still fight back. Even when his vision was clouded by their spraying blood, he could still fight back. They couldn't bring him down. Now some of them had managed to tangle their arms in his and had pulled them until they were twisted behind his back. His shoulders should've screamed the pain, but instead they passed a polite note onto his brain that another injury was taking place.

His fists may have been out of the fight, but his legs weren't. Teeth broke, noses smashed, cheeks ripped as he kicked and swung his legs in every direction, meeting enemy faces wherever they flailed. He hadn't been aware of movement, but suddenly he found himself outside in the wet, twilit alley, which smelled no sweeter than the shit-hole tavern. And then, finally, one of the useless cronies pulled out a blade. It was very shiny. The blade was as wiggly as a snake, and on the hilt the cross-guard and pommel were pointlessly decorated with all sorts of gems and jewels. This was clearly an instrument to demonstrate wealth, not a weapon to instil fear.

Now Jaymes *did* laugh. "What fancy mansion did you steal that letter-opener from?"

The crony pulled back his arm to finish the job, and stretched out his lips in a frightful grimace that revealed his broken and rotten teeth.

"Stop!"

The bellow was enough to make all the cronies release their grip on him and the weapon-wielder to spin and hide his hands behind his back. Had Jaymes accidentally ambushed a bunch of kids? He leapt to his feet, hoping the father would provide a more interesting fight, in that case.

But in this case, the father turned out to be the ugly fucker he'd punched in the mouth in the first place.

"What for?" whined the weapon-wielder. "We had him!"

"Barely," said the ugly fucker with a sneer. "Which is why the Chief should meet him."

"Who the fuck's your chief," said Jaymes, "and can he actually fight?"

"*The* Chief likes nothing better than a bit of violence." The cronies grunted laughter. "And he'll happily ply you with it for trespassing."

The Chief, was it? Jaymes grinned. "Then lead the way."

JAYMES SCOWLED when he finally saw the Chief.

At first, the journey had seemed promising. Alleys got smaller and filthier and more dangerous, and then one of the cronies covered Jaymes' eyes with a stinking rag so he wouldn't know where their secret lair was kept. Blind he may've been, but it didn't stop the sound of their scuffing feet, or distant savagery or close up fucking reaching his ears. Nor did it stop the wretched reek of human effluence pouring up his nostrils and into the back of throat until he wanted to gag. Orc's bollocks, he knew Keep'Out Quarter was a shit tip but he'd forgotten it smelt this bad.

Finally they reached a building, and he guessed it was the Chief's. He'd done what he could to reduce the stink by lighting scented oil-lamps and incense. With the front door shut and him having been shoved up and down steps and through into different rooms, the place didn't actually smell that bad. He even got a whiff of food. Then they took the rag off his eyes, which resulted in his current disappointment.

The Chief was nothing but a big fat fuck smeared across a seat.

Next to that seat, which was easily big enough to sit three Rebels comfortably next to each other or both of this Chief's arse cheeks, was a little decorative table piled with plates of little balls of food. Even if his eyes were fully accustomed to the light after his recent blindness, and even if they weren't still covered with the drying blood of his combatants, he'd never have been able to work out what those little balls of food were. Smelt fucking delicious though.

"You're a Rebel," said the Chief. Jaymes was surprised by his voice; it was rich and deep. Almost cultured. "And while you might be suffered up in In'Keep, you're trespassing down here. It's called Keep'Out for a reason."

Jaymes said nothing. He couldn't be bothered. This wasn't the Chief he'd imagined from the Keep'Out legends. This man was soft and powdered, his clothes laved and perfumed, his hands bloated and covered with jewellery. This was no fighter. He paid other people to do the fighting for him.

"So what I'd like to know," he said, rising with surprising grace and walking over to a cabinet on the other side of the room, "is what you're doing down here."

"Starting fights," said Jaymes.

The Chief filled a fine glass with thick liquor, then turned and swept his gaze over his men before settling it back on Jaymes. "Oh I can see that," he said. "For any particular reason?"

Jaymes shrugged. "I like to fight."

"Not unexpected from a Rebel, I imagine. But I've never seen any of your ilk venture down here to do so."

He shrugged again.

"I have an acquaintance in the Rebels," said the Chief, returning to his chair. "How's Kole?"

"Dead."

"Ah. Shame. Sweetmeat?" He lifted a silver platter of food balls and held it out towards Jaymes.

He scowled.

"Suit yourself," said the Chief, then popped one in his mouth. When he'd finished eating he said, "So does that mean the mission failed? The Healing Glass remains hidden and the plague remains free?"

Well, that was a bit of a surprise. "No."

"Which question does that answer?"

"All of them."

The Chief raised an eyebrow, sending waves through his pudgy forehead. "And yet I still have no answers."

"Who are you really?" said Jaymes. "And how do you know Kole?"

"Ah, forgive me, I've been remiss. I am the Chief. In'Keep has the Prime Minister. Out'Keep has," he inclined his head gracefully, "me. And you, my angry friend, are Jaymes Balos."

"How do you know Kole?"

"I know you Rebels are supposed to sever all ties with family when you join your," he fluttered his fat fingers about, "illustrious band of brothers, but Kole was a good boy. He looked after his mum and dad from Out'Keep. He assured me he didn't want anything...untoward happening to them, so therefore he agreed to look after me too."

"You sound like a right bastard."

The Chief exploded with laughter. A pleasant sound. "That I am, my dear Jaymes, that I am. But there are none who'd be brave enough to tell me so. Except you."

"So, what, you're going to ask me to be your new spy now you know Kole's dead?"

"You see, that's what I like about the Rebels: you're strong *and* intelligent. The two don't often go together, you know. But I don't ask. I tell."

"Fuck you."

The Chief smiled. Then looked up at one of his cronies. "Bring in the girl."

There was movement behind him but Jaymes refused to look. He was too old and too dead to give a fuck about this shit.

And then a little girl was pushed past him. When she got her balance back, she stepped slowly to the Chief's side. Her entire body was trembling like it was cold. But with the great fire burning in the ostentatious fireplace, it couldn't have been that, even though she was only wearing a raggedy old tunic that barely covered her limbs.

"Over you come, dear," said the Chief, beckoning with his fleshy fingers. "And now turn around, let our guest get a good look at you."

She did as she was told, and Jaymes saw the terror clearly in her eyes. He also saw bruises around her mouth and covering her arms and legs. As pale and thin as she was, they stood out all the more starkly.

"This is Kole's sister," said the Chief. "Jaymes is a friend of your brother." Hope flickered slightly across the girl's face. "Tell him how old you are, dear."

She opened her mouth to speak, but no sound came out. She stopped, swallowed and tried again. "Ten," she said.

"Ten," said the Chief with a smile. "And, ah, Jaymes, she has been made to do things that no ten-year-old should ever know about. But I'm a willing teacher and it didn't take me long to break her." He chuckled. "And she is very broken. No man would take her now. I'm afraid I can't tell you her name because I never bothered to learn it."

"Why is she here?" said Jaymes, and now he really was

surprised. Surprised how sickened he was by the Chief and protective he was towards the young girl. Kole's little sister.

"Kole was kept in line by the threat to his family," said the Chief. "But I needed to keep the family in line by the threat to this little one." He stroked her cheek and she whimpered. "On your knees, dear."

She glanced down at the Chief's pudgy crotch and covered her mouth with tiny hands.

"We're not doing that today, dear," said the Chief. "I want you to keep looking at your brother's friend."

She sank down to her knees, relief on her battered face, and directed a look full of pleading at Jaymes. A lump heated his throat. And a sudden feeling of dread froze his heart.

"What are you doing?" he whispered to the Chief.

"This." He brandished a dagger, a much more practical one than that of his crony, wound his fingers through the girl's hair, and pulled her head back. She squeaked in pain, but she hadn't yet seen the dagger. Somehow, Jaymes was relieved by that.

In a heartbeat, the Chief had the dagger at the girl's throat and he sliced through it slowly. She tried to scream but there was only a bubbling gurgle. That, and a dreadful fountain of blood that rushed over the Chief's dagger-holding hand and all the way down her dirty tunic to pool on the expensive rug on the floor. The Chief kept her head pulled back long after he'd finished cutting to make sure that Jaymes saw every last drop of blood fall. Then he pushed her limp body forward and it thumped and cracked as it hit the floor.

Time passed, and eventually Jaymes could speak again. "Why?"

"Oh, you know," said the Chief, wiping his bloody hands on an embroidered silk napkin. "Now Kole's dead, that family is of no use to me. Besides, I find people more will-ingly do what I want them to do if they are scared. So I scare them. Now, I realise that child was nothing to you, but I can find people who are. And I wanted you to be aware that my depravity has no depth. Do you understand?"

"Yes."

"Good," he said, folding the napkin and placing it back on the table. "Because you work for me now."

For the longest time, Sab saw the whole world laid out below her. But not with her eyes, that wasn't quite right. She saw with her whole body, and she saw everything from the crashing waves under the 'Sphere, and the fish that swam through them; green carpets of forests and the birds that flew around them; red dunes of the desert, and the insects that buried themselves under them. Intoxicating wasn't the right word.

And then she was whole again, standing on her own feet, looking out of her own eyes. It was hugely disappointing.

Tugging around her ankle made her look down. Claws. Her face, staring up at Sab's with incomprehension, was drained of all colour. Sab squatted down and helped her friend up.

"What was that?" Claws whispered.

"Probably our newest recruit," she glanced sidelong at Volos, who was busy looking proud of himself, and lowered her voice. "Showing off his magic."

"But what did he do to us?"

Sab looked around. Oceanwall was nowhere to be seen.

Actually, nothing was anywhere to be seen. Everywhere was flat and scrubby, rocky grey sand underfoot, spiky plants doing their best to make a living from it. The distant horizon smudged into the overcast sky. A chilly breeze plucked at her t-shirt, brought with it the smell of rain.

"Well," she said, "I'm going to go with transportation."

"I feel like I was ripped apart, then thrown back together again."

"Yep. That's pretty much what happened."

Claws's eyes widened at that, then she spun around and vomited over the nearest rock. Prisca gasped and ran over.

"Mutants," said Volos with disgust. "They're useless."

"Ignore the bully," said Sab. "The first time's always a bit of shock to the system. You'll get used to it."

"I don't want to."

"And you probably shouldn't," said Prisca, reaching into her bag and pulling out some bread. "Eat this. It'll help settle your stomach."

"Will she be all right?" said Sab.

"I think so. But I don't know how using such strong magic on someone like Claudia will affect her. We'll just have to keep an eye on our girl."

Sab nodded, then looked over to Volos. He was wearing the kind of expression that said if he could dismiss these three women and complete the race on his own, he would. The lord and lady had a pretty effective leash on him in Oceanwall, but that was way beyond the horizon now. No knowing just how far they could take him before it snapped.

"So where'd you bring us?" said Sab. "Hinterland Deeps was the next city on the itinerary, so where is it?"

Volos laughed, the translucent skin around his jowls wobbling. "You think we're playing by the rules of your patriarch? We're far from the Deeps, and far from the other team. We're in the lead and we'll win this race for the lord and lady."

"Cheating, nice," said Sab. "We'd better make sure we do win then, or the Patriarch'll definitely have something to say about that."

Volos spat on the ground.

"Eloquent," said Sab. "Anyway, if we're not near the Deeps, then where are we?"

"Nearer to our goal. Follow me." And with that he lurched off.

Sab rolled her eyes. "Urgh. Enigmatic statements to simple questions. What a twat. I hope Audra kills him first so I get to watch the smugness fade from his eyes."

"He scares me," said Claws.

"Don't you worry," said Sab. "We'll keep you safe. Won't we Prisca?"

The old woman gave a tight little smile, and followed their unasked-for leader.

"We'll keep an eye on Prisca too," Sab said out of the corner of her mouth to Claws. "Just until we get our old one back."

"What about my brother's team?"

"Well, if we can trust anything that comes out of bully-boy's mouth, we're ahead of them. Don't worry—we probably won't have to put up with them again for a while now."

"Ain't what I'm worried about."

Sab looked at her.

"The little boy the lord and lady put on their team," said Claws, then stopped.

"What about him?"

"He's…he's like me, isn't he?"

"How'd you know?"

"Mutants don't need magic to spot each other. It's like an instinct. I could just tell."

Sab nodded. She didn't really understand because she relied so heavily on her magic, even the sparse amount grudgingly doled out to the Stratians, to give her all the information she needed of the world around her. For true Mages, instinct was a dead behaviour, all but bred out of them. Who needed instinct when you had magic? But she trusted Claws's feelings.

"Well," she said. "I'm sure he'll be safer with those lot instead of out here with Volos."

Claws turned on her, teeth bared. "What do you know about it? You ain't got no idea what my brother is like. The lord and lady may as well've killed that little boy themselves."

Then she stomped off to catch up with Prisca.

Sab pulled a cigarette out from the air, flicked a flame from her thumb to light it. She inhaled long and deep, savouring the sharp flavour. Then she blew out a long, thin stream of smoke.

Shit on a stick. That was two of them who were acting weird then.

DRAYKE

"You've been given your orders, Rebel," said Drayke. "Several notches ago. Why are you still here?"

Claytun looked up at him, his eyes wide, skin pale. "I don't understand."

"And you thought sitting in the barracks while the day turned to night would help you? Your brothers have gone to Out'Keep to weed out the criminals, I expect you to do the same. You're a good fighter. You'll be needed there."

"But Audra's an Academician, she can't give us orders. Why has the Prime Minister allowed this?"

Drayke sighed and walked over to the Rebel's bunk. Packing up his dead comrade's effects to send to their families was a chore he was happy to take a break from. "I've already explained all of this to you, Rebel."

"But it makes no sense. How can a girl imprison all the ministers by herself—while you were standing there too? I saw her at the gate when you arrived. She's tiny!"

"She has magic—"

"Magic doesn't exist any more," said Claytun, shaking his head.

"I explained all this to you too. I explained to everyone what happened on our mission. Whether you believe it is irrelevant. This is the way things are now, and I'd rather my Rebels obeyed my orders regardless of who gave them to me. Especially if she's able to punish at will."

Claytun stared at his feet for a moment. "We'll never weed out the criminals living in Out'Keep. And where are we supposed to put them? Everyone living down there is a criminal in some way or other."

"And even if they're not, they likely know people who are," said Drayke. "We all know what it's like down there, no matter how long we've been living up here. But we have our orders, Rebel, and orders must be carried out."

"My parents sacrificed everything to get me up here," he said. "I can't betray them."

"Then don't disobey orders and have me expel you."

Claytun's shoulders sagged. "If Audra's got all this power why doesn't she just do it herself?" He snorted a laugh through his nostrils. "Perhaps we should be protecting the people from her. You know how Keep'Out Quarter works?"

Drayke nodded.

"Then you know what happens to people when they've got all the power. It never works out well for the rest of us."

Drayke considered this. Clearly this lad was stalking about the Chief. Everyone who lived in Out'Keep had heard of the Chief, even if it was only to scare their children with stories, or give nightmares to people they didn't like. Those who lived in Keep'Out Quarter, however…they lived in their nightmares. The Chief was a man with as much power as the Prime Minister, but twice the fear. Even those who'd escaped from lower down were still too afraid to speak his name.

But In'Keep didn't have the Prime Minister any more.

What would the Chief think about that if he ever found out? So far, only the Rebels and Audra knew, but even now his men were in Out'Keep, where old friends and family lived. Men who spoke, men who would answer questions if asked them. Questions regarding their sudden appearance lower down when they should be higher up protecting their city's leader. Perhaps he should never have told them, but after the events of the last two months he was fucked if he was going to keep secrets from his men.

If the Chief would indeed try to extend his little empire then they would have to trust Audra to help them. A woman with magic. Power. Not the same as the Chief's, but was it any less corruptible?

"I'm giving you new orders, Claytun," he said.

The lad looked up, a little hope in his eyes.

"Stay here, pack up our comrades' effects and see they're delivered to their families."

"Yes, Drayke Rebel Leader." He stood from his bunk. "Does that mean you're going down to Out'Keep in my place?"

"It means I'm going to find out as much as I can about our new leader," said Drayke. "Know your enemy if you want to defeat her. We're Rebels, Claytun. It's our job to protect the people from autarchs, isn't it?"

NIGHT WAS FALLING AS QUICKLY as the rain, but at least Drayke had his bear skin. He lit a lamp at the entrance of the Rebel barracks, making sure the glass lid was fixed well enough that the rain wouldn't drip in and extinguish the flame, then he made his way out into the night.

Perhaps he should go to the library? No. He didn't know what information to look for, so staring at a room full of books would be a waste of time. Besides, he didn't want to see Audra. She'd ask him what he was doing there. Instead, he'd go to the Academy.

He wasn't fond of those people, but collectively they knew everything about everything. Mages and magic were the stuff of legends, and while the folk on the street might not know any more than that, the Academicians would surely know how those legends started. Orc's balls, Audra had found that cursed journal by that cursed Mage, so who knew what other secret information lay hidden there?

The problem was, everybody knew how jealously those people guarded their knowledge. It was the only thing they had over the common folk and they didn't give it up easily.

Halfway down Library Walk and still trying to work out how he should approach Academicians, he almost collided with one. Stupid Academician! All that intelligence yet he didn't think to bring a lamp out in the dark!

"Oh gosh, I'm so dreadfully sorry!" said the Academician. A female one. Drayke scowled.

"No harm done," he mumbled.

"Oh, you're a Rebel," she said.

This wasn't the right weather for conversation so Drayke walked on.

"Were you one of the ones on Audra's mission?" she called after him.

Audra's mission? He stopped, but he didn't turn. "Why?"

"Maybe you can tell me what's going on?" she said. "Audra was too tired to say anything earlier and now the Academicians—well, my husband—seemed a little panicked when I told him she was back. I'm to fetch her back to the Academy, but… Well, you succeeded, didn't you? The plague's over?"

Now Drayke turned. "Yes."

"Then why aren't people happier about it?"

"I'm sure you'll find out soon enough. Good evening to you." He turned around again and hurried onwards. The

Academy wasn't too far, he could see the glow of lamps in the near distance. Even if he couldn't find what he was looking for there, at least he'd be able to dry out before heading back to the barracks.

He jogged to the main entrance, a pair of plain but over-sized doors. Lamps hung on either side of the lintel, upon which was carved: Truth, Unity and Harmony. Drayke snuffed a laugh through his nose. What did the Academicians know about that?

He pulled open one of the doors only to startle another of the white-robed idiots.

"You could at least apologise," he said. This time it was definitely a man.

"It's rude to stare," said Drayke.

"You're a Rebel."

"I see privilege has made you astute."

"Were you one of those who went on Audra's mission?"

"I am Drayke Rebel Leader, and the mission was mine as given by the Prime Minister of Kingston City. Audra Academician was merely there in an advisory capacity."

"So Jenna was right—you did come back."

Drayke scowled. "Weren't we supposed to?"

The Academician's eyebrows shot up at the same time as his hands. He looked guilty. "No, no, that's not what I meant," he said. He wasn't a short man, this Academician, nor was he slight. He was soft and flabby, and when he flapped his hands the flab on his face shivered. Drayke didn't like flabby men. It was unnatural. Men should be strong. For him, a flabby man was a lazy man who sat around doing nothing.

"Then move out of my way," said Drayke. "I have work to do."

"What work could you possibly have to do here?" said the Academician, his guilt transforming into a sneer.

"Matters of state. And you'd do well not to hinder me."

"Is it about Audra?"

"What do you know about her?" said Drayke, finally stepping over the threshold and out of the rain. The flabby man stepped back, instantly out of arm's reach. A coward as well.

"Nothing, nothing. She's a friend of my wife. And me. She's a friend of mine. In fact, I was on my way to see her. Now I know she's back."

A coward *and* a liar. But it was no secret that the Academicians had wanted the Healing Glass for themselves. That was why they'd agreed to let Audra come in the first place. If they didn't know that the Rebels had come back empty handed they soon would—and they'd also know that their Academician had come back imbued with magic. The thought of these flabby intellectuals having access to that kind of power made him uneasy.

"Then let me accompany you," Drayke said, stepping back and holding the door open once more. "Audra's my friend too. I should make sure she's settling back in after our long and difficult journey."

The Academician offered a poor smile and even poorer thanks, but he stepped out into the darkening night anyway. It seemed to Drayke that he knew something, and even though he wasn't sure what it was, he was sure he wanted to find out.

"AUDRA ACADEMICIAN!" shouted Drayke when he and his companion entered the library.

"No, she's not here. It's just me. Oh, it's you again," said the woman from earlier. Her eyes flickered to his companion. "Konrad? What are you doing here?"

"Coming to find Audra," said the flabby man. "I told you to bring her back to the Academy, Jenna."

"I was going to, but she's not here."

Drayke looked from one to the other. "Do you know each other?"

The man called Konrad frowned. "She's my wife."

Drayke raised an eyebrow. From the looks of it, the only thing these two had in common were their white robes. How could a woman like that find a flabby man like him attractive enough to marry? But then, she was an Academician. Who knew how their minds worked?

"If she's not here," said Konrad, speaking to his wife again, "where is she?"

"I don't know, that's why I'm still here. I'm waiting for her to come back."

"Then you needn't wait any longer." Everyone swivelled around. Standing by the door was Audra, the scrawny lad still by her side. "I don't think I've ever had so many visitors. What do you all want?"

The man called Konrad sneered. "I see you've taken to wearing civilian clothes since you've been away from the Academy."

"Tell me what you want, or leave. I've no mind for idle conversation right now."

The sneer slipped a little. "You're to come back with me this instant."

"Is that so?" said Audra. The scrawny lad beside her— what had she called him before? Squirrel?—shifted and closed his eyes. Drayke didn't take that as a very good sign at all.

SQUIRREL

I don't know who the fat bloke in the white dress was, but the minute he ordered Audra about I knew something bad was going to happen. She was wearing that smile, a joyous smile that told the world she was about to do something she really loved. And there was no mistaking the fact that she was in much better humour since she'd used her magic a couple of times.

"Is that so?" said Audra, grinning.

I couldn't help it—I had to shut my eyes. Whatever she did this time, I didn't want to see.

"All right then," she said. "It's been a long time since I was last invited to the Academy, it'll be nice to see everyone again."

I opened my eyes, frowned and looked at her. To say that was unexpected was like saying the Chief was a bit of a bad'un. But I can't deny that I was relieved.

"Let's all go," she said. "Then Drayke and Jenna can tell me what they wanted along the way."

"Drayke and Jenna aren't invited," said the fat bloke.

Drayke frowned, but the woman called Jenna looked a bit

deflated.

"Very well," said Audra. "But Squirrel is coming with me. He's my charge."

"Squirrel?" said the fat bloke. "What kind of a name is that?"

"Mine," I said. I didn't like him.

"Bring him if you must. But I suggest you don't keep the Sages waiting any longer."

"The Sages?" said Audra, already turned and on her way back to the door. "I am honoured." She looked down at me. "This should be *fun*."

"Not for them, I shouldn't think," I said.

I'D SEEN the Academy before, course I had—I'd nicked from enough places in this quarter. When it came to writing things down, Academicians didn't stint when it came to gold pens and inkwells. But even their paper was worth a coin or two to us lot in Keep'Out, so long as you knew who to sell it on to. A couple of thieves I knew made their living from buying paper from kids in Keep'Out and selling it on to merchants up in their quarter. So I'd seen the Academy, all right. I'd never been inside it though.

Compared to the elvish mansion I'd been in earlier, it wasn't much. Clean, lots of wood and light and countless times better than anything found on the lower slopes of Kingston, but I'd always imagined it more decadent. A bunch of people so rich they all had time to just sit around reading and talking about stuff? Yep, definitely thought it'd be plusher than it was.

We walked along a lamp-lit corridor for a while, clearly just going around in a big circle, when the fat bloke suddenly stopped at a door. It was plain, no name tags on it like I'd seen on the others so far.

"I shouldn't keep them waiting any longer if I were you," he said.

"Are you not coming up with us?" said Audra. His sneer faltered. "Ah, I see. You're not important enough for this meeting. You can run errands for the Sages, but you can't listen in on their secret discussions."

"You're a Historian, I'm a Very Academic Philosopher," he said. "You'd do well to remember your place."

I had no idea what any of that meant, but it made Audra laugh. She was still giggling when she pulled open the door and stepped through.

It opened onto a sloped corridor; polished wooden floor, walls and ceiling, all leading softly upwards. There were only a couple of oil lamps, but they were more than enough to light the place with a soft honey glow. I didn't know where it led, but I decided it was a pleasant enough way to get there.

"There are four of these little passages," said Audra, looking back over her shoulder at me. "One leading up from each of the four disciplines, and only highest Esteemed from each field is ever invited to be a Sage."

"Important people then, these Sages?"

"Oh, they very much like to think so. Even though they all hate each other." She shook her head. "Knowledge is supposed to be inclusive, but the Philosophers think they're better than the Mathematicians, who think they're better than the Historians, and all of them think they're better than the Artists and Musicians. Ridiculous really."

"Bit like everywhere else then," I said. "Everyone wants to feel they're better than someone else. I'm a thief, but at least I'm better than beggars."

Audra raised a questioning eyebrow.

"'Cause I work for my money."

She dropped her eyebrow and gave me a sad smile instead. "We'll change all that soon enough."

"I don't know how you can change people," I said. "And when you say knowledge is inclusive, that means only for the people as can afford it, right? Ain't no Academy in Keep'Out Quarter as far as I can remember."

The corridor ended at another plain door. "We'll make this city a better place, Squirrel, I promise."

She looked so sincere. I almost believed her.

So, while the rest of the place hadn't impressed me too much, when Audra pushed open that door I'll admit to gasping a little bit. It was circular too, but this room was made all of glass. I knew it was, because it was night outside and all the lamps within had turned the whole place into mirrors. I looked down; even the floor was glass. I could see my astonished face in it quite clearly. How had they managed that?

Looking around I saw three other doors just like the one we'd come out of, standing at each of the compass points, and I guessed they led up from the other disciplines that Audra just told me about. Flowing from them were timber tracks that perfectly dissected the round glass room into four equal quarters until they reached the middle, where four men stood beside four very comfortable armchairs. It looked to me like being a Sage was a very cushy job indeed.

"The tales of your return are true," said one of the Sages.

They all wore golden robes which flickered in the lamp light as though they were made of a million tiny flames, but the talker had the longest moustache I'd ever seen. No beard, just a grey moustache that reached all the way down to the floor. I looked at the rest of them. One had a great big bushy beard the size and colour of a storm cloud; another had a shaved face but ridiculous eyebrows that reached up and up then over until it became part of the white hair flowing down over his shoulders. The last one had decided to opt out of the facial hair fashion altogether and had a face and scalp as shiny as a new-born babe's, although he was markedly older. They were a queer bunch, and that was a fact.

"You sound a little surprised, Sage," said Audra. "Did you not think we'd be successful on our mission?"

"Frankly, Audra, no," said Moustache.

"Then I'm not sure whether I've pleased or disappointed you. However, it's with great regret that I inform you that I don't have the Healing Glass. It turns out that it doesn't exist."

Moustache blinked but he didn't say anything.

"I expected more of a reaction than that, I must admit," said Audra. "Considering that's what you ordered the Prime Minister to give you in return for letting me go along."

"Well done, you got one of the Rebels to talk to you during your two-month excursion," said Moustache. "Now if you'd be so kind, tell us how it is that you're back."

Audra frowned. "How it is that I'm back?" She stepped forward. "Didn't you expect me to come back?"

Now the Sages moved for the first time; they looked at each other, then back at us.

"Why didn't you expect me to come back?" Audra said. Her aura flared red and I gulped.

"Audra Academician, no one ever comes back from these…missions," said Moustache. "They're not supposed to. And you were such an embarrassment to our institution. We deemed the sacrifice worthwhile. But now that you're back, well! That puts us in quite a difficult situation."

"You know," Audra whispered, stumbling back a few steps. "You know what the Mages do. Do you *know* what the Mages do?"

She was shouting now and I could barely see her through her aura. Deep down I knew I should've done something but I was rooted to the spot.

"Calm yourself, girl," said Moustache. "These Games have

been played for longer than you or I could possibly imagine and they work in favour of all of us. We regulate the population of the lower slopes, while the Mages—"

Whatever the Mages got out of it I never learned because Audra roared. A wordless sound of rage. Even my old man Bear had never managed anything so terrific as that roar. And then the Sages' heads exploded. All four of them. *Pop pop pop pop!* Spraying blood and brains and bits of bone all over the glass room, while their bodies crumpled slowly down and forwards by their comfy chairs. As I looked on in utter shock, wisps of white and grey hair floated down around us.

Then we both fell to our knees, groaning and gasping.

"Can you feel it?" whispered Audra hoarsely, clutching at my shoulders. "Can you feel all that power?"

I could. Half of me was in ecstasy, the other half disgusted. But ecstasy won, and I threw my head back and cried out as the power released from four dead Sages filled my body and made me strong.

It seemed to last an eternity, but soon enough Audra and me had quietened, and we just looked across at each other, kneeling in the gore of the four old men she'd just killed. And then the door opened. We both looked around at the same time to see that fat bloke in the white dress peer in. He'd obviously been alarmed at all the roaring and screaming he'd heard and come to check everything was all right. From the look on his face now, though, he clearly wished he hadn't.

First he puked. Then he started screaming. Looking around, grabbing his hair, screaming.

"Let's go," said Audra. "I think our meeting with the Sages is over."

She pulled me up onto my feet and I clutched at her all the way out of the glass room and back down the corridor, the sound of screaming running after me.

*B*y the time Sab finished her cigarette, some two hundred yards later, she'd caught up with the others enough to overhear Prisca and Volos fighting. She pulled another cigarette out of the air, lit it with her thumb, and handed it to Claws.

"They're fighting about me," she said, taking the offered smoke, sucking on it so hard it clouded out of her cheek.

Sab listened. "Sounds to me like a simple chat about how best to go about our adventure."

Claws huffed at her through her nostrils, smoke curling out. "You *know* it's my fault we can't transport anywhere."

"Did you choose to have different genes from the rest of us?"

Claws scowled her confusion.

"Look," Sab rolled her eyes. "It's not your fault you can't transport—you were born that way. It's not your fault you're different. You can't take the blame for everything." She nudged Claws with her shoulder. "Otherwise there'll be nothing left for the rest of us to feel shitty about."

They were silent for a few moments. "Can you stay back here with me?" said Claws. "That Volos freaks me out."

"Course!" said Sab. "Probably better if the grown-ups believe they're in charge anyway."

At least that got a chuckle. Forced, yes. But it was better than fretting.

As landscapes went, it was pretty dire, Sab had to concede. The land under foot was so dry it crunched like gravel, and any plant life they happened to come across was nothing more than bundles of spiky leaves and thorns. Most of them, however, did sprout outrageously orange berries, which added a splash of colour to the general drabness of the surroundings.

For Sab it was glorious though. Her whole life, Ages, she'd been cooped up in the 'Sphere. If she'd gone up to any of the levels where windows were fashionable, the view only ever consisted of sky and sea. Sometimes seabirds. Sometimes rich dicks, if their sky-diving had gone horribly wrong. That was always hilarious to watch.

The point was, as ugly as the landscape was, it was still better than that place. Out here there were different things to look at because the landscape changed every time they descended into one valley and climbed up out of another. Flying insects droned, staggering from plant to plant like drunkards looking for snacks. And the wind! All right, it didn't exactly carry the best aroma she'd ever smelled. Kind of smelled like there'd be a lot of rotting carcasses in the not too distant future. But it riffled through her hair, lifted it up and swirled it around before throwing it in her face. The sensation was exhilarating. And it didn't stink of salt! That was the best thing about the wind.

Stinky smells, but also voices. The wind was a useful thing. "...been traipsing for hours now! It'll take days to reach the mountains at this rate!" That was Volos. No one could mistake his rumbling grumbles.

"Then so be it," said Prisca, still avoiding his eye. "I'm not risking either one of my girls with magic."

"There's only one of them that can't transport," he said.

Before he could finish that flying pod of thought, Sab shouted, "If you're so desperate to get to the mountains, go on ahead. Not one of us here will stop you. We'll meet you in Taurë."

Volos turned slowly, then ambled over to her, his hairy jowls jiggling with each stomp. Obviously the brute believed personal space was just a myth, and when he finally came to a stop in front of her, she was staring squarely at his nipples. She could bite them off from down here, but getting all that hair getting stuck in her teeth? Ugh, gag. She looked up at him instead.

"Ooh," she said, blinking once. "I am very scared."

"You should be," he growled. "These are the scablands. Only degenerates and vicious animals live out here."

"Like I said. Go on ahead. We'll meet you there."

He bent down so he could look her in the eye. Sab sincerely wished he hadn't. His breath was foetid. "I'm not leaving Prisca out here undefended."

"Fuck you," said Sab. "That old hag can take better care of herself than you ever could."

"My lord and lady commanded it."

"Yeah, all right," she said, pushing him away from her. Then was disgusted by how squishy and fleshy his belly was, even under his clothes. "Yuk. Can we just get on? Or do you have more posturing to get out of your system?"

"I won't lose this race because of some mutant."

"We're not gonna lose," said Sab, plucking her tobacco and papers out of the air and passing them across to Claws. "We're miles ahead of the other lot. And I'm guessing those spiky things along the horizon are the mountains? How about we just walk for now, and see what we can do a little bit later on?"

"And if the other team uses magic to get to the mountains?" said Volos. His expression suggested he thought he'd outwitted Sab.

"They've got a mutant too, remember?" She took the cigarette Claws proffered and lit it with her thumb. "They're not going to go any faster than we are." She blew out a thin plume of smoke, which the wind picked up and scattered as soon as it left her mouth. "I'll lead the way then, shall I?"

Before her first step had even finished falling, Volos was already marching out in front. Sab smirked, shook her head.

Claws took Sab's cigarette and lit the end of hers with it. "His name's Lian," she said.

"What? No, girl, that's Volos."

"Not *him*!" said Claws, and even though her voice was quiet there was anger in her eyes. "The kid on Emil's team. His name's Lian. Even mutants have names, you know."

Shit it. "I didn't mean... Look, I was just..." she sighed. "I'm sorry, Claws."

They walked in silence, Claws smoking her cigarette like she had a grudge against it. She flicked the butt off into the distance then glared sidelong at Sab. "I ain't no use to you lot now you have *him*," she said. "I want to go and find Lian."

That stopped Sab in her tracks. "No way!"

"Why not?"

"Because!" There were so many reasons Sab didn't even know where to start. "It's dangerous out here!"

"More dangerous for me than in the 'Sphere surrounded by Mages who hate mutants?"

"Yes! It's much easier to survive when you know what the dangers are!"

"Then come with me," she said, grabbing onto Sab's flayed

arm. "We can find him and be back before the other two even know we've gone."

Sab huffed a laugh. "You're kidding, right? We have no idea where they are, no idea where *we* are, and even if Emil doesn't want the kid on his team, he's certainly not just going to hand him over to us if he knows we *do* want him. Besides, I am *not* leaving Prisca on her own with that...Mage."

Claws scoffed. "You think a Mage like Prisca will have a harder time protecting herself against one man than a little mutant boy will against six Cirrocumulans?"

"No, of course not." She huffed. "Look, if we could save everyone who needed it while we're out here, I'd love that. But we can't—"

"Ain't asking you to save everyone. I'm asking you to help me save one little boy."

Sab flicked her own butt out into the gritty wastes. "Claws, you're a free woman now, and I'm not going to stop you from doing anything. But I'm not going to stop looking for Audra."

"Wow," said Claws, shaking her head. "Never thought I'd see the day when couldn't-give-a-fuck Sabina started playing the same games as all the other Mages." She marched off, just far enough to be away from Sab, but not so far that she caught up with Prisca and Volos.

It sucked, saying something like that to Claws. Sab knew she'd never leave on her own. It was a brave idea to save that little kid, but no way was Claws brave enough to do it by herself. She was a bitch to've given her the choice to leave when she knew she'd never take it. She should've just said no, she wasn't allowed to leave. At least that would've left Claws with a little bit of dignity. Now, for every day that Claws was still here, they'd both know it was because she wasn't brave to go out on her own.

But she was wrong, Claws was. Sab wasn't staying

because she wanted to play the Patriarch's game. She probably only said that because she was trying to goad her. But she had to find Audra first. Had to. She was the only one who could put a stop to all this.

TIME PASSED. Scenery changed. The mountains on the horizon didn't look any closer. The gritty scrub became a kind of tough grassland, dotted here and there with mean-looking trees, their trunks all twisted, spindly branches sprouting tight clumps of dense leaves that looked like balled-up fists. Those orange-berry bushes were still ubiquitous though.

"We're stopping for a breather," said Prisca, and promptly sat down on the ground.

"No," said Volos. "Get up."

"My girls need to eat, and so do I."

Sab grinned over at Claws, but she only scowled and looked away. Still not friends, then.

"*Mages* can subsist on magic for as long as needed," Volos said.

Prisca pulled out two packets of waxed paper from her bag. "One for each of my girls."

"Is that porridge?" said Sab, grinning.

"Course it isn't," said Prisca. "Although it is quite oaty. Eat up. We're not stopping long."

Sab unwrapped the packet. The wind plucked at the waxed paper, spilling crumbs onto her lap. She looked down at a thick disc of oats. She sniffed it; it didn't smell of anything. She looked up at Prisca.

"Can't we just eat those orange berries off all the bushes we see around here?" she said.

"I wouldn't," said Prisca. "They're firethorn bushes. The berries are poisonous. They'll make you sick."

"Not you Mages," said Claws. "You've got magic."

Prisca shrugged a shoulder. "Everyone's got their vulner-abilities."

"So what do they do to Mages?"

"Make us very sick."

Sab held up the packet. "More than this?"

"Just eat it," she said. "It's good for you."

Sab did as she was told. Once she'd managed to bite through it, all the spit in her mouth was used up instantly in an effort to soften the lump. It was bland and crunchy.

"Delicious," she said to Prisca with a smile. She could feel chunks of oat sticking to her teeth. "Hey, Volos! Aren't you joining us?"

The man scowled then turned his back on her. Kept his gaze fixed on the distant mountains.

"Who is he, anyway?" said Claws. She'd crumbled her oat disc into pieces and was genteelly using her fingers to eat the crumbs. "Why'd your mum and dad pick him to be on our team?"

Prisca sighed. "He's been their pet ever since he... dismissed his own parents."

"The fuck?" said Sab. Claws looked at her quizzically. "Dismissed is Al and Silly's word for murdering people with magic."

"What?"

"They're not murdered," Prisca mumbled.

"Right, sorry," said Sab. "Our friend over there uses his magic to imprison people in the solid water that makes up the plaza and palace."

"Those were *real* people?" said Claws.

"They're not dead though," said Prisca.

"You do see that that's worse, right?" Sab said to her.

Prisca folded the waxed paper over her unfinished oat disc. "Of course I do."

"But how come someone so dangerous is your parents' pet?" said Claws. "Ain't they afraid of him?"

"Afraid of him?" Prisca echoed. "They created him. His parents were mutants, both of them, living as farmers on the outskirts of the city. A life of hard labour wasn't what Volos wanted though, so he dismissed his own mother and father in the plaza in front of everyone, and said that he wanted my parents instead."

"Wow, said Sab, raising an eyebrow. "That must've been quite a spectacle."

"He only got away with it because of his extraordinary power. Any normal Mage would've been exiled for such a demand, and for putting two perfectly adequate farmers out of commission."

"Well," said Sab, "as...disturbing as that story is, doesn't really tell us why Al and Silly dumped him on us."

"Because he's the strongest Mage in all of Oceanwall, aside from my parents. And they'd do anything to beat the 'Sphere."

"Ah yes," said Sab. "The three great cities and their ridiculous power grabs. Immortality really makes us shallow, doesn't it?"

"His parents were mutants," Claws whispered. "Like me."

Prisca flicked her eyes towards Sab, then nodded.

"Both of them?"

Prisca nodded again.

"Then how come he's so powerful?"

"The exact same way that you're a mutant even though both of your parents are Mages. Our magic is genetic, so is the mutation, but from time to time these things can skip a generation, or pull something up from our dim and distant genetic history. You could mate with a third-generation mutant and still bear a child that's as powerful as your father."

155

Claws shuddered. "That'd be horrid."

"It's out of our control. That's why, in Oceanwall, it's forbidden by the lord and lady for mutants to mate."

"Wait," said Sab. "Then how did two mutants make Volos?"

"What do you think he was doing at the plaza in the first place?" said Prisca.

Sab whistled. "He ratted out his own parents?"

"Proved his loyalty and got rid of his shame in one go."

"Why are you so surprised?" said Claws. "Ain't nothing like a mutant in the family for bringing on shame. You don't think my parents banished me to Stratus because they loved me, do you?"

"No, of course I don't, but—"

"And don't think shame can't turn into hatred, because it can. If I could *dismiss* my parents I would. They're dead to me anyway." She scrunched up her waxed paper into a tiny ball and threw it to the ground. Then she launched herself up to a standing position—no easy task with legs as long as hers— and stomped away from them for a few paces before dropping back to sit on the ground. She shoved her chin in her hands and glowered at the scablands.

"You girls had a falling out?" said Prisca.

"Whatever makes you think that?"

Prisca gave a brief, tight smile. "We're all we've got, Sabina. We can't let anything get in the way of that."

Sab held her gaze. "All right. Then tell me what the deal is with you and Volos. Don't tut at me like I'm making stuff up. You've been weird ever since Oceanwall. And you know I'm going to keep pestering you about it until you tell me, so you might as well just tell me. I'll just keep on and on, and on and on, and on—"

"All right!" She threw a handful of oat crumbs at Sab.

"Fine. Let's just say, my parents had…high hopes for Volos. And just as high for me. Until they got a better offer."

Sab huffed. "You know how I feel about enigmatic bullshit. Just tell me straight what happened with you. How come you ended up in the 'Sphere?"

"My parents sold me, all right?" There was anger in Prisca's voice, but she kept it low. "They were so desperate to have one of their scions in the great and mighty 'Sphere that they sold me. There. Happy now?" Then she also launched herself up to standing and stomped off towards Volos.

"You'd think I would be," said Sab, even though no one was listening to her. "Except everything you just said was probably bollocks."

JAYMES

*J*aymes was surprised the Chief had let him go so easily. Granted, he wasn't an undernourished pre-pubescent kid unable to fight back if a bunch of debased grown men wanted to have a go, but he'd expected a few more horrors back at the lair before he was let out into the world again.

That wasn't to say he was completely off the hook, oh no. He'd been blindfolded when the ugly cronies from the tavern had brought him here, but he was released with his eyes wide open. Turned out the Chief's lair was closer to In'Keep than anyone could've possibly guessed. So close, in fact, that when Jaymes had stepped out into the reeking, dripping morning, looked around and saw the In'Keep walls towering up behind him he'd taken an involuntary step back. The Chief's lair had almost mythical status here in Keep'Out Quarter—only those closest to him knew where it was; if anyone else did, they wouldn't be privy to that information for very much longer. But once Jaymes had got over the brief shock at the Chief's audacity at setting up the black and rotten heart of his criminal empire so close to In'Keep, the fact didn't really surprise him. One look at the fat bastard's penchant for finery—food, clothes, wine and jewels—and it was obvious he thought he should be living up on the higher slopes of the city. But he was fated to stay down here with the rest of the low-born, so he made their lives as miserable as possible.

Just like the man, the lair was dark and sprawling, spreading along the In'Keep walls like some kind of mould. More like a bloated spider, whose web reached out into every corner of Keep'Out, and he sat there patiently, waiting for his prey to become enmeshed in it.

And he was, now, following the lines of that web through the less crowded but still stinking alleys of Keep'Out as they slipped and twisted their way down to the old moat. He knew where he was going, which was unfortunate because it meant it wouldn't take nearly long enough to get there. An old hovel, no better or worse than the other ramshackle huts in these parts, was his destination, and as bad luck would have it, the proudless owner was squatting outside shifting through the detritus that the night's wind had drifted up against his door. The splashing of feet in greasy puddles alerted him to Jaymes's presence and he looked over his shoulder, ready to defend his newfound treasures to the death if need be, only for his face to spilt in a smile of recognition.

"Jaymes, you little bugger, I thought you were going to nick my stuff!"

"No chance, Badger, you're far too quick for me."

Badger wheezed a laugh which turned into a meaty cough, then he spat out a sticky gob of dark mucus and wiped his mouth. Putting his hands onto his knees, he pushed himself up slowly until he was standing and took small steps around so that he faced Jaymes. He wasn't that far past his middle years, but he looked as though he'd been living for more than an Age.

"What you doing here, Jaymes? Not often you Rebels come down to visit us. Kole well?"

Jaymes tried not to lose his smile. "He's why I'm here. The wife home?"

"Scraping a few oats together to take down to the cook fire," he said, thrusting his chin back towards the hovel.

"Kids?"

Badger looked down at his feet. "My two lads are working, Jaymes. You know how it is. Chief's taking care of our little'un. Ain't that something?"

He nodded. "Well, what I've got to say is for both of you. Mind if we go in?"

Badger shook his head, looked up and down the alley, then beckoned Jaymes in with his head.

"Thought I heard your voice out there, Jaymes! Good to see you again, love!"

"You too, Cat, you too."

"Was just about to go and make some porridge. You hungry, love?"

Jaymes looked at the meagre amount of oats sitting in a cracked pottery cup, and shook his head. There were barely enough there to feed one, let alone three. But after Jaymes had finished here, neither of them would be hungry any more.

"Kind of you, Cat, but I came here to tell you both something."

Husband and wife glanced at each other, then back at Jaymes without saying a word.

"It's about Kole," he said. The cup in Cat's hand started shaking. "Badger, Cat; Kole's dead. I'm so sorry."

"Was it you who killed him?" said Badger.

"Course not," said Jaymes. "We were on a mission outside the city. He was killed in battle."

"Then you've nothing to be sorry for."

"Battle?" said Cat. "Why was he in a battle?"

Jaymes stepped forward so he was only an arm's reach from the both of them. "There's things going on that even I don't understand," he said. "All I am is the bringer of bad news."

He whipped his hands up to the twin daggers strapped at his shoulders, pulled them out and across the couple's throats before they even had a chance to blink. Their corpses sank to the floor, blood seeping out and into the packed earth floor. Jaymes looked away from them and around the room. Nothing had changed here. Still cramped, still cluttered with little treasures that In'Keepers would consider less than rubbish. And even though Cat had done everything she could to keep it as clean as was possible despite being built on a slope of shit, it stank of human waste.

One thing had changed though, and that was the addition of two new dead bodies. Jaymes closed his eyes tight and clenched his jaw even tighter.

"You did well."

Jaymes opened his eyes. The weak light coming in through the hole of a door was now obscured by the bulk of the Chief's crony.

"I don't want your approval, bastard."

The crony laughed. A spiteful sound. "We're comrades now, you and me, so you probably want to call me by my real name. I'm RibCage."

Jaymes stared down at the two bodies, wondering how long before someone found them. He hoped it wasn't either one of their remaining sons.

"Ain't you going to ask why I'm called that?"

Jaymes swung around slowly until he was staring into the crony's obscured but no less ugly face. "Couldn't give a shit."

RibCage lifted his leather shirt. "Because of this."

Jaymes looked but refused to let any reaction show on his

face. Despite the lack of sunshine, there were distinctive parts of RibCage's torso that shone dully, parts of his torso that had been skewered by sharp flats of metal following the general outline of his ribs and overlapping each other like dangerous fish scales. It was as impressive as it was gruesome. Jaymes sniffed.

"Ain't you going to ask why I done that?"

"There is still a dearth of shit in my vicinity," said Jaymes, opening his arms and looking around himself.

"Because I get bored sometimes. I like to stick sharp things in myself when I get bored," said RibCage, grinning a revolting grin and lowering his shirt.

"Then I'd suggest something longer and more pointed, and if you stick it a couple of inches higher and deeper we'll all be saved from having to look at your ugly fucking mug."

"That how you speak to your friends, is it? You might want to watch that. Some of us could take offence."

Jaymes took a step forward and pointed back to the corpses. "I kill my fucking friends, you piece of shit, or hadn't you noticed? You and your recreational piercings don't scare me." That said, he pushed passed him and stepped out into the damp morning.

"Where d'you think you're going?" Jaymes didn't look back at RibCage. "You think that's your job done for the day? That was just a warm-up. Making sure you're the clever sort who does as he's told. We got a busy day ahead of us, you and me, and the notches are moving on."

"Where we going?"

"Left at the end of this alley. I'll tell you more as you need to know. Now, move it."

For the notch-being, Jaymes didn't have much of a choice so he complied. For the notch-being. But soon enough people were going to pay their dues, and he was the one who was going to collect them.

SABINA

*N*o one was talking. Actually, no one was even walking next to each other. It wasn't as though Sab had expected the race to be a fun-filled adventure of laughter and fond memory creation, but she'd thought she and her friends would've been, well, friends for the duration of it. Stupid Volos. He'd thrown everything off balance.

Another clump of firethorn bushes were coming up. These ones had branches so stuffed with those bright orange berries that they drooped to the ground. And they were rustling. Sab swerved towards them to investigate. It wasn't like anything else interesting was happening.

Sitting in the middle of the nearest bush was the cutest little critter Sab had ever seen. Granted, there wasn't much in the way of wildlife on the 'Sphere unless you went up to the zoological gardens on Cirrus level. Which, for someone like Sab, was approximately never.

"Hey, Claws!" she shouted across to her friend. She was glad when she stopped and turned to look back at her. "You've got to come and see this thing!"

"Shit on a stick!" Claws exclaimed when she reached Sab. "That's the cutest thing I ever seen!"

"Right? Couldn't you just eat its fluffy little face right off?"

Claws giggled. "I want to cuddle it to death!"

It was a tiny little thing, probably small enough to sit in the palm of Sab's hand, if it didn't mind dangling its legs over the edge of it. Soft, tawny fur covered it from head to paw, the front two of which rummaged expertly through the orange berries until it found the ones it wanted to eat. But only one of its heads ate the berries.

Normally, you'd think something that had two heads would be scary to look at. But this critter's heads were just as fluffy as its body, with huge tufted, pointy ears on top of them, and the biggest amber eyes that Sab had ever seen. Its snouts were flat, tipped with leathery brown noses, and its mouths looked small and delicate. While one was busy nibbling at all the berries, the other chittered and trilled. Every now and then, it would rub its heads up against each other and purr. It was the most adorable thing Sab had ever seen.

"Get away from that thing."

It was Volos's voice, but there was an urgency to it that Sab had never heard before. She looked around at him. He wasn't exactly scared, but he was certainly uncomfortable in the critter's presence.

"Get away from it," he repeated.

"Why?" said Sab. "It's completely harmless. Look how cute it is, sitting there eating berries—oh look! He just dropped one!"

Claws balled up her fists, held them to her mouth and squealed into them.

"They're dangerous!" hissed Volos.

"Fuck they are," said Sab. "I want to keep it."

She took a step forward, about to reach her arms out to it,

but Volos grabbed on to her and yanked her back. He pulled Claws out of the way too. Then kept dragging.

"Get your filthy paws off me," said Sab, reaching for her power so she could twist out of his grip.

"Shut up," said Volos. His voice was still lowered. "You're lucky it hasn't spotted us yet."

"It's a cute, furry, little fur ball," said Sab. "How can something as monstrous as you be scared of it?"

"Listen, 'Sphere bitch," he said through gritted teeth. "You don't know the scablands. I do. That fur ball'll burn you alive."

"It's true," said Prisca just as Sab opened her mouth to retort. "That's why they eat the fire berries."

Sab shook her head. There was no way she believed them. But...neither of them looked like they were joking. She cocked an eyebrow at Claws, shrugged, then tiptoed with exaggerated care away from the two of them.

"Do you believe them?" she said to Claws once they were crunching their way across the wastes once more.

"I'm still mad at you."

"That's fine," said Sab. "Can you be mad at me and still talk to me? Pretty boring journey otherwise."

Silence. Which worked well enough as an answer. She considered trying her luck with Prisca, but it looked like her old friend was deep in conversation with Volos the Terrified of Cute Critters. Interesting... They were far enough away that Sab couldn't overhear them with all the wind that was blowing about the place. But if she improved her hearing with just a little magical help...

"...waited for you for an Age," Volos was saying in his raspy voice. "You didn't even try to contact me once in all that time."

"Don't blame me," said Prisca. "The lord and lady do what they like. It's not like I had a choice."

"But you were supposed to be *my* mate," said Volos.

"I didn't have a choice in that either."

"My mate, not some ponce Mage from the 'Sphere."

Shit all over a stick. Then shit on it some more. Those two had been earmarked as a *couple*? Sab didn't know whether to burst out laughing or gasp in horror. Yuk, imagine having to mate with that hairy mountain and his rotten breath. Obviously, Mages who sought to beautify themselves with magic were pathetic and shallow. But Volos was definitely one specimen who could've done with a bit of a tidy up. She'd never say that up to his face though. But if he was as powerful as Prisca said he was, why wasn't he showing that off by making himself glorious?

Hang on just a second—was that why Prisca was acting so weird now? There was definitely a whine to Volos's voice that suggested he had some kind of feelings for Prisca. And Prisca... Well, Prisca... Actually, she sounded just like she always did when Sab and Claws were trying to be unreasonable with her. Like, when they asked her to cook them something hot and fatty and delicious even though they knew that the only things left in the stores until the next dump were oats and sprouting potatoes. A fed-up tone, but held in check because she didn't want to start an argument.

Huh. Well, that was unexpected. And here she'd been thinking that Prisca was scared of the brute. Wait—she didn't...? No. She couldn't possibly have feelings for him too? That would be far too weird. And back up just a minute—had he said *not some ponce Mage from the 'Sphere*?

So many things to talk about, and not one friend who was currently on speaking terms with her! She turned off her hearing, just in case Volos got it into his giant head to declare his undying love, or something equally horrifying. Sab would never be able to control herself if she overheard something like that.

Well, there was nothing for it; she'd have to try and get through to Claws. There was no way she could keep something like this to herself for very much longer. She jogged over to Claws, moved in front of her and kept jogging backwards so she could look up to her face.

Claws tutted, stopped. Then walked slower.

"Still not talking to me?" said Sab.

"Still not helping me rescue Lian?"

Sab rolled her eyes.

"Then I'm not talking to you," said Claws.

Sab looked over her shoulder conspiratorially, then inched her way closer to her friend. "But I've got some mad gossip about Prisca. Please talk to me!"

"Ain't interested. And I ain't a child. Stop talking to me like one."

With no warning, Volos barrelled into both of them. "Get away!" he bellowed.

For a crazy moment, Sab thought he'd felt her listening in and was bent on punishing her. But her peripheral vision caught sight of Prisca's face. She looked terrified. She was running to keep up with them, but she kept looking over her shoulder.

"Down here!" roared Volos.

"Your mouth is right by my ear," said Sab. "You don't need to fucking scream into it."

They slid into a gash in the ground, grit scratching its way into the fibres of Sab's forearms. She gritted her teeth against it. Pain she liked, irritants not so much.

Once they were still, all breathing heavily from the sudden burst of energy, Sab said, "I hope there's a good reason for fucking up my lovely walk."

Prisca gave her one of her ice-white looks. The one that warned her not to say anything else because it was bound to be stupid.

Claws scrambled out of Volos's grasp, her breath coming faster than everyone else's, and Sab knew she was going to bolt as soon as she'd got her feet organised again.

"Wait," said Sab, laying a hand gently on her shoulder. "I can feel something."

"What?" said Claws. Her frown conveyed disbelief, but there was a twinge of fear in her eyes.

"The ground," said Sab. She looked up at Volos. "Is something coming?" Then she tutted at herself. She had plenty of magic to spare now, she could find out for herself. She reached down, plucked out a few tendrils and flung them out into the scablands.

"Woah…" she whispered.

"What is it?" said Claws. "Sab, what is it?"

"I don't know—some kind of animals…"

"They're woolly rhinos," said Volos. "A herd of them. I've never a seen a herd that big before. And they're charging."

"At us?" Claws whimpered.

Volos shook his head. "They eat grass. Something spooked the herd and now they're charging. You get in the way of charging woolly rhinos, you die."

"But they're massive," said Sab. "I felt it. What could spook giant beasts like that?"

Volos glared at her. "If we stay out of the way, we should survive."

"*Should?*"

"I feel it too," said Claws, her palms pressed flat against the ground. She cocked her head. "I think I can hear them too."

Sab nodded. There was definitely some pounding going on somewhere up there.

Volos pushed himself back against the ledge of the gash as far as he could. No easy feat for a man of his bulk. "Get back here," he said to Claws.

She didn't argue. But she did make sure she was in between Sab and Prisca.

Sab let her head loll to one side so she could look up at Claws. "Friends now?"

"Not really the time, is it?" said Claws through gritted teeth.

The pounding was louder now, and definitely closer. Grit and small pebbles slid down the ledge onto them. Sab pulled her feet in close and wrapped her arms around her knees. Something told her that making herself as small as possible was probably the best thing she could do right now.

Just when the pounding reached a deafening pitch, and just when the vibrations of it had rattled Sab's bones to powder, she caught her first glimpse of a woolly rhino. It flew from the ledge above them, soared through the air for a couple of seconds because of its momentum, then crashed back down to the ground so hard that Sab was sure she'd lifted off it a couple of inches.

The thing was enormous. Easily six metres long, and a couple of metres tall, all covered in long, matted fur the same kind of browny-grey as the grit and rocks of the scablands. Two ridiculously long horns protruded from its snout, the front one about twice as long as the back one. What did a grass-eater need such vicious weapons for? It stumbled a bit as it hit the ground, then pounded off into the distance, raising great clouds of grit and dust as it went. Yep. If slaves rioting could do in Sab's mum, she didn't doubt for a second that being trampled by that brute could do in her.

For a hopeful second, Sab thought the danger had passed. But she'd sensed a herd. She closed her eyes and prepared for bladder-loosening terror. It arrived way too quickly.

Hundreds of the beasts leapt from the ledge above them.

Rocks and dust fell from their hoofs, smacking Sab on the head and face. Claws squealed in terror, and Sab covered her

169

head with her arms, pulled her down so that she was spared some of the tumbling stone.

The torrent of mammoth beasts was endless. Sab's ears hurt from the onslaught. Then she remembered her vast store of magic, and wove some tendrils together, pushing them out so that they covered the four of them cowering beneath the ledge. It kept the rocks off them, but she wasn't sure how it'd hold up if one of the rhinos fell on it. The protective dome also lessened the noise a little, and Sab heard Claws's breathing slow a little, her heart beat calm. She kept her head buried though.

Sab looked out at the panicked animals. In their haste to escape whatever was chasing them, many crashed into each other as they landed, sending out shockwaves that tripped many others. One poor beast was skewered by its neighbour and its bellow was horrific. So was the resulting fountain of blood. The injured rhino thrashed about in evident agony, while still trying to escape. The scent of blood must've spooked the rhinos even more, because the charge seemed to level-up its urgency, until the thundering hooves were accompanied with mad bellows of primeval fear.

Just when Sab thought she'd go mental from the constant barrage against her senses, the tide of charging rhinos lessened. A dozen or so jumped over the ledge, trampling their fallen friends, skidded in the blood, and then it was all over. She was about to release the protective bubble, but more creatures arrived on the scene, jumping over the ledge and into the carnage. Little fluffy creatures with two cute heads and two pairs of enormous amber eyes. Sab burst out laughing.

"Don't tell me those giant rhinos are afraid of those cute little critters!" she said.

Claws looked up. "They caused this?"

The critters were jumping delicately over the fallen

rhinos, some of which were still moving, trying to get back up to join their herd, bellowing out their agony.

The critters jumped up and down and trilled to each other excitedly, and hopped over to the rhino that almost had its feet again. It saw the approaching critters and bellowed in fear. It was obviously trying to run, but its legs were too injured from its fall. The critters surrounded it, trilling to each other all the while. Then, as one, they opened one of their mouths and belched out bright orange flame.

Sab jolted in shock. Claws and Prisca did too, she felt them. The rhino's wool caught fire instantly and the stench was appalling, though not as appalling as the shriek of fear and pain the rhino released.

It took an Age for the poor beast to die. And Sab just knew she was going to be haunted by the sight of its charred and burning body still trying to run away from its tormentors, even though there was clearly no hope of it surviving.

When the beast finally collapsed and the flames died, the cute little critters began their feast.

"Right, that's it," said Sab, "time to go. This is disgusting."

"Stay where you are," said Volos. "Once they've eaten they'll go away. If we move now, they'll chase us. We'll be safe as long as we're still."

Sab wanted to argue, but she had precisely zero good points to make. She had no idea about the land and creatures beyond the 'Sphere, where Volos obviously did, the bastard. Plus, the adrenaline that had coursed through her body during the charge finally ran out and she realised she was exhausted. Staying still appealed to her far more than trying to make a dash to safety.

She tutted at him, just for the sake of it, then rested her head back against the rock. She closed her eyes too, just in case they were drawn to the sight of feasting beyond her protective dome. Not something she wanted to witness.

The next thing she knew, she was being nudged awake.

"Were you asleep?" said Claws, accusation in her voice and furrowed brow.

"I think I must've been," she said, scrunching up her eyes to get the dust out of them. "Those critters gone?"

Claws nodded and gazed out at the rhino carnage littering the wasteland. All that was left of the poor incinerated beast was a pile of blackened bones. Not a critter in sight though. That was a good thing. It was also noticeably darker than it was before she closed her eyes.

She released the protective dome, stood up and stretched out her stiff limbs. She reached a hand down to help Claws up, but she pushed herself up on her own. Ignoring Sab's help, or not seeing it, she wasn't sure. She plumped for the latter because she was far too tired to feel pissed off right now.

"Lead on, then, Volos," she said. "I'm sure we can cover a few more miles before it's completely pitch black."

"Easy for you to say," Claws mumbled. "You just had a kip."

"Well, there was nothing stopping you from shutting your eyes while we waited for those critters to finish their dinner."

"You're kidding, right? With them things only a few feet away, munching on that rhino?"

Sab rolled her eyes. "I was protecting us."

"You were protecting *you*." Claws stomped away. Not too far though, Sab noted. She wouldn't want to separate herself from the group. And she certainly wouldn't want to be too close to Volos. She just wanted to get away from her.

"Was there subtext in that sentence?" Sab called after her. "You know, because I feel like you were really referring to something else. Come on, share it with the group. Maybe if we all put our heads together, we can work this thing out."

Claws spun around. "Just shut the fuck *up*, Sab! You're

such a fucking bitch sometimes!" She spun away again and carried on walking.

Sab blinked a couple of times, momentarily stopped in her tracks. They'd bickered before, of course they had. You couldn't live in such close confines with someone like these two had and not bicker. But Claws had never been angry at her before. Not like this. Sab had felt her fury from ten metres away.

"What is going on with you two?" said Prisca, sneaking up on her unannounced. "I've never seen Claudia so upset before."

Should she tell her? She kind of really wanted to, just to spite Claws. Spill that Claws had wanted to leave Prisca on her own with Volos while the two of them went off looking for that kid. And she opened her mouth to do just that. Except. Claws was pissed off enough with her. If she spilt that secret too, it might just be the final spell that broke the slave's back. Yeah. No point making it worse.

"Nothing," she said eventually. "I think she's just embarrassed about the whole can't-transport-like-the-rest-of-us thing."

"That's clearly not true. Well, she may well feel that way, poor love. But it's absolutely not the reason why she screamed at you. But," said Prisca, then sighed. "Who am I to meddle in other people's business?"

"Ha! The whole reason you're here, old lady, is because you meddled and invited yourself along!"

"That's not meddling, it's keeping an eye on each of my girls. Now, come on." She linked her arm through Sab's. "She can stay in front of us if she wants to, but I'm not letting Claudia go too far ahead on her own. There's dangerous creatures out here."

"What, like Volos?"

"He's not as bad as all that. Now move it." She tugged on

Sab's arm. Sometimes it annoyed her that Prisca and Claws were the only two people in the whole world who weren't disgusted by their lack of skin and grabbed them at will.

She rolled her head back and released an exaggerated cry of exasperation, but allowed herself to be pulled along anyway.

Then, not too far above them, she spotted something. Did She? The twilight was doing funny things to her vision. She wasn't used to it. Thanks to the non-stop nature of her work back on the 'Sphere, the lamps on Stratus level were lit every notch of every day because the slaver shifts were constant. The constant use of magic to keep said lamps lit was another reason, according to the great and mighty Patriarch, why the Stratians weren't entitled to as much personal magic as the other levels. The only time she wasn't surrounded by light was when she was sleeping back in her cell and it was lights-out. So, light or dark. Those were the two settings her eyes were used to. Not this weird twilight that made distances and objects make no sense at all.

So what was that thing up there? A cloud? It was up in the sky and totally nebulous, so maybe. But clouds weren't usually that black. Could be a warning about a sudden down-pour. That would cheer Volos up no end.

But clouds didn't usually swirl like that. Fog, then? Nope, the reason why fog was fog and not clouds was because it was already on the ground.

She considered telling Prisca about it. She'd lived beyond the 'Sphere, after all, so maybe she knew about all the weird shit that went on out here in the world.

But before she even had a chance to lower her head and open her mouth, that swirling blackness descended at an astonishing rate and eclipsed the rest of the world.

SQUIRREL

$\mathcal{A}$s he did every morning to let me know he was hungry for his breakfast, Mouse jumped on my head. It never hurt because he was a scrawny little thing, just like me I s'pose, but there are nicer ways of greeting the new day. Like waking up and realising all the horror you'd seen the day before was just a hideous nightmare and not really true at all. I'd yet to have a day like that. Past experience suggested that was never going to happen to me, but what's life without hope?

I rubbed my eyes hard, hoping that'd dislodge the seared images of exploding heads from the inside of my eyelids, but it didn't. So instead I reached over to Mouse, pulled him close and nuzzled the fur on his neck. He miaowed and wriggled because he wanted food not cuddles and eventually I let him go.

But at least I wasn't sleeping in a tree. The library, it turned out, had some pretty ample living quarters hidden underneath them which Audra had made her own. Apparently she had a big old house in the Academician's Quarter that had been in her family for generations, but she didn't want to go back there since her dad died in it a few months ago. Besides, she preferred it here in the library and it meant the Academy didn't have to find another librarian, so when she left her family home she'd decided to stay. They were out of her way and she was out of theirs. Because it turned out that the Academicians didn't like her all that much, and that was before she started blowing up their heads. She'd told me all this last night when we got back and I only listened out of terrified politeness before she let us go to bed.

"We can't stay here, can we, Mouse?"

A plaintive miaow was his response and I took that for a yes.

The little room she'd given me was almost bigger than the cot I'd slept in, and never had I had such a night of comfort. Didn't hardly sleep, thanks to nasty images and my own fear rattling around inside my head, but at least I was bricking it in cosiness. I wanted to steal the soft woollen blanket, because I'd miss that as the wet season became the cold season. But I didn't want to give Audra any reason to find me.

Concentrating, I couldn't hear anything beyond the closed door. Not a great surprise, because if the darkness outside the little window was anything to go by, the sun hadn't risen yet. I could sneak out and be safe in the dangers of Out'Keep before Audra even had a chance to think about breakfast. It took a few attempts, but finally I had Mouse in my arms and I slipped out the door as quietly as I could, making sure to close it again after me so that my gracious hostess wouldn't know I'd already gone.

I remembered from last night that my little room was at the end of a short corridor. Hers was a few steps along it, and at the end was a room especially for washing in, which still, quite frankly, had me gobsmacked. Past that, the corridor turned sharply right and led into a main living area with a little kitchen leading off that. I didn't want to go that way though, I wanted to walk through the living room and up the stairs that led to the library and, hopefully, freedom. I fervently hoped that Mouse wouldn't twist in my arms and jump away in an effort to find some food out here. He seemed to understand the tension of the moment, though, so he kept nice and still for me.

I was halfway across the living room when Audra appeared out of the kitchen holding a thick slab of bread slathered in butter and honey.

She raised an eyebrow. "You're up early."

Now, I was a thief, and I'd schooled myself Ages ago not to react guiltily when caught out.

"When a cat jumps on your head, you know it's time to get him breakfast," I said.

"You're lying."

"Bloody am not."

"Your aura says otherwise."

Well, shit.

"Where were you off to?"

"I don't know, Audra. You exploded four heads right off the top of four men's bodies last night, so I s'pose I was going somewhere where I'd be able to keep mine."

She sat down in one of the room's two armchairs, looking a little surprised. "You think I'd do that to you?"

Mouse chose that moment to leap out of my arms and investigate the buttery treasure that Audra held. Little traitor.

"What can I say? We said we were going to do great things with our magic, but so far alls I've seen you do with it is paralyse the government, disappear a fortune, and kill a bunch of old men. I think you and me have got wildly different ideas about what 'great things' means."

She wiped a bit of butter off the crust of her bread with a finger and held it out to my cat. He lapped it up, like the little back-stabber he was. "All those people are the reason why Out'Keep is the way it is. We won't cure anything if we treat only the symptoms and not the cause. My father taught me that."

"A wise man he was, and I'm sorry you lost him to the plague. But I'm just not happy about witnessing the violent deaths of old men I don't know."

"Thank you for being truthful," said Audra.

Like I had much of a bloody choice.

"And I'm sorry for what you saw last night," she continued. "Though it can't have escaped your notice that they admitted to knowing about the Game. In fact, admitted to being a party to it. To keep the population of Out'Keep *regulated*, as they so sensitively put it."

I shifted my feet. "I'm not saying they weren't complete bastards. But what does that make us if we go around killing people we think ought to be killed? Apart from more powerful." This time I shuddered as my body remembered what it felt like to have the rest of those old men's lives pour into mine. "I don't like it when it does that."

She smiled a soft smile and it made her pretty. "Go and get yourself and Mouse some breakfast before all of mine is stolen," she said, scratching my cat behind his tabby ears. "Then you can tell me what you think we ought to be doing. And I promise that's what we'll do."

WHICH WAS how we found ourselves in Out-Keep later on that same day, old leather cloaks (that had been left in the library by previous careless owners) wrapped around us against the rain. It had lessened off, the rain, as the sun marked out the notches in the sky, even though it was hidden behind steel clouds, but it was still damp. You couldn't see the raindrops falling, but just being outside and walking around was enough to get you dripping. Rainy season wasn't my favourite time of year.

She'd wanted to go to Keep'Out Quarter, seeing as how she knew that's where I was from, but I managed to convince her we needed to take this a step at a time. I hadn't told her about the Chief. Wasn't brave enough yet. Telling her would mean admitting what I'd done when I first used my magic, admitting the horror I'd seen in my mum's eyes when she found out her son wasn't normal. That he was a killer. If I didn't say it out loud then it wasn't true. So I'd told Audra it'd be best to go to a less unsavoury quarter in order to try out our plan, test the water. Because there was certainly enough of that around.

So this was our plan: to find out how the poor folk wanted to be helped. Bit of a broad plan, I'll freely admit, and I'm sure there's enough merchants out there that'd balk at it. But today wasn't about doing, it was about seeing. Conducting research, as Audra so happily put it.

I took her to the quarter which was as far away from Keep'Out as it could be while still being on the lower slopes. It was the quarter that lay just beyond King's Gate and sprawled out to the right of King's Route. That was a lovely road, mind; all flat flagstones and lined with straight trees so tall that I fancied they disappeared into the low-hanging clouds. And bugger me if there wasn't gold in that road! Not gold I could pick up and shove in my pockets, more was the pity. This gold was sunk deep into the flagstones, like they had been dug up that way, but I doubt that nature would've seen fit to spell out the names of all Kingston's past kings in such a fussy way, dates and all. Even though I knew it was impossible, and even though I imagined that countless other people had done so before me without success, I couldn't help but bend down and scrape my fingers along the name of the first dead ruler we came across. Just in case.

Take a few steps off King's Route though, past all the pretty little merchant's cabins that line it in order to tempt the wealthy traveller, past the impossibly tall trees, and it's a different story altogether. Well, that's obviously why they planted all those trees there—they don't want all those wealthy travellers on their way to the Palace Quarter to see what the city's really like. Don't want them to be offended by such squalor. Or maybe, they don't want these poor folk to see what wealth looks like. Just in case they fancy a bit for themselves.

Keep'Out was no doubt the most dangerous quarter, thanks to the Chief and his cronies, but this one I found myself in now was definitely the worst. After a few steps off the golden-veined track, both of us were stopped in ours as we took in the sight before us.

"All this used to be the Kings' private lands," Audra whispered. "Up there were their orchards. Down towards the moat, their hunting grounds."

"Get that from your books?"

"Of course I did."

"Seems like they might need some revising."

Audra nodded, but it seemed the scenery had finally stolen all words from her. Not surprising really.

This side of the Kingston City hill sloped more sharply than the others so from where we stood we had a great view of the acres of human desolation before us. Even in Keep'Out you could see patches of green, if you were on the roofs on the way home from a job, where some poor bastard decided he'd grow his own food to feed his family. Course, it was always taken by the Chief, and because he'd grown so accustomed to his free fresh food, the little allotments were allowed to stay. But here, it was just a vast swathe of grey. No doubt made worse by the incessant drizzle, but I think even at the very height of warm season it would still look pretty grey. It would certainly smell a lot worse at any rate. I had the impression that most of the shit was running downhill with the rainwater.

"Still want to go down there?" I said.

"We can make this place better." I looked up at her. She looked so earnest. "We can make it so much better." And off she went.

There weren't so much as roads or even paths, more just places where people hadn't stuck a bunch of rubbish together in order to make some kind of shelter. They made the hovel I'd grown up in look like the swankiest of abodes. But the people that filled these non-roads and shelters of refuse gazed at us with a mixture of suspicion and fear. Now, this quarter was far too vast for everybody to know everyone else, especially without the Chief's network making sure that people knew who was who, so it wasn't because they didn't recognise us. It was because we looked so different. Spat out and dragged up in Keep'Out I may've been, but before we'd gone to visit the Prime Minister the day before, Audra'd used her own coin to buy me new clothes to replace the stinking, threadbare rags I'd been living in ever since I left home with my mum. I'd never pass for aristocracy up in In'Keep, but I think I did down here. Plus, we had cloaks and shoes. I only saw one shoe during the first notch we were down there, and it was being used to beat a kid.

Then we came across something that was quite unexpected. It was a beautiful building. Audra spotted it from many paces away and finally we had something to aim for.

On reaching it we discovered that beautiful it may've been once, but now it was in ruins. A two-storey affair which had it towering above everything else in this quarter, but the white stone it was built from was stained and crumbling. Five windows graced the front of it, all smashed in now, strips of unidentifiable rags placed in the holes as some kind of pointless protection against the elements. The door looked as though it had been boarded up with scraps of metal, but not very well; I could see gaps on either side showing the uninviting blackness of the ruin beyond.

"You can see where there would have been pillars," whispered Audra, pointing to crumbling grooves running from ground to roof on either side of the door. "And those walls next to it? I think that would have been a stable."

She was pointing to a line of barely standing stones, though they did give the impression that they'd been built parallel to each other.

"If you know all that," I said, "does that mean you know whose house this used to be?"

"It would have belonged to the kings. I don't know who was the one to build it all those Ages ago, but I do remember from some text or other that hunts could last for days and days, and so the king and his guests would pass the nights here in his hunting lodge. His staff would stay in tents, of course, once they'd finished tending to the king."

"Of course."

"Squirrel, this is fascinating! This was a king's hunting lodge—it could be Ages old! I didn't realise any historical monuments existed outside In'Keep!"

I wanted to explain that she was highly unlikely to, being as how, up until very recently, she'd never left her nice, safe world, but she looked so excited I didn't have the heart to say anything.

"If fact, I'm not sure any Academician does. Think how much we could learn from it!"

"It's a broken down old building," I said, completely confused. "What could you possibly learn from it except that it's taken a long time to fall down?"

She looked at me as though I'd just said something worse than scandalous. "This is *history*," she said. "There's always something to be learned from history. And I'm not just saying that because it was my chosen discipline at the Academy; I'm saying it because it's true. I can't believe we've let it fall to such neglect."

And then she marched right up to it with no thought that there might be frightened and dangerous people inside and pushed on the scrap-metal door, which fell over very noisily as soon as she touched it. The riff-raff around me were instantly drawn by the noise, but Audra was heedless of everything save her find, and she marched right on in without a care in the world.

"All the floors have fallen in," she called out. "I can see right up to the roof. I think there was a grain store up there!"

I raised my eyebrows and pulled my cloak around me a bit tighter. I didn't really know what to say to that. And then I saw a faint red glow from inside.

"Oh no," I whispered, thinking the worst. Whoever she'd caught desecrating her historical monument was going to pay heavily for it. I took a step forward, telling myself that I wouldn't let her take another life with her magic, when the earth moved beneath me.

I stumbled backwards, as did the crowd we'd drawn. Stumbled over the moving stones. And then we all witnessed something we'd be hard pressed to describe to someone else who wasn't there. I reckon even an Academician with all his fancy words would have difficulty describing what happened next.

The house rebuilt itself. Kind of. The rubble and stones littering the ground around it that had obviously been a part of it, unexpectedly leapt up and reattached themselves to the hunting lodge's skeleton, like it was the most natural thing in the world for them to do. But not all of the original pieces were just lying around on the floor waiting to stick themselves back on. Where Audra magicked the glass for the windows and wood for the door from, I'll never know. And an entire roof made of slate! That stuff was expensive. I'd only ever seen it in the Financial and Academician Quarters —not even the merchants in their wealthy quarter could afford it. They had to make do with tiles, the poor sods. The last thing to go up were the pillars, and I fancied that Audra did that for my benefit, once she knew she had my full attention. Impressive pillars they were too, complete with carvings of rich folk with weapons on horses chasing beasts for sport.

Within a surprisingly short amount of time, the hunting lodge gleamed bright, and so out of place in this filthy quarter. The door opened revealing a beaming Audra.

"As good as new," she said, stepping across what had now become a short lawn. When she reached me she turned back to look at her handiwork. "And now we can study it."

"Study?" I echoed with a little chuckle. "By the end of the day that place will look just like it did when we found it."

"How can you possibly know that?"

"Because the people who live here have nothing. Their homes are made from rubbish. You've just given them a free source of materials to make them a tiny bit more liveable. Once the riots and the fights have stopped, that place'll be stripped back to it bones again."

She looked a little shocked at my prediction. "Not if I tell them the historical significance of it, surely they won't."

"Historical significance don't mean shit when you're

working out how you're going to survive the day. Look at them."

I turned and pulled her with me. The crowd was much bigger now. And while they were all struck motionless for the moment at the incredible sight they'd just witnessed, it wouldn't take long for one of them to make a move towards it. And when one did, all would. And then it was just a question of who was the strongest with the least to lose.

"I know you've got a bit of thing for history," I whispered, "but wasn't the point of coming down here to find out how we can help these people? Alls you've done is give them a reason to kill each other."

"You're right. I didn't think." She looked crestfallen. Then her face lifted in a smile. "But perhaps I can rectify it. Hello everybody!" she called so loudly, I jumped.

She took a couple of steps forward so she could address the crowd properly. "What you see before you is an ancient building from a past Age—"

"How'd you do that?" a voice called out.

"I don't know really, I'm still finding out how the magic works—"

"Magic?" cried another, which opened the floodgates. Audra tried to talk over the din, but it wasn't possible. Then she glowed red, something only I could see judging from the complete lack of reaction from the assembled throng, until the ground beneath their feet started shifting and sliding, the piles of rubbish melting into each other and sinking down until alls we were looking at were smoothly cobbled roads. From the pockets of noise that drifted up from different parts across the quarter, I guessed that what we were seeing here was happening all over the place.

"What the curses is going on out here?"

Audra and I both turned to look at the new speaker who'd just appeared in the doorway of a shack next to us. We knew he was a man, not just because of his voice, but also because he was completely naked and sporting a very erect manhood.

"Good gracious me," Audra mumbled, which was lost amongst the smattering of laughter and jeers from the crowd. Then a naked lady appeared which just made the crowd jeer more.

"What the blazes is going on over there?" Audra was so scandalised I couldn't help but laugh.

"It's a brothel," I said. "They're everywhere. Don't tell me you don't have them up in In'Keep?" But even as I asked the question I knew the answer. None of the men wealthy enough to live up there would want to tarnish their reputations by being seen in a whorehouse on their own doorsteps, and none of the women up there were so poor that they needed to sell their bodies in order to buy food. Of course all the whorehouses were down the slopes in Out'Keep. And now that I looked at the man properly, his arrogant stance told me he was no Out'Keeper.

"Brothels," said Audra, disgusted. "Women paid to have sex whether they want it or not. I don't think so." She raised her arm and made a rapid clenching motion with her fist and the whorehouse collapsed. Now, in full view of all, a handful of men could be seen committing unspeakable acts to handful of women. Some of them weren't even old enough to be called women. In fact, some of them weren't even female. All of them looked shocked to be in such public view all of a sudden.

"Get away from them!" Audra cried, swatting her hand, and the men were flung away like so many dead leaves in a wind storm.

Audra's aura lit up once more, and before I had time to worry about the men's safety, as depraved as they were, I saw the spot where the brothel had once stood begin to turn green as grass pushed its way up through the rubble and shit, followed by flowers and then a few trees, which popped out fruit the moment they were grown. I strained my eyes to see as far possible and saw more patches of green spring into life.

"Pretty," I said to her, relieved no one was dying or being horribly injured.

"And not at all difficult," she said, smiling at her creations, "thanks to all of this once being orchard and forest. And now there are no more disgusting brothels around here and those poor women are free."

The crowd around us were now oohing and ahhing at the splash of lush life in the midst of their rubble wasteland. A couple were even jumping up and trying to snag some of the ripened fruit on the low-hanging branches. I didn't have much time to admire the beauty before one of those poor women spoke up.

"The fuck have you done?" she screeched at Audra, pulling at her shawl, which had been snagged by the growing foliage, in an effort to cover her nakedness. "Where am I supposed to work now?"

"Anywhere you like," said Audra, unperturbed. "You're a free woman."

"Oh, am I? People I owe money to ain't gonna call me a free woman! How'm I supposed to earn money?"

"Any way you—"

"Yeah!" shouted a young man from the crowd. He could only have been a couple of years older than me. "And you've turned all the scrap into stones," he said, pounding his foot against the brand new cobbles Audra'd conjured. "How'm I supposed to earn *my* money? My dad'll wallop me black and blue if I go home empty!"

"But I've cleaned up your quarter, given you food," said Audra, confused.

"Apples ain't gonna to pay my debts, love," shouted the

whore. "If you got magic, why couldn't you just magic us up some coin?"

That sparked off a lot of agreement amongst the horde around us, and a lot of fuming looks were thrown about the place. Far too many of them in our direction.

"Audra," I said as quietly as I could, "I think we should probably scarper."

"But I helped them," she said, walking towards me but stumbling a bit, even though the ground was flat and clean now. I caught her outstretched arm. "I did something good."

"You did, but for them it's not good enough. What they need and what you *think* they need are completely different things. Now we've really got to get moving."

Truth be told I was getting quite alarmed. The whore was rallying people around her with angry words, and the naked In'Keeper was hurrying to get his clothes back on.

"They won't be happy until they've taken everything from us!" she was saying. "Ain't enough that we're their servants and whores, that we live off their shit while they dine on fresh meat and gold! And now they send down this bitch to take away what little we *do* have!"

The crowd roared their agreement, and even though In'Keepers think they're so high and mighty, the whore-buying bloke was looking as nervous as I felt. Although he made the mistake of trying to sneak past her across the new grass while she was mid-rant.

"I'm done with being fucked by In'Keepers!" she shouted, pointing directly at him.

The raging mob needed no further encouragement. They leapt on the bloke and he disappeared amid a writhen mass of flailing arms and kicking legs, but despite their braying for his blood, the bloke's screams of agony pierced the air while the whore stood there and laughed at his demise.

"Audra, get us out of here," I whispered. "Or we'll be next."

"But I helped them."

"Just get us the fuck out!"

I shook her until understanding came back into her eyes.

"We can't stay here," she said at last. And then everything disappeared.

SABINA

"Sab? Are you there?"

Claws's voice fell strangely flat in this unexpected darkness.

"Yeah. I'm here," said Sab. Her voice sounded weird as well.

"What's happening?" said Claws. "Are you doing this? Is it because you're angry with me?"

Sab tried to look around. She knew she was moving, but she couldn't see past the smoky greyness clogging up her vision. It looked like smoke, but it didn't smell like smoke. Fog? Had they somehow stumbled into a random patch of fog? Anyway. She wanted to scowl at Claws and ask her just what kind of friend she thought Sab was, but Prisca's voice came from somewhere and beat her to it.

"Sabina isn't doing this, my girl," she said. "I don't know—what's that noise?"

Sab cocked her head. There *was* a sound. Faint, but echoey, even though all three of their voices had a flat quality in this place. Whispers. It sounded as though hundreds, thousands, of people were whispering all around her, above and below, in different languages that she couldn't understand. Some seemed to reach her from miles away, others were right by her ear, making her turn this way and that to see if she could catch the culprit.

"Is this you, Volos?" she cried out, the unceasing susurrus finally getting to her. "Volos!"

The whispering got louder, much louder, and much too close, until her ears and head were filled with millions of moths.

Then, for a second, there was absolute silence. Until a voice spoke.

"Volos is not here."

It was exactly the kind of voice that you didn't want to hear in the dark, when you couldn't see your friends and you were all alone.

The whispering moths returned. Claws whimpered somewhere out there in the darkness.

"Okay," said Sab. "Volos isn't here, but you are. Mind telling us *who* you are?"

A second of utter silence, then, "We are the grey sisters," said the voice.

Before a clever retort could come to her, the smoke-fog shifted, kept shifting, like some gale had blown in from somewhere, but Sab felt nothing. The susurration came back with a vengeance though. Who knew whispers could be so deafening?

It seemed to Sab that the swirling fog was reforming itself into a solid shape right in front of her. A solid shape that she could *see*. She looked around, saw Claws off to the left, Prisca hurrying over to her. Once she'd grabbed her arm, she dragged her over to Sab.

"I don't know what's going on, my girls, but we stay together, you understand?"

"Yes, Prisca," Claws whispered.

Sab nodded. She could see. There was no light source, at least none that she could make out, and it was definitely still dark all around them. She shouldn't be able to see. Unless the fog was the light?

But the fog had disappeared. Now three people faced her. Well, 'face' wasn't exactly the right word, but—

The one in the middle opened her mouth and the whispering stopped. Almost like she'd sucked it up.

"We are the grey sisters," she said, in that peculiar voice of hers. And when she went quiet, the whispering started up again, but not quite so ear-splitting as before.

More unnerving than her voice though, was the eyeball she held aloft in her fingers. The iris was as charcoal grey as the rest of her, but it swivelled to look at Sab and her friends of its own accord.

She should say something. "I'm Sab," she said. "That's Prisca and Claws. Um."

Silence. "We know who you are. We brought you to this mooting." Whispers.

Now, Sab would be first the person to point out that looks aren't everything. She'd seen beautiful Mages, like Emil, behave like total dicks to people. Whereas self-mutilated Claws was the kindest, most timid soul Sab had ever met.

These women though... Sab was disappointed that Volos wasn't here, because they'd even give that brute the creeps. The one who'd done all the talking so far had a face that was just mouth. Actually, that wasn't quite true. She probably had a face somewhere, it was just that it was covered with some kind of leathery cloth, the seams hideously highlighted with ghastly thick stitches. All that showed was her mouth. Her lips were cracked and oozing, and Sab was overjoyed that she couldn't see beyond them to her teeth. From out of the back of her head was an explosion of frizzy grey hair that swayed gently on a breeze that didn't exist in this place. Maybe it swayed to the beating wings of the whisper moths. The other thing about her was that everything, from the tips of her frizzy hair to the tattered rags of her, well, rags, was a charcoal grey colour.

The sister to her left was the grey of thunderheads, and her hair fell in long, thick braids that dragged along the ground. Her face, though, was pretty special. This one had her mouth stitched up so tightly her nostrils and cheeks were distorted. And where eyes should've been were two black pits. Deep and hungry. Sab looked away quickly in case she got sucked in.

The third sister to the right was the colour of pale ashes, but Sab couldn't see her face because matted locks of hair fell down in torrents in front of it. She could just make out the ragged edges of her ears though, and they seemed to twitch this way and that, as though picking up sounds only she could hear.

And while each sister was her own distinct shade of grey, they all wore the same tattered, threadbare clothes, which seemed to meld seamlessly from one sister to the other.

That eyeball, though.

"S-Sab?" said Claws. "What's a mooting?"

The whispering stopped when the middle sister opened her raw mouth. "You yondfare to the distant highbergs, and that is good. You must seek out your werekin beclosed by galdercraft and release them."

The whispering came back.

Sab scowled. "Prisca, do you have any idea what they're saying?"

"Not…really, no."

Utter silence. "They do not understand us, sister. We are

too olden, their tongue has wended. We must make them understand before the sunderborn one beshrews us all."

Even though it was only the charcoal sister speaking, because the other two literally had no mouths to speak from, Sab would swear that each sentence she uttered sounded different. Almost like she was having a conversation with herself. Or perhaps Thunderheads and Ashes were speaking through Charcoal's mouth.

"I hold with you, sister," said Charcoal, in her own voice. "Take it and see the woundswathed one."

She passed the eyeball to her left, and Thunderheads took it easily, even though she couldn't possibly see out of those black, eyeless holes in her face. When the eyeball touched her fingers, as thin as burnt twigs, the iris changed colour to match her.

She closed her fingers gently over the eyeball, then held up her fist to Claws's face. When she opened her hand, the eyeball was nowhere to be seen.

Until a wrinkly eyelid in the middle of her palm suddenly flew open.

"Shit on it!" Sab cried and stepped back, as did Prisca.

Claws, however, seemed to be caught in the gaze of that revolting eye. It wasn't swivelling now; its unblinking regard was fixed on Claws.

Sab's wits returned and she was about to make a grab for her friend, but Claws suddenly shuddered, Thunderheads closed her fingers down over her palm, and Claws was released.

"Are you all right, my girl?" said Prisca.

Claws nodded. "I think so." She blinked several times, then rubbed her eyes. "I saw things."

"Those things were only for you to see," said Charcoal in Thunderhead's voice. "You and no other."

Thunderhead now had the eyeball back in her fingertips,

and she passed it carefully back to Charcoal. She also made a fist over it, and held it up to Prisca's face.

"Oh great," said Sab. "Looks like we're all getting a turn."

"Looks like it," said Prisca.

Sab shoved her arm. "Well don't look at it!"

"I want to see."

The eyelid in Charcoal's palm flicked open, and Prisca stared at it for several seconds, swaying slightly, before she was released.

"Fucking hell," said Prisca. "That was intense. How long was I entranced for?"

"A couple of seconds," said Sab. She watched the eyeball change fingers, until Ashes held her closed fist up to Sab's face. "Well, I guess it's my turn."

Sab stared at the ash-grey palm, trying to find the eyelid amongst the wrinkles.

Then she was looking into an ash-grey eye. Just for the fun of it, she tried to close her eyes and turn her head away, but she couldn't. She was stuck. And she wouldn't be released until she'd seen whatever it was her friends had already seen.

Wouldn't've had to fuck about with all the gross eyeballing if they'd've just let them talk to each—

The grey eye turned green. Sab knew she was standing still, but she also knew that she was falling down, down into that orb of green until it enveloped her completely. She heard the wind whistle past her ears as she reached terminal velocity. Wherever the green spat her out, it was going to be as a squelchy, steaming puddle.

It came as quite a nice surprise, then, when the falling stopped and she was standing upright once more. The green had shaped itself into a forest. The scent of it was all around her, damp earth and growing leaves. Even though she knew she'd spent all her life on the 'Sphere, she also knew that she'd grown up with this scent, that it was in her marrow, as much a part of her as her flesh and blood.

So was the singing, although she didn't remember that until she heard it. Beautiful voices that chased each other around a melody, harmonising with each other, and singing of such happiness that Sab laughed. Accompanying the voices were silver bells, chiming every time the breeze soughed, all throughout the forest from the canopy to the roots.

She'd stood here for an eternity, but all too suddenly the singing turned to screams. The bells turned to drums. The green light that suffused the forest dimmed and turned black—not the black of night, but the black of storms overhead.

Lightning struck. It struck several times before Sab realised it wasn't coming from above like it should if there was a real storm. It came across the forest, ripping through trees as though they were of no consequence.

The forest screamed.

It was in agony.

She was in agony too. Every time the lighting struck a tree and shattered it, she shattered too. The lightning was killing her, but she didn't know how to stop it. She couldn't see what was causing it. Except that...she knew *she* was the one who was causing it. It was her fault that the forest was suffering and dying. That knowledge, even though it made no sense to her, was worse than the searing agony that ripped through her body.

Through the torment and grief though, she was aware of other images.

Audra, awash with red. Blood, perhaps.

A great army, filled with fear but also determination.

Great clouds falling from the sky and into the ocean, raising it up until it drowned entire lands.

And this was her fault too. She was the root of all destruction, and the knowledge tortured her.

Surely the only release from such pain was death? She wished it would come for her. She almost believed her wish was granted when she was sucked backwards, enveloped in green again.

Then she was looking at the orb.

Which became an ash-grey eye.

The eye blinked, and Sab rocked back onto her heels, finally released.

She looked down at her flayed arms, momentarily confused as to why they weren't branches. She flexed her fingers, wondered why they weren't leaves.

She glared up at Ashes, annoyed that the grey sister's face was hidden behind a filthy curtain of hair and couldn't see Sab's fury.

"The fuck *was* that?" she roared, although in this place it fell flat. "You could've killed me!"

Charcoal opened her mouth and sucked up the whisper moths. "You all saw what was needful to see."

"Why did we need to see it? Apart from excruciating agony, none of it made any sense!"

"You saw what was needful to see," said Charcoal. "You will understand when you have to."

"Shit on that," said Sab. "I've never liked puzzles, and all that enigmatic bollocks is just annoying. Either tell us, with proper words that everyone understands, what we're doing here, or let us go. We've got a race to win."

"You need to do more than that," said Charcoal. "For each of you, your part in this is eyeseen. The ereworld is dying. The Mages are taking all the galdercraft from it. Should they stay unbefought and the galdercraft goes, the world will die. This is your oughting."

The whisper moths swarmed then, so much that Sab had

to cover her ears, even though that barely made a difference. The grey sisters were fading back into the fog again, or maybe becoming a part of it. Sab had no idea what those creatures were, and before she could ask them, they'd gone.

Only silence and darkness remained.

"Don't tell me," said Sab, "that we just got a mission from a bunch of creepy weirdos."

JENNA

*J*enna's beloved daughter Calla had sensed her disquiet this morning, because when she left her at her mother's boutique in the Merchant's Quarter she bawled. She never bawled, except that time when she had the coughing fever, but she was always such a good and quiet girl. Naturally, her mother had demonstrated concern in the form of countless questions, but Jenna hadn't wanted to answer them. Explaining that Konrad hadn't returned home last night would not answer any questions, it would merely start a thunderstorm of others. Jenna had to get to the Academy as quickly as possible to find out what happened after he'd taken Audra and that skinny boy back there with him.

The morning was grey and dry for the moment, but that wouldn't last long; the fat black clouds promised that. Usually she walked to the Academy after leaving Calla with her grandparents, and she enjoyed the notch-long march, whatever the season. Today, however, was an exception. She hailed the first carriage she saw outside her mother's boutique and asked the driver to get her to the Academy as quickly as possible.

Fortunately there wasn't too much traffic on the roads between the quarters, and for that she was grateful. Her panic peaked when they left the main thoroughfare and turned onto the lane leading to the back of the Academy. Numerous white robes rushed around in apparent confusion, leaving no space for a horse and cart. The driver reined in the horse, pulling the carriage to a gentle stop, then looked around at her.

"You can leave me here," she said, handing a silver coin over to the driver.

"You sure, miss?"

"Yes, please. It looks easier on foot."

"Not wrong there, miss." He accepted the coin with thanks.

Jenna jumped out as quickly as she could, first walking then jogging to reach her colleagues who seemed in such distress. She grabbed the sleeve of the first one she came to and asked what all the fuss was about, but his ashen face simply stared blankly at her. When she released his arm he took off once more.

The excitement must have something to do with Konrad and Audra, but she forced them out of her mind until she had evidence. Asking her fellows was useless. She'd have to find out for herself.

Unlike the main entrance, the southern entry was nothing more than an archway leading through to the courtyard at the centre of the building. She enjoyed taking her midday meal here from time to time. The grass was soft, and many, many seasons ago now, an Artist had created a wonderful pond and waterfall in the middle, which was as relaxing as it was beautiful. The thick glass tiles that made up the floor of the Sages' chamber covered the entire courtyard, which was why it was such a clement spot to lunch. Even during the rainy and cold seasons.

The moment she reached the other side of the arch, a door opened from the Historians' quarter and a robed figure peered out and looked up. He cried out, then swooned forward in a dead faint. Jenna rushed to his side, but luckily the grass softened his blow. His breathing was deep and regular. What could he have seen up there to cause such a reaction?

Obviously, Jenna had look up.

Curiously, since yesterday, the glass tiles had turned red. She frowned. No, that wasn't it... It was more like a great quantity of red liquid had been spilt over the glass floor of the Sage's dome. She saw the spider-leg trails of it stretching from the centre outwards. Had the Artists gone up there and drenched everything in red paint?

And then she saw a hand. Just one, flat against the glass directly above her, fingers splayed as though it were waving to catch her attention. Her frown deepened; why was there a hand on the floor?

Unfortunately for her stomach, it didn't take long for her to notice that other body parts, internal and external, were scattered all over the place up there. She heaved up what little breakfast she'd managed that morning, and it landed on the poor Historian who was still insensible beside her. The poor creature had had the shock of his life before he collapsed, and it wasn't going to be any pleasanter for him when he awoke.

Despite all the lectures she'd attended, she'd never learned anything that could help her in these circumstances, so she pulled the inert Historian back into the corridor, leaving a trail of semi-digested bread and butter behind him. Then she did the only thing she could when all was beyond her understanding. She went to find her husband.

. . .

HE WAS IN HIS LABORATORY, which wasn't a surprise; gibbering under a workbench, which was.

"Konrad," she said, rushing to his side. "Why didn't you come home last night? Calla and I were dreadfully worried about you."

He looked up at her with wide eyes, then relief when he finally recognised her. He was trembling and had a thin sheen of sweat across his brow. In fact, he looked very much like he was the grip of a fever.

"S-s-sages," he mumbled.

"Yes, dear. We should probably get you home, you look awful. Which isn't very surprising if you spent the whole night cooped up in here with your chemicals."

"The Sages," he said again, his voice a little stronger now.

"Yes, dear, I've just walked through the courtyard and seen the mess. Was it the Artists, do you think? A new instalment perhaps? Or perhaps a silly trick. I don't think the Sages will be too amused when they arrive this morning."

For several heartbeats Konrad's mouth worked while he tried to find some words. "No, you silly woman, that *was* the Sages! I saw it! It was Audra and that, that Out'Keep boy of hers! They did this!"

"Nonsense, Konrad, you just have a fever. I'll take you home and—"

He pushed her hand away from him then scrabbled up from under the bench.

"Do you think the Academy would be reacting the way it is if this were just a prank pulled by the Artists?" he said, leaning forwards and speaking into her face. "All morning I've heard people running backwards and forwards along that corridor out there, panicking. The Sages are dead—all four of them! Audra did it and I witnessed it and I'll be forever haunted by that image!"

Jenna stumbled, reached out a hand and balanced herself on her husband's workbench. "Audra? But she's my friend."

"She's a Mage!" Konrad hissed.

"She's an Academician."

Konrad slapped her across the cheek and it was so unexpected that Jenna didn't even cry out. "Listen to what I'm telling you. Something happened when she left the Academy to find the Healing Glass. She didn't come back with it, but she came back with something far more dangerous. We need to know what happened out there so we can work out what to do about it. People don't just turn into Mages."

Jenna nodded. "Do you think she's always been a Mage?"

Konrad sneered. "If she had, she would have known those ridiculous theories of hers were false. No, something happened to her. And you have to find out what it was."

"Me?"

"You're her friend. You're always gossiping like Harbourton wives. Ask her and she'll tell you."

"But you're the one who witnessed...the Sages."

"Listen," he said, turning to his bench and moving his beakers around. "I've got far too many duties here to be chasing after Audra and her Out'Keep rapscallion. I'm very busy and my work is incredibly important. Now just do as your husband tells you before your friend decides to murder any more of her superiors."

JENNA WASN'T A STUPID WOMAN. If she were, she wouldn't have been chosen from amongst all the In'Keep applicants to join the Academy. But right now nothing made sense to her. She traipsed along Library Walk, grateful to be away from the chaos, utterly at a loss as to how she could complete her husband's task. Was she supposed to march into the library and ask Audra if she was a murderer? And what good was an Academician like her at something like this anyway? Surely they should be involving the city guards? Or if Audra were as dangerous as Konrad suggested, perhaps the Rebels should be the ones investigating her. After all, a group of them did accompany her on the mission to find the Healing Glass.

She stopped in the middle of the pathway as an idea struck her. Of course! She should seek out Drayke Rebel Leader! He could answer any of Jenna's questions, once she'd come up with some. Plus, he wouldn't be able to do anything nasty to her with magic if he got angry.

Magic! Everybody knew that had died out with the Mages, the Academicians especially. Why, it was they who told the rest of the population this well-known fact. Evidently, she wasn't denying anything her husband had seen, he certainly looked shaken enough by it. But magic…?

Just as she reached the palace enclosure the rain started. She pulled up her hood and looked at the dismal sky from underneath it. A storm was coming; she'd heard thunder rumble like a crowd of discontents, but it was a long way off yet. She decided to take the long way round to the barracks, past the palace instead of past the library, because the idea of being stopped by Audra and questioned on what she was doing up here if not visiting the library worried her a little. Because even though she doubted the existence of magic, she also knew that Konrad wasn't a liar.

"HELLO? I'm sorry to come unannounced. Hello?"

She'd never had cause to come to the barracks before, and even though it was unlikely the place was forbidden to her, she still had a funny tingling sensation in her belly when she stepped over the threshold. The door, unassuming and wooden, was open and led into an atrium made of undecorated raw stone, the monotony broken by metal pegs marching around the wall. A few even had thick bear-skin cloaks dangling from them. As silent as the place was, and even though no one had answered her, there was at least some evidence that the barracks were occupied. It smelt of damp leather and boots, hardly surprising considering a large group of men used this as a cloakroom. Directly opposite her was another door leading to the main living space. No one was there to either greet or halt her, so she went through.

First she noticed the aroma of roasting meat, then she noticed the two serving boys. Both looked up at her when she entered. Both wore matching palace staff uniforms and expressions of surprise.

"I'm looking for Drayke Rebel Leader," she said. "Is he here?" One look around the surprisingly luxurious room told her only she and the two boys were present.

"He's back there," said one of the boys, indicating another door at the end of the room.

"Can I go through to see him?"

The boys looked at each other. Evidently this was an unprecedented situation.

"Perhaps," said Jenna, "it would be better if one of you were to inform him of my presence and ask if he'd be kind enough to come out and see me."

The same boy nodded his head, looking a little relieved, and jogged to the adjacent room.

"I hadn't expected it to be quite so cosy," she said to the remaining boy. "Lots of rugs and sofas. Would you mind if I waited by that lovely fire? I got ever so damp on my way over."

"Not at all, ma'am."

"Which part of Merchant's Quarter are you from? I can

tell by your accent. And because I always used to call people sir and ma'am when I left to join the Academy."

"The Boulevard, ma'am."

"Very nice," said Jenna, raising her eyebrow. "I was always envious of the people who lived there when I was growing up."

"My father said I had to learn the value of money by working for none."

"A wise man," she said with a chuckle.

"Working, not gossiping."

They turned to look and there stood Drayke Rebel Leader, in all his leather-strap glory. Jenna wondered if he ever wore clothes that covered his torso, and she had to admit it would probably make him look a lot less daunting. Perhaps that was why the Rebels wore the strange straps-and-trews ensemble. She also noticed his hair was much longer than hers.

"I'm sorry to come unannounced," she said again, "but I really must speak with you most urgently. May I? It's about Audra."

Drayke's frown deepened. He motioned to the serving boy next to him to leave with one swift flick of the head, then he stood aside so Jenna could pass. She looked longingly at the hearth she was about to leave.

"There's a fire in this room as well," he said. She blushed, and strode across the room.

Considering the number of beds in this new chamber, it was evidently used for sleeping. All the beds were exactly the same; simple cots with simple mattresses covered with simple blankets, wooden headboards lined up against the walls so the sleeping Rebels' feet pointed into the centre of the room. There were even two or three cots stacked on top of each other, separated by metal poles. With so many men crammed into the chamber every night, she was surprised that it smelt of lavender and not stale sweat.

"I didn't realise you all slept at the barracks as well," she said, looking around.

"Once we join the Rebels they become our family and this our home."

"What about your actual families?"

"They don't exist for us any more."

"Oh. Well, that's nice."

"Why are you here, Academician?"

"Jenna, please," she said with a smile. "I don't think I'll ever really get used to titles. Well now, that's a very big book!" She'd spotted a little writing table and chair at the far end of the chamber in between a couple of thrice-stacked cots, and upon it sat a tome of magnificent proportions. She would never have taken any Rebel as an avid reader. "May I see it?"

"When you've explained why you're here. What has Audra done now?"

"Um, this isn't a pleasant story. You may want to sit down," she said. He folded his well-muscled arms across his chest, scowled, and remained standing. "Right. Do you recall when my husband, Konrad, came to the library to take Audra and her young charge to see the Sages?"

He nodded once, and after a brief pause Jenna recounted all she'd seen that morning in the Sages' dome as well as her conversation with Konrad. Drayke's expression didn't alter even a fraction.

"Konrad suspects she's a Mage, and he entrusted me to find out from Audra precisely what happened on her mission to find the Healing Glass. But I came to you because..."

"You're afraid of her."

"Well—"

"You should be. She's dangerous."

"But I find that so hard to believe. I've known her for years." She walked to the nearest bed and flopped onto it. "She was the first Academician ever to speak to me. Outsiders aren't always welcomed at the Academy, but Audra didn't care that I came from a family of merchants."

"She's not the same woman. The mission changed her, not least because she came back with magic." He marched over to a single cot placed nearest the door and pulled a loose sheaf of papers from beneath the pillow. In a few steps he stood before her and held it out. "Read this."

"What is it?"

"Read it."

She took the sheaf. "Could I trouble you for a cup of tea?"

He glowered at her then swung around and left the chamber. Jenna grimaced at causing so much trouble then lowered her eyes and began reading.

What wonderfully neat handwriting! And the tale the words told enthralled her. True enough, they weren't very descriptive words but they recounted the mission of the Healing Glass in great detail, culminating in a great battle, at a place called the Blasted Glade in the forest to the east. Between the Rebels and...orcs, apparently. The last page was an account of how Audra slew two Mages, then came back to the battlefield and woke all those who had fallen during the short but vicious skirmish—humans and orcs alike. And the orcs were no longer savage. Audra then explained that all of them had been deceived into playing a Game the Mages had devised countless Ages ago in order to create bloodshed, but the Game ended when she killed those two Mages. So did the plague in Kingston, and whatever affliction had caused the orcs to travel to the forest.

She lowered the pages to her lap.

"You didn't drink your tea."

Jenna looked up at Drayke, who had returned without her

noticing, then down at the cup by her foot. It was probably cold by now but she needed a cup of tea more than ever.

"Did you write this?" she said once her drink was finished.

He nodded once.

"You said she was dangerous. According to this, she saved everyone."

"She killed two Mages with no help."

"That's a good thing, isn't it?" she said looking back at the last page. "They were taking lives by making you kill each other. It seems Audra did what was necessary to stop them taking more."

"You understand nothing."

Jenna rolled her eyes. "Then tell me so I do."

"We used to think the Mages were good people; extinct, but good. It turns out they're neither, and after Audra's confrontation with them at the Blasted Glade she came back with power."

"How did that happen? You made no mention of that in here."

"I don't know. I was busy defending myself against extinct orcs. I imagine it's because she killed them."

Jenna shrugged with her mouth. It sounded implausible to her, but she wasn't there, and she certainly was no expert.

"Since we've been back she's used her power to imprison the Prime Minister and his government."

"How—"

"With magic," said Drayke. "Trust me, it would take the same to free them. I've recently heard that she also visited Lord and Lady Worthy and taken all their money because they wouldn't give it to the poor in Out'Keep."

Jenna blinked. "Did she give it to the poor once she'd taken it?"

Drayke shook his head once. "It vanished."

"Vanished."

"And now she's killed your Sages. I can't pretend I had great love for them, but I certainly never wished death upon them. You have my condolences."

"Thank you."

"While she may have been your friend, you must understand that she now has Kingston at a disadvantage." He gestured to the bundle of papers in her hand. "I learned that the Mages we once remembered so fondly are evil. Mages were the only humans with magic. Now Audra has that magic. She can do whatever she pleases and none of us can stop her. That makes her dangerous."

"If all that really is the case, then our situation looks entirely hopeless, doesn't it?"

"What are you three doing just standing there?"

There'd been moments, several of them, in the long Ages of Sab's life, that she'd got so brain-meltingly drunk on hooch that she passed out right in the middle of talking or fighting or fucking. Except she never knew she'd passed out until her consciousness came back. Because it wasn't really passing out. There was no coma-like sleep until she woke up in a strange position in an even stranger corner of Stratus level. No, she'd still be doing her talking or fighting or fucking, it's just that everything would blank out for an unspecified period of time, and then her consciousness would switch back on, and there she was. Still talking or fighting or fucking. It was a really weird sensation and she didn't know how it worked, but she always found it truly astonishing. In that vocal way of astonishment that only true drunks have mastered.

Coming out of that black fog or smoke or whatever it had been, into the raging face of Volos felt just like those times.

"Shit on it, man," she said, covering her nose with her

hand. "You're stuffed full of magic. Can't you use it to do something about your breath?"

"What's wrong with you three?" he said, glaring at Sab but not rising to her jibe. "What did you do?"

"Me? Nothing! Why are you blaming me?"

"Then tell me why the three of you were rooted to the spot for the past half-notch! Nothing I did snapped you out of it!"

Now that he mentioned it, Sab did feel something... She shoved the sleeve of her t-shirt up to her shoulder and saw a purple ring of bruises on her upper arm. And the other.

"Oh, nice," she said. "I bet it really broke your heart to have to lay hands on an unresisting girl. Claws, you all right?"

Volos snorted with disgust. "I'd never touch *her*."

Sab ignored him, waited for her friend to check her arms and belly, was relieved when her friend nodded.

"What happened?" said Volos. His voice was quiet, but somehow that was more threatening than when he was shouting.

"Look," said Prisca, laying a hand on his hairy forearm. "I've been thinking about how we can all transport safely. I don't know what just happened to us, but there's something very strange going on out here, and I think it'll be for the best if we get to the train as quickly as possible."

During her little speech, Volos's face had melted from rage to attentiveness. Astonishing. "Tell me."

"It was Sabina's dome during the...the rhino stampede that gave me the idea," Prisca said. "Volos, if you use your magic to transport us, Sabina and I can channel ours into Claudia, protecting her from any negative side affects."

"Yeah," said Sab, realisation dawning. "Like billions of mini bubbles protecting each of her particles during the transport, and making sure they go back to the right place when it's over!"

"Exactly right," said Prisca, beaming at her.

"Are you sure it'll work?" Claws whispered.

"Are you questioning a skilled Mage?" roared Volos.

"Of course it will," said Sab, ignoring Volos and pulling Claws close. "I can't believe I didn't think of it before. I'm sorry about that. Still not used to being able to cast magic at will, I guess."

Claws smiled down at her. A tentative little smile, but it was enough for Sab to know that they were friends again.

"All right," she said quietly. "Let's do it."

"You heard the girl!" said Sab, grinning. Then she turned to Volos. "Don't do anything until me and Prisca are ready, right?"

Prisca stepped to the other side of Claws so that she was in between the two of them. "Thank you, Volos," she said.

It was enough to wipe the scowl off his face for a second or two. Sab kept her face neutral.

"All right, Prisca," she said. "What do we do?"

"Don't touch her, but see your magic enveloping every part of her. Claws, you won't feel a thing, I promise."

Sab imagined her best friend was made of a billion bubbles, then turned her focus inward, to that part of herself where the magic waited, still amazed at how much there was. She beckoned to it, sent out gentle tendrils towards Claws and watched as they spread around and through her. Sab's magic was a buttery yellow colour, and it surprised her when she noticed Prisca's was a deep blue. When they met, they made Claws glow green.

"We're ready," said Prisca.

Volos nodded, flung his arms apart and then Sab was flying, caught up in the invisible breeze and somehow able to see all of the world at once. Exhilarating! But also terrifying

—she'd only ever transported in the confines of the 'Sphere before. Out here, it would be all too easy to let her component particles disperse further and further away on that invisible breeze, to never let herself be whole again, remain pain free forever as nothing but a sense of elation.

But then pain struck every part of her all at once. Excruciating pain. As though someone had taken those component particles and set fire to them.

Then she was falling to the ground. She barely felt it as her back hit it, there was already too much pain. But it did punch the air from her lungs.

"What the fuck, Volos!" she screamed when she was capable of doing so. Although the scream wasn't quite so ferocious as she'd wanted it to be.

When she'd managed to push herself up onto her feet, she cast about for Claws. She looked a little dazed, but not like she was in any pain. Sab stumbled over to her.

"You all right?" she said.

"Did it work?" Claws said. "I can't tell if we've moved, it's too dark."

"You're not in any pain?"

She shook her head. "*Did* it work?"

"That fucker over there," she looked around for Volos. He was on his knees, vomiting. "Um. Is puking. Okay, I wasn't expecting that."

Prisca was already up and tottering over to him, hands clasping her head. "Volos, what happened?"

"Don't know," he gasped when his mouth stopped spewing. "My spell. Something stopped it."

Sab looked around. It was proper night now, but even without the raggedy toenail of a moon up in the sky, she would've been able to see all right. And there was nothing *to* see. Nothing that could've stopped a transport spell mid-movement.

Oh. Shit it.

She sent out, very carefully, a tiny tendril of her own magic. She quested for a moment or two, then yep. Just in front of her, a little electric shock as it fizzed out of existence. On a small scale like that, kinda felt nice.

"We crashed into a magic dead zone," she said.

"What's a magic dead zone?" said Volos.

"Didn't you have any dead zones in Oceanwall?"

Volos blinked once, slowly. "I feel my original question is your answer."

Sab rolled her eyes. "Simple *no* would've done."

"Dead zone..." said Claws. "You mean, like the one at Terminal?"

"Exactly," said Sab. "But it's different. Look."

She sent out another tendril of magic to the place where she got zapped last time, but instead of letting it fizz out, she kept a thin stream going. The electric kind of shock was doing pleasant things to her teeth, fingers and toes.

"You guys seeing that?" she said.

There was a chorus of quiet agreement. Sab chose to think this was because of the sight bursting in front of them. Forks of pink and purple lightning, with the odd mini-explosion of turquoise. It was really pretty. And totally silent. Eventually, Sab stopped sending her magic out there. A couple of her back teeth were starting to feel a little loose.

"What was that?" said Claws. "It was gorgeous!"

"That was the thing that crashed the transporter spell," said Volos, frowning.

"So," said Prisca, "it's actually more of a...more of a wall, than a dead zone?"

Sab shrugged with her face. "Maybe. A protective barrier of some kind, yeah, why not. I've never been out here before, so I really don't have any idea."

"Can we pass through it then?" said Claws. "Or are we stuck on this side?"

"Um," said Sab. "Well, we could all pass through the Terminal on the 'Sphere with no problem. "I don't see why this should be any different."

"I know," said Volos. "How about you go through first, and if you fry, the rest of us will know that you were wrong."

"Ha ha ha!" said Sab. "Volos cracks a joke! But I think comic Volos is more of a dick than hot-stick-up-his-arse Volos. But you know what? Fuck it."

And with that, she walked forward ten paces.

"Sab, no!" Claws cried out.

But nothing happened. "It's all good, guys. Come on over."

"Maybe we can try the transport spell again," said Claws. "Apart from the landing, it really didn't hurt last time with you two protecting me."

"I'm not trying that again here," said Volos. "What if magic still doesn't work?"

"Well, let's have a look, shall we?" said Sab.

She summoned a ball of blue light into the palm of her hand, then threw it up into the air, where it shattered into a thousand scintillating pieces.

"Well, shit," she said.

Not because the spell hadn't worked, or even because it had. It was because of what the light had illuminated.

In front of them, on the gritty wasteland that made up this place, were hundreds of very angry-looking faces, attached to bodies that looked just about ready to attack.

And then they charged.

JAYMES

esterday had been an unpleasant one of killing and torturing—punishment for unpaid taxes, according to RibCage. Jaymes had been glad when it finished, even though he assumed he'd be spending the night in a foul little cell beneath the Chief's lair. So when RibCage pushed him into a comfortable room to pass the night... It'd been locked, of course, but it wasn't a filthy cell in a dungeon. And he'd been fed meat stew, fresh bread and strong ale.

It was still unexpected when he woke this morning. The part of him that despised himself more than he despised the Chief wished he was in a cell. The atrocities he'd committed yesterday shouldn't be rewarded with a soft bed and hot food. Perhaps this was all part of the Chief's plan: to break him with his own self-loathing.

An almighty crash against the door startled him a little. "Wakey, wakey, comrade!" The unmistakable voice of RibCage. "Stop fucking your hand, I'm bringing in breakfast." The door opened and the scent of eggs and bacon wafted in before RibCage's self-mutilated form, a leering smile slashed across his face. "You're a quick finisher. We had a girl here so long that most of the men forgot how to do it themselves. Telling you, waking up to the sound of neglected hands tugging the slug ain't the best way to greet the new day. You're lucky you got a room to yourself. Here." He shoved a plate of greasy meat at Jaymes. "Better eat up. Busy day ahead of us."

And here was another surprise: even though Jaymes wanted to do nothing more than punch the ugly fucker in the face again, he did as he was told. But a lifetime in the Rebels had taught him obedience, and even though some little woman with unnatural powers had disbanded them, disobeying a given order, clearly, was a difficult thing to do. That, and he was fucking famished.

RibCage waited patiently while he ate, leering every now and then at his own thoughts, scratching at his torso with a metallic rasping sound, breathing heavily through his nose. Once Jaymes had eaten his breakfast, he gestured him towards the door with his head and pushed him out into the corridor, as gilded and gaudy as the rest of this den. A few strides along then down a staircase lined with ostentatious bannisters and he was once more in the presence of the Chief.

The fat bastard was seated at a table erected in the centre of the room, one which hadn't been there yesterday, and was laid with colourful silk linens, sparkling cutlery and glasses, and tureens full of different kinds of meat. While he shovelled food into his mouth with a silver fork and surprising grace, Jaymes noticed the beads of sweat that formed at the top of the Chief's bald head and chased each other down the side of his face. Every now and then he would swipe at them with a lace napkin, but they reappeared as quickly as they were dealt with. Jaymes's own breakfast turned sour in his belly at the sight of it. Not to mention the fact that he shared his breakfast table with another young child.

"I trust you slept well," said the Chief, laying his cutlery down on his plate with a delicate clatter, reaching for a silver goblet.

"Well enough," said Jaymes. "Who's the boy?"

"My new friend," said the Chief, with a grin like a snarl. "And watch your careless questions or you might hurt the poor tyke's feelings. Tell him who you are, child."

The boy had been stuffing meat into his face with considerably less grace than the Chief, but now he looked up, almost guiltily, and blinked a few times at Jaymes before answering.

"Mole," said the boy. He looked back at the Chief, who indicated with a wave of a pudgy hand that he should continue speaking. "Mum's Sparrow. Dad's Hare. From Midden Pit."

Jaymes straightened. He knew those names well enough. "What you doing here, lad?"

Mole shrugged. "Mum's dead of the plague now, Dad's dead in a fight. His crew took me on. Then the Chief comes along and says he's found Stag."

"Name's Jaymes now."

Mole giggled. "Mum said you was a Rebel and was given a funny name. She always talked about you. Said *her* mum always knew you'd leave Midden Pit because you was so big. Biggest of all the Rebels, Mum said. Is it true?"

So he had a nephew. Now he looked, he could see his sister's face staring back him, the large, green eyes and dark hair. The narrow nose and sharp cheekbones. He even had the same habit of rubbing his nose with a clenched fist when asking a question as she had. And now the Chief had his claws in him.

"I'm big enough," said Jaymes. "But you should see the Rebel Leader. He's a fucking giant."

Mole's eyes widened. "Honest?"

"Honest. Makes the Chief here look like a beetle."

"Cor!"

"Well, now that the two of you have been reacquainted," said the Chief. "It's time you and I, Jaymes, discussed today's business."

"Why's he here?"

The Chief looked as though he were disappointed at being asked such an obvious question. "As little Mole so recently pointed out, Jaymes, you're a big man. And though I have many big men of my own," he looked across to RibCage, "keeping those who'd rather be somewhere else than under my fair roof is considerably more difficult than keeping young boys with me." He tousled Mole's hair and the youngster grinned at him with his greasy mouth. "There's only so long hot food and a warm bed will keep you here, I wager."

"I dunno, mister," said Mole. "This is the first hot food I ever ate. Don't reckon I'll ever get bored of it."

The Chief chuckled, a warm and friendly sound. It scared the shit out of Jaymes.

"If your Uncle Jaymes does as he's told," he said, "then you're both welcome at my table, any time you like. Without harm coming to your person afterwards, no less." Mole, still chewing, looked at him in confusion. "But if he upsets me, even just a little bit, I'm afraid RibCage here will have to do all those dreadful, dreadful things I employ him to do. And it wounds me to say he enjoys it far too much than is probably tasteful."

"I fucked a woman to death once, using this blade here in fact," said RibCage, lifting his shirt and tapping one of the filthy blades stuck into his torso. "Then I ate her face because she was so pretty. And that was just for fun. Chief didn't even ask me to do it." He leaned over the table and peered into Mole's face. "I just like hearing people scream. I call it their blood song. Chop off my own stones to hear your blood song, little boy."

Mole burst into terrified sobbing, mouth hanging open, half-chewed meat spilling out onto his silver plate as fat tears spilled down his cheeks.

"Now, RibCage," said the Chief. "Is that any way to talk to our honoured guest? Don't listen to him, dear Mole. He's quite, quite insane. But he does get quite explosive at the sound of children crying, so you might want to stop that noise sooner rather than later."

"Let him go," said Jaymes. "You have me here already, I'm not going anywhere—but only if you let the boy go."

The fat bastard roared with laughter. "It's adorable that you think you have any power to bargain with me, Stag, was it? But Mole is my newest friend and he'll be staying with me for as long as I want him to. Don't worry though, Stag, he'll be perfectly safe. You have my word."

"How can I possibly trust your word? After what you did yesterday?"

"Well, you can't, can you? But you have no choice. Do as I say, and this sweet boy here will be safe, fed, and unmolested by any of my men. Irk me even a little, and I send him out to the wolves."

"Wolves?" squeaked the poor boy.

"Not real wolves, my dear. I mean my men. They're far worse than wolves. They hunt for pleasure, not necessity, you see, and they like to make it last as long as possible."

Mole's face had lost the flush of a good meal well eaten. Now it fell slack, the grease and gravy accentuated obscenely against the pallor of his skin.

"But it won't come to that," said the Chief, clapping his

hand down on Mole's shoulder so hard that the poor boy jumped. "Your uncle will see to it. Won't you, Jaymes?"

What choice did he have? He nodded. He might not know the boy, but he was family, and he was fucked if he was going to have the wretch's death on his conscience.

"Good! Down to business then." The Chief pushed his platter away from him and pulled his goblet closer. "While you and RibCage were out on your jaunt about town yesterday, news reached me of an interesting occurrence in Out'-Keep beyond the Palace Quarter. A riot, I believe. Do you know what started it?"

Jaymes frowned and shook his head.

"One Audra Academician, according to my eyes and ears." He took a genteel sip of wine. "You know her well, yes? She led your expedition out to the Blasted Glade last season."

"How did you—?" but Jaymes was silenced by a wave of the Chief's hand.

"I know everything. You'd do well to remember that. But that little story of yours is of no relevance to me. What is, however, is the stir she caused."

"I don't understand."

"Of course you don't." The Chief picked up his goblet with one hand. With the other, and with shocking violence, he swept the silver breakfast crockery off the table. The din as it clattered to the floor was terrible. Poor Mole was trying to sink into his own chair.

When the last fork had settled, the Chief spoke again, quite calmly. "That girl could be a considerable source of trouble. Your job today, Jaymes, is to fetch her to me so I can make her a valuable asset instead."

"Why?" said Jaymes. "What do you intend to do to her?"

The Chief grinned. "Oh, dear Mole will find that out for you if you don't do as I say. Now, your Academician still lives up in the library despite her father dying and leaving her that big Academician house of his. Off you go."

"Don't leave me on my own here, Uncle Jaymes," said Mole in a tiny voice.

"Be back before you know it, lad." He looked up at the Chief. "No one touches him while I'm gone."

"You have my word."

Jaymes scowled. Fuck his word, but there was little he could do about it. Little, except bring him the woman who'd got him into this mess in the first place.

CONVINCING the Chief to keep RibCage back at the lair for this job was surprisingly easy. That self-deformed fucker had no way with words. Jaymes simply had to point out that, alone, he'd be able to move about up in the Royal Quarter without a hitch. The barracks were right next to the library and no one would question his being there. RibCage, on the other fucked-up hand, would stand out like a mutilated thumb. Of course, the Chief had his nephew. He'd already demonstrated that he had the oversized stomach for slaying youngsters, so it wasn't as if Jaymes could use the opportunity for escape.

Not that it hadn't crossed his mind.

But where would he escape to anyway? Where could he possibly go that could give him back his life the way it was before Audra came into it? If he had to trade her life for his nephew's, then so be it. He'd gladly hand her over. It was nothing more than she deserved anyway. Let the Chief kill her. After all the deaths she'd caused, it was only fair that someone caused hers. And while the Chief was busy with her, Jaymes would get his nephew out of that rotten place and put him somewhere safe.

It wasn't a great plan. He'd never had to worry about

making plans before, that was Drayke's job. Jaymes had always followed, because that was *his* job. Not a great plan, but a plan nonetheless, and that gave him a purpose. Any purpose was better than trying to find answers for the questions that tormented him. Questions that fucking Audra had burdened him with in the first place.

By the time he reached the palace enclosure a notch or so later, the drizzle had ceased. By the time he reached the entrance to the library his anger at Audra had reached heights that almost frightened him. Scored deep into the white stone above the lintel was the library's maxim, *Healing for the heart and mind*, and he barked out a rough and humourless laugh. What healing had Audra's little book brought his dead comrades? What about those, like him, who should be dead? The Healing Glass was nothing but a lie, and so was the book she'd found it in. So was she. Healing for the heart and mind? Thanks to Audra, Jaymes's heart and mind were totally fucked. Let the Chief have her. She wasn't innocent, but his dead sister's son was. He kicked open the door and stomped in.

The first thing he saw was a cat. Not a very big one, but it was covered in thick, tabby fur that gleamed in the lamplight. It was licking its lips as though it had just eaten the most delicious meal in its life, its pink tongue reaching out and combing through its white whiskers, first one side, then the other. To Jaymes it gave the most withering look of disdain that he'd ever seen on a creature that wasn't an elf or an Academician. It pushed itself up from its seated position and padded over to the base of a marble bust of some dead librarian or other, and jumped with liquid grace onto the top of its head, all the better to glare down at Jaymes with its yellow eyes.

Tutting, Jaymes plodded through the atrium and pushed open the doors to the library proper. This place was as familiar to him as the barracks were, because the first years of any Rebel's life were spent studying. Muscle and strength was what got a man into the famous army. Learning was what kept him there. Jaymes would happily admit that it wasn't his favourite part, but he'd had no especial hatred for it. In fact, there were times, when bruises were fresh and joints were sprained from too much fighting practice, that he found the silent place more restful than the barracks. If Drayke found a new recruit lying on his bunk he'd be kicked out to fulfil some unpleasant task or other, usually involving latrines or middens. Sitting in the library with a book propped in front of him, though, meant he could sit down for a while and let the superficial hurts heal, so long as he read enough to withstand a conversation with the Rebel leader later on about his chosen book.

But not now. Audra had even taken that away from him, because he knew she lurked here, somewhere. The silence grated on his nerves, the air seemed heavy and stale, and the sailing dust motes caught in the shafts of lamplight made him feel itchy.

"Audra!" Fucked if he was going to stand around and wait for her to make the first move in her territory. "Audra!"

"Oi!" a voice hissed. "Pretty sure you ain't s'posed to shout in here."

It wasn't Audra. Unless she'd become a scrawny lad, which he wouldn't put past her, quite frankly. But the lad lacked that look of arrogance that Academicians saved for everyone that wasn't them.

"Who are you?" he said.

"No one you know. Who are you?"

"No one you do."

"Well, then," said the lad. "Seems we've reached the end of our conversation."

"You look more suited to Midden Pit, lad. What you doing up here in the library?"

"You're standing in here judging a book by its cover? I could be heir to one of the great houses in the Financial Quarter for all you know. Probably be wise to show me a bit of courtesy while I'm here reading up the historical importance of my clan."

Jaymes chuckled despite himself. "If you're an elf, I'm a fucking Mage."

The boy paled at that. Seemed his sense of humour had fled. Probably for the best. Jaymes wouldn't want to pass on someone he liked to the likes of the Chief.

"How long you been in here, lad?" he asked.

"Why?"

"I'm looking for someone. Audra. She lives here."

"Ain't seen her."

Jaymes walked forward slowly, looking into each dim aisle of books as he passed it. "I find that difficult to believe, elf. If she weren't here the place'd be locked up tight. And if she knew she had an elvish visitor she'd be only too pleased to spend time with him. She's got a bit of a fondness for the clans. Course, you know that, being from one yourself."

"Look," said the lad, stepping away. "I only came in here to get out of the rain. I ain't seen no one else. What d'you want with her anyway?"

"I don't want anything from her. Other people do. And if you don't give me her, I'll have to give them you. So what's it going to be, lad? You going to speak to me, or them?"

"She's not here, all right?" said the lad, his pale face showing the first signs of fear. "She asked me to keep an eye on the place while she went out and I said I would. That's alls I know, honest."

Jaymes sighed and shook his head. "People who end a sentence with "honest" have usually just told a lie. My dad told me that once, and he was the most dishonest person in all of Kingston, so he should know. How do you know her?"

"Audra?" The lad was looking around like he was trying to find an escape. The only one was the front entrance that lay directly behind Jaymes. The poor tyke wasn't going anywhere. "She...found me lurking in here. Place had been empty for Ages and I was hiding out. Might be full of books, but it's still better than Keep'Out Quarter. I s'pose she took pity on me. Ain't asked me to leave yet."

"You managed to sneak into a locked up library?"

"I was a thief. Sneaked in anywhere, I could," the lad said, a hint of pride in his scared voice.

"And she left you in charge while she went out...where?"

"I don't know! She don't tell me stuff, she just lets me stay here!"

Jaymes had had enough. The lad was clearly lying, but he couldn't understand why. How could Audra command such loyalty from someone? There was something strange going on here but he was too impatient to figure it out. He just wanted to get his nephew out from the clutches of the Chief and both of them away from that Quarter for good. Besides, if this lad was important to her, she had enough power to get him back for herself, didn't she? Maybe she'd even do the lower slopes a good turn in the process and get rid of the Chief for them. Before he could think about it any further, his fist lashed out and struck a fearsome blow on the lad's temple. It lifted him off his feet and deposited him, senseless, a couple of strides away.

"Sorry, lad," he said, bending down to pick him up. Hefting him over his shoulder was no difficult task, he was a bag of skin and bone weighing no more than seven stone. Less than half of what Jaymes himself was. "Nothing personal. It's Audra I've got the grudge against."

The tabby hadn't moved from its spot atop the marble head when he walked back out into the atrium.

"Take that look off your face," Jaymes said to it. "Or I'll take you to the Chief in all."

The cat jumped off the bust and trotted into the library proper before the heavy double doors closed.

"Thought as much," said Jaymes. Then he stepped out into the damp greyness of the afternoon and made his way back down to Keep'Out Quarter.

"*W*hat the fuck are they?" screamed Claws. "Sab! What the fuck are they?"

The panic was clear in her friend's voice, but Sab was a bit too busy making sure the protective dome she'd thrown over them—just in time, thank fuck—stayed in place. The creatures were throwing themselves at it like maniacs with a death-wish. She really had to concentrate.

But there was more to it, she was sure. Just like the barrier earlier felt a bit similar to the 'Sphere's dead zone, there was something more to these creature's attack on her protective dome. It wasn't just physical.

Then Claws's screaming reached fever pitch. "They're coming underneath us! They're coming underneath us!"

Sab looked down. Sure enough, there were fingers, then hands, then arms reaching up through the gritty ground beneath them. Volos stomped down on them, filling the dome with nasty crunching. Prisca joined in, but less gleefully.

"Extend the dome!" she cried out. "Make it a bubble!"

Sab did so, but it took a bit of time. Ground was well-known for its resistance compared to, say, just fresh air. Eventually she completed the sphere, and, apart from their heaving breaths, there was relative calm on the inside again.

"What are they, Sab?" Claws whimpered. She'd buried her face in her hands now. Seemed that just watching these things bashing themselves stupid against the bubble was too much for her.

"I don't know, gorgeous," she said. "Never seen them before. But they're strong little fuckers. Never had to concentrate quite so much on maintaining a spell before."

"Are they...are they like the things that...ate that rhino?" she said.

Sab held her tongue. Why did Claws always think she knew the answer to everything? Besides, if she just looked up from her hands for a second, she'd see that these things were much more humanoid than those critters had been. Sure, they had vicious little teeth, all sharp and pointy, on fine show thanks to their grimaces of rage. And their skin was far more leathery than Sab had ever seen on anyone. But they had two arms, two legs, and covered themselves in a semblance of clothing. If scraps and strips of old and random cloth could be considered clothing. And while their eyes were contorted into various shapes of hate-fuelled anger, there was definitely intelligence in them. No dumb beast could express the level of loathing these creatures did.

Besides, there was something else that was niggling away at the back of her mind. Something to do with the amount of concentration she had to give to maintaining her protective bubble... But she couldn't quite put her finger on it.

"They're elves," Volos rumbled.

"What?" said the three women in perfect unison.

"Elves," said Volos. "Badlands elves. Evil little bastards, every last one of them."

"Oh, so we've levelled-up from scablands to *bad*lands?" said Sab through gritted teeth. "That's nice."

"Elves?" Claws whimpered. "But they're extinct! Everyone knows that!"

"Oh, really?" said Volos. "Then I must be mistaken. We're being attacked by nothing more than a figment of my imagination."

"All right, Volos, give her a break," said Sab. "It's something everyone on the 'Sphere is told. The last of the elves were wiped out in the last great Mage War."

"And who told you that? Your Patriarch? He's a liar."

"Well, obviously," said Sab. "Oh shit it! That's what I'm feeling! Elf magic! Man, it's weird."

"Because it's not real magic," said Volos.

"Riveting discussion, everyone," said Prisca. "But I think our time would be best served figuring a way out of here. We can't stay in this bubble forever."

"Can't we transport again?" said Claws, her voice still muffled by her hands.

"No," said Volos. "All that would do is disperse us inside this bubble. And then all our particles would get mixed up with each other."

"And the second we drop the bubble," Prisca continued, "those...elves'll be all over us."

"It's not possible to cast both spells at the same time?" said Claws. "Like you did earlier when you protected me from the transport spell?"

Prisca grimaced and hissed air in through her teeth. "That was different. Mine and Sabina's magic made sure your particles went back to their proper places after the transport spell. Our spell was simultaneous to Volos's. That's one thing. Trying to cast one spell the instant another has been dropped so that we don't get mauled alive by, well, elves, apparently, is quite another matter."

"Quite the conundrum," said Sab. She was sweating now. Been a long time since she'd sweated from casting a spell. Had she ever? She'd never had enough magic in her for a sustained spell that'd even cause her to sweat. And what the fuck did that matter anyway? There were far more important things to concentrate on. Why was her mind so intent on wandering?

"You know what's weird?" she said aloud in order to keep control of her focus. "I always thought elves were gorgeous, graceful creatures. Not these slavering savages. You seem to know your shit, Volos. What's up with that?"

He sighed. It was more like a growl, but Sab chose to hear it as a sigh. "Because beyond our cities there's nothing but degenerates, I already told you. Whatever the elves used to be hundreds of Ages ago, they're not like that any more. You have other questions, or can I go back to thinking of a way out of here?"

"Just one more question," she said. "Is it exhausting being such a dick all the time?"

"Sabina."

If Sab's eyes weren't squeezed shut with effort she would've rolled them. "Sorry, Prisca," she said instead.

And then it was gone. That awful pressure against her protection bubble was gone. She didn't let it drop just yet, she wasn't that stupid, but it was nice to be able to breathe through her whole mouth instead of just her teeth.

"They're going away!" Claws cried. "Aren't they? They're going away!"

Sab opened her eyes. Certainly looked like it.

"I don't believe it," said Volos. "They're up to something."

"Want to transport right now while we have a second?" said Sab. She was glad to notice that Prisca was already sending some of her magic into Claws in preparation. "Don't think I'm gonna be able to help you this time," she said to her.

"You've done enough, my girl."

"Drop the bubble the instant I say," said Volos.

Sab nodded.

"Now!"

She dropped the bubble.

She felt herself scatter. But now she could see-sense why the elves (really? Elves?) had backed off her bubble. There were...creatures being led to where their bubble had been. She couldn't see-sense if they were magical creatures or not, but they were certainly fuck ugly. About three times the height of the elves even though their frames were hunched and bent. Thinner than a slave corpse, with mops of matted, black hair exploding out of their heads, covering most of their faces. Sab was all right with that. Their bodies were bad enough, she didn't want to see-sense their faces too.

Those bodies, emaciated beyond belief, had normal sized torsos, but ridiculously long arms. Their forearms were far longer than their upper arms, and they used the knobbly knuckles on their hands to help them walk. Their legs were too long too, and Sab couldn't work out if they had two knee joints, or whether that second joint was an ankle at the top of a monumentally long foot. If the latter were the case, then these creatures walked on their toes rather than their feet. Toes which had shockingly long talons at the end of them.

As her being passed overhead one of these creatures, it shrieked, a hideous sound of rage, and flung its too-long arms up at her. Turned out that the thing didn't have fingers after its knuckles, it had blades. It brought its hands together as though to clap, then it interlaced its blade-fingers until they were perpendicular to the backs of its hand. And then... and then it *spun*. A spinning disc of deadly metal came soaring up towards her, and if she'd still had her mouth she would've screamed.

Maybe Volos got a good look at one of those creatures

too, because the next thing Sab sensed-saw, was a dark rushing landscape and a blissful sense of getting away. Far, far away.

Hopefully to safety. But she was beginning to learn that the world out here was just as untrustworthy as her old world inside the 'Sphere.

JENNA

Though Jenna had been in Drayke's company for a couple of notches now, she was suddenly aware of his nearly naked torso. It looked nothing like her husband's. Konrad. That was her husband's name. And his torso was soft and, while not exactly fat, it was definitely wobbly around the edges. Drayke's looked as though it could cut through glass. How did a man get a torso like that? And was the rest of his body the same?

A blush started in the pit of her belly for thinking such thoughts. It was his fault though; he'd sat down so close to her, filling her nostrils with a faint scent of sweat and leather —which wasn't that unpleasant, she was surprised to find— and her eyes with the sharp definition of his trunk. She looked up briefly into his eyes and was rewarded with a sharp glare. She blinked, looked away, and shuffled the papers she still clutched. As comely as his form might be, his face was less so. It was far too angry to be comely.

"You understand the danger we're in, don't you?" he said.

"I'd be fibbing if I said yes," she said. Drayke scowled at her. "But how can I understand? This is all so unlikely. I don't doubt that it's true," she added hurriedly, "but understanding is not the same as believing. We Academicians spend our lifetimes in research, you see, so I find it quite remarkable that this is the first I've heard of it." She held up Drayke's sheaf of papers. "Aside from all the legends, of course."

"Legends come from somewhere," said Drayke.

"Of course they do, but they're legends because the stories and events took place in the past. They're not supposed to be in the present." She frowned, chewing the inside of her cheek while she thought. "We know that five Ages ago, in the Age of Darkness, any records that had been kept were all lost and destroyed—"

"Because of the four Ages of Rebellion, Sacrifice, War and Loss that became before it," said Drayke. "This history is well known to me."

She smiled. Of course it was. That was when his Rebel order was born after all.

"Two Ages ago was the Age of Intellect," she continued, "when the Academicians established themselves in order to record history once more so we wouldn't make the same catastrophic mistakes we had in the past. According to these antique texts, the first sightings of orcs occurred some nineteen hundred years ago in the Age of Nightmares, and their savage attacks continued unabated right up until the Age of Mages, some five hundred years later. Those Mages helped our ancient ancestors build fortified towns so that we'd be safe from orc attacks. The next time we see them is when a plague struck, nearly wiping out all of those who hadn't been killed in rebellion and war."

"The Age of Loss. Nathaniel ScourgeMaster was the Mage who came to our aid—it was his journal that Audra found. His writings led us on our false quest to a Healing Glass which only existed as a means to lure humans into battle with orcs once more."

"But it doesn't make sense. Why would they do that, when in the past they'd been so helpful?"

"What we know of them in the past is only what's been written down," said Drayke. "And I think ScourgeMaster's journal is proof that not all that's written is truth. You said yourself that the Academicians were writing about such events hundreds of years later, when all past documents had been lost. Who's to say what they'd written was correct?"

"There'd be the odd discrepancy perhaps," she said. "But they wrote of wise and helpful Mages, when you say they're blood-thirsty killers. Which is how they described orcs, when you say that's only a symptom of a curable malady called the Rage. How could they have got it so wrong? Oh," she said suddenly, a memory flashing up before her eyes.

"What?"

"It's probably nothing, but I've just recalled my husband's reaction."

"Is it relevant to our current discussion in any way?"

"I'm not altogether sure," she said, ignoring his icy tone. "Konrad knows Audra and I are friends, and he took great pleasure in mocking her when she first told the Academy about the Healing Glass and her mission. Just like everyone else there, really. But when I told him she'd returned he didn't believe me at first. I had to tell him several times that I'd spoken to her that morning. Almost as though her return was the last thing he'd expected. Then he became quite agitated and told me I had to fetch her over to the Academy right away."

"For what reason?" Drayke's icy expression had melted to one of grave interest.

"He didn't say—he stormed out of his laboratory in a very disquieted manner. And he would *never* leave me alone in his lab. I sometimes think he has more love for his equipment and experiments than he does for his family."

"Do you know where he went?"

Jenna shook her head. "He left before I could ask, but I imagine it was to seek out a colleague. Maybe even the Sages."

"And the Sages were found dead this morning after Audra visited them," said Drayke, his face clouding over. "I do not condone her bloody actions, but I think she may have been goaded into her murderous rage. The Prime Minister incited her and she reacted...so the Sages must have said something to her, or done something..." He inflicted the full force of his blue eyes upon Jenna. "I think some of your colleagues know more than others. Your husband included. Come," he said, standing.

"Where are we going?"

"Back to the Academy," said Drayke, taking the papers from Jenna's hand. He stalked across the room and shoved them back under the pillow on his cot. "Your husband wanted you to speak to Audra, but I'd like to speak to *him*. If he expects you to face danger for him, it's only fair that he give you all the information about it, don't you think?"

DRAKE

THE ACADEMICIAN'S fat husband was found easily enough; in his laboratory, where she'd expected him to be. Less expected, to judge from her gaping mouth, was seeing him slumped over a wooden bench, pale jowls jiggling as he mumbled to himself, a jar of liquor clutched in a sweaty fist.

"Konrad," she said. "What are you doing? What are you *drinking*?"

The fat husband howled. Fortunately it was muffled because his head was buried in the crook of his arm on the bench. "I saw what she did! It will haunt me forever! I close my eyes and the image is before them, a spine-chilling sweven that will steal my sleep until my final day!"

Drayke grunted. "Give a man an ale pot and he becomes a balladeer."

The fat husband's head shot up. "I'm a Philosopher, not a Musician," he said with slurred venom.

"You're a disgrace," said Drayke. "You shame your wife and your peers." That earned the Academician a sneer, but at least her fat husband sat up.

"What are you doing here, Rebel?" he said.

"Your wife recounted the circumstances which befell your Sages when you brought Audra to them," said Drayke. "I have some questions for you."

The fat man spluttered. "Me? What could you possibly want to ask me? It's Audra you want! Go and find her!"

"I take my commands from the Prime Minister only," said Drayke. This fat man was foul. He wanted to hit him. "And I will speak to Audra once I understand what I'm dealing with. I have no wish to be turned inside out. It seems a painful way to die."

The fat husband covered his face with his hands and moaned.

"So you will tell me what I need to know," continued Drayke, "and you will tell me quickly and honestly."

"Ask your questions then, Rebel," he said, "but my wife knows Audra better than I do. Perhaps you should interrogate her instead of an innocent man."

"What knowledge of the Mages have the Academicians suppressed?"

The Academician gasped in shock, which Drayke ignored. The fat husband spluttered and scoffed a false denial, which he didn't. Two steps and he was at the bench. His fingers grabbed a fistful of white robes and hauled the fat husband to his feet. Orc's balls, but he was heavy. The muscles along his arm contracted, as well as those across his back and torso. He even had to engage his legs to bear the weight. How could the Academician suffer to marry such a lump?

"You know something about her," Drayke said, relieved that the strain didn't show in his voice, "and you will tell me. Otherwise *I* will turn you inside out, and without magic I expect it will take longer, be more distressful, and last far longer than anything Audra conjured on your Sages. Now speak."

"I know nothing except what I overheard, I swear it!"

Drayke dropped the fat husband back onto his stool, and he scrabbled at his bench to keep himself from toppling over. Drayke tutted in disgust. "Tell me what you overheard."

But the fat man was sneering at his wife. "You stand by and watch this Rebel abuse me? Shame on you!"

Drayke smashed his fist on the bench, scattering glass containers. "Speak!" he roared.

The fat man whimpered, but at least his eyes were back on Drayke. "I overheard the Sages! When the Prime Minister arrived with his entourage it caused a stir here—the Prime Minister never visits the Academy unless there's a special public lecture. He told the Sages that Audra had found a cure to the Plague and that she must be allowed to join his Rebels in the search for it. They agreed without debate, which surprised me. When the Prime Minister left, I heard them say that it was the perfect way to be rid of Audra because she'd never come back. She wasn't supposed to come back, that's all I know, I swear it!"

"Why did the Sages want rid of her?" asked Drayke. He hadn't liked Audra on their first meeting but he hadn't ever wished harm on her. He'd even put his own life at risk when he saved her from the burning barn in that strange, unmapped village they'd stopped at. The memory released a complex slew of sentiments about her, so he dammed it up before he was flooded by them. "Why wasn't she supposed to come back?"

The fat husband's mouth twisted in contempt. "She's a disgrace to the Academy. Her researches make a mockery of this great institution. I hypothesised that the Sages wanted rid of her because they feared she'd become her mother."

"Konrad!" said the Academician, scandalised.

"That woman was insane and all knew it," said the fat husband with disdain. "And with the researches she carried out, Audra was evidently on the same road to madness."

The Academician looked as though she were ready to cry while the fat husband was huffing and puffing from the exertion of his contempt. Drayke was grateful that the Rebel order kept him from such relationships and their petty hatreds.

"Did you hear the Sages give that as their reason for getting rid of her?" he said.

"No," said the fat husband sullenly. "But it's obvious."

"How could they know she wouldn't come back?" said the Academician, though Drayke barely heard, her voice was so small.

"What kind of question is that?" spat the fat husband.

"A good one," said Drayke. "If the Prime Minister had only come to the Sages with news of the Healing Glass that day, how would they know Audra wouldn't return?" And all the Rebels who accompanied her, and the little lord and lady from the most powerful elvish clan. But matters were already complicated enough. "What knowledge had they already? Speak!"

The fat husband jolted. "I don't know! She wasn't meant to return, that's all I heard!"

"How?" said the Academician. Both men's eyes swivelled

towards her. She was frowning with thought. "If the meeting was conducted in the dome, how did you hear even that?"

Drayke looked back at the fat husband, and his pale jowls had blushed pink.

"You're a Historian, not a Philosopher," he said. "You wouldn't understand even if it were your business. Which it isn't."

So the fat one had been spying on the dead ones. Drayke cared little for that, but he was annoyed he hadn't gleaned more useful information from the misconduct. Whatever the Sages knew about the Healing Glass, they'd been willing not only to squander Audra's life, but also those of his comrades. Many of his comrades hadn't come back. Except those who'd fought at the Blasted Glade. They'd died, he'd died too, but... No. Now wasn't the time to dwell on that.

And Audra came back to Kingston. She'd come back changed. Whatever the Sages' plan had been, it had failed.

He turned back to the Academician. "Audra believed she'd discovered new information in the Mage's journal, but the Sages knew better," he said. "We need to find out what they knew. Regrettably they're unable to help us now." The fat husband whimpered but Drayke ignored him. "Where do you people store your researches?"

"It's all written up in books and stored in the library," she said. "Those deemed worthy for publication, at least. But if anything was there, Audra would have read it and known about it. She's read practically everything in that library. She knows it better than anyone."

Drayke nodded, disappointed. "Where else do you store your knowledge?"

She shook her head and shrugged. "If a submitted paper is deemed unsatisfactory by the Sages, it's destroyed and remains unpublished. There are approved texts currently being written by the scribes, but they would be newer researches…" she trailed off, her eye caught by her fat husband. "Do you know something else?"

Drayke swung around to glare at him. "Tell me!"

"I know nothing else," he whispered, looking at his wife with fury. "The only person who knows what the Sages did is Audra. Perhaps you should do as I told you in the first place and go and speak to her!"

Drayke scowled and slammed his fist on the bench again. He wanted to reach up, pull his axe from his back and stick it in the side of the fat man's head, but Rebels were prohibited from cutting down unarmed civilians for no good reason. Obnoxiousness wasn't considered a good reason, unfortunately.

"We'll speak again," he growled into the man's flabby face. Then he marched away towards the door.

"Where do you think you're going?" he said. Drayke turned, but the fat husband was talking to his wife.

"I'm going with him," she said.

"You've no business cavorting with Rebels. Your place is here at the Academy."

Drayke stepped forward. "She's needed if I'm to clean up the mess your Sages created," he said. "She's the least useless Academician I've come across and her knowledge is useful."

The fat husband scoffed. "*Her* knowledge? Don't forget how you came to be here, Jenna," he spat at her. "Take her then. And good riddance to you both!"

Drayke closed the door behind them before he'd even finished his remark.

"*W*hat the fuck," said Sab, when her body was fully whole again, "were those *things*?"

"Those long, thin people?" said Claws. "Were they even people? They looked scarier than the elves."

"I've never seen the like before," said Prisca, a deep frown creasing her brow. "Volos?"

He shook his head. Not that he'd ever admit to such a thing, but Sab could tell he was shaken. His skin looked paler and clammier than usual, even under all that hair.

"Not far to go now," he said. "The entrance to the train is just down that valley."

Sab followed his finger. The gritty badlands had been replaced with rocks. Everywhere. Some small and throwable, but most were mountains. Or the foothills at least. It was pretty difficult to tell in the faded light.

"Can't we wait until morning?" she said.

"Seriously?" said Volos. "After everything we just saw?"

She rolled her eyes. "Yeah. All right. Let's go."

It wasn't a difficult climb down, mostly because Sab pretty much slipped all the way. There must have been rain here recently because the ground was wet, making it difficult for her tatty, worn-out boots to grip. Especially when bits of stone came loose the moment she set foot on them. But they reached the bottom of the valley without encountering any more monsters, and for that Sab was grateful.

"So, how far to these famous mountains then? What are they called?"

"The Impassable Mountains," said Prisca.

"Yeah, them. How far till we reach them?"

"We're already there," said Volos.

Sab blinked. All right, so it was dark, but you'd expect a thundering great mountain range to be visible. She threw up another ball of light.

"Shit on a stick," she breathed.

"Language," whispered Prisca, but she was looking up too. So far up, in fact, that she was almost bending over backwards.

"Impassable's a good name for them," said Claws.

Volos just harrumphed.

It wasn't as though Sab knew precise distances, but she knew that those balls of light flew high up into the sky. Like, *really* high. And when they did their silent explosion, they'd light up the place from horizon to horizon. That was the point of them, after all. To give you a bit of daylight when the darkness was all around.

But all around them now was just mountains. Grey rock, from horizon to horizon, and so high even the sky was blocked out. She shouldn't be surprised, it was right there in the name, but still… Knowing something and seeing it right up close so that nothing else was visible was another thing entirely.

"And a Mage did this," she said, neck aching from twisting it around in so many unnatural angles.

"Well, not just one, but yes," said Prisca. "Mages did this."

"And there's a train here?" said Claws, disbelief very evident in her voice.

"Not far," said Volos. "Follow me."

He led them through an impossible labyrinth of stone corridors and gullies and ledges and tracks that descended and dropped, twisted and doubled back on themselves.

"How do you even know where we're going?" said Sab. "You've done a Game, have you?"

"No," he said. "I just know."

"That's why I love these chats," said Sab. "You always teach me something new."

Volos ignored her. But it occurred to Sab that she could make out the thick, curly hair on his arms a little better now than before. Eyes becoming accustomed to the night?

No. Probably something to do with that faint green glow that seemed to come from…somewhere.

Then they turned a corner and Sab was confronted with a sight so startling she actually stumbled. "No fucking way," she said.

Glowing there, on the side of a mountain where it looked unreal and out of place, was a green portal. There was no other word for it. Circular, its shimmering surface undulating like a vast cloak in a stiff breeze, and surrounded by a coppery frame, it was definitely an exit out of this world and the entrance into another. A portal.

"Train's through there," said Volos, not even an ounce of awe in his voice.

But it wasn't just the unfeasibility of such a thing that gobsmacked Sab. It was the fact that she'd seen it before. Quite recently, in fact.

"This is what they showed me," she whispered.

"What are you talking about?" said Volos, but Sab turned to Prisca and shook her arm.

"The grey sisters," she said, "they showed—"

"Stop," said Prisca. And Sab did, because the command was so unexpected.

"But the—"

"No."

She huffed in frustration. "But this is what I—"

"Sab, for fuck's sake, just stop talking!" hissed Claws. "Why can't you ever take a hint? We ain't supposed to talk about it, so just stop fucking talking!"

"What's going on with you three?" said Volos. "What are you talking about?"

Sab, much to her surprise, was speechless.

"Nothing," said Prisca. "Time to go. Maybe we'll win this stupid race after all." And she marched off towards the portal that the grey sisters had definitely shown Sab in her vision, although her friends wouldn't let her point that out to them, for some peculiar reason.

"What were you talking about?" said Volos once Prisca had passed him.

"I really want to tell you," said Sab, "but Claws is right behind me. And I gotta tell you, Volly, those two scare me a bit when they gang up."

Claws snuffed an unamused chuckle onto the top of Sab's head.

Volos scowled up at her, but didn't press. He simply spun away and stalked on after Prisca.

"Well if we can't talk about what I actually want to talk about," said Sab once they were picking their way through the maze of boulders again. "Can I tell you about something else?"

"What?" said Claws.

"Those two," said Sab, gesturing with her head to where Prisca and Volos couldn't be seen because the stony path was too bendy.

"What about them?"

"Dunno, something though. I heard them talking earlier—way back before the fire-breathing puffballs. You know, I think there was something going on between them once."

Claws burst out laughing, stopped pretty quickly when she realised Sab was serious. "No. Why would you even think that?"

"Because," she hissed, hoping they wouldn't catch up with the other two before she got this mad gossip out. "I heard him say to her that they were supposed to be mates. He's jealous that Prisca got sent off to the 'Sphere to be with another Mage."

"What? But she isn't with another Mage. She's down in Stratus with us."

"Yeah, all right, there's that to think about later—but Claws! He was all whiny about the fact she never got in touch with him after she left Oceanwall."

"Volos?"

"Uh huh."

"Whiny?"

"Yep."

"Because of Prisca?"

"Right."

"So, what? He's in love with her, or something?"

"I don't fucking know, but it's weird, right? I mean, he's a hairy, clammy mountain of a Mage. And Prisca's all…proper. You know?"

"More like he's mean and cruel and horrible to mutants. But Prisca's a mother to everyone."

"If you like. But it *is* weird, isn't it? It's not just me, is it?"

"No, it's weird," said Claws after a moment of thinking. "Why would her mum and dad set her up with their pet Mage and then send her off somewhere else?"

"That's not the weird part I was referring to."

"If you girls stopped gossiping, you wouldn't have kept us

waiting," said Prisca, suddenly appearing in the green glow. It was pretty bright now, this close to the portal. Sab really shouldn't have missed her. "What were you gossiping about?"

"Nothing," said Sab.

"Nothing," said Claws, a split second after.

"You're both liars, but it'll have to wait," she said. "Ready to board the train?"

"Fuck yeah," said Sab.

"Language."

"These mountains are doing my head in," she finished.

"Then stop wasting time," growled Volos. "After you."

She flipped her middle finger up at him, then said, "Claws, I better load you up with some more protection. That's a lot of magic making up that portal."

Claws stepped closer, grabbed Sab by the hand. When Sab was satisfied that Claws's component parts wouldn't be smeared across the mountainside once she neared the undulating green, she turned to Prisca and said, "See you on the other side."

Then, with Claws matching her every step, she stepped up the little bronze stairs leading to the rim and climbed through.

It felt like the sound *gloop*. That was the only way she could describe it. Not unpleasant exactly, but it had the distinct possibility of getting very uncomfortable if she stuck around in it.

But it was over in a couple of seconds. And on the other side...well.

On the other side, it did *not* look like the mountains any more.

You'd think that, right inside the belly of a mountain, it'd be dark and, well, really stony. But no. On the other side of that portal it was bright, clean—luxurious, even. Oh, they were definitely still *inside*. But the space was immense. And it looked like the underside of those mountains were gold-veined marble. The whole vastness of the place twinkled from hidden lights, although ripples of green from the portal still painted the odd surface. Either somebody had done one hell of refurbishing job in here, or it was all glamour. Magic washed over her, but it was difficult to know if it came from everywhere, or just the portal.

And that was just the surroundings.

Ahead of them was the train. In her mind, Sab had expected something not too dissimilar to the capsule that got them off the 'Sphere. But this vehicle in front of them was no capsule. It was long and cylindrical, as shiny white as the surroundings on its lower half, smoky glass on its top half. It hovered just above a smooth groove in the floor, and every now and then Sab caught a cyan crackle of magic between the groove and the train, which was obviously its source of locomotion.

Claws whistled through the hole in her cheek. "Fuck me," she said.

"Right?" said Sab.

"Well don't just stand there," said Volos, walking past them and on towards the train.

"I'm glad you got through all right," Prisca said to Claws, cupping her hands on her cheeks. She stepped across to Sab. "Thank you, petal."

Sab shrugged a shoulder. "Right. Well, let's get our arses to Taurë, shall we?"

Volos reached the train first. There were no obvious doors to be seen, but when he reached out and touched it, one appeared. A rhombus-shaped hole that was suddenly there, as though it had always been, with flashing green lights around it. A sleek slope slid out from the bottom, inviting them to step aboard.

He waited for the three women to enter, then he stepped

up last. When Sab turned around, the door had already gone, replaced with a marblesque wall and dainty light fixtures.

The whole carriage was long and well-lit, with comfortable sofas and divans scattered about it, fully loaded with blankets and cushions. Expensive vases crammed with fresh flowers decorated finely carved tables that were only big enough for said vases, and across the marble floor, deep-pile rugs were casually strewn. Only vast wealth could conjure up this kind of laid-back luxury.

"Well, at least we'll be able to catch up on our sleep," said Prisca, the first one brave enough to break the awed silence.

"Shouldn't we try to find out how to make this thing go, first?" Claws whispered.

Volos grunted, then stomped off towards the front of the train. Sab decided it was the front, because where they'd got on, there hadn't been anything that looked like a control panel.

The walk through this carriage was long, probably because of its astonishing grandeur but also sameness. Was it possible to get bored of decadence? Sab was a Stratian, living out her whole life in the shittiest level of the 'Sphere, hating on those Mages above her who jealously guarded their level from the ones below. She'd dreamt of luxury. She didn't think she'd ever find it boring. But perhaps that was what the mind did when it couldn't really comprehend what it was experiencing.

Eventually, though, they came to a section that definitely looked like it controlled the train. The panels of flashing lights were a dead giveaway. But there was also something else here that hadn't been evident in the rest of the train.

Or rather, some*one* else.

"The train comes with a driver?" said Sab.

The someone, who'd clearly been engrossed in all the flashing lights and buttons of the control panels, spun around at her voice, lost his balance a little because of the stuffed backpack on his back. It was a young someone, a young man. Although age and gender didn't really mean anything to a Mage. They changed themselves with a thought. Mouth dropping open, eyes growing wider though… Didn't really look like someone who expected passengers.

"No," Volos grunted. "*Who* the *fuck* are *you*?"

He did his best angry scowl and his best threatening loom. It worked a treat on the young Mage, who seemed to shrink down inside himself.

"I-I-I-" he said. Gulped. Took a couple of steadying breaths.

Sab rolled her eyes. "You gave it too much, Volly," she said, pushing him out of the way. "Hi there," she said, smiling brightly. "Name's Sab, these are all my friends. Don't mind Volos. We haven't fully trained him yet. What's your name, buddy?"

The Mage blinked at her, seemed to calm down now that he wasn't faced with a hairy, clammy giant. Wow. First time Sab had ever seen a Mage that wasn't squirting arrogance out of every pore.

"Hello," he said, trying out a smile. It still looked manic, but he was getting there. "I-I'm not trying to steal your train, I swear."

"Never said you were," said Sab, still smiling. "Just want to know your name, so that we can all be friends."

He actually breathed a sigh of relief. "Oh. All right. Great. Well, my name's Jason. And I've really got to get to Taurë. Something bad's happening there."

AUDRA

*D*espite the blackness she can still hear their shouting, their calls of anger. Their hatred flows from them like lava—slowly, reticent because they're afraid as well as angry, but if it were to reach her she would be swallowed up and burnt to cinders. The pain would be unbearable.

The pain.

She feels it. Eating through her entire being. Melting her skin. Burning her bones. Boiling her blood. And it hurts! Skies above, it hurts more than her mind can understand!

AUDRA FORCED HER EYES OPEN, hearing her ragged breathing and feeling the sweat pour from her in seething torrents. Fingers of panic clawed at her heart—what was happening to her? She tried to focus her thoughts but the pain batted them away, like an angry parent to an unwanted child.

Her eyes swivelled wildly in her head and she forced herself to take note of what they saw; a pale ceiling, walls covered with sheets of paper, themselves covered with writhing scribbles. She knew this place, she told her panic, she knew it and it was safe. If the fingers would only leave her heart she would be able to catch the memory...

A room. Her room. This was her room. And that meant she was in the library. The library was a safe place, she told her panic, there was no shouting here. No mother. No anger, no hatred, only books. Safe books. Beloved books. No one would hurt her here.

Her breathing softened, her heart settled down, and she relished the feeling of it. Her body still ached ferociously but at least her mind was under control once more. Gritting her teeth and whimpering only a little, she pushed herself up onto her elbows, then to a seated position. She was in her bed, her blankets soaked and twisted around her legs. Only a nightmare? But if that were the case, why was she in such pain?

She closed her eyes and nudged her mind back to the last time she was awake.

Squirrel had been there. Afraid before she was. Her mind threatened to unweave again when she remembered the fear but she grasped the fingers of panic before they got to work. He'd been afraid, yelling at her to get them out. Out of where? They were outside already. They were outside on the north-western slopes of Out'Keep...and she'd found an ancient royal building, yes! A magnificent old hunting lodge that had fallen into ruin but she'd restored it to glory. And then she'd saved the prostitutes from the licentious men and regenerated the whole area with fresh grass and ripening fruit trees and flourishing plants.

A moment of pride cooled her sweating brow, until she remembered what came after. They hadn't been pleased. None of the inhabitants were thankful for her help. They'd killed a man. They would have killed her and Squirrel. That's why he'd bellowed for her to get them out.

Now she remembered. She'd used her magic to get them out. She didn't know how, but that's what had happened. Flashes of imagery returned to her. Squirrel's anguished face looking down at her. Movement beneath her body as she was pulled into her room. Blackness creeping in at the edge of her vision as exhaustion took her.

And now the pain. This she couldn't fathom, for she'd returned them both to the library before the mob beset them. So why such agony?

Because she'd used up a great deal of power. The answer came to her, sudden and obvious, like knowing it was morning because dawn had broken. She'd been weakened after her confrontation with the Sages before their life essence restored her, but she'd ignored it; this pain, however, wouldn't be ignored. It snapped at her, as the hungry wolf snaps at the deer. It wouldn't stop until it had fed.

She groaned, a pathetic sound deep in her throat. Unlike the wolf, there was only one thing her magic wanted to eat.

"I can't," she whispered, disentangling her legs from the blankets and placing her feet on the floor. The rug beneath her bed scratched at her naked soles, but she knew the cold flagstones of the room would be a balm. Grimacing, she heaved herself up until she stood, the room and all its sparse furniture tipping wildly. She closed her eyes, clutched at her belly, waited until everything settled once more. Pain and nausea—was this the price of having the power to change everything for the better?

No, came the sly reply from her mind. The price is much, much greater than that. You know it. You've done it already, you can do it again.

"They deserved to die," she whispered behind closed eyes. "They deserved it. Not everyone does."

But everyone dies. Eventually. Why not make use of it? Use it and feel better. Use it and change the world.

Audra sobbed. This wasn't a conversation she wanted right now. Perhaps all she needed was food and good strong black-tea. She opened her eyes the tiniest crack, and once she saw the room was still, she opened them fully. Daylight filled the small space and stabbed needles into her head. She shuffled across the rug, feeling the razor sharpness of the textile with every step. She pushed her body forwards even though every movement shattered bone and tore flesh.

Finally she reached the flagstones and she could have wept for the coolness of them. Walking became a fraction easier, but it still took an Age for her to reach the kitchen. Another Age to prepare the tea; yet another to bring bread, butter and honey from the pantry and put it on the table. When she sat down on a stool her body was trembling as though she'd undertaken intense physical labour, which only added to her discomfort. She drank and ate ravenously, and while it made her feel a little better, it didn't take away her pain. Maybe she ought to take her mind off it by talking to someone. Squirrel. he might even be able to give her some counsel towards easing her pain. He certainly couldn't know any less than she did.

"Squirrel." She'd intended to call out, but all she managed was a broken rasp.

It caught the attention of someone though. Not Squirrel; Mouse. The scrawny mog trilled a greeting as he poked his head around the kitchen door, rubbed his cheek against it a few times, then strode fully into the room, purring like a thunderstorm.

"Ready for breakfast, are you?" she said with a wan smile. Yesterday it had pleased her that she was beginning to learn the cat's personality traits—overt friendliness and almost bird-like trilling meant he wanted food—but today she was too tired.

In response to her question, Mouse sprung up onto the

table, found the fresh pat of butter and set to it with great relish. Also yesterday, Audra would have reprimanded him and pushed him off the furniture. Today she barely had the strength to keep looking at him.

Until one hand whipped out and caught up the cat by his scruff while the other grabbed the bread knife. Within in a blink she'd opened up Mouse from neck to belly, his intestines snaking out to land wetly on the table, spattering the bread with gore, while a dark crimson puddle pooled before her.

Instantly the pain lessened and she breathed a happy sigh behind closed eyes, purposely ignoring the voice in her mind that told her it wouldn't be enough.

Then she opened her eyes, took in the destruction before her and screamed.

HE'D KNOW it was her. He'd come home from wherever he'd been and know it was her who killed his beloved cat. How could he not? Only they two lived in the library. Not even other Academicians knew there was a living space under-neath it, let alone any of the public. It would break his heart —skies above, he'd named the creature after his dead mother! —and then he'd be angry and there was no knowing what he'd do to her if she lost control. He was as powerful as she was, she knew that from his aura. He could destroy her with a thought.

The air was thick with drizzle, the streets slick with it, but she paid it no mind. Her only concern was to get away from the library, far enough away so that Squirrel couldn't immediately find her, so that she had time to think about what to say to him. What to do.

What to do...

Her stomach dropped. What she should've done was

clean up the mess she'd made. If she hadn't given in to her panic and run away then she would've come to that decision at a vastly more appropriate moment. Instead, she'd scarpered out of the library, past the palace and out towards the King's Gate before her mind started functioning again. She should go back. She should go back and clean up the mess she'd made, before Squirrel came back to see it. Although she had no notion of where he could be, the lad used to be a thief in his old life. Perhaps it was customary for him to spend the day outdoors. It certainly wasn't normal for him to spend his days cooped up in the library. Obviously then, while she was sleeping, he'd taken the opportunity to take to the streets. Perhaps reignite past acquaintanceships. Audra would have plenty of time to tidy up before he returned.

She cursed herself bitterly—why had she done that to Mouse? The poor creature was innocent of anything, save his constant pilferage of food. It wasn't her fault! The memory of her waking agony was still fresh in her mind, howling like an angry mob; surely Squirrel would understand when she explained. He would understand why she'd needed to kill his blameless cat.

In an agony of indecision, she dithered out of the drizzle under the boughs of a giant oak, just one of the hundreds that surrounded the palace enclosure, so that those at the very pinnacle of society wouldn't have to see the fence that protected them from the commoners. Eyes as rich and powerful as theirs should only ever have to look upon things of beauty.

Audra's own eyes were drawn to the palace. Even in ugly weather it shrieked its beauty and splendour. And inside was a cluster of creatures who certainly weren't as innocent as poor Mouse had been, for they had been responsible for creating the Kingston City Audra now lived in, shaping it to

suit their whims and wants, while those on the lower slopes
struggled just to survive. She'd vanquished the Sages for
allowing Nathaniel ScourgeMaster to decimate the population, her father included, in order to play their Game, but the
Ministers were safe from harm in their resplendent palace.
Why shouldn't they be used to help her build a better city?
They were as much to blame for the iniquity as the Sages
were. Besides, those bloated bodies would give her freedom
from pain for an Age, no doubt. It was evident to her that
such pain only caused her to lash out and injure anyone,
which wasn't how she wanted to behave. The innocent had
suffered enough under the tyranny of the city's rulers and
she'd vowed to make it better for them. If anyone had to
sacrifice themselves for the benefit of the city, it should be
those who'd taken advantage of it for their own selfish ends
without care or thought for others. The Ministers in their
palace were no different from the Sages in that respect.
Moreover, keeping them bound and alive in there was
undoubtedly using a constant supply of her power. The
quicker she was rid of them, the better it'd be for all.

Her mind finally made up, she stepped out from underneath her shelter and headed towards the palace.

But the unexpected surge of power halted her.

She gasped. It wasn't coming from the palace. Her body
turned without instruction from her mind, as though it knew
before she did. It was coming from King's Gate. Beyond the
King's Gate. The lower slopes where she and Squirrel had
been only yesterday. She ran. Evidently something terrible
had happened, someone had died, but not because of her. She
could reap the benefits of another's ill deed. She shouldn't be
this thrilled about that, but she was.

The fence surrounding the palace enclosure was
unguarded now that the Rebels were down in Out'Keep,
actually putting their brawn to good use. Soon enough, she

was on King's Route, racing through the least populated quarter of Kingston, where past kings walked their queens through meticulous gardens, past majestic fountains, and along charming pathways. The common people had to cram themselves on to the lower slopes, but that didn't matter so long as the ancient kings had plenty of space. Audra promised herself that this would be rectified along with all the other injustices of the city.

But first she had to feed.

Feed? No. That was absolutely *not* what she meant. She was merely going to investigate the cause of the power surge in Out'Keep. Something which, distressingly, didn't take too long once King's Gate was in sight.

For the first time in her memory, the gate was closed and heavily defended by countless city guards and a handful of Rebels, all of whom seemed to be simultaneously ferocious and confused. Rammed against the ornate and gilded iron-work of King's Gate were Out'Keep inhabitants. The noise was atrocious, mostly she heard the angered ranting of the very people she'd tried to help yesterday, but all too often it was punctured by a squeal of agony, and below it all were the groans of those too broken to do more. Those people unfortunate enough to be at the front were disturbingly silent, their heads and faces slack, eyes unseeing but bulging from their sockets at the immense pressure coming from behind.

Walking now, she approached a city guard who was doing nothing but shifting from foot to foot while his gaze was fixed on the scene.

"What's happening here?" she said.

"No idea, miss," he said without turning to look at her. "Apparently there was a riot. They managed to shut the gate in time, but… I was only sent as back-up. Why won't they go back? Can't they see they're killing themselves?"

"What caused the riot?"

"No one knows. No one can speak to them. I don't understand why they won't go back."

Audra walked away from him, not that he noticed, and moved closer to the gate. There must have been a dreadful number of people crushing themselves to death for she could feel life-force replenish her own, strong as a punch, more welcome than a kiss. She had to do something for them. The guards and Rebels were useless. But what could she do? If she didn't know why they were rioting, she couldn't help them.

Money. The memory hit her as forcefully as the power surge. They'd been angered by her replenishment of their quarter because, even though they'd been literally living in a rubbish heap, that's how they made their money. When she'd cleaned it all away, she'd taken away their livelihoods, such as it had been.

The Worthy Clan's fortune! She'd removed it from beneath their noses and put it somewhere. It was bound to be...around. She made another mental note to find out precisely how this power worked. For now, however, she needed to concentrate on all those piles of gold coins and make them...

...Rain down over the King's Gate Quarter. She smiled. That seemed to work. And she couldn't deny it brightened up the grey day when a little gold coin suddenly winked into existence about head height and tumbled over and around before hitting the ground. She'd had the wherewithal to focus the golden rain some distance behind the crush at the gate, away from King's Route, and it took a little while for people to notice what was happening. But when they did, the calls of anger turned to squeals of delight. Within a few heartbeats the gate was all but clear.

Unfortunately, that was when the death toll became awfully apparent. Those that had been pressed up against the iron bars fell back or slipped down to join the many hundreds that were littered over the ground in different aspects of self-protection, but nothing could withstand the heavy crush of humanity that had borne down on them. A sob burned Audra's throat even as tears burned her eyes, for a treacherous part of her mind told her that this was her fault.

It also told her that she could save them if she wished it.

"I do wish it," she whispered to herself. "No more death."

Now that the crowd had dispersed and the air beyond King's Gate was hazy with cascading gold coins, the Rebels and city guards had lost all discipline and were simply staring through the bars or around at each other. No one paid her any mind as she jogged to the gate. She almost had it open before a man's hand on her wrist stopped her. Her eyes tracked the length his naked arm and up to his face. It was one she knew very well.

"Calum," she said.

"Leave them be," he said.

"But I can help them. You know I can."

"Leave them *be*. They're dead. They should stay dead."

"But it was needless, it was—" she was halted, but not by any words. It was his eyes. There was something in them that... No, not in them. It was more like something was missing from them. Despite her great power, she was afraid.

"You did this," he whispered, and she knew he wasn't talking about the riot. She shrugged herself from his grasp, turned and ran back to her library.

The day was getting darker, the rain heavier. Both mirrored her heart. Needless death she still couldn't bear. But some would have to die. Otherwise *she* would.

SABINA

*W*hat started out as a shocked silence turned into such a long pause that even Sab was beginning to feel awkward.

The Mage calling himself Jason (and what kind of a name was *that*?) kept looking at each of them in turn, his face getting redder by the second, massively uncomfortable by the four pairs of astonished eyes glaring at him.

The Mage called Jason swallowed and Sab heard his throat click. She was fascinated by his distress. You didn't often see it on a Mage.

"Honestly," he said. Whispered, really. His eyes darted about as though seeking out ways to escape. "Something b-bad is happening. Going to happen. Has happened. Um." He breathed in a shuddering breath. "This isn't another G-Game is it? Have I stumbled into a Game? But no, that doesn't make any sense, one just ended. But you're Mages, aren't you? You have to be, otherwise you wouldn't know about the train. So why aren't you—?"

Finally, Prisca stepped forward, hands raised in a placating gesture. "Jason," she said. "Jason, you said?"

The young Mage nodded.

"This isn't a Game, no," she said.

"Tell him nothing," Volos growled.

Prisca swivelled her eyes around to him. It seemed to convey everything she wanted to say, because Volos grumbled an assent. She turned back to Jason. "It's just that...we really weren't expecting anyone else to be here."

"Nor was I!" said Jason.

"Can you tell us what you're doing here?" she said.

"It's such a long story," he said, sagging his shoulders but creasing up his face. "But when the Game ended... Look, there's a New Born human in Taurë and something bad's going to happen. I n-need to get there."

"Why's it so important to you? *Jason*." Sab wanted him to know that she knew that Jason wasn't his real name.

"Because," he said, clearly floundering for what to say next. "She's a *New Born*. And also, one of the Mages from the Game was Messina. She was my m-mother."

Wow. Okay. So *that* was unexpected.

"Messina was your mother?" said Prisca.

"So, what? You're a Cirrun?" said Sab.

"You want your revenge?" said Volos.

There was another pause while Jason looked between them, probably deciding which question to answer first. Sab was sorely tempted to send out a tendril of magic to find out for certain who this Jason was, but it would be so obvious at such close quarters. She didn't really care if this Jason thought she was shockingly rude, but she didn't want the subsequent lecture that Prisca would give her if she tried something like that. Besides, he hadn't tried to find out who they were either. Say what you like about Cirruns (massively arrogant thundercunts, said Sab's hindbrain), but they were all up in that honour shit.

"Really, it's such a long story," Jason repeated. "Can't I explain everything to you once we get going?"

Volos barked out a laugh that contained precisely zero humour. "You can't possibly think we're going to take you on your word, do you?"

"Why not?" asked Jason, genuinely surprised by the look of him.

"Because we're Mages," said Volos. "We can't be trusted."

Sab caught the flicker of his eyes towards Prisca, but she didn't think her old friend had.

Jason rubbed his hands across his face. "All right, fine. Yes. Yes to all three. Yes, she's my mother. Yes, I'm a Cirrun. And yes, I want r-revenge. She's a New Born human, isn't she? You can't tell *me* you're taking the train to Taurë to welcome her into the family."

"No, we're racing another bunch of Mages to see who can kill her first," said Claws.

"A race? What *race?*" Jason's eyes boggled.

But not as much as Sab's, Prisca's and Volos's.

"I said—"

"I know what you said, Volos," said Claws, staring at the floor. "But you're all being ridiculous. We all want to go to Taurë, don't we? Then let's just go. It ain't like you can kill each other, is it? And if this Jason person wants to find her too," she flung a hand in his direction but still didn't look up, "then he can help us. End result is still the same. He ain't part of the race. If we get there first, we'll still win. Fuck's sake, you Mages can be such dicks sometimes."

Sab burst out laughing. Then she pulled her friend down so she could kiss her forehead.

Still no one spoke. Sab rolled her eyes. "Well, she's not wrong, is she?"

"But we—"

"Volly, Volly, Volly," said Sab, reaching up to put a hand

on his shoulder. "There's four of us and one of him. And if that's still not enough for you, send out a bit of magic and find out what he's about, if that'll ease your mind."

Volos looked horrified at the suggestion. She grinned up at him.

"You can if you like," said Jason. "I've got n-nothing to hide."

"See?" said Sab. "He's offering. Can't be rude if someone's offering."

Volos sucked his teeth and shrugged her hand off his shoulder. "Let's go," he said.

"Hooray!" said Sab. She spun around and winked at Claws. "Well done, gorgeous."

"You know how to work the train?" Jason said to Volos.

The hairy giant bent to loom over Jason, so Sab tugged at his sleeve, grabbed hold of Claws with her other hand, and pulled them both into the carriage proper.

"Our dear friend doesn't like to be bested," Sab whispered. "So best just let him get on with it."

She pushed Jason down onto an obscenely overstuffed armchair, squatted down in front of him so he couldn't take his backpack off, rested her forearms on his knees. People always got awkward around her skinless arms. Awkward people generally had difficulty lying.

"So, Jason," she continued, her gaze unflinching and unblinking. "Can I?"

"Use your magic to test me?" he said. "Of course. I've got—"

"Nothing to hide, yeah, you said. Genuinely innocent people rarely say shit like that though."

"Train activated," came an androgynous voice from everywhere at once.

Sab didn't break her gaze. Neither did Jason.

"Oh good," said Claws in a monotone. "He got it to work."

"If it will make you feel better," said Jason, "use your magic. I don't m-mind."

Sab cocked her head, allowed her gaze to travel across his face, looking for the tell-tale signs. He looked genuine enough. Problem was, this close, sending out a tendril of magic was a two-way path. However much she found out about him, he'd find out just as much about her. And there were way too many things she didn't want even Claws to know about, let alone this…stranger.

"Destination in three hours," said the train.

"Why didn't you know about the race?" she said instead.

Ah. Interesting. A little twitch in his eyebrow.

"If you're a Cirrun," she continued, "and your mum was Messina, that means you're a scion of House Lix-Tetrax."

He nodded. "I am."

"Then why didn't you know about the race?"

"Hang on a sec," said Claws, bounding over and jumping onto the plush chaise long next to Jason's armchair. "If he's a scion, and *you're* a scion, does that mean you're related?"

Jason's eyes widened a little and he looked at Sab with new interest.

"Pfft," said Sab. "Those Lix-Tetrax dicks fuck everything. We're all over the place. We get everywhere. Being related doesn't mean shit. Your brother's my cousin, remember? A billion times removed, but still."

"Was Messina your mother too?" Jason asked Sab.

"Oh shit," whispered Claws.

Which was a strange reaction for her friend to have, considering there was no way she'd know who Messina was.

"Well, well, well," said a voice that was *not* part of their team. But it was one Sab knew and hated very well. And now Claws's reaction made sense. "You got the train up and running for us. What a good little slave you are."

Sab finally broke eye contact with Jason, pushed herself up to standing and turned around to face her cousin.

"Emil, was it?" she said, frowning in mock concentration.

"You know very well who I am," said Emil. He looked as fresh and handsome as the last time she'd seen him. As though the journey across an entire continent of danger and fucked-up creatures hadn't fazed him in the slighted.

The utter bastard.

"And now," he continued, smugness smearing itself across his face, "this train is ours."

SQUIRREL

There's something to be said for being unconscious, and it's this: it's hugely preferable to being awake. Especially when you come from Keep'Out Quarter and the majority of people there are working for the Chief in order to save their own threadbare hides, and your head has got a sack of gold coins dangling above it.

Oh, and the excruciating pain.

I knew I was waking up again because I wasn't so much a person with a body, more a burning ball of agony that desperately wished to be put out of its misery.

"What the fuck...?" I managed.

"Ah, our little guest is finally awake."

Well, shit. I knew that voice. I'd hoped never to hear it again, but there it was, insinuating its way into my ears like the worst form of venomous serpent. And then the memory of the big bloke from the library walloping me over the head after asking about Audra came back to me. That, and his promise to take me to the Chief if I didn't give her up. I groaned.

The Chief laughed. "Music to my ears, Squirrel. And let me assure you that my men will keep you singing for days and days and *days*. I've looked forward to our reunion for too long to let you go away too soon."

"Fuck you," I growled through teeth clenched tight with pain.

Then my head exploded in a shower of red sparks. I didn't see where the blow came from because I'd yet to open my eyes, but I didn't need sight to know that someone had just smashed his fist into my temple. Too much to hope that the Chief hadn't restocked his supply of thugs once I'd done for his last bunch, I s'pose.

The Chief chuckled, warm and throaty. "I might fuck *you*," he said. "And I happen to know amongst my men there's a little queue forming for who gets to fuck you afterwards. But you'll never fuck me, little Squirrel. Not in all your pathetic and truncated life."

I opened my eyes. It took a while and a lot of effort, but I forced myself to get a good look at him. He was even fatter than I remembered, his swollen body swamped in lavish clothes, his bloated hands squeezed into more jewellery, but he was still every inch the bastard I'd been desperately trying to hide from for the past few months.

I could feel my fear. Felt it like a physical presence right next to me, like Mouse; a part of me, but also separate. I'd been scared of this man since the day I was born, and rightly so because he was a cruel and depraved scumbag who'd made his shitty life better by making every other life around him even shittier. But it dawned on me that, even though I hadn't yet reached manhood, and even though his thugs outnumbered me countless to one, and even though he outweighed me dozens of stones to one, I was more powerful than him.

All right, so there was a part of me that was actually more

scared of my magic than of the Chief, because I'd wiped out the last band of brutes he sent to deal with me and my mum. I'd seen Audra wipe the Sages from existence in the blink of an eye. I was terrified of it because I'd seen what it could do.

On the other throbbing hand, I'd seen what it could do. Petrifying for me, oh yes. But surely more for those on the receiving end of it. I didn't have to fear the Chief any more. I could annihilate him and his cronies with little more than a thought. Which was lucky, because my body was next to useless right now.

"Fair enough then," I said, moving my head and shoulders about, testing them. "Let's get it over with."

"Not so fast, my dear Squirrel," said the Chief. "Before I hand you over to my men for raping and flaying and torturing and whatnot, I'd like us to have a little discussion." He draped a hand over the arm of his luxurious recliner and plucked a tiny cake from a massive pile of them. "A discussion about a certain woman we have in common. A mutual friend, if you will. Someone who I'm very anxious to meet because—"

"You mean Audra," I said.

The Chief frowned. He didn't like the honey tones of his voice halted mid-flow. "Yes. Audra. And you will tell me where—"

"She's at the library. Sleeping downstairs after a bit of a tiring day, even though it wasn't even lunch time by the time we got back home. She's probably still there. Though that might all depend on how long I've been here. If I was unconscious for any length of time then she's probably popped out somewhere. Or not." I shrugged. "I'm not her keeper."

The Chief's frown deepened, but this time he wasn't directing it at me. I shifted my head around a bit so I could see who the unlucky bugger was. It was that big bloke who'd nabbed me. Even though he was bigger than all the others crammed around the edge of the sumptuous room, he looked less frightening. He didn't have that smug look smeared across his face that all the others did, didn't look quite so much like he was enjoying the interrogation of a little lad who was beaten and bound in the presence of the Chief.

I'd still be having words with him about what he did to me, mind.

"You checked the entire library, I imagine," the Chief said to him. "As much of a prize as Squirrel is to me, for I'm looking forward to punishing him on reneging on an agreement, I did, in fact, send you there for Audra. So I'm sure you inspected her lodgings thoroughly, didn't you, Jaymes?"

The big bloke called Jaymes just shrugged his shoulders. "Kid said she wasn't there. People don't generally lie to me."

"Then you're a fool," spat the Chief. He turned his gaze to another thug, nearer the door, and gave him a little nod. "I have no time for fools."

"Kid just told you where she was," said Jaymes. "What's the problem?"

The Chief launched himself to his feet. Every time he moved I was always surprised at how quick he was for such a bloater.

"The problem is that she should be here already, you fucking imbecile!"

I quailed a little bit. The Chief angry always meant something unexpectedly bad was going to happen. I mean, it was always bad in the Chief's company. Bad enough when he was in a good mood, anyway. When his fury got the better of him though…that's when shit started flying and you didn't know where it was going to land.

"I reckon if you just sit tight, she'll come right to you," I said. The Chief's look of astonishment that I'd spoken without leave made me smile. "She's grown quite fond of me and I reckon she'll try to help me out."

"Even if she knew where you'd been taken, she'd never find her way in here," he said, sneering as though I was a maggot wriggling through a dead dog's eye.

"Right, of course," I said, feeling such a surge of bravado at being cheeky to the Chief that it almost felt like an inrush of power. "Ignore me then. Get back to your tongue-lashing of…Jaymes, was it?"

The Chief turned his bulk towards me, opening his mouth in readiness for saying something undoubtedly terrifying—but the door crashed open before he managed it. His face of fury turned into something vastly more frightening: a smile.

"Well, here you go, Jaymes Rebel!" he said with a chuckle. "Here is what your incompetence buys you."

A bundle was thrown into the centre of the room, completely distracting me from the fact that Jaymes had been called a Rebel, flopping onto the thickly woven rug with a wet crunch.

I heard Jaymes roar, but it was drowned out by my own horror. The bundle was a little boy. Or rather, he had been a little boy. Now the poor rascal was nothing but a dead bag of skin and bones. Bones which were all too visible through his lacerated flesh. He hadn't died well, this little boy. But from his oozing blood, it was clear that he'd died all too recently. My hand shot to my mouth after realisation had slapped me across it. It hadn't been courage I'd felt at speaking back to the Chief at all. It had been this poor tyke's life force.

I looked up at the Chief, looked across at Jaymes. He was flaming mad at the Chief, so much so that four thugs were holding him back, just in case he landed one on their boss. There was something odd about him though… Couldn't quite put my finger on it. Perhaps it was just a level of rage I'd never come across before.

The Chief though. He just stood there grinning, his shoulders shaking in silent laughter.

What happened next took everyone by surprise.

The mirth never leaving his face, the Chief whipped out a heavily jewelled dagger from somewhere about his person, lunged across to Jaymes with that peculiar grace he has, and slit his throat. The thugs released him, probably fearing that one of them'd be next if they didn't move out the way of that maniac. The Rebel's hands flew to his neck at the same time as he crumpled to the floor.

I'd had it with him.

"Stop murdering people, you fat fucking fuck," I said.

He wasn't laughing any more. And I'd definitely caught his attention.

Remembering the storm I'd felt deep down inside myself when I'd destroyed his last lot of thugs, I reached in and pulled it out. Pulled it out, pulled myself out of the chair and binds, and threw everything I had at the Chief and all the other bastards in that room.

The Chief I held suspended in the air so's he could get a good look at was I capable of. One by one, and with nothing more than a sweep of a hand, I ripped the thugs in half. Blood and gore and probably their breakfast, as well as their shit and piss, showered the room. It was disgusting, but I was past caring at this point. When I'd done with them, so much stronger now than when I started, I looked up at the Chief hanging there like a grotesque, gibbering balloon.

"You never wondered what happened to those fucks you sent after me and my mum?" I said to him. Funnily enough, the love of his own voice had dissipated. "*I* happened to them, that's what. Should've come for you sooner, I s'pose, but I've only just realised that I'm not scared of you any more. But don't worry, Chief, I'll make your death nice and slow. Wouldn't want you to die without suffering, now would we? Not after everything you've put *us* through."

I was as good as my word. And to be honest, those screams will haunt me for the rest of my days. I started with his feet. You think it's bad when you stub a toe? Imagine what it feels like to have each individual bone crushed into liquid. And then having that liquid drip out through a hundred little gashes in your soles. That was what I did to the Chief's feet.

I moved up his legs, snapping bones and tearing skin—but not too much tearing. I didn't want all his blood to seep out and kill him before I had the chance to make him suffer. But as each flower of blood bloomed, I grew stronger and hungrier to inflict more. And *angrier*! I remembered the beatings he gave me, and all the other Keep'Out kids like me, for no other reason than he loved the sound of kids in pain. I remembered his pleasure and it fuelled my fury. His blood-lust fuelled my bloodlust. I remembered what he did to my mum, remembered her screams, her bones snapping. I'd screamed at him to stop hurting her, screamed so hard I spat blood. And he just kept on laughing at us, while he wiped our blood off his tools. I remembered my mum—

I remembered my mum.

"What've you done?"

The memory of her colourless face, staring at the remnants of RazorHand and his cronies after I'd dealt with them, crashed into my fury, made me stumble back.

"I'm sorry, Mum, I didn't mean to. I wanted to save you."

She couldn't even look at me. She was horrified. Even after I'd fixed her legs and she could walk, she still couldn't bear to look at me. It was why she'd cut her own throat to get away from me. And if she could see me now…

If she could see me now…

My fury started boiling again, but this time it was at myself, not the Chief. Fury for letting the magic take hold of me like this, for letting it turn me into something my mum was scared of.

I turned tear-blurred eyes back up to the Chief. When I'd first suspended him up there, he was a bloated balloon. Now, he was a deflated, gibbering puddle of a thing. He was crying. His tears cleaned tracks down his grey, bloody cheeks. I screamed my boiling fury up at him, and he *became* my boiling fury. His skin bubbled and seethed, turned red, steamed—

—and he exploded across the room. Blistering gobs of flesh and fat and innards splashed everywhere, filling the place with the stench of over-cooked pork and burnt hair.

Orc's balls, it felt so good to hurt him, mind. But equally shameful. Didn't know I had such viciousness in me. No wonder my mum wanted to leave me.

Once I'd finished, and once the storm inside had calmed, and even though I was strong enough now thanks to all that fresh power pouring into me, the shakes set in. I knew I'd pay for my actions, but first I had to get out of the blood-soaked shit-hole before I added vomit to the gruesome mess.

The silence of the aftermath was broken by a low groan. I fair nearly squealed like a girl—surely no one had survived that?

"He killed Mole, the bastard!" A bloody fist rose and slammed back down onto the equally bloody floor, causing a little shower of red.

"Hello?" I said. Wasn't anything else I could think of.

A body unfurled itself, his back entirely covered in gore, his front clean of it because he'd fallen flat on his face. It was the Rebel. And it was funny that his front should be so free of blood, considering his throat had been slit, and all. There was a wound, all right; the flesh on his neck was parted like some sort of ghastly mouth, but there wasn't any blood coming from it. I blinked a little bit. The Rebel looked around the room.

"You did this," he said.

I nodded.

"With magic."

I nodded again.

"Fuck's sake," he said. "You're just like Audra."

DRAYKE

"I trust you're taking me somewhere useful," Drayke said to the Academician. She ignored him. It seemed she was too intent on chewing the inside of her cheek. "Academician," he said sternly.

"Please, call me Jenna," she said, finally out of her reverie.

"I trust you're taking me somewhere useful."

"He knew something."

Drayke refused to be drawn by enigmatic statements.

"Don't you think so? The look on his face when I told you about unpublished research… I would swear an oath that he looked guilty."

"You're talking about your husband."

She nodded. "But if he knows something, why wouldn't he tell us?"

"Perhaps because he uses his great intellect and the Academy's resources to spy on his peers and superiors. He's nothing more than an eavesdropper."

The Academician gawped at him but he ignored her. Soon enough he would lose his temper with her; they were literally walking around in circles, following this endless corridor. He was a Rebel. He should be protecting the Prime Minister. He didn't like that he had to find the answers to secrets in order to do his job.

"I wonder if… But no, that's just something we say."

And he didn't like that the Academician refused to speak plainly.

"Tell me," he said.

"Well, we have an expression, you see, about research that has been rejected by the Sages. We say it's been sent to the hall of extinction."

"And?"

"I thought it was just an expression, but what if it isn't? What if there's truth to it? What if there really is a hall of extinction?"

"I'd appreciate your answering your own questions."

She stopped him by laying a hand on his arm, the gentlest of touches. "What better place to keep a secret document than in a fictitious room?"

"Finding such a place would be difficult."

She nodded again, turning her head. Her face paled and her hand dropped from his arm. Turning to see what caught her attention, Drayke noticed that they'd stopped before a door leading out to the circular courtyard. Above hung the glass floor of the Sage's dome, still awash with blood. Of course, the idea of cleaning up hadn't occurred to an Academician; it was far too beneath them.

He walked into the courtyard, the grass cushioning his feet, still looking up. "The dome could be your hall of extinction," he said. "The Sages would read the papers up there, no doubt. I imagine that's what they needed such comfortably expensive armchairs for."

"There's not enough space," said the Academician. She

hovered in the doorway, keeping her eyes fixed on the grass. "The Academy's been around for Ages, there'd be uncounted thousands of rejected papers, the dome's not nearly large enough. Besides, we'd see them." She sighed. "It's a silly idea. I'd heard the expression shortly after I arrived here years ago and Audra explained that it was just a joke amongst the Academicians. Nothing more than a local legend."

"You told me yourself that legends had to start somewhere."

It was possible the rejected papers were simply destroyed. For a group of people as arrogant as the Academicians, pointless research wouldn't be worth keeping. Nor would research containing dangerous ideas, like Audra's assertion that humans weren't native to Taurë. Nor handwritten clues that Mages weren't as history described them. Drayke's instinct told him that if an Academician had conducted research that was correct but dangerous for the public to know about, the Sages would have kept it, passing the secret on to the next generation as they passed on the torch of their authority. And while they were privy to all the knowledge, everyone else was kept in the dark. Considering the utter hubris of these people, there was only one place they would keep such information.

"It's beneath them," he said.

"I beg you pardon?"

He cursed himself silently for becoming as enigmatic as his acquaintance. "I believe if your Sages came across any research they didn't like they would bury it beneath them, where it belonged."

"The floor of the dome is made of glass. If they buried anything beneath themselves there wouldn't *be* a dome any more."

He reached up over his shoulder to grab his axe, then swung it down so that it bit deeply into the grass.

"What are you doing?" squealed the Academician.

With a flick of the wrist, a great damp sod flipped up and landed a stride away. Good, the ground here was soft so wouldn't take too long to remove. Soon enough, however, it became apparent that an axe was not a proficient digging tool. A brief look around and Drayke noticed a wheelbarrow and a tidy rack of equipment lined up against the wall, among which was a spade. Within moments he was back at his task, digging with an energy that almost surprised him, considering he'd hardly slept since his return. He was aware that the Academician's appeals to stop had petered out, and as he shifted enough soil so that he stood first knee deep, then waist deep, he was beginning to think perhaps he should stop too, for perhaps he'd made a mistake.

Holding the spade like a spear he threw it towards the ground in annoyance—and it stuck with a wooden thunk. He looked up at the Academician, forcing his mouth not to smile at her. Within a heartbeat, he'd tossed the spade aside and taken up his axe again. After the first few strokes, the Academician spoke up.

"Don't you think it's dangerous to break through the ground like that?" she said. "What if the garden collapses? I'm not sure a falling fountain will do much good."

"It was built for the express purpose of holding this garden up," he said between strokes. "I doubt I'll affect the integrity of the structure."

When he'd finished, she looked about and sighed. "But now there's a big hole in here."

"If people refuse to share their secrets," he said, strapping his axe to his back once more, "something always gets destroyed."

~

JENNA

TRULY IT WAS A BIG HOLE. Poor Garth would be devastated when he came back to his garden, he took such good care of the lawn. Nor did Jenna doubt that he'd be as surprised as the rest of the Academy that their indoor circle of outdoor calm actually covered a wooden floor, which itself was the ceiling to... She peered as close as she dared. She saw nothing but darkness. For all she knew, Drayke could have dug out a hole to the very centre of the world, but she doubted that it would have a wooden ceiling. Whatever was hidden in the gloom definitely involved people at some point. Considering it was in the very middle of the Academy, those people could only be the Academicians.

She sighed. More and more it seemed to her that these people, whom she'd admired for so long, weren't the simple seekers and recorders of knowledge she'd always thought them to be.

"I wish it weren't my Academy being destroyed though," she said.

"Do you need help climbing down?" said Drayke, though he didn't offer up his hand.

"I'd rather you went in first to see if it's safe. If plunging into a pitch black hole doesn't break your neck, I'll follow you down."

"As you want," he said. And plunge he did, without even looking first. He simply walked to the edge of the hole he'd created and jumped through it. Jenna shook her head at his stupidity. The Rebels probably called it bravery.

"Is it safe?" she called out after a few heartbeats had passed.

"I see nothing that says otherwise," came Drayke's voice, surprisingly close.

"So you can see down there?"

"No. It's dark."

"Well, would you like me to bring down a torch?"

"Our eyes will become accustomed soon enough. Stop asking questions and come if you're coming. It's not far. You won't hurt yourself."

Shaking her head slightly, perhaps at Drayke, perhaps at herself, she walked over to the edge of the hole and sat upon its edge, conscious of the soil that would no doubt stain her white robe, and not enjoying the unpleasant sensation of the ripped wood poking at the back of her thighs. She shuffled forwards, her robe hitching up from the tiny fingers of splinters that grabbed at it, and still she couldn't see into the gloom.

"I don't want to break my legs," she said.

"You won't." Drayke's voice was reassuringly close. "Hurry up."

She braced her hands against the edge of the hole, readying herself to jump through. Although it might be easier and safer to enter with her belly against the edge, then lower herself down with her arms instead of a blind jump. Wriggling around, she couldn't quite find a position that would allow her to do that without spilling herself into the blackness. She twisted back around so she perched on her backside once more.

"Orc's balls, Academician, what are you doing? Just jump."

"I don't want to hurt myself—eeeek!" Her ankles were grabbed and with no warning or consent she was pulled through the opening. Ragged wood scratched along her thighs, rump and back at the same time as hands grabbed her legs and waist. Within a heartbeat she was standing upon solid ground, the dark form of Drayke staring down at her, his hands still clasped around her middle.

Jenna pulled her hand back and slapped him across the face as hard as she could, only to be astonished and ashamed in equal measure at her behaviour. Before she could apologise, however, Drayke barked out a short laugh. It sounded unpleasant and unpracticed.

"There's a spark of fire inside you after all, Academician," he said, removing his hands. "You're a little less detestable."

"And you're more so," she said, pulling and straightening her robe. To her horror, it had risen up around her hips during her ordeal. She kept telling herself that Drake couldn't possibly have seen her small-clothes in the dimness, but it didn't stop her cheeks from burning. "I'm scratched all over, and I wasn't ready! You had no right to pull at me like that!"

"You were taking too long. I'd already told you it wasn't far. Stop your snivelling and look around you. Our downward journey isn't over yet."

The urge to slap him again was so strong she almost couldn't fight it; until she looked around. The little light shining down from the rent above them vanished into the vastness of the underground room. The coolness of space was all around her. For a moment she was dizzy and almost reached out to Drayke for support, but she managed to control herself just in time.

"What are we standing on?"

Drayke moved away from her cautiously, testing with his feet each time he stepped forward.

"It sounds wooden, don't you think?" she said.

"Yes. And it's narrow." He trod on a little more. Then, "It continues into the darkness, I think, but there's a ladder here."

"Oh. That's very useful. Shall we go down it?"

Evidently, Drayke didn't think a response was necessary.

He crouched down, then disappeared out of Jenna's sight. A brief panic enveloped her and she walked as quickly as she dared along the narrow path. She was about to ask him where he was when she heard him chuckle mirthlessly.

"What is it?" she called out.

"You'll see soon enough."

Finally she espied two hooks biting deep into the wooden pathway; she'd found the ladder at last. She turned carefully, crouched slowly, and then dropped a foot over the edge, moving it around until it caught a rung of the ladder. She breathed out her relief slowly and quietly so Drayke wouldn't hear.

A few steps down and she realised her eyes had finally attuned themselves to the darkness. She blinked a few times. "Oh my," she said.

"You see where we are," said Drayke from far below.

"I do, yes," she said. Books. Hundreds of them. Thousands. Stretching out on both sides until they were lost from view. "We're climbing down a bookshelf." She chuckled. "This is ridiculous. I'm climbing down a bookshelf in near total darkness after jumping through a hole a barbarian made in the Academy courtyard. Mother and Father will never believe me when I tell them about my day."

By the time she reached the bottom, her arms ached from having gripped the ladder so tightly, and her legs were sore from the unaccustomed and uncomfortable movements. It had been a long, long way down. The hole in the garden was nothing but a pinprick in the ceiling, like the first star that came out at night.

"The first thing we must do is find a torch," said Drayke.

"Easier said in the gloom than done." She heard him tut.

"We make our way to the walls. That's where the torches will be."

Well. Put it in that tone of voice, of course it's obvious.

Fortunately the bookshelves were too huge and high to bump into—and they made for useful, if dusty, handrails. This wasn't a place for study; it was a place for storage. There were no desks or stools lurking in the dark to bruise hips or shins. It was, however, a labyrinth. The shelves marked out corridors, and as soon as one ended, she turned into another. She had no idea where Drayke was—his hulking form took a different turn when she wasn't looking, and she wouldn't call out to him. She resigned herself to zigzagging through corridors of bookshelves for the rest of her days. Surely there were worse ways to die. Feeling the bite of Drayke's great axe through the neck for one. Or being turned inside out like the poor Sages. At least down here she would be able to stop now and then to read one of these books. Except that there was no light. She'd likely die of boredom. Yes, there really *were* worse ways to die. She sped up a little, determined to find a torch so that at least her final days could be spent reading.

Time passed, and Jenna only knew it did because her feet became sore from so much walking, and finally she was free —only to be blinded by an explosion that ignited right before her eyes. She squealed a little, which annoyed her. She'd been doing far too much of that recently, and it wasn't the pleasantest of sounds.

"I thought I'd have to go in and search for you," said Drayke.

"But instead you thought it'd be more fun to wait until I arrived so you could blind me by lighting a torch?"

"It's a lamp, and I hadn't realised it would cause such a fright. For that I apologise."

Jenna sincerely doubted it. She heard the smug laughter in his voice even though he didn't so much as titter. She'd keep her tongue, though. When she was growing up in the

Merchant's Quarter, there was a boy from the Boulevard who used to pick on her because she lived in Kettle Alley, a considerably less fashionable neighbourhood. He taunted her, called her names, pulled her hair or pushed her over every time he saw her in school. At first, it made her cry. As she got a little older, she picked herself up and shouted at him. Finally, she stopped reacting altogether because she just couldn't be bothered any more.

It was then that he stopped picking on her. She realised the fun part for him was seeing her reaction. Drayke was precisely the same as that little boy, and she wouldn't give him the satisfaction. Particularly since he could see so well now with that bright lamp clenched in his brutish hand.

"If there's another one," she said, "perhaps we should separate. We're only two and there are so many shelves! We don't know if anyone will come down to escort us back up for trespassing in an out-of-bounds area."

"No one knows we're here."

"There's a bloody great hole in the courtyard."

He snorted a laugh. "But your idea is logical. There's another lamp a few strides along this wall."

He held out his own lamp and she saw he spoke true. Once she had her own, dusty but with a full reservoir of oil, she marched back into the maze to conduct her search.

How many denounced ideas were down here? The Academy was instituted two-and-a-half Ages ago. Two hundred and fifty years. Countless thousands of Academicians, countless thousands of ideas. No wonder they'd had to build shelves so high and wide in such an impossibly large room. Each shelf had its own ladder to reach the uppermost levels but if she could avoid climbing, she would. She'd trust to luck that texts about the Mages would be at eye level, before willingly getting on one of those rickety things again. She plucked a book out at random from the shelf before her.

It was quite thin, leather-bound, as all submitted papers must be, and covered in a fine dust. Wiping it down, she read the title: On Orcs And Their Lineage With Ancient Realm Elves, Tristin Barros Academician, 2108. She smiled; no wonder this one was sent to the hall of extinction—the elvish Clans of Kinston City wouldn't have liked being set in the same family tree as the orcs at all.

She placed Tristin's work back where she found it and pulled out the one next to it: On The Benefits Of Execution For Any Misdemeanour, Haydyn Feyn Academician, 2172. She frowned. Not just because the subject was so frightful, but because the paper was submitted nearly seventy years after the previous one she looked at. She pulled out the remaining texts on the shelf and a brief glance told her that there was no order to the way they were placed; different names, different subjects, different years of submission. That was going to make searching for anything related to the Mages much more time-consuming. It would take an Age to go through every single rejected text in this cavern!

"Academician!" Drayke's voice sounded far away.

"Yes?" she shouted back, but there was no answer. Of course there wasn't. He'd called, so he expected her to go running to see what he'd discovered. Well, it could take forever to find him in this labyrinth and she certainly wasn't going to rush. She wasn't even going to give him the satisfaction of asking him where he was. He could jolly well wait for her.

Soon enough she saw the soft glow of lamplight emanating from a distant corner of the room. How long she'd been walking she had no idea, but she was glad Drayke hadn't decided to hurry her along by calling out cutting remarks. One last corner and she came upon him, crouching down, flicking through a text, a great pile of them laid haphazardly along the lowest rack of the shelf.

"Took your time getting here," he said.

"Did you find something about the Mages?" she said.

"No." He stood and held out the text he'd been reading. "Plenty on Audra though."

"On Human Evolution In Taurë," she read from the leather cover with a smile. "Arguably her most famous piece."

"If it's down here people shouldn't know about it."

"No, they shouldn't," said Jenna, "but Audra's nothing if not persistent. When the Sages rejected this work, she handed in another fairly innocuous paper, I can't even remember what it was called now. Academicians can lecture on their accepted paper if they choose, and Audra did choose; only—"

"Only she lectured about our people coming from else-where instead," Drayke said.

Jenna smiled. "It caused quite the scandal. She'd done paintings of Elvish ruins she found in the High Beach Barrens and everything. Academicians were talking about it the whole time she was away, until the Sages forbade it. There were a few of us who thought it unfair, but most people were happy enough to ridicule her. Going against the Sages is the best way to get your papers rejected, you see."

"Yet she willingly risked being ostracised just so she could talk about her researches."

"She really believed in them," she said with a shrug.

Drayke looked thoughtful but he said nothing. A moment later he took the book from Jenna's hands and slotted it into a pocket in his trousers.

"You can't take that!"

"Nobody will know," said Drayke. "It may be important. I'd like to know about the evidence that was compelling enough to risk her profession."

"I can tell you all you need to know. Audra and I spoke of it enough times."

"I'd rather read the original." He turned back to the bookshelf. "Everything you see here is about Audra."

Jenna's eyes widened as she took in the texts and piles of paper that littered the place. "She wrote all of this? I hadn't realised she'd been so prolific. Mind you, I suppose stuck out there in that library—"

"I said *about* Audra, not by her. Her mother and father too. I can't imagine it's usual to keep such records of one specific Academician, and then hide them away down here."

"Not at all," she said, shaking her head. She reached out and took a sheaf of papers at random. A quick scan revealed they were about Audra's mother. "Poor woman. No one ever did find out what caused her madness. But that's why her father took to healing." She sighed. "And then he was taken from her too."

"That fa—your husband," said Drayke. "He mentioned the mother's illness."

Jenna nodded. "Karyssa. She was a respected Academician in her own right, even before she married Raynard, Audra's father. She was a historian, and made it her life's work to chart the history of the elves. That's why Audra is such close friends with the Worthy Clan, you see. She spent a lot of time with Adàm and Faër. Grew up with them, really—and it's why she's got such an interest in language despite being a Historian. Although she always liked to combine the two by charting the evolution of our language. The Worthy Clan's library was full of ancient books that she would read just so she could see how our language had changed over the Ages. She told me once that the servants at the Worthy mansion would call her and Karyssa 'Lady' just like the elves because they spent so much time there." Jenna smiled but it was sad. "She wouldn't speak of her mother much."

"If the mother did so much research into the history of the elves, why isn't more known of them?"

"Because of her madness. At first, her papers only included the odd remark, though nothing too outrageous. Then they became...peculiar. Then she gave impromptu lectures at improper times, then she was rambling all the time. The deterioration was very quick, apparently. A season later, Karyssa was bed-ridden and Raynard had given up his post as Esteemed Philosopher and became a healer so he could look after her. I think he wanted to cure her."

"Obviously he didn't."

Jenna shook her head and dropped her voice to a whisper even though they were alone. "She took her own life in the middle of the night."

Drayke said nothing, and while his face remained motionless, Jenna was sure she saw emotion in his eyes.

"If you were to ask Audra about any of this though, you'd get no answer. Anything she told me of her mother was by accident, and when she realised, she'd clam up and not speak again for a while. I felt such deep pity for her."

Drayke turned his attention back to the shelf, scanning the papers, as uneager to speak as Audra always was. She turned her own attention back to the papers in her hand, glancing through the information, which was written in a lovely neat script and easy to read despite the poor light.

"Oh," she said. "I never knew that."

Drayke turned his head towards her.

"Karyssa had a sister."

"Is that remarkable?"

"It wouldn't be...except her sister lives in Out'Keep. It was well known that Karyssa's family came from a long line of distinguished Academicians. The whole family."

"So what was her sister doing in Out'Keep while the rest of her family lived in privilege?"

Jenna read a little more, then looked up at Drayke. "Because Karyssa believed she was an only child."

He indicated the sheaf of papers with his chiselled chin. "Is there a name?"

"Allysun. A tanner's daughter near Midden Pit, it says here. People call her Swan."

"It seems a trip to Out'Keep is next on our list."

"*W*hat did you just say?"

For the first time ever, Sab wanted to cheer Volos. A little bit of that was because he was on her team, but mostly it was for the look of just-shat-my-pants terror that flickered across Emil's face. Didn't take long for the arrogance to smear itself back into place, but it was just long enough for Sab to see what kind of person Emil really was. A coward.

"I said this train is ours," said Emil, although not quite as cock-sure as the first time.

"I don't think so, little 'Spherian," said Volos, taking a step forward. "We were here first."

"Can I just p-point out that the train's already moving?" said Jason. "I don't think it'll let anyone off until we've reached our destination."

"Who the fuck's this?" said Emil, glaring down his noble nose at the interloper. "Can't be anyone you picked up at Hinterland Deeps, because we know for a fact you didn't go there. You bunch of dirty little cheaters."

Sab burst out laughing. "Oh *please*! We enslave human

beings in order to keep our magic levels topped up, and you think we play fair?"

Emil looked genuinely confused. "*Humans* are nothing more than animals," he said. "Lower down on the food chain. It's what they're there for. Mages are an honourable race. We abide by the rules of our Games."

Sab widened her eyes for a second at such nonsense. "Fair enough. Well, how come when you got to Hinterland Deeps you didn't just think you were ahead of us?"

"Because you were sent out of Oceanwall first," said Emil. "There was no way you were behind us."

"Right," said Sab, nodding. She'd caught the looks Emil's lackeys had shared behind him. You'd have to be a dick not to. Rich and entitled as they were, they were neither clever nor subtle. "You didn't go there either, did you?"

"Well, why should we?" Emil whined. "*You* didn't! And I'm not going to lose this race to some stupid Stratian slaver slut!"

Sab gave him a slow blink but didn't bother responding. Far worse things had happened to her in her long life, and being called names by a privileged prick didn't even make the list.

"Then how did you know?" said Prisca.

"Know what?" said Emil, giving her a filthy look.

"That we didn't go via the Deeps?"

"Because," said Emil. "I'm a Mage. We know things."

"True," said Prisca. "But if we're not worried about staining that honour we were so recently proclaiming, then we normally don't mind bragging about it. Your reticence to explain how you know we didn't go there ourselves leads me to suspect you had an underhanded way of finding out that information."

"Look, you can shut up too, you Stratian whore."

This time Sab's eyes widened and stayed like that. She turned to look at Volos.

"*What* did you call her?" whispered the big man, his clammy body trembling with fury.

Sab turned back to Emil and grinned hugely.

"Look, all right, I g-get it," said Jason then. He stood up, swung his backpack to the floor, effectively breaking the spell. "We still haven't evolved past the posturing and backstabbing phase, but perhaps while we're all stuck on this train together for the next few hours it'd be best if we stayed on opposite ends of it. You can take up your fighting, racing, whatever, when we get to Taurë, but let's keep the train as neutral territory, shall we?"

"Well said, young man," said Prisca.

"Who the fuck *are* you?" said Emil.

"He's a member of our team," said Prisca, before anyone else on her actual team could speak up. "And we all agree with him, which means you're outvoted. Now do the honourable thing and wait on the other end of the train until the race starts up again."

Emil snarled at her, but he still turned to go. That's when Sab noticed something.

"Hey, cousin?" she called. "Where's Lian?"

"What?"

"Lian. The boy from Oceanwall."

All six dicks looked at one another and sniggered.

"Oh, *that*," said Emil, summoning a sphere onto his palm and throwing it over his shoulder to them. "That was hilarious. Have a watch."

And then, still chuckling amongst themselves, they walked to the other end of the train.

Sab looked at Claws. Her friend was grinding her teeth so hard the muscles along her jawline pulsated.

"We don't have to," Sab whispered. "Maybe we shouldn't."

But they didn't have a choice. It was a sphere. It opened up and started playing automatically.

There was no sound, thank fuck for minuscule mercies, but the visuals were horrific enough. There was Lian, poor scrawny mutant boy that he was. He was running away from the screen, but every now and then he glanced over his shoulder and the look of sheer terror on his face broke Sab's heart. Which surprised her—after all the atrocities she'd done to human slaves in the name of house Lix-Tetrax, she kind of thought she was beyond sympathy. But Lian was just a little boy, and he was so confused and afraid.

From the left-hand corner of the screen a light flashed; one of the dicks releasing some magic. It shattered across Lian's back, slicing through his clothes, then his skin. Blood bloomed. Lian's head shot back, and even though Sab couldn't see his face, she knew full well he was screaming at that point.

The magic flashes and slashes continued until the poor boy sunk to his knees. He hadn't tripped, hadn't fallen. He'd simply given up. He fell forward onto his face, which made Sab jump when it connected with the gritty, hard ground.

The flashes ceased, but the angle of the screen shifted so that they were looking down on Lian's prone body. A foot appeared at the bottom of the screen, nudged the boy's leg, then torso. No movement from Lian. The nudge became a kick, kicks which became ever more violent when the dick behind the foot realised there was no more life left in Lian to play with. Other feet joined in until the boy that had been Lian was nothing more than a red, lumpy, pulpy mess, no longer recognisable as a person.

Then the screen folded back up into a sphere, diminished in size and popped out of existence.

Jason threw up. The sour stench quickly permeated the

carriage. "I'm sorry," he whispered, hoarse. "I've never... How could they...?"

Sab ignored him, focused all her attention on Claws. Her best friend wasn't making any sound, but torrents of tears streamed from her eyes, and her whole body convulsed from sobs kept silent. Sab moved over to her, went to put her arms around her, but Claws batted them away, her eyes filled with such loathing that Sab actually stepped backwards. There was nothing she could do or say that would ease what they'd witnessed.

She looked at Prisca. The old woman had her eyes closed, hands pressed firmly against her lips. She looked at Volos. Even the giant man, the man who had dismissed his own parents in the deep-freeze prison of Oceanwall, looked paler and clammier than usual. And his eyes were round and blinking, still fixed on the spot where the screen had been. Despite everything, his reaction pleased her. It meant he wasn't the same kind of thundercunt as the Cirrocumulans of the 'Sphere.

"When you've finished watching our little movie, Claws," Emil's voice came from everywhere at once, "my men and I need some refreshments. You're the closest thing this train has to a slave, so get to it." The guffaws of his lackeys were audible before Emil cut the sound.

"Fuck you!" Sab screeched at the carriage door. She didn't know how to throw her voice like Emil had done, so screeching would have to do. "Fuck all of you!"

But Claws wiped her face and stood up.

Sab reached for her arm. "You don't have to."

"Yes, I do," said Claws. She put a hand in her pocket and balled up her fist, as though she clasped at something in there. "You know I do. What else am I good for?"

She watched her friend stumble out of the carriage, but she didn't follow or even call out to her.

Talking didn't seem appropriate right now, so Sab found a little chair at the end of the carriage and curled up in it. After seeing such casual hate and violence, she just wanted to pretend she didn't exist for a while.

At first, it was just a tingle. Then she was naked in a hailstorm.

"The fuck?" asked Sab, trying to understand why her limbs were all knotted together.

"Prisca!" That was Volos.

She stopped trying to move for a moment, because it clearly wasn't working anyway, and instead concentrated on opening her eyes. Just in time to see Prisca running out of the carriage.

"What's going on?" she said. Then, "Did I fall asleep?"

"Didn't you feel the release?" Jason whispered.

She turned to look at him. He was very pale.

Tingling and hailstorms. "That wasn't just a dream? Shit."

Sab eventually managed to get her limbs sorted out and she pushed herself up from the chair. Her neck was one throbbing crick, and her knees screeched at their prolonged misuse. A little bit of magic sorted that out, and when she was pain-free once more and fully conscious, she made to dart out of the carriage.

Volos grabbed her arm. "The train has stopped. We get off it together."

Sab gazed wildly around. The place still reeked of vomit, even though the sludgy mess had been cleaned up. But there was no door.

"Then how do we get off this thing?" she said to Volos.

"We wait for Prisca."

"I don't… That didn't answer my question."

But Volos wasn't giving up any more words. When his eyes widened and he straightened up, Sab turned around.

There was Prisca, all right. And she was leading Claws by the hand.

Claws had a faraway look in her eyes, and an almost peaceful expression on her face. But the most startling aspect of her, was that she was covered head to toe in blood. Dripping with it, in fact. There were little droplets all along the floor where she walked.

"Fuck, Claws," said Sab, running over to her. "What happened to you? Are you all right? What did they do to you?"

"Nothing," said Claws, her voice distant and sing-songy. "It's not my blood. It's theirs."

A little bit of coldness made Sab's heart shiver. "Theirs? Then what did *you* do?"

"Mages can't kill Mages," she said in that same voice. "But I'm not a Mage. I'm a mutant. Mutants *can* kill Mages, did you know that?"

"You killed them?" Sab looked up at Prisca. "She killed them?"

"They were sleeping," Claws sang.

"Their throats are cut," Prisca whispered.

"Not cut," said Claws, shaking her head. Then she raised her hands, flexed her fingers. Her pointed nails were thick with gore. "Torn and ripped. All torn and ripped."

She giggled then, and it was the single-most terrifying sound Sab had ever heard.

JAYMES

*F*ucking kid's just like Audra.

Jaymes looked at him, surrounded by the massacred corpses of the Chief and his goons—there was even a bit of RibCage stuck into the wall just above the kid's head, but he decided not to point it out—and shook his head. He was nothing but a scrawny little lad, probably older than he looked because none of the kids here in Keep'Out ate near enough to make their bodies grow properly, with a great shock of messy auburn hair exploding out of his head. His face was pale, his wide eyes were ringed with dark circles as though he hadn't slept for the past Age. His bunched fists, nothing but knuckles and bones, were rammed onto his ears like he could still hear the frightful wails of grown men being torn apart at the seams. Tearing which this boy had been responsible for. But seeing his horror at the scene splashed in front of him, it was easy to think that it wasn't the boy who'd done it. Only Jaymes had seen it happen. And it'd been fucking brutal.

So even if he didn't look like he could possibly be the same as Audra, he fucking was.

That said, the Chief and his bunch of bastards weren't going to be missed.

"Squirrel, is it?" said Jaymes.

The lad nodded his head, blinked, stared at Jaymes' neck, and blinked again.

"The fuckers killed people and kids every day. They deserved this."

"You're one of them," said the lad.

"No. I'm a Rebel, but thanks to your friend Audra," he sighed and rubbed his eyes. "It's a long story and I can't be arsed to tell it. Wanted to kill the Chief myself after what he did to my family," he surveyed the carnage. "But this'll do."

"You're still alive."

"You want thanks for that?"

Squirrel looked confused. "No. He slit your throat. I thought you were dead."

Ah, yes. After killing poor Mole he'd jumped over and cut his throat as payment for his incompetence at not finding Audra. He remembered feeling the cold blade part his skin, remembered the pain, remembered falling to his knees and then his face. He thought he was dead too. But then, he'd been dead before. There was nothing for it, he was going to have to touch it.

"Does it look as horrid as it feels?" he said.

Squirrel nodded his head. "Can't go out looking like that."

Jaymes barked a laugh. "Reckon people round here have seen much worse, but you're probably right. Might get them asking questions I wouldn't be able to answer."

"I could probably fix it up for you," said Squirrel, stepping forward.

"You keep your fucking magic to yourself!" Jaymes roared. The kid crumpled backwards into the seat he'd been strapped into.

"I'm sorry," he whispered. "Just wanted to help."

In truth, Jaymes hadn't meant to holler quite so loudly. Hadn't realised he was so afraid of being touched by magic again. But the words were out now and he wasn't one to take them back. What the lad had said was right enough though— he couldn't go out with his neck flapping open. It was bad enough with just him asking himself what he was.

"If you want to help, go and find something I can wrap around it. Not one of the Chief's poncey scarves though. I have to see to my nephew."

Squirrel scurried out, his eyes never leaving Jaymes—for a kid with the power to do anything he wanted just by thinking it, he was surprisingly nervous. Then the Rebel turned his attention to his nephew. He was glad Sparrow wasn't alive to see her little Mole like this. Her heart would've broken into as many pieces as her son's body was. He scraped as much of the gore off as he could, closed his eyes, and pretended that Mole's expression was one of peaceful relief.

"I got a blanket for your nephew too."

Jaymes looked up. Squirrel stood in the doorway, a deep blue woollen bedcover draped over one arm, and a black cloak over the other.

"Thanks, lad." The cloak was rich wool, heavy, with a high collar that clasped at the throat with a silver button. No doubt it was meant for the cold season, but it wouldn't look too out of place in the rain. Besides, it covered up his wound. Just like the blanket covered up his nephew. Poor blighter weighed nothing in his arms.

"You going to burn him?" said Squirrel.

"Course. Least I can do."

"What about this lot?"

Jaymes spat. "Let them rot."

. . .

WALKING down Intellect's Path didn't take long. Despite the name, they passed no Academicians nor would they, this deep in Out'Keep. They'd all be tucked safely behind Intellect's Gate in their special quarter, where the dead bodies of little boys weren't carried to an early pyre. If the son of an Academician were to succumb to an early death, there'd be more pomp to the occasion. All he got for his nephew was a few suspicious stares, but mostly, for the people around here, it was an ignorable sight.

Once they were through the main unguarded gate, the stench of shit and dirt was replaced with that of ash, and the odd salty exhale as the wind blew across from the sea. The harbour was a notch's march from here, and he knew that place would be awash with fishermen and their colourful boats. Here, though, nothing but desolation. What trees there had been, were gone, food for the constant pyres that burned throughout the plague, and now it was nothing but a scorched wasteland, the air foggy from the cinders that the breeze picked up and swirled around.

"They call it Pyre Pits now," said Squirrel behind him.

Jaymes nodded, unsurprised. And just like Midden Pits, this place wouldn't see anything grow again for Ages to come.

"We'll burn him here then?"

"All this place is good for now," said Jaymes. "Besides, I reckon my sister was probably burnt here with the other plagued, and it seems right that Mole should be with his mum's ashes." He spotted a likely pile of charcoal and headed towards it, his feet churning up the wet ground and smearing a black paste up his boots. Even though the rain had stopped for now, everything was so sodden he doubted that the pyre would burn at all.

"I got some oil," said Squirrel.

Jaymes turned, and sure enough the lad was there, both

hands clutching a jar, as long as his forearm but many times wider. It was wonder the boy could lift it at all. But Jaymes had been an Out'Keeper long before he'd become a Rebel and these people were tougher than they looked. Some of them, anyway. The survivors.

"Where from?" he said.

"There's a bunch over by the gate," said Squirrel. "Considering the amount of people they were burning every day, s'pose it made sense to keep the oil roundabouts."

He nodded his thanks, made sure Mole was well wrapped in his blanket—partly to keep from having to see his nephew burn, partly to provide his body with as much kindling as possible—and laid him gently on top of a pile of damp charcoal.

"We'll need more to go on top of him," he said. He heard Squirrel place the jug down and move away. After a heartbeat or two he rose and had a look around himself. Within half a notch, both of them were gazing down at the grey-black mound and Jaymes was pouring oil all over it. He had a flint and striker in a pocket in his trousers, all Rebels did. After several false starts, a tentative flame crawled within the pile of blackened wood and eventually took hold. Despite the smell and the sound, Jaymes wouldn't leave until his nephew had gone for good. Far too young, but considering the life he was born into, maybe it was for the best.

"Do the Academicians know yet what happens to us when we die?" asked Squirrel.

Jaymes shrugged. "Nothing. We're born, we live, we die. The world turns, and no one really gives a shit."

"Is that what they said?"

"No. But if they knew they'd delight in telling us. I reckon if they don't know, it's because nothing happens."

Squirrel took a long breath in and blew it out through his nose. "My mum said nothing could be worse than here. She reckoned that once we were free from our bodies we were free to go wherever we wanted. I hope she's where she wants to be."

Jaymes looked at him, another lad who'd lost everything and everyone to the Chief, no doubt.

"She always fancied Farmerston," said Squirrel. Jaymes laughed, a soft snort through the nostrils. "S'pose 'cause of all the fields. Alls we had to do was leave, but we never did. Maybe a shit-hole's too sticky and too deep to climb out of though. Anyway. I hope she's there now."

"So do I, lad. And I hope she's there with Sparrow to welcome Mole."

"Reckon she is."

He had big eyes, this Squirrel, the same auburn colour as his hair, and they looked at him so earnestly. So desperate to believe his own tale. It was almost too difficult to believe he'd taken out all those men on his own. That he had the same terrifying power as Audra, to call on as he willed it. Jaymes didn't know if that made the boy bad or not. He didn't look bad. He looked hungry and exhausted, but not bad. Mind you, nor did Audra.

"Better get back to the city," said Jaymes. "Stuff to do."

"What stuff?"

"Chief's dead. Shit's going to be flying about in Keep'Out like the worst kind of storm." Might be his...talents would come in useful during a riot, but he didn't tell the lad that. He also didn't tell him that he was going to hand him over to Drayke as soon as he got the chance.

So when they came upon Drayke on the way back up Intellect's Path it was something of a useful coincidence. By the looks of him, the Rebel leader was just as surprised to see Jaymes as he was to see him. He had his own companion in tow, a lass, and an Academician by the looks of her. So probably less of a companion than a necessity. But what would Drayke want with another one of those lot?

As they drew nearer, he saw that her robes swamped a tiny body, while spectacles on her face made her brown eyes huge. There was nothing about her that appealed to Jaymes.

"Didn't expect to find you marching up Intellect's Path," said Drayke when they'd reached each other. "Least of all with Squirrel."

Jaymes raised his eyebrows. "You know him?"

"One of Audra's...friends."

"Doesn't surprise me." He flicked his eyes to the Academician then back to his leader. "You know about him then."

Drayke was about to speak but Squirrel got there first. "How about speaking to me like I'm actually here?" he said. "And being as that one weren't at the Chief's with us, he knows a lot less than you do."

There was warning in his voice but pleading in his eyes. If Jaymes didn't know any better, he'd've thought the lad didn't want people knowing what he could do. He couldn't tell if that surprised him or not.

"You were at the Chief's?" said Drayke. "Fuck were you doing there?"

"Killing him," said Jaymes. That got a gasp from the little Academician and a raised eyebrow from Drayke.

"You killed him. You fancied turning all of Keep'Out upside down then?"

"Who's the Chief?" said the lass.

"No one you'd know," said Jaymes, not looking at her.

"But why did you kill him?" she said.

When it was obvious that Jaymes wasn't going to answer her, Drayke said, "I trust there was more to it than just wanting a new cloak."

"Unexpected bonus."

"Hope it's keeping you warm enough in this mild weather."

Jaymes shrugged. He didn't feel much of anything. Except anger. But that was no one's business but his own. "You come down here looking for me? Got new orders from Audra, have we? When you going to tell her to fuck off?"

"We came down here looking for someone, but not you," said Drayke. He turned to Squirrel. "You might know her, she lives in Midden Pit."

"Ain't lived there for Ages, mister."

"Her name's Allysun. You might know her as Swan."

Squirrel's mouth dropped open. "What do you want with Swan?"

"So you do know her," said Drayke.

"My mum did. Mum used to look after her a bit, before her legs got broke. Made sure she ate and stuff."

"Why would your mum do that?" said Jaymes. No one looked after other people in Keep'Out, not unless they were tied by blood. And even then only if they got something back from it.

"Because she was fucking mental," said Squirrel. "Swan. Not my mum."

Drayke and the Academician looked at each other, passing some kind of message with their eyes. Jaymes frowned. Drayke trusting an Academician had fucked them all over last time, and he was doing it again. Whores and pub sluts weren't enough for him any more, so it seemed. Jaymes wanted to punch him.

"The fuck's so important about some bitch in Midden Pit?" he said. "Audra's the one you should be going after. Or you too scared? Scared of a little girl?"

Drayke's arm whipped out and he grabbed the collar of Jaymes' cloak in a fist, yanking him towards him so he could glare directly into his eyes.

"She's no little girl," said Drayke. "But there's plenty about her to be scared of. You saw with your own eyes. So we reckon we need to find out exactly who she is before we tackle her."

"How's Swan going to help you do that?" said Squirrel.

Drayke pushed Jaymes away. "Because she's the only family that Audra's got left now."

"Family?"

"Swan is Audra's aunt," said Drayke. "And if you know where she is you must take me there."

SABINA

"We have to clean her up first," Sab hisspered to Prisca. "We can't go through Taurë with her looking like that!"

"There isn't time," Prisca said. Her voice was even, and to an untrained ear it would've sounded calm. "We don't know how long the door stays open for."

Sab looked across at the gaping hole in the carriage's side again. A couple of seconds after Claws started giggling—which she was still doing, and it was starting to fray Sab's nerves—the wall just dematerialised. A ramp unfolded itself, leading down to the platform. Obviously in response to the train's stopping, and probably at this end because the train knew where its passengers were.

The ones left alive, anyway. She looked back at Claws.

"She's head to toe in blood," she said.

"We can find a stream or a river or something," said Jason. "We'll still be in the mountains. There'll be plenty of water around before we reach civilisation."

"How do you know?" said Sab.

He didn't answer, and Prisca was already pushing her and

Claws firmly towards the ramp. Jason led the way, and Volos exited last. When they were all on the platform, the train sealed its door, and a few moments later it slid noiselessly away, back through the mountains. Taking its murdered cargo back with it.

"Me and Emil made a blood pact," said Sab, her words muffled because her face was buried in her hands. "Which broke when his magic was released. Now everyone in the 'Sphere knows and we're in so much trouble." She threw her hands up and let them slap down on her thighs, spinning to face her friend. "They were Cirrocumulans, Claws. What were you thinking?"

"More importantly," said Volos, a scowl threatening to cleave his flabby face in two, "how did one mutant girl best six Mages?"

Claws shrugged. "They said I'd do something like that. I didn't believe them because Emil always scared me, but I did it. Just like they said I would."

"Emil and his dick pack told you you'd murder them one day?" Sab said.

"Not *them*, silly! Those boys didn't say anything. They were too busy sleeping. Lazy boys! Angry slaves have fire in their bellies, you know." Claws giggled. "Or their pockets! Let's go this way!"

"What are you talking—?" But Claws was already skipping over to a shining arch.

This station was completely different from the other one. It was just a cavernous space hollowed out of the mountain. There was a groove on the floor where the train ran, but other than that, it just looked like a cave. Just in case any of the locals wandered in by accident. Unless the train actually here, it wouldn't look like anything other than a cave.

Except for the shining arch, which was clearly the way

out of this place. Sab jogged to catch up with Claws, not wanting her to exit first. Sab had never been to Taurë before, she didn't know what awaited them outside this cave. For all she knew, these humans knew all about the Mages and their Game and had a lynch mob on standby for when they arrived.

So it was definitely a glamour, that much was obvious when she reached it. It had that cyan twinkle to it that denoted magic hard at work. She stepped through it a couple of steps ahead of Claws, made sure the outside was free of angry mobs, then turned back. From this side, it looked just like rock. When Claws stepped through, it looked like she'd walked through the solid wall of a mountain.

Sab blinked. "The glamour didn't hurt you?"

Claws shook her head. "Stung a bit, but nothing serious. Aren't these the same mountains?"

Sab looked around too. Admittedly it looked exactly the same as the spot where the green portal had been, mountains so high they blocked out the sky, but it was unlikely they'd spent the last few hours sitting on a motionless train.

"No," said Volos. The friends swung around at his voice. "We're in Taurë. Follow me."

Sab looked at Prisca, but the old woman just raised an eyebrow.

"You've been here before then?" said Sab.

All she got for her troubles was a resounding silence.

"And what about you, Jason?" she said. He looked startled at hearing his name. "Been here before?"

He shook his head, lingered behind Prisca instead of catching up with the rest of them. Sab didn't let that put her off. She simply waited for him with a smile on her face.

When he eventually reached her, she said, "You never did tell us your story. Where are you from?"

"A long w-way away," he mumbled, not looking directly at her.

"Bit suspicious, all that lack of detail. What are you hiding from us? For all we know, you could be a dangerous maniac, and I'm not sure if I'm comfortable having you tag along."

He didn't say anything to that. He glanced across at Claws though, before lowering his gaze back to the ground. It said more than words could. And even though she'd never say it out loud, she had to admit he kind of had a point.

"I-I don't know you either," he whispered. "My silence is my protection. But I don't want to hurt anyone. I just want to find Audra."

"Why?"

"Why do *you*?"

Sab shrugged. "The Patriarch shat his pants at the thought of there being a New Born human out here. Invented this race so we could catch her and bring her back to the 'Sphere."

He looked at her, clearly surprised that she'd told him the truth. Well, the official truth, at least.

"Race?" said Jason. Then he glanced over his shoulder back at the mountain they'd just come out of. They hadn't walked far so it still loomed over them. Would do for Ages yet, she reckoned. "Those other men in the train were…"

"Yep, the other players. Looks like we're going to win now."

"B-But she'll kill you. The New Born. They can kill Mages."

Sab snorted a chuckle out of her nose. "Well, we've got a mutant. And as it turns out, they can kill Mages. Probably New Born humans too, if we can't."

"Well, you know, if the New Born killed Messina and Nathaniel, it probably means we can kill New Borns. I don't see any reason why it shouldn't go both ways."

"Maybe," Sab said with a shrug. "But better safe than not, right?"

She saw Jason's eyebrows twitch, but he didn't say anything. Just kept his head down. Kept on walking.

Weird, but fascinating, this Jason. She'd never come across a Mage who wasn't as arrogant as all fuck. But this one... He looked nervous. And while she didn't doubt that Messina had been his mother—Mages rarely lied about their lineage, because what was the point? It was too easy to prove or disprove with one little tendril of magic—the difference between Jason and, say, Emil, for example. She shivered mentally at his name. Not because she was horrified by what had been done to him. He deserved it. No, she shivered because she was disappointed that she hadn't gone to look. And that probably wasn't very healthy.

Anyway, Jason was nothing like Emil. For a start, he wore clothes that were sensible. Not poor and badly made by any stretch of the imagination, but...well, appropriate. Durable fabric that had seen wear, but wasn't ostentatious, nor was it ugly. And he had very sensible boots, perfect for travelling long distances. A Mage who dressed appropriately for the situation, rather than to impress and demonstrate wealth. Upper echelon Mages just didn't behave like that.

And while he wasn't difficult on the eye, nor was he of that breath-taking beauty that told everyone you had the kind of magic to spare that allowed you to change your appearance. He didn't look old, but his face was creased around his eyes, across his forehead, and the corners of his mouth, which suggested he never bothered to iron out his face with magic. Immortality was one thing, but Mages were also obsessed with the appearance of eternal youth. It was how you differentiated between the levels. Sab had never bothered to look in a mirror, but she didn't doubt her face was just as creased as Jason's. She'd been alive for a long time now.

But it was his demeanour that fascinated her more than anything. The way he never looked at her directly in the face. His stutter. His hunched way of walking. As though he was supremely uncomfortable with himself. Or perhaps even scared...?

She looked at her swinging forearms, flesh-free and all-over exposed muscles and bone. She looked over at Claws, bloody great self-inflicted hole in her cheek, half her head criss-crossed with scars—oh yes, and covered head to toe in blood because she'd single-handedly massacred six Mages. So, yep. Scared was probably a sensible emotion for someone to feel when faced with people like them. But he was a Mage too. You might *feel* scared, but you certainly wouldn't *show* it. That was a giant flashing neon sign of weakness, that was.

So where had he come from? Certainly not from the Mage-lands, where the main cities were, that was for sure. Otherwise he would've known all about the race, and he didn't. Well, asking him certainly wasn't getting her the answers she wanted, and using magic was out of the question because he'd know. She'd just have to wait and find out. And if she were honest, she kind of liked the idea of that. She couldn't remember ever having come face to face with a mystery before.

"There's a pool just up ahead." Volos's gruff voice bounced around the mountain ravine. We can...clean up there."

"I've got some spare clothes," said Jason, hefting his shoulders to indicate his backpack. "She's taller than me, but it's better than...you know."

"Walking around in clothes drenched with blood?" said Sab. "Yeah."

"Thank you," said Prisca. "That's very kind."

He swung his bag around to his belly, then crouched on

the floor to open it up and riffle through it. There was quite a bit of clinking, as of glass jars knocking together, but also plenty of spare clothes. Now there was a Mage who came prepared. Almost like he didn't always rely on his magic to get things done. Was he someone who'd always had little to spare, like Sab herself? She knew very well that old habits like that didn't die easily.

"Here you are," he said, passing up a bundle of well-folded linen. It looked a little worn and frayed, but also spotlessly clean. Sab also caught a whiff of dried flowers or herbs as the bundle exchanged hands.

Prisca smiled at him, and when she turned back to Claws and saw that the girl was teetering on the edge of the pool, she called out to Volos. "Don't let her jump in!"

"I'm not going anywhere near her," the giant man said and walked away from the pool, plonking himself down on a boulder to watch.

Prisca tutted, but ran over to Claws, speaking soothing words, even though Claws was still giggling and didn't look at all like she was in any kind of distress. Maybe Sab ought to go over there and help, but she didn't want to stop talking to Jason just yet. Which surprised her.

Prisca placed the clean clothes carefully on a rock beside the pool, then managed to coerce Claws into taking off her gory ones. Sab couldn't hear what they were saying from this distance, but so far there was no trouble. In fact, Sab was surprised that Claws wasn't putting up more of a fuss. Back in Stratus, the bathing rooms were communal, and Claws had always hated using them. She hated the vulnerability of being naked and wet when there were other people around. But now, here she was, letting Prisca tug her shirt over head even though Volos and Jason were strangers to her, and men to boot.

Jason gasped when Claws was finally naked though. "What happened to her?"

Sab frowned for a second. He couldn't possibly have forgotten the massacre already, could he? Then she looked at Claws too, and realised he must be talking about the hundreds of scars that criss-crossed Claws's body. Some were old and silvery, others were recent and violently red.

"Self-defence," she said with a shrug.

Jason looked at her and frowned, shook his head with incomprehension.

Sab sighed. "Down in Stratus, some of us cottoned on to the fact that if we were so disfigured as to be disgusting, the higher ups coming down for a bit of raping and pillaging would leave us alone. Rape's not about sexual attraction, obviously, it's about power and control. But revulsion can be an even stronger force than that." She held up her own arms. "My thighs and stomach are the same." She chuckled with grim satisfaction. "More than one Cirrocumulan got the fright of his life when he saw them."

"I'm so sorry," Jason whispered.

Sab looked up at him, astonished to see tears in his eyes.

"I'm so sorry that was the only way to escape your cruelty," he added.

Sab blinked. "You escaped as well, though, didn't you?" she whispered.

He paused for only a second, then nodded.

"How?"

"The privileged have more choices." Disgust contorted his face as he said the word *privileged*. "And I had to protect my sister." His eyes widened, as though he was afraid he'd just given away too much information.

Sab held up her palms. "Your secret's safe with me. We've all got them." She gestured with her head to the rest of her group.

"Thank you," he said, and this time he held her gaze. There was gratitude in his expression, and a little bit of hope.

Nope, he was not like any other Mage at all.

ONCE CLAWS WAS clean and dressed, her scarred ankles showing out of the ends of slightly too short trousers, they continued on their journey out of the ravine. None of them spoke, except for Claws who was busy having a conversation with herself, and a jolly one it seemed to be; there was a lot of giggling. Every now and then, Prisca, who hadn't let go of her arm since she'd dressed her, looked at her with concern, but didn't say anything. Or try to join in with the conversation. Sab wondered if she should go over and try to help, but if Prisca didn't even know what to do, what good would Sab be? As it was, she was happy to let Volos take the lead. A bubbling stream was his guide and he seemed to know where it would take them.

Finally, the walls of rock turned into leaping hills carpeted with grass and trees, and eventually they flattened out too.

"This stream turns into a river a little further south," he said. "Big enough for boats. We can take one of those or use another transportation spell."

"I hate boats," said Jason.

"Transportation spell," said Sab at exactly the same time. "Well then. That's an easy decision. Prisca?"

The old woman nodded. "Come and help me with Claws?"

"Sure."

"What do you need?" said Jason. "Maybe I can help?"

"We give her a bit of our magic so she won't explode during the transportation spell," said Sab. "Wouldn't say no to a bit of extra power."

Jason nodded. When they were ready, Claws as unaware as ever, Volos cast the spell.

What Sab noticed most about this land, as her component parts were diffused across it, was that it was mostly forest. Some bright spots around the edges suggested towns, but considering the trek they'd endured to get here, it looked like a pretty land.

And then she was standing on her own two feet again, looking up at another tall hill. But this one was all alone, not part of a chain that led to ridiculously high mountains. And it was also covered in city.

"Kingston City," said Volos. "Where the plagues always start. Figured this would be the best place to look for our New Born."

"Bit damp, isn't it?" said Sab. "Does it always rain around here?"

"Skies above," whispered Jason.

"I know where the rain comes from," said Sab, turning to look at him. But he wasn't talking to her—he was staring at the city. With a deep look of concentration creasing his face. "What's wrong?"

"It's not just one New Born human," he said, looking confused by his own words.

"What do you mean it's not just one?" growled Volos.

"I mean there's two of them in there," said Jason pointing to the city on the hill. "There are *two* New Borns."

SQUIRREL

So at this point it was fair to say my head was reeling because of two things: the big brute Jaymes saying he killed the Chief instead of me. Not that I wasn't grateful—I didn't fancy having to tell Drayke and Jenna how I'd managed to do that all by myself. Far too skinny for that, me. But I did wonder why. I didn't know if he was protecting me or everyone else with that fib.

Then there was finding out that Swan was Audra's auntie. That was just weird. I'd known the crazy old lady ever since I was a little'un. Mum would take me round to her place every morning after we'd made up our porridge at the cook-fire, and the three of us would eat breakfast together before Bear even woke up from his night of boozing. If he'd come home, of course. I was always pretty sure that that porridge was the only thing Swan ever ate all day, she was that spindly. And once Mum had made sure she'd eaten it all, she'd leave me there for a bit to talk to the old bird while she went to fetch some rainwater in order to wash her down a bit. I never saw the point in it, even when I was that little.

The little hut was nothing more than a pile of mud with

sod and sticks for a roof. It stank of shit constantly, being that close to the middens, and despite Mum always looking about the tiny space secretly to make sure Swan hadn't shat anywhere that wasn't the slops bucket. Mum always emptied that too. Rotten job, but alls she had to do was walk around back with it and chuck it into the pits where everyone else did. She never complained about it, Mum.

And when it was time to go, she always apologised about having to leave, and made me go and give the old bird a big hug. I did what I was told because I knew Mum always hugged her after me, but it always made me feel awkward. Not just because she smelt so bad, but because she always had tears in her eyes. I asked Mum once if she was my gran, but Mum just smiled sadly and said she wasn't old enough for that. And then, when I was older and working in the family business, Mum would ask me every now and then to keep my eyes peeled for a spare blanket, or some warm clothes, or a bit of simple crockery so we could make Swan's life a little bit more comfy. Didn't mind doing that at all. By then I was working nights, so was never back in time to go around and see the old bird any more. And then Mum's legs got broke and the visits stopped altogether.

And now it turns out that she was part of Audra's family. Well, if Audra was some rich Academician living up in In'Keep with her rich mum and dad, what the blazes was Swan doing down in Midden Pits?

I suddenly felt all sorts of sympathy for the poor old bird. No wonder she was so sad all the time—her family had abandoned her to live a life of squalor, while they all lived it up with the rich folk. Seemed bloody unfair to me. I got a wash of guilt for thinking so poorly of her when I was a little'un. Granted, I'd lived in Keep'Out my entire life, but I'd always had a mum who loved me and a little shack she'd made up all nice. All right, it wasn't no Academician's mansion, but there was always food to eat, clean rushes on the floor, and the roof kept the rain out. And it was no where near the middens. Poor Swan.

"I'll take you to her," I said to Drayke then. "Don't know if she'll still be alive, mind. She was pretty old when I knew her and that was a bunch of seasons ago, and she wasn't living in no rose field."

"If she's dead, so be it," said Drayke. "But I need to know for certain."

Bloody charmer, that one.

So off we went, me, Jaymes with his sliced-open throat (something else he'd neglected to mention to the Rebel Leader), and Drayke with his Academician companion, Jenna.

The moment you step off the chipped flagstones of Intellect's Path, your feet seep into mud up to your ankles. At least, they do during the wet season, even when the rain's stopped for a bit, like it had now. The sky was grey and heavy though, and I knew this little let-up wouldn't last long. No one spoke. I gathered they were all too busy watching where they were putting their feet, like I was. Maybe they were caught up in their own thoughts. Maybe they were all wishing they weren't beyond In'Keep. I knew I was, and I'd only been in there a short while. A bloke gets used to the air not stinking of shit quite quickly, it seemed.

No conversation drifted amongst our strange group, but the sound of Keep'Outers shouting and animals shrieking and our feet squelching meant it was anything but quiet. I was glad Audra had fixed me up with some decent clobber, even though it meant I got a few stares, and even though it was roughed up and bloody after my run-in with the Chief, because at least it meant my feet were dry. I'd never had a pair of boots before. Real leather ones with no holes in them. Hadn't known walking could be so comfortable.

But that was all besides the point: I needed to concentrate on getting this lot to Swan's. Finding Midden Pits wasn't the problem, you just needed to keep going down. Along Market Street for a bit, then right down Cut Throat Alley; along Peddler's Lane then right down Gropers Alley. I heard Jenna gasp when she caught sight of her first whore. Lucky it was midday and not midnight that I was leading her down here. She probably would've died of shock. Zig Zag Street came quickly enough then it was just a matter of turning right down Squeeze Guts Alley and we were on Tanner's Street, the backbone of Midden Pits. Alls I had to do was remember whereabouts Swan's little mud hut was amongst all these others.

"That ain't you, is it, Squirrel?"

Now, back in the old days, I wouldn't have looked around at someone calling out my name because that's just asking for trouble. You never admit who you are in Keep'Out until you know who and why your name's being called out in the first place. But an Age had passed since I was here and I'd forgotten all my lessons. I turned and looked across the street.

"Bloody is you, in all," said the bloke. "No mistaking that hair, and you got your mum's face, in all. We all thought you was dead. Looks like you been in a nasty fight, mind."

"Hound," I said, suddenly remembering who he was. He was as long and lean as a whippet, skin just as grey. He used to gamble with my old man Bear. And by gamble I mean fight over coin then spend it all on whores anyway. I liked him as well as I'd liked Bear. "Just visiting friends. Won't keep you." I turned to walk off but he wasn't done yet.

"I heard tell the Chief was looking for you," he said.

"Well I made it this far, so it can't be true."

"Been looking for you for a good long while, in all," Hound continued, giving my companions a long look-over.

He probably liked his chances against me and Jenna. It was Drayke and Jaymes who were clearly making him pause and hurt his head with thinking. "Come on over and see the missus, we'll have a chinwag. You know Bear's dead?"

I didn't even blink. "Plague, was it? Got my mum too."

"Bastard owed me a purse-full. Weren't plague though. Heard tell the Chief done him up. As a traitor."

"And that's surprising to you, is it?"

The Hound laughed, a vicious, grating sound. "Serves the fucker right. Come on over, we'll chinwag."

"Things to do, Hound."

"Enough," said Drayke. "Squirrel's with us. We've got business to do, so we'll leave you to yours. Squirrel." He gestured with his head for me to carry on.

"The fuck are you anyway?" said Hound. Then he raised his voice. "Don't look like you're from round here. None of you."

I saw flaps of doors twitch open at that, then all shapes and sizes of men were stepping out onto the street. Some of them went and knocked up others who hadn't already been roused by the noise. Well, shit.

Drayke straightened up, placed one hand on the axe-handle poking over his shoulder. "We're Rebels here on official business."

Personally, I wouldn't've fucked with that tone of voice, but Hound just smirked. "Rebels from the palace, eh? Your business might be official up in In'Keep, down here it don't mean shit. Only official business is from the Chief. Chief know you're sniffing round here, is it?"

"Your Chief's dead, now leave us alone!"

As one, all of us in that street turned to look at Jenna. Me, Jaymes and Drayke all had "oh shit" expressions on our faces of varying degrees, mine being of the slacked-jawed persuasion at the upper end, theirs being the slight frown of the lower end. Everyone else started mumbling, a heartbeat later they were shouting the news all over the place. It wasn't going to take long for every Keep'Outer to know.

Jenna was trying to hide behind Drayke's back. "I probably shouldn't have said that, should I?" she said to me.

I shook my head.

"Oh dear."

"Chief's dead, is it?" said Hound, walking towards us now that he had a burly group of mates with him. "Means there ain't no one here to give a shit about what happens to a bunch of In'Keepers then."

"Prime Minister'll have a shit or two to give, I reckon," said Jaymes.

Hound unleashed his laugh again. "Prime Minister don't give a fuck what happens down here. Chief was the only law here. And now you say that law is dead, is it? Well. Reckon that means you probably are, in all."

I groaned. Fucking Keep'Out. Always trouble somewhere down here, and lucky me gets to see it right from in the middle. I shouldn't've killed the Chief, that was the problem. I mean, no one deserved a horrible death more than him. The man was a right bastard. But I'd opened a gaping Chief-sized hole in Keep'Out, and now that word had got out about his demise, every second bastard who thought he was something special was going to try and fill it. Better the orc you knew, as my mum was fond of saying. And I could tell by the look on his face that Drayke blamed me, in all, even though Jaymes said it was him what killed the Chief. He knew me and Audra were the same, and that was enough for him to pin the blame on me anyway. Even if he didn't know he was right. Or maybe he was just pissed off that his little mission of hide-and-seek was going to be more difficult now. Coming from Keep'Out, I was quite skilled at reading the nuances of a scowling face, but Drayke didn't seem to have much in the way of subtlety in his.

I shrugged. Next-in-line-Chief riots were something for future Squirrel to worry about. All I wanted to do right now was get back to Audra and Mouse. But before I could do that, I had to get this lot to Swan.

Then I got pins and needles all over my body. Started off faint, then they got pretty uncomfortable, and all of a sudden I was whipped up into the air, looking down on all of Kingston City. Not looking, exactly. Sensing, maybe? It was difficult to explain, because it felt like my brain was scattered into a million different pieces. I reckoned I could be at peace up here, looking down on the city instead of being a part of it, except for the rising panicked terror that seemed to come at me from everywhere at once.

And then I was standing outside the city. On grass. In front of a bunch of strangers. One bloke, one giant and three really weird women. One of them was lying on the ground trying to plait grass into her hair. I was obviously having some kind of post-murder traumatic dream.

Until I saw Audra.

SABINA

"*H*ow can you possibly tell," said Sab, "that there are two New Borns in there?" She waved her hand at the city on the hill.

"He's right," said Volos, squinting into the distance. "There are."

"Urgh!" said Sab, frustration made vocal. "How can you tell?"

"You can't?" said Jason.

Sab took a deep breath, only spoke again once she'd released it slowly. "How did my question make you think otherwise?"

"S-sorry, it's just that… Well, I've always been able to see Mages' auras."

"Huh. And what's an aura?"

Jason's eyebrow twitched, but he refrained from asking any more ridiculous questions. "It's…I suppose it's a mental manifestation of magic. It surrounds all of us. Well, us Mages. Humans haven't got one, and they can't see ours, either."

"Why can't I see them?"

"I don't know…perhaps you haven't trained your mind to see them. It's not like they actually exist as something physical, like the grass or anything else you can see and touch. It's more like…" he paused, clearly trying to think of a way of explaining that Sab would understand. "You know when you close your eyes after you've looked at something bright, and you can still see an image of that thing against your eyelids?"

Sab blinked. "Yes, I think so."

"Well, that's what a Mage's aura is. It's like a person's afterimage, caused by their magic."

"So I have to close my eyes in order to see your aura?"

Jason shook his head. "No, it doesn't work in the same way. It's just something you can automatically see with your physical eyes if you've trained your mind's eye."

"I still don't get it."

"All right, well try to think of it as—"

"No, look, it doesn't matter," said Sab, waving her hands at him. Another peculiar explanation wasn't going to help her. "It's probably because I've been a Stratian my whole life. We're slavers and survivors. Anything outside of that is just frippery."

She looked over at Claws, who was busy picking daisies, then apologising to them before she ate them. The girl had really lost it.

She turned back to Jason. "So I've got one too?"

"Of course."

"What's it like?"

Without even a pause, "It's pink."

"Fuck off."

"With a few flecks of gold. It's pretty."

She huffed her disgust at him, swivelled her head to look at Volos. "You can see it too?"

He nodded, grinning.

"And you?" she said to Prisca.

"Yes, my girl. I've always seen it."

"What colour's yours, then?"

"We can't see our own auras, Sabina."

"What colour's hers?" she said to Volos.

"Deep blue," he said, without even turning back around to look at her.

She turned back to Jason, eyebrow raised in question. He looked at Prisca, then back to Sab and nodded.

"Well, fuck me," she said. Then to Prisca, "How come you didn't tell me about this before? We've known each other forever!"

The old woman shrugged. "I just thought you knew."

"It's not hard to learn," said Jason. "Simple training will help open your mind's eye so that seeing them will become second nature."

"No time for that now," Sab said. "We've nearly finished the race. Let's just get it done."

"We've still got to get her back to the 'Sphere," said Prisca.

"That. Right," said Sab.

"Except now there's two of them," said Volos, frowning.

"And what colour are *their* auras, that everyone can see except me?"

"One is a very bright red," said Jason, eyes glazed towards the city again. "That's the closest to us. It's near the top of the hill. The other's fainter, on the slope on the other side of the hill. A kind of violet colour."

Volos grunted in agreement.

"You can see the aura *through* the hill?"

Jason nodded. "The mind's eye doesn't have the same barriers as the physical eyes."

Sab widened her eyes briefly. "If you say so. Well, then, which one's Audra?"

Jason started. "You know her name too?"

"Yeah. Came to me during the surge. Same for everyone, right?"

"Of course, of course," said Jason. "But unfortunately, our auras don't tell us each other's names, only that we're Mages."

Sab nodded. "Right. Which is why we need to send out a tendril of magic to find out who someone is."

"Exactly."

"So if we can't tell which one is Audra," said Sab, "how do we know which one to bring here?"

"Easy," said Volos. He concentrated fiercely on the hill in the distance, flung his hands apart, then dragged them towards his chest. "They'll be here in a second."

"He favours the transportation spell," Jason whispered towards Sab. "It's common for Mages to perfect only a few spells."

"He's done that one a lot out here," she said. "But in Oceanwall he's famous for another one."

"Which one?"

But Sab didn't have time to tell him.

Because two very confused New Born humans had appeared and were gaping at all five of them.

AUDRA

The sky had been dry for well over a notch but still Squirrel hadn't returned. Audra didn't know whether to be relieved or worried, but the greater part of her was glad that he hadn't yet discovered the death of his beloved cat.

Death? She snorted a sardonic laugh. Murder. She'd murdered Mouse just so she could feel a little bit better. Is that what her life would be from now? Constantly seeking a living being to bleed in order to escape the pain? She was a monster from the Age of Nightmares. A dæmon.

She blinked. She'd forgotten all about that word, and the woman from the unmapped village who'd bestowed it upon her. Forgotten it even though she'd promised herself she would find out what it meant when she returned. There were many things she'd intended to do when she got back to Kingston, but all she'd achieved was death and riots. And losing her friends. Squirrel had probably run away while she was asleep because he was so afraid of her. And Adàm had walked away from her because he'd been so disgusted with her. Adàm. She hadn't even thought of him since that day at his parents' mansion. What had she become?

A dæmon. She needed to find out what that meant. If that woman and her villagers knew what it was then there must be some mention of it somewhere. Not in her library—she'd read most of the texts in there and hadn't come across the term once. But perhaps in her secret store, the same place where she'd found Nathaniel's journal.

Wait—Nathaniel's journal... She'd become this dæmon because of her confrontation with the two Mages, Nathaniel ScourgeMaster and Messina LandSlayer. When she'd killed them she took on all their powers. Perhaps there was something in his journal about what had happened to her at that moment. Perhaps there would even be a cure! When Messina's life-force became her own, she understood that Messina had been responsible for creating the race of orcs, that they became Raged by the taste of blood, and that unRaged blood was the cure. Maybe there was a similar cure for her and Squirrel.

Oh, but wait... Squirrel hadn't been at the Blasted Glade with her when she'd killed the Mages. His powers had manifested before that. She tutted and shook her head; thinking around in circles wasn't going to help. She needed to read the journal again. It would still be in her bag, after their journey back from the forest. She hadn't unpacked her meagre belongings since arriving home. Briefly she considered locking up the library so no one would disturb her, only to set the idea aside just in case Squirrel returned. Besides, the Academicians would be in no fit state to study after the gruesome events that recently took place. The library wouldn't have visitors for a while.

Having a plan at last gave speed to her feet and she trotted down the little staircase towards the living chambers. Only to be greeted by the cloying aroma of drying blood.

Mouse. He was still on the kitchen table. His tabby fur was matted with blood, the wood beneath stained a deep crimson-brown. Panic flared as quickly as regret, but Audra had no time for that. She had to clean up. Bad enough that Squirrel's beloved companion was taken from him, he didn't need to see his torn corpse as well.

Wait. She could bring him back. Just like she'd brought back the Rebels and orcs and men after the battle at the Blasted Glade. Then Squirrel would never have to know what she did to his dearest friend! It was easy. All she had to do was—

Leave them be. They're dead. They should stay dead.

Calum's voice. His eyes... She'd brought him back. What did he know now?

She looked down at Mouse's cold corpse again. "I'm so sorry," she whispered.

From her bedroom she took a blanket, then carefully wrapped up the little body, trying to ignore the gruesome gash along his belly, quailing at the touch of cold innards that had spilled onto the table and now slid over her fingers, an obscene contradiction to the rigor mortis of the corpse. Finally the task was done and she closed the blanket around Mouse. She'd burn the body, as befitted the death of a friend. But first she had to clean the table.

No amount of soap and scalding water lifted the stain, and finally she had to return to her bedroom, take a clean sheet and drape it over the offending taint. Once that was done, she carried Mouse back up the stairs, placed him on a basket of wood next to the fireplace in the library, and carried her burden out amongst the trees surrounding the palace enclosure. Her boots squelched across the saturated grass. There were no Rebels to see and ask what her business was, no Ministers wandering around to wonder what she was up to, so she built her little pyre free from prying eyes.

The rain had stopped for now, but beneath the trees, a few drops fell from dying leaves like tears, but it wasn't enough to put out her fire. Within a notch, all that was left was a smouldering pile of ash. If she couldn't find a way to reverse what had happened to her, she may well be burning more friends like this, and Kingston would contain nothing *but* smouldering piles of ash. For a heartbeat she wished the plague had killed off everyone while she was away. At least then she wouldn't have any more deaths laid at her feet.

She pushed herself up from the sodden ground and walked back to the library.

DRESSED in dry leggings and a long-sleeved woollen middy, Audra sat on her bed and stared at ScourgeMaster's journal. When she'd taken his life she'd also taken his knowledge.

"It's so soft," Adàm had said a thousand Ages ago. "What's it made from?"

"Hide," she'd answered, "although I don't know which animal's."

She knew now. It was human skin, flayed from a slave who had passed his use once his blood had been spilled to feed the immortality of the Mage. But she didn't see the face of the unknown slave who'd died Ages ago in another part of the world. She saw Faër's face. And Kole's. And all those Rebels and men and orcs who'd died because she'd found this journal and asked them to come with her on the journey written within its pages. And here she was again, hoping to find answers when she knew all she'd found before were lies.

She opened the cover and looked at the first page. The first three words.

Undeadlicnes þurh æmtignesse.

Immortality through emptiness.

She blinked. She understood the archaic language perfectly.

Blod biþ þa ea þe us abiraþ æt æmtignesse.

Blood is the river which carries us to emptiness.

That was important, but she didn't understand why: the words may well be legible to her now, but deciphering the enigmatic phrases of an ancient Mage was a different matter entirely. She would ponder it later. First she had to find out if there was a cure to her affliction.

For two notches she read, while rainclouds pummelled each other and made the day dark, but learned nothing she hadn't already known. When she came across a note she'd scribbled in the margin she found herself in equal parts amused and disgusted—amused because her translating skills had been less than accurate; disgusted because she'd defaced the skin of a human corpse. All she learned was that the journal really did just describe the plague and the way to find the Healing Glass. As though it were written for that purpose alone.

She looked up. The room was dark enough for lamplight but that would have to wait. ScourgeMaster's journal hadn't been the only text she'd found. When she'd first been banished to the library, she'd found these disused, dusty old quarters that she'd cleaned and taken as her own. She'd found the staircase leading down to the hidden vaults beneath the library. The staircase that sat behind a locked door, itself behind a thick hanging tapestry in this very bedroom. Many of the ancient texts she'd already saved, meticulously cleaning them and tracing fresh ink over faded words: they stood in that very cabinet where her wardrobe used to stand, black velvet draped over them to protect them from dust and sunlight. Ages of knowledge that could hold all the answers she sought. She leapt from her bed and raced to the cabinet.

*Audra Academician, no one ever comes back from these...
missions. They're not supposed to.*

The memory stopped her hand dead before it reached the
gilded handle of the cabinet. The Sages knew. They knew
about the Mages, they knew about the Game. And when she
became an embarrassment to them they banished her to the
library, where they knew she'd find the rooms and the vaults
and the ancient texts. She was meant to find them, so that
when the plague struck she would have an answer.

She dropped to her knees, sending lightning strikes of
pain along her thighs. She'd been a part of the Game long
before the first Out'Keeper had succumbed to the plague.

A wordless cry of rage erupted from her throat and she
smashed her fist against the cabinet, shattering glass. Then
she pulled herself up and snatched the journal off her bed
and threw it into the fireplace, setting a flame on it before
she could change her mind—burning a book was the worst
kind of desecration.

But it wasn't a book, it was a collection of lies. It wasn't a
book, it was a dead human. It should've been burned a long
time ago. Any hope she'd had of finding answers in her not-
actually-secret stash turned to ashes with the journal. The
only people who could've answered her questions were Than
or the Sages, and she'd killed them all. She smiled a bitter
smile at the irony.

The only person she had left now was Squirrel. As much
as she wanted to put off seeing him, she didn't know how
long this lucidity of hers was going to last. If the pain started
again, the only thing she'd be able to think about was making
it stop, instead of finding a permanent solution. Before she
had a chance to think herself out of it, she snatched up a
hooded cloak from the top of the clothes chest, ran back up
to the library and out into the darkening afternoon.

Not far from the palace enclosure she found a horse and

carriage at rest, the driver outside smoking a pipe, frowning up at the heavy sky. She was just about to run over to him when she realised she didn't know where she was going. She doubted the driver would respond very well to "find Squirrel, please." How was she ever going to find one skinny boy in a city full of millions of people? Briefly she smiled when she found the answer. None of the other people in Kingston were surrounded by a violet aura like Squirrel was. Casting her gaze as far as she could, she let her sight fall across the city. Up here in In'Keep, she stood upon an outspread plateau that had been colonised by the wealthy and their mansions. If he'd decided to seek out his old haunts down on the slopes of Out'Keep it was very unlikely she'd see his aura from up here.

By now, the driver had shifted his frown from the sky to her, a strange young woman in civilian clothes loitering outside the palace enclosure. She smiled as she approached him. His frown didn't budge.

"I'd say good afternoon but it's almost as dark as evening," she said.

"Aye."

"I wonder if I might hire you?"

"If you've got silver, I'm free for hire."

Audra tried smiling again but it still didn't work. "I need to go to Intellect's Gate."

The driver nodded and put out his pipe with his thumb. "I'll take you to the Gate but I'm not going no further—there's riots going on in Keep'Out and I'll not have my horse frighted nor injured."

Now it was Audra's turn to frown. "I thought the riots were at King's Gate earlier this afternoon?"

"That was nothing compared to this'un. My lad's been back and forth telling me the news. Chief's dead, it seems."

"Oh." Audra had no idea what that meant, least of all its

significance. "They're not rioting for the same reason as they were earlier then?"

"I s'pect the Keep'Outers are just as unhappy as them that rioted this morning," he said, giving her a funny look. "Don't reckon people would be rioting at all if they was happy. Been a long time coming, I reckon."

"I had no idea," she said.

"No. But like I say, I'll take you as far as the Gate but no further."

"That will do very nicely, thank you," said Audra. All she needed was a good view of the slopes and then she'd be able to find Squirrel's aura.

A strange sensation set her body tingling. It was a little bit like being filled with power. She stopped and looked around again. Not exactly like being filled with power, more like it was in reverse… More like someone using it. It wasn't her, so there was only one other person it could possibly be. And that meant she'd found Squirrel.

"I didn't mean Intellect's Gate," she said once her foot was the step of the carriage. "I meant Merchant's Gate. I'm always getting those two confused."

"Right you are," said the driver, stepping up into his seat.

Audra settled herself on the cushioned bench and tried not to think about Mouse.

THE DRIVER REINED in his horse several strides away from Merchant's Gate. Torches were already lit around it and the portcullis was down. Several city guards were lined up before it, looking so much like the calamity at King's Gate that her steps faltered for a moment. Only a few heartbeats passed before she noticed the difference however; these people weren't angry, demanding to be let in. They were terrified, pleading to be let in. Audra looked back at the driver, but he was smoking and frowning again. He'd forgotten all about her. She marched up to the nearest guard and tugged on his arm until he noticed her. He looked a good deal younger than she was.

"Why aren't you helping these people?" she shouted.

"We didn't get orders to," he said. "Captain always keeps the portcullis down because of where we are, and it's a good job too—we'd be overrun with Keep'Outers by now if we didn't."

"They need help!" And then she felt it. The powerful stream of energy piercing her, meaning that someone was bleeding. "They need help!" she said again, this time pushing her way through the guards until she was at the portcullis, dreading what she would see there but compelled nonetheless.

The grille of the portcullis was made from oak shafts as thick as her arm, bolted together with iron; and while it was three times as high as a man, it was narrow, not even able to admit two horses and their riders abreast. But the torchlight shone down on those who were pushed up against it, their mouths hanging open but no sound emanating from them, their eyes vacant, their bodies limp. It was only the crush of the crowd behind them that kept them from falling to the ground. They'd been pressed to death by the sheer force of humanity behind them, their breath strangled in their lungs, their innards liquified within unbroken skin. But no blood spilled.

No blood... Then why was she being filled with delicious power?

Immortality through emptiness.

Looking into the vacant eyes of the filthy creature before her she knew: that emptiness was death. Her power came from death, not blood. Blood was merely the river which carried people to their deaths when it was spilled.

The realisation drowned out the stricken cries beyond the Gate just as the power was drowning out her mind: she was a creature whose life depended on death. The thought struck such a blow that she stumbled back from the gate and doubled over. An image of her cold father dead in his favourite armchair flashed into her mind. She didn't want to be responsible for the deaths of the people she loved! Because what if she couldn't stop it? What if the urge to

feed

increase her power overcame everything and she couldn't stop herself? She didn't want to live like that...did she? No! Of course she didn't. Then why the question?

But there was no time to answer it. Something outside the city, to the north. A strong wind pushing against her, but there was no movement in the air.

Was it magic? It felt like it could be magic.

And then she was no longer outside the gate and the dead bodies crushed behind it. She was up, up, up above the city. A snowflake's view of Kingston. And it was peaceful up here, like all her problems and worries had been scattered to the furthest corners of the land. Had she done this to herself? Perhaps it was the result of seeing too many corpses, of realising she was a creature of death.

But then she was standing on grass. Grass? Not the flagstoned road outside Merchant's Gate? And instead of the portcullis and corpses, there were five people. Alive. Gaping at her. Her mind struggled to keep up with events.

"Audra?"

She looked around—Squirrel! Her flash of relief at seeing him running towards her was instantly doused by the sight of him. He was covered in blood. Covered in it. The result of the power she'd felt earlier when she'd got into the carriage, perhaps?

"What happened to *you*?" she said. "Are you hurt?"

"No, I ain't—" He stopped and looked down at himself. "I did something bad. But it was for a good reason!"

Audra wanted to reach out and embrace the poor boy, but a bellow from behind made her jump. Squirrel too.

"New Borns!"

Audra turned slowly, remembering the five people she'd first seen. There was a giant among them, pale and hairy, flabby around the jaws. She knew instantly it was he who'd bellowed. She could tell by his rapid breathing and deeply scowling face. Anger ignited in her. He was a Mage, she knew by his aura. In fact, they all had auras. Except one young woman, who was lying on the ground and braiding— was she braiding strands of grass into her hair?

She refocussed her attention on the giant, gathered her anger around her like a cloak. Then she marched right up to him and pointed up into his face.

"You did this, didn't you?" she shouted. "Why? *What* did you do? How are we here? Answer me right now!"

SABINA

"*A*udra?" said the smallest New Born human, running to the woman. He was no more than a skinny little boy. And just like Claws had been not that long ago, he was head to toe covered in blood. "What's happening?"

Audra, just as shocked but able to keep herself in check, glanced over towards the sound of her name, then double-took as the sight of the boy registered.

"What happened to *you*?" she said. "Are you hurt?"

"No, I ain't—" he stopped and looked down at himself. Dropped his face into his hands and then looked back up her, distress on his face. "I did something bad. But it was for a good reason!" he added quickly.

"New Borns!" shouted Volos, and the two of them jumped, turned back to look at them.

The woman called Audra wasn't that much taller than Sab, although she was certainly cleaner and infinitely less scarred. Her skin was flawless and her hair was deep auburn. She also wore splendid clothes. How typical, that an already powerful woman in this society would get even more power. Sab watched as her face morphed from an expression of shock to one of anger. Then she stormed across to Volos as though he wasn't a hairy giant that literally every other person on the planet was afraid of.

"You did this, didn't you?" she shouted, pointing a delicate finger up at his bulbous nose. "Why? *What* did you do? How are we here? Answer me right now!"

Sab kind of got the impression that Audra was a woman who was used to getting her own way, but she did enjoy watching Volos's confusion. Not so many people called him out on his behaviour.

But enough was enough. Sab came here for one reason only and now it was time. She stepped forward.

"Audra, my name's Sab," she said.

"How did you know my name?"

"The second you killed Nathaniel and Messina," said Sab, "every single Mage on the planet knew who you were. Things might get tricky for you in a while." She looked across to the skinny boy. "And for your friend."

"Every single Mage...?" Audra shook her head. "But..." Then her eyes widened a little in realisation. "You're all Mages too. Than and Messina weren't the only ones."

"Well, they were the only ones in Taurë at that time. I'm guessing you know all about the Game?"

Audra scowled and nodded.

"Well, there's a lot more of us," said Sab.

"And that's why you're here?" said Audra. "Is this another Game? How many more people have you come here to kill? I won't let you!"

Sab put on her angriest face and stepped up close to Audra. "We're not here to kill humans. This isn't a Game. This is a race, and you're the end of it. We're here for *you*, Audra. And probably your boy too. Yes, we're here for both of you, and we're going to take you back to the Patriarch and he's going to do terrible, terrible things to you. You can't stop us! There's no way you can stop us! Except death. And also it's just me. Everyone else here is my prisoner, so don't hurt them. Apart from Volos, he's a dick. Do whatever you want with him. But if you want to escape, the only way is to kill me. Otherwise, you know. Bad things will happen to you. And your boy there."

Audra blinked.

Prisca ran forward, grabbed her arm. "What are you doing?" Then she looked at Audra. "Don't you dare touch my girl!"

Audra blinked again.

Then Jason's hand was on her other arm. "That's why you came all this way? To get yourself killed?"

For the first time ever in her long, long life, and because she wasn't on Stratus anymore and didn't need to keep her reputation intact, and because Claws had finally lost her mind and wasn't listening, Sab cried.

She cried so hard that it hurt her throat, her chest, her nose. Her eyes stung with boiling tears, and her legs went weak from the sheer release of it all.

"I can't bear it any more!" she wept. "It's too hard! The things we do to those poor slaves, just so the higher ups can have more and more magic! The things the higher ups do to *us* just because we're Stratians and we're not worth shitting on! It's too much, Prisca! I'm tired. I'm so fucking *tired* of it all. I understand why my mum did what she did now. I get it. And I don't blame her. If I was as brave as her, I'd do the same thing, but I'm not." She turned back to Audra, and now the woman's astonishment had turned to pity. That expression just made Sab cry all the harder. "Please help me," Sab said. "You're the only one who can do it. And you can do it quickly. But please, don't hurt my friend, Claws. She isn't a Mage. And she needs looking after. And don't hurt Prisca either. She's only here because she wanted to look after me and Claws."

It was the longest speech Sab had ever given, and what with all the tears and sobbing, it took the last little ounce of strength she had left and she sank to the floor.

Prisca sat down beside her, arms around her, sobbing into her hair.

Then Audra knelt down in front of her. She smiled at her, and it was a kind smile. It was so bizarre to see kindness from the face of one so clearly privileged that Sab stopped crying.

"I'm not going to kill you," said Audra. "But I am going to help you, if I can." She reached out and took one of Sab's hands in her own. And she didn't even flinch when she saw the extent of Sab's flayed arms.

But Sab did when Audra's skin touched hers. It was like that feeling when another Mage is sending out a tendril of magic to find out who you really are. Except...not. As impolite as it was, that kind of questing magic was only a feather in a breeze. Audra's touch was...invasive. That was the only word that fit. It didn't hurt exactly, but it was like Audra had stripped her of more than just her skin, and from her entire body, not just her arms. She saw all of her, past and present, feelings, secrets, knowledge, fears. She was more vulnerable now than she'd ever been, even when the cruelest Cirrocumulan had come down to Stratus to rape her before she started flaying herself.

Except... Audra wasn't doing this intentionally. She knew, because whatever this was, went both ways. And she could see it in Audra's face too. The tears of distress that overspilt her eyes. This...invasive connection was a result of her being a New Born human.

"Than was your father," Audra whispered, so only Sab could hear.

Sab nodded.

"And you hate him. For what he did to your mother."

Sab nodded again. "I should never have been born. My mum killed herself because of me. Every time she looked at me, she saw him." Sab started sobbing again. "I can't take it any more. This much anger all the time…it hurts. Please…"

Audra broke the connection and wiped her eyes. "You poor, poor thing," she said, then gave a brittle smile. "I'm angry at my mother too. For the way she died."

"I know."

"We're not so different, you and I."

Sab laughed, but it was bitter. "How many humans have you enslaved and murdered?"

Audra's face clouded over. She glanced briefly at the skinny boy, then leaned in closer before speaking again. "I'm terrified that I might be able to answer that question in the near future. This…power frightens me. The things it wants me to do…"

Sab blinked. Audra spoke of magic like it was its own entity. But she'd felt her terror right enough. And she knew about the cat. That's why she'd looked at the skinny boy. The cat had been his companion before Audra murdered him for his blood. Yes, she supposed it could be a terrifying change to a human, suddenly having magic.

"I won't kill you," said Audra. "But I will help you."

She stood up, and Sab followed suit. "How can you help? *Why* would you?"

She looked around at all of them, her eyes resting a little longer on Claws. Sab followed her gaze, noted that her friend was weaving unpicked blades of grass into her hair.

"I think we can all help each other," Audra announced.

The skinny boy tugged on her arm. "The fuck you doing? Them's Mages! They'll kill us, or something worse!"

She placed an arm around his narrow shoulders, then looked back at Sab. "No, I don't think they will."

Sab shook her head.

Then, much to Sab's surprise because she'd quite forgotten he was there, Jason said, "No, we won't. You made the world a better place when you rid it of Messina and Nathaniel. But we can do more."

"We can," said Audra, nodding. "There's rot festering here in Taurë, and beyond the Impassable Mountains, it seems."

Sab nodded again. It wasn't often she was rendered speechless, but that's what Audra had done to her. This moment was supposed to be her final release. Now what was she going to do with herself? She literally hadn't thought this far ahead.

"Then let's cut it out," Audra continued. "We can start here, by telling everyone the truth about the Mages and their Game. And then we can build an army right here in Taurë to bring down your Mages."

"A human army?" said Volos, then coughed out a sardonic laugh. "They'll be dead before they've even caught sight of their first Mage. How can humans stand against Mages?"

"Not just humans," said Audra, with a smile. "Elves too. I know many. I know they'll help."

"Elves?" said Sab, remembering those atrocities in the badlands. "They're your friends?"

Audra nodded. "And orcs too. I know they'll definitely want to help, after what Messina did to them."

"What," said Sab, relieved her words were coming back to her, "the fuck are orcs?"

"We have a lot to talk about," she said, smiling. "And I'll tell you everything, I promise. I'm sorry your journey didn't end the way you'd planned, but I need you. All of you. We can make everything right again. Will you help me?"

Sab looked into Audra's eyes and they were full of pleading. She imagined a world with no Patriarch, no slavers and slaves. Maybe even no 'Sphere. She *loved* that idea. She thought about the huge amount of effort it would take to change the whole world. The danger. The time. But she was immortal, so what did danger and time mean to her? Plus, it would be fun to fuck the higher ups over for once.

"You know what?" said Sab, "fuck it. I'm in. Let's burn this fucking world to the ground and start all over again."

"Language," said Prisca.

Audra smiled uncertainly at her. "We'll maybe not need to burn the *whole* world down, but I'm delighted that you agree with the principle."

"I agree too," said Jason. "And I also know of many... people who can join our cause."

Audra beamed at him. Perhaps she hadn't noticed the slight pause before *people,* but Sab did.

"I go where my girls go," said Prisca. "And I've only ever wanted to keep them safe, so I suppose I agree with shaking up the status quo too."

"Prisca!" said Volos. "You would declare war on Ocean-wall? On your mother and father?"

Prisca tutted. "This from the man who dismissed his own parents. And don't you dare try to defend your actions by saying they were mutants, they were still your parents, and they hadn't done anything wrong."

Volos, to Sab's astonishment, looked chastised by Prisca's words. "But the lord and lady—"

"Shit on them," said Prisca. "They *sold* me to the 'Sphere. *Sold* me. For enough magic to build that ridiculous fucking city of theirs. Oh yes, they told everyone that I was marrying into an auspicious Cirrun family to join the two houses together, but actually they *sold their own daughter* just so they could be more powerful. And they *knew* the Patriarch was going to use me as a slaver. His little way of reminding them that he was still more powerful than them. So I'm with Sabina—fuck them. I'll happily watch their stupid city burn to the ground."

"Except it's made of water," said Sab, grinning.

"Then I'll watch it fucking boil."

And Sab watched Volos boil. "They *sold* you?" he hissed. "My beloved Prisca? Sold you into slavery? I'll see them BURN!" he roared.

"Boil," said Sab.

"BOIL!" roared Volos, without missing a beat.

Claws looked up, snapping all the grass braids entwined in her hair. "Ssh please," she said.

"Wonderful!" said Audra, squeezing the skinny boy in a hug. "Let's go and plan a revolution then."

"I think one might already be starting, actually," said the skinny boy. He looked guilty about something.

"What's that supposed to mean?" said Sab.

"It's all right, Squirrel," said Audra. "I won't be mad. Tell me what happened."

"Well. I accidentally killed the Chief," said the skinny boy, whose name was Squirrel, apparently. Bit of a strange name for a human, but who was Sab to judge?

"You know," said Audra, "someone mentioned that name to me just a moment ago. Who is this Chief? And why in all the world would you kill him?"

"He was a bastard!" Squirrel cried.

Sab choked out a surprised laugh, but the distressed look on the boy's face made her rein it in.

"He killed this little boy, Jaymes's nephew, for no reason. And he's killed loads of people for no reason. He crippled my mum, and he was a total bastard! And he was gonna kill me, and Jaymes, in all...and I, sort of, lost it. And I killed him. With my magic. And I'm really sorry, because it's caused a right mess down in Keep'Out. But I'm also not because he deserved it, the fat *bastard*."

"Good for you, kid," said Sab, and she meant it. "Nasty bastards get what they deserve."

"Indeed," said Audra. "Although it does rather mean we'll have a little mess back in Kingston to clear up before we can organise *our* revolution."

Sab shrugged. "Fine with me. We clear out your place of all your scum, that'll make your lot more willing to help us clear out all of our scum. Let's do it."

This was better. Dying could wait for a little while longer. It was much better to be doing something useful. Her whole life she'd bitched about the world in the safety of her own mind. And now she was out *in* the world getting ready to change it. Change that would bring the Mage Houses down forever.

And she was all over that shit.

END OF BOOK TWO

Book 0 in the *Age of Academicians* series

Discover the first orc
Discover the first Mage
Discover the truth about
the academy

ORIGINS reveals the secrets
that were kept hidden
from the humans of Tauré
throughout the Ages.

Get Your Free Gift Now!

Claim your FREE BOOK here: https://www.mariaherring.com/free-book/

ACKNOWLEDGMENTS

Writing a book isn't a solitary endeavour. In fact, the shortest part of the whole process is when I'm alone at my desk, thumping the keyboard, and hoping it'll all turn out all right.

The longest part of the process involves a lot of people, and it's thanks to them that I have this book to show for it. I'm lucky to have people patient enough to support me and my imaginary friends.

First, Liz Williams, my editor. Without you I wouldn't have had the confidence to pursue this career in the first place. And my books are *definitely* a billion times better after you've finished with them.

Next, my trusty tribe of proof-readers: Cécile, Chelsea, James, Fabrice and Ian. Thank you for your eagle eyes, honest critiques, and encouraging feedback. I'm so grateful for the time and effort you give to me. There will be beers in our future!

And then there's my family. You're a certified bunch of nutters, but thank you for being there for me.

Finally, but most importantly, you, dear reader. Thank you for taking the time to read my book. I'm not renowned for my super-short, quick and easy reads, so I'm overjoyed that you stayed with me until the end! If you enjoyed Awakening Mages, I hope you consider leaving a short review. Us writers rely on these more than you can imagine! And it would make me and my imaginary friends very happy.

Thank you.

ABOUT THE AUTHOR

Besides reading and writing and teaching English, Maria Herring is known for:

- taking great long hikes up the side of mountains so she can chat to the trees

- drinking a small fortune in coffee

- drawing fantasy maps

- dropping stuff

She lives in the Mont d'Or in France with her partner, Fab, and Bilbo their cat, but can often be found in the UK visiting family. Other bits and bobs can be found on her website:

www.mariaherring.com

Pop on over. The kettle's always on!

ALSO BY MARIA HERRING

AGE OF ACADEMICIANS SERIES

The Healing Glass

Awakening Mages

Fairer Tales (with Catherine Herring)

Legacy of a Warrior Queen

Printed in Great Britain
by Amazon